SUE McCA

The author is a writer and a journalist. She has worked on the staff of several newspapers, and as a freelance journalist has contributed reviews, articles and regular columns to many magazines. Her short stories have been widely published and broadcast on radio. She has also written several plays for radio which have been broadcast in New Zealand, Australia and Great Britain, and has had three television plays screened. In 1986 she was appointed Writer-in-Residence at the University of Auckland. She lives in Northland, New Zealand, and writes a regular column for the *New Zealand Listener*.

Her other novel, OTHER HALVES received widespread literary acclaim, won New Zealand's two major literary awards, became an immediate bestseller, and was made into a feature film.

Sue McCauley

THEN AGAIN

sceptre

British Library C.I.P.

McCauley, Sue
   Then again.
   I. Title
   823[F]

   ISBN 0-340-43105-9

Printed and bound in Great Britain for Hodder and Stoughton Paperbacks, a division of Hodder and Stoughton Ltd., Mill Road, Dunton Green, Sevenoaks, Kent TN13 2YA (Editorial Office: 47 Bedford Square, London WC1B 3DP) by Richard Clay Ltd., Bungay, Suffolk.

To Nathan, Keely and Pat.

Heartfelt thanks to the New Zealand Literary Fund, without whose assistance this book would not have been written

February 4th

SHE'S STILL AT the top end of the gangway when she hears Mickey scream. She's sardined between all these people whose faces show their threadbare patience while her baby is being trodden on.

She can't see him. Somewhere down there ahead. Other faces craning forward, shrugs to shorter companions; can't see anything. Where's Alan then? Oh god. She'd told him, bending down to eye-level, keep hold of Mickey's hand.

A new scream, angrier but less urgent. Maureen breathes. If her smallest son is being trampled on it is now only by casual footwear. And if she could see him what good would that do? She has a knapsack on her back, a cardboard box containing Alice's chipped plates and crippled cutlery and used magazines under one arm and in the other hand the metal ring of a birdcage. The cage is draped with a torn blue towel, intended to make the guineapig within think comfortingly of summer skies.

Somewhere ahead of Maureen, down on the deck, the bottle-neck has cleared. As the line begins to shuffle forward and downward, an irritable human escalator, Maureen sees her loud and youngest son lifted high and slung across a wide female shoulder. Where he wriggles and kicks but at least has stopped screaming. So in the comparative silence she is able to hear Carly whimpering behind her and ask helplessly, you all right? Not sure among so many bodies if her sweater is still being held onto. Not able to turn far enough to see. Carly answers with a watery, reproachful sniff.

A young man, trying to gain a few inches, edges up and gets caught by the trousers on something sharp at the bottom of the birdcage. He tugs himself free and the cage whacks against a little woman carrying a bar stool with an engraved leather seat. They both blame Maureen with shrivelling looks.

Unable now to see Mickey she searches for Alan; who, having abandoned his brother had no doubt pushed and prised himself to the front of the queue and would by now be triumphantly on board examining, exploring. Drawn by some secret force to the engine room where he probes among moving parts. Maureen sees splintered bones and pleads for a clean amputation, left hand.

They've stopped again, backlogged while the people on deck agonise over the choice of seating they've pushed so hard for: inside, outside, top deck, middle deck, dark and airless hold. And for a second Maureen glimpses Mickey, held now by solid arms, his cheek resting against a curtain of pale gold hair. Maureen sees the desolate droop of his mouth and the glistening tear trail on his free cheek. She feels something similar, fluid and probably salty slide in the region of her belly. Or is it the womb—that internal receiver of all their disconsolate bleeps? She would wave if she had a free hand. She waves her head, her mouth, but he's gone again. Hidden by a proud new knapsack with a humiliating label, *Gadabout*, enclosed in butterfly wings.

They are on board. Room to move the arms, to check that Carly the whimpering barnacle is still attached behind. To wonder if Giggles the guineapig has survived this far. To recognise the sleek gold hair and follow it down in search of Mickey; in time to see him diving beneath the skirt of the woman's white tent of a dress. His plump bare legs, the faded red and blue sneakers between her putty coloured sandals. Surprisingly shapely ankles.

Maureen puts Carly in charge of the birdcage and the cardboard box. Tells her, no, leave the towel on or Giggles might get nervous. Says he's probably sleeping—in case Carly peeks and sees him lying ominously still.

The woman in the white dress straightens. She's been talking to Mickey upside down through her skirt. The bushy man beside her cups his hands around his mouth. 'You're surrounded,' he says, though not loudly. 'I'll give you five seconds and then we're coming in to get you.' The woman giggles and the man's face crumples into a grin, as if without her amusement it wouldn't have been a joke at all. The man has a leathery outdoor face and a wild mane of grey-white hair.

Maureen owns up. 'It's mine I'm afraid.' She gives them her all-purpose rueful mother smile. 'I'm sorry. I saw you rescue him. I had both arms full.' She crouches down, 'Mickey.' She touches his ankle. 'Mick. Come on love.' A small sound that could be Mickey giggling. The woman smiles down at Maureen like a distant pale moon. Maureen raps her knuckles across the small ankles. Mickey hops then stands still. The woman grasps a handful of white cotton and twitches it up gracefully as if she's about to bossa nova across to the hatchway. A grinning Mickey retreats between two vast white thighs. Maureen grabs and hauls. 'It's not a game, Mick.' The man laughs, taking Mickey's side.

Maureen stands with the boy straitjacketed in her arms, trying to find the thing to say. The woman adjusts her dress and pats Maureen on the arm, 'I used to have a dog that did worse, to perfect strangers.'

'He doesn't usually do things like that,' Maureen smiles at them gratefully. She and the woman stand looking at each other as if there's more to be said, until the man says the seats are all being taken and the two of them turn away. Maureen stands for a little while watching them. Sometimes she gets this great longing to hang around with the grownups.

Back to Carly sitting primly on the edge of the carton. A set of fork prongs have bitten their way through a corner fold. 'You haven't seen Alan?' No.

'I'll have to look for him, love. If you just stay here. I won't be long.'

Carly's bottom lip quivering. Her eyes staring mistily past the rails at the slurping sea.

'You can't slide through. There's rails and that thing at the bottom there.' Carly's face turns to her, disbelief in the vague hazel eyes.

'Oh god. Come on then, we'll put this stuff somewhere and . . .' Feeling now the knapsack's dead weight on her shoulders. Others have left their baggage on this top deck clustered around a funnel unattended.

What kind of thief, among all that, would want to steal a knapsack of kids' clothes, Alice's white elephants or a guineapig of doubtful health? A dumb thief.

If she told that to Alan he would laugh immoderately. Alan has no sense of humour. He laughs loudly and uncomfortably and often in the wrong places. He thinks jokes are to do with pattern and repetition and sometimes he invents his own; pathetic legless things that go nowhere.

Free of luggage Maureen hoists Mickey onto her left hip and offers Carly her right hand. Carly, Maureen realises with that vortex feeling of a plug just pulled, is empty-handed. 'The bag, Car? Where is it?' Carly looks down at her hands and shrugs.

'What did you do with it?'

'I never had a bag.'

'You did. The green bag, remember? Car, you didn't leave it on the wharf?'

Carly's eyebrows pucker. Her bottom lip trembles.

'Oh never mind. Never mind.' But Maureen hears the cold anger behind her own words.

The green bag contained nothing that was valuable. Nothing, strictly speaking, that was necessary. Liquorice allsorts for bribing, a damp facecloth for wiping, a ballpoint and a newsprint pad for occupying, two oranges for dividing and some clean pants for Mickey just in case.

Maureen takes Carly's hand and they begin to move towards the stairs. Engine rooms are surely somewhere low.

'I feel sick.' Carly tugs at her mother's hand.

'You can't feel sick. We're not even moving yet.'

As she says it the motor comes to life. The gangway is being dismantled. Men in rolled-up jeans and unlaced sneakers shout to each other and throw armfuls of rope. Goodbye green bag.

'They're like pirates, don't you reckon?'

Alan has appeared from nowhere, dancing up and down, his face wide and wild with delight.

'I told you to hang on to Mickey. People were treading on him.'

'I couldn't help it. He wanted to go back to you. I told him, but he just went.' Alan's too excited to sound properly misjudged. 'You wanta see the engines?'

'No.'

'You'd like them. It's not far. You'll really like them. Carly wants to, don't you Car?'

'Later, okay. I just want to sit down. Did you see any empty seats anywhere? We have to find somewhere to sit.'

There are passengers everywhere; standing, walking, squeezed onto benches.

'What about downstairs?'

'You wanta come?'

'No. Just did you see any seats?'

'There's lots of people.' But he sees how tight she's wound. The urgency of the need. 'We could go out the back, there.'

It looks like a great distance. Legs, bags and baskets to be got past.

'You go and see if there's empty seats. Okay? We'll wait here.'

Watching him push his way through with more determination than tact. And sitting down, in the meantime, beside the baggage surrounding the funnel. Mickey squeezing his small self beside her. Carly looking doubtfully at the wooden floor and sweeping it with her hand before she sits.

Alan returns. 'There are sort of seats.'

'What sort of?'

'Just sort of. I dunno. It's good out there anyway.'

'It's all right, love. We may as well stay here. No one's stood on us.'

'Here. On the floor.' He's horrified. He has no confidence in his mother's ability to lead, provide, nurture. Every time Maureen makes a decision she can tell by Alan's face that his fears are being substantiated.

'It'll do,' she says, leaning back against a suitcase.

Alan looks around for scandalised faces. He crouches tentatively, then stands up.

Mickey pulls at Maureen's shirt for attention. 'Dwink.'

'I haven't got any, Mick. You'll have to wait till we get to the Island.'

'Yes you have,' prompts Carly. 'You got oranges.'

Maureen shakes her head. 'They were in the green bag.'

'You lost it?' Alan takes such pleasure in Carly's transgressions.

Maureen says, 'No one lost it, it just got lost.'

Alan looks at his mother pityingly. She doesn't meet his eye.

Carly's face has crumpled and now she begins to sniff. 'I want an orange so much.'

'Hard luck,' says Maureen sourly.

'We all want an orange,' says Alan, 'but we can't have one 'cos someone lost the bag.' Maureen gives him a warning look.

Carly sniffs. 'Oh shut up,' says Maureen too loudly, so heads turn. Alan walks away from them, his shoulders hunched in shame. Carly pushes herself around so her back is to her mother. She folds her head in her arms. Maureen can feel the girl's back trembling with stifled sobs.

'Dwink,' says Mickey.

Maureen takes a long deep breath. Something knobbly prods between her shoulder blades from the vinyl wall of a stranger's suitcase. The ferry trip takes fifty minutes and they haven't even left the wharf yet.

*　　　*　　　*

Josie McBride is fair, fat and forty-six. That was how she put it to Geoff before they first slept together. Except then she said fair, fat and pushing forty—which she was at the time. She'd said it with bravado, as if saying it would remove the sting of truth. As if once acknowledged by her it would no longer be apparent to him.

She can remember the day, that moment of saying, with rare clarity. The anxiety, the inevitability. The way they moved and spoke. The way their looks collided when trying to edge politely past. Oh Jesus, no, she'd thought, recognising the tremors. Knowing even then that this one was going to be the most devastating upheaval yet. It's like an old movie many times replayed. The woman is at once familiar

11

and remote. Good god; was I really so defensive, so insecure?

Fair, fat and forty-six. Saying it to herself now, and the words have a proud resonance. Optimism. Like a peal of morning bells.

McBride is Josie's maiden name. It's the name she began with and the name she intends to end with. She has been Josie White and Josie Stevens. In other old familiar movies.

Josie McBride and Geoff Patterson sit side by side hand in hand on a wooden bench open to the weather. They are aboard an old and unceremonious ferry which sails between Auckland city and the island of Motuwairua. The ferry rides low in the water burdened by its Saturday rash of passengers. Every few minutes people searching for a seat, or for friends or fresh air push their way along the narrow space of deck between the bench where Geoff and Josie sit—squeezed between an old woman reading a race guide and three Asian students—and the boat railing. Then Geoff and Josie tuck in their knees and lean back against the peeling green wall.

Even when Josie's toe is stood on, and when Geoff is whacked across the jaw by a string bag full of leather sandals it feels like part of the entertainment. Josie and Geoff are day-trippers; baggage-free and footloose on a small unpremeditated adventure.

And when she frees her hand from his to find a cigarette and light it and then reaches between them to find again his hand it's not just for comfort. Between his hand and her hand there is still a current. At least there seems to be. She's almost sure.

Only half an hour ago the two of them were sitting among the orderly concrete of Auckland's Downtown park. Josie making tentative plans: 'We could go and see Sandi. If she's back.'

Geoff seemed not to be listening.

'Or Paul and Juliet? We *ought* to see them.'

Geoff sighed.

'Oh well,' said Josie after a decent interval, 'we'll just sit here then all bloody morning and watch the concrete grow.' Which she did for a full thirty seconds. 'What're we going to do then? Go home?'

'That's not home,' he said. Making her sad for him, and a bit for herself. So she touched his thigh in comfort.

A girl walked across the park. She carried a canvas bag with a rug slung between the straps. For a few minutes the clouds cleared and the sun caught the gold threads in her skirt.

They watched her cross the street and be met by another girl. This one in baggy khaki pants, black shirt, army surplus knapsack. The two of them going into the ferry building, which is busy as a railway station on this quiet weekend morning.

'Where are they all going?'

Josie shrugged. 'Devonport . . . the islands maybe.'

'Which islands?'

'The Gulf islands. You don't think they'd be off to Tonga with their overnight bags?'

'Let's go then.'

'Where?'

'Wherever. Does the boat come back again?'

'I think so.'

'Coming?'

'What say it rains?'

'It's not gonna rain.'

Always such certainty. As if he had inside information: on the weather, the future, the election prospects, the national debt. And despite herself she is always inclined to believe him. As if by making his prediction he has placed upon fate an obligation to perform. The same way he's lucky with dice and always winning pub raffles for a bag of mussels or a haunch of wild pig.

So she followed him. Not even a jersey to pull over her cotton dress. If it rained she would say I told you so and get wet and cold. If it didn't rain she would half-believe he had kept the clouds at bay. Always a tinny bastard.

Today they had been up by the silly Saturday hour of six o'clock. And Josie awake for an hour or so before that. Hearing Sarah running a bath, padding up and down the passage, talking to herself or probably Hogg . . . to someone or something who didn't reply. Josie wondering if she should get up and make some parental speech, say I love you, like the Americans do on TV, spelling it out in case they haven't noticed.

Who's being pseudo, Sarah would say. Pronouncing it swaydough. Plagiarising Josie's little old joke.

At eight thirty-five, departure time, Josie and Geoff were standing at the viewing deck at the International Airport watching the Jumbo turn for take-off. Josie was poised to wave—feeling dutiful and foolish for surely they wouldn't be able to see her. Possibly they wouldn't even think to look. Beside her Geoff stood with his hands in his pockets. They're not his children.

13

She wanted him to be feeling, as the plane tucked in its wings, some emotion that might pass for paternal concern. She suspected him of feeling only relief. She thought, if he wants to leave now while the plane is still there, while Daryl and Sarah may just conceivably be craning wistfully for a last glimpse of their mother, then she will hate him.

'I suppose,' he said, 'you want to wait here till it's halfway across the Tasman?'

'Just till I'm sure it won't turn back.'

'It won't turn back.'

'Well, just for a while.' The shrinking silver gleam on the sky was draining her. She felt, suddenly, the chill wind. Then the release; the marvellous selfish joyful realisation that she was no longer in the middle. In the months ahead . . . perhaps for the rest of her life . . . she would no longer be the mediator, negotiator, placator. She squared her unburdened shoulders.

Geoff took her hand as she turned away from the glint in the sky. 'That's it.'

'Mm. That's it.' Oh hell, she thought, now he'll want to go to bed. The minute they've gone; it would feel like betrayal.

'Geoff, let's not go home. Not yet.'

'Okay. What d'you wanta do?'

'I dunno. I just feel . . .' Restless. Excited. Weepy.

Bereft.

'Come on then. We'll find somewhere classy for breakfast, then we'll do whatever you want to do.'

Which seems to be sitting wedged on this trundling boat feeling for her bruised middle toe and watching the select seafront homes of the North Shore slide slowly past like first act scenery being carried off stage.

Geoff has been watching her. 'You're not worrying about plane crashes?'

'I wasn't, but now you've mentioned it.' They're on the right side if the sun comes out.

'I hope there's a lot of room on the island or some of us are gonna be paddling.'

'It's about sixteen miles long or something. I imagine we'll all squeeze on.' She hears herself sometimes sounding like an infant mistress.

'Have you been there?'

'Actually I think I have. I'm pretty sure. Years ago. My memory's getting so bad. There's things . . . I don't know if I remember them or maybe dreamt them. D'you find? Perhaps it's television . . . too many images so that after a time we can't sort out reality?'

'It's because you've led such a long and full life.'

She digs her nails into his hand until he laughs in pain. Geoff claims to be about forty-one. His exact age, his origins are a mystery. His adoptive parents were, he claims, either secretive or uninformed. His birth certificate was made out after he was adopted; at which point in her estimates he was already about two years old.

—How do you know, Josie has demanded, if your parents didn't tell you anything?

—Well, if you went by my age there I would've started school when I was three and left when I was fourteen—pubic hair and my voice broken years before. So maybe I was a prodigy. Only when I started school there was this story I heard that I'd been dumped off by a drover heading south. And he never came back for me.

—But you asked your parents?

—A few times, but I didn't get any real answer. They didn't talk much anyway. Only what time's the tide and which hens were clucky and who was stealing the calves this time.

—But adults in the district . . . neighbours . . . didn't you ask them?

—Most of them'd moved by the time I really thought about it. Anyway if I'd made a big thing of it it might've upset my old folks.

If it was Josie she wouldn't be able to leave things so raggedy; it's as if his life began frayed.

'Are there bushes and things? Privacy?'

She looks at him, oh you . . .

'It's all this sitting still. Anyway you can't talk, we were hardly on board and you were shoving young men up your dress.'

Josie looks sideways to see if the Asian students have a grasp of English, but they're exclaiming incomprehensibly over a passing tug. The woman is still studying form. Now she keeps her voice low. 'I knew what you were thinking. While his poor mortified mother—'

'So you should.'

'Should what?'

'Know what I'm thinking. After all this time.'

For no reason she begins to feel sour. She makes it an accusation: 'Alone at last—that's what you were thinking.'

He doesn't hear her changed tone. He turns to face her with an unsuspecting leer, but she is distanced from him. She sees this woolly haired man pushing his face at hers, smirking with victory. Suddenly she misses her children terribly. If there is a victor there must also be the vanquished.

Yet they'd wanted to go. They were agreeable if not wildly enthusiastic. They were both old enough to decide.

And she had wanted them to go. That was the truth of it. Being a mother had gone on too long, she wanted a time of just being Josie. She'd never have said so, but they knew all the same.

Another three or four years. It hadn't seemed so long till the chance came up – then it suddenly seemed like forever.

'What's the matter?' A defensive edge to his voice.

She smiles at him. 'Nothing.'

Reassured, he smiles back. His face is friendly with curves and crinkles. She sees he is lovely. She lets him slide in through her eyes and caress her mind, just a little indecently. She is amazed . . . as she always has been, as she increasingly is . . . by the astonishing evidence that he loves her, admires, desires her. Still; after seven years. In this throwaway world.

Which begins to look like third time lucky, but she lacks absolute faith. One corner of her mind is ever prepared for departure – lists of places to stay while she reassesses her options, an inventory of possessions which are indisputably hers, a few salient phrases to hurl behind her as she sweeps out the door and a – diminishing – collection of friends who could be expected to care and understand.

For seven years there has been a part of her poised always for a quick getaway. In forty-six years the one certain rule she has come to believe in is that the one who is left weeps the longest. She suspects it's the uncertainty that has prolonged their affair. It still feels like an affair. She can look at him now and make her mouth water. He's cashew nuts, gherkins and cheese, strawberries blotted with icing sugar. Josie has always been a greedy pig.

She moistens her lips. Geoff, who is watching, takes it for granted she has him in mind. 'Hullo.'

'Hullo,' she says back.

He nudges in closer. Her thigh is very aware of his thigh. There do seem to be times when life is prepared to let her have her cake and eat it too. Even to lick the bowl.

So is it ungracious of her to resent having to wash the eggbeater and the baking tin? And dry them? And put them away? The question, in one form or another, is always lying about in Josie's mind; having to be edged behind or pushed aside or stepped over. Waiting for a confrontation.

Now she rummages in her bag for cigarettes. When in doubt put something in your mouth—it's a rule that's served her from as far back as she can remember.

She flicks the dead match out over the boat rail. 'I hope the sun comes out.' Talking to Geoff is like talking to herself, that comfortable. Nothing seems banal.

'It will.' It is now obliged to.

But thinking of the sun, of that golden reflected heat up there on the wrong side of the clouds has reminded Josie of flying, of plastic trays with circles for plastic cups, of Daryl and Sarah.

So even though here they are Geoff and Josie in love and finally on their own and going nowhere in particular just for the hell of it . . . Josie is looking down at herself from an unfathomable height. Seeing them as two undistinguished dots on board a matchstick craft, frail in a vast and unpredictable ocean.

Free after twenty years of maternal cares and duties Josie feels more than anything . . . forsaken.

*　　　*　　　*

The Shelleys had warned him about the boat trip. Myra has said, with the kind of appalled pride with which someone might describe a homicidal relative, *absolutely ghastly*. But at least the holidays were over. Around Christmas those ferries . . . talk about primitive . . . little better than cattle trucks.

And Keith had at once felt mildly hopeful. Even began to look forward to the trip.

'Tell me about the Island itself. What's that like?'

'Motuwairua? Oh god, where to start . . . ?'

The Shelleys looking at each other, eyes widened, eye-brows rearing. Keith hunching down in his white wrought-iron chair watching them with uneasy wonder. Cowed by the glossy perfection of this scene: the Parisienne café table, the fresh strong coffee, croissants, paper napkins, the cobbled path leading past the ferns to the spa pool, the drooping entangled thatch of grapevine, passionfruit, clematis. And Mort unselfconscious in a dove grey suit . . . even his hairless scalp somehow seeming co-ordinated . . . Myra in a dazzling white dressing-gown affair soft as cottonwool, a gold chain on a tanned neck. Her head held high and swivelling graciously, like a goose.

They don't, thought Keith, just think they're neat; they're absolutely certain.

How could people change so much in just a few years? Where had they found this flawless confidence?

It's this city, he thought. Perhaps any city, but certainly this one. I've been feeling it in the still stale summer air. In the shops, the streets; something off-centre. Vanity and arrogance, struttings and self-satisfaction . . .

Motuwairua . . . ? Well it may be different now. No—places like that don't know how to change. There are, or have been . . . phases is the word I'd use. Yes, definitely phases . . . when it's been fashionable in certain circles to live over there. Oh god yes, for a while everyone was rushing over there and setting themselves up in gruesome little fibrolite baches . . . Subsisting on cockles and blackberries. My god yes, remember that Walter whatsisname? Until they grew out of it . . . Came to their senses. No, to my mind it was more a matter of growing out of it. Well six of one half a dozen of the other. I always found the place quite depressing. When did we last go over? Five . . . no it was . . . d'you know it would've been five years at least. Anyway the point is there's not a lot there except native forest reserves and retired people and a bunch of self-styled eccentrics . . .

Keith not wanting them to go on but not knowing how to stop them. Feeling as if he'd stumbled into a rehearsal and must wait politely through the whole script.

And there must have been something in his eye, some small particle of the city which made him touch his right eyelid without even thinking. For suddenly Keith felt something almost imperceptible, lighter than a moth's wing, touch the back of his hand.

He didn't hear it land.

He closed his left eye and looked past Mort's shoulder through the grapevine and the wisteria. The bay windows of the house next door were hazy golden brushstrokes of reflected light. The grapevine leaves were fuzzy edged.

Oh shit.

Nothing among the croissant crumbs or under the plate. Mort and Myra broke off their routine and watched Keith peer urgently into their coffee cups before lurching under the table.

The verandah floor is slats of mahogany-stained wood. A few

withered leaves, fresh crumbs, a couple of squashed grapes, one childsize sneaker. And the gaps in between.

Mort's executive shoes and navy blue socks, Myra's pale blue canvas things, surprisingly large. It could've bounced anywhere.

'Is something the matter?'

'No. I always throw myself under the table after breakfast.' Keith hearing the petulant anger in his voice. Rebuking himself; it's not their fault for godsake. You're a guest here.

'I've dropped a lens.' The secret is not to give up too easily, the thing exists and therefore can be found.

'A lens?' Myra was always thick. Some things no amount of redecoration can change.

'Contacts,' said Mort. 'Of course. I knew there was something different. I thought the haircut . . . something.'

Mort getting up, scraping back his chair, a lot of unnecessary footwork by the grey suede shoes. Leather sole on a small concave plastic teardrop, flattening, shattering?

'Right. Now what does it look like.'

Mort looking at Keith between the table legs. Myra's tanned ankles in canvas blue flipping into action.

'Heavens look at the time and I haven't woken the children.' Sounding to Keith like a pre-rehearsed exit line. To get her away, no doubt, from the unseemly sight of Mort crouching in his custom-made summerweight grey. As if this confirmed her fears that Keith's cloddishness was contagious and given another couple of days Mort would revert to draught beer and audible farting.

'It's tiny, clear, like a dewdrop,' Keith told Mort. 'I felt it hit my hand but I don't like the chances. Is it possible to get under here?'

'Only if you wormed your way. I wouldn't fancy. Costs a lot to replace?'

A lot by Mort's criteria or Keith's?

'Enough,' he said. A sudden surge of joy and he reached out for something small and glistening.

A fragment of cellophane from a cigarette packet.

So now Keith sits watching his fellow passengers—and beyond them, out the spattered greasy windows, the receding shores of Auckland—through a kind of visual warp. If he closes his right eye the faces, the buildings, have a sharp-edged precision. If he closes his left they melt and merge.

He is squeezed between an enormous lump of a young man wearing headphones and a couple of teenage girls who whisper and giggle and stuff themselves with marshmallows. In this back section of the boat they sit in rows like movie-goers without a movie. Keith debating whether the prospect of losing his seat for the rest of the trip outweighs his desire for fresh air and an unsmeared view of the harbour.

The numb fatalistic mood that's hung about him for the last week is being infiltrated by flickers of childish excitement. Perhaps it's the boat ride. Or the relief of getting away from that city.

He needs a drink.

In the public bar of the Everton DB, Lynn will be stacking up glasses, wiping down the pool cues, smiling. Thinking about it is a kind of homesickness.

Keith checks his back pocket. The key is still there. Tied to the key is a luggage label telling the lot number and street of Jerry Veale's bach in Hoki Bay, Motuwairua. Hoki Bay . . . the name sounds contrived. A token plastic tiki place full of American tourists and Jerry Veales. Small town sharpies wearing Hawaiian shirts under their reefer jackets.

Jerry Veale was and is the advertising salesman for the *Everton Times*. Keith Muir was and may again be the reporter for the *Everton Times*. The *Times* and a shared generation was about all the two of them ever seemed to have in common. But already Keith can look back and see there was more than that. They were both small town blokes. Just thinking about it he can feel a sentimental bonding.

Good old Jerry. Sliding into Keith's office when Tom was safely out of earshot.

'I admire you, mate. Courage of your convictions, eh. Not the boot Wendy says, just—how did he put it?—leave of absence?'

'That's about the size of it.'

'What'll you do?'

'I dunno Jerry.' Wouldn't tell you if I did.

'Well a holiday never goes amiss.'

'That's right.'

'If you were thinking of going away—well I got this bach up north. Motuwairua. Bought it in the sixties . . . four thousand would you believe, from the wife's old uncle. Just sitting there. We used to get up before the price of gas . . . hell when you add it up it's cheaper to hop over to Tahiti these days. Worth hanging onto though; time's gonna come when that place is some fancy suburb for the money boys.'

'It's empty, this place of yours?'

'Right. I pay some local bloke to keep the section tidy. God knows if he does. Should check that out. Always getting letters wanting to rent the place but you know how it is, tenants such a bunch of rip-off artists.'

Keith—always a tenant or a boarder—let it pass, accepted, offered rental payment which was refused.

'After all what are friends for.'

A vexed question. Keith's friends—the people he considers to be friends—are those who frequent his corner of the Everton DB public bar. Improvident and usually impoverished. Not handy in a crisis.

Edging himself out past the earphones Keith shares a few escaped notes. Distinctly honky tonk. And feels foolishly pleased at the unpredictability of things.

In the stern of the boat it's standing room only. Keith finds an unoccupied piece of wall and leans. The sun has come out and the gulf water is an extraordinary and translucent green. The city is behind them, distant and incidental; on Keith's right is the last strip of mainland, the last few palatial homes with private jetties and vast latticed windows. How would it feel to live in one of those, to be the owner of this constant view . . .? Ferries, ocean liners, weekend sailboats; the gulf islands scattered and aloof . . .

How must it feel to live in such splendour in a country at present so rancorous and fearful? To have a bedroom, a dining room, a leisure room, a den. Some people living in packing-cases, tents, even cars while other people have empty holiday homes lying round like loose change.

Which Keith could've had, might've had if he'd . . . Coveted more? Boozed less?

So what? My money, earned by me, I'm entitled. Which is what (he supposes) they're saying up there behind those big wide latticed windows. *I'm entitled.* The cry of the common kiwi. Clutching his rights to his breast and screeching; blind in the daylight of a dissolving world.

Water churning in the wake of the boat, clear and cold as ice-cubes. Jesus, thinks Keith, I could do with a drink.

He has no expectations of the bach. He hadn't thought to ask if it was furnished or how far from the shops. It's a long way from Everton; that seemed enough. A holiday bach in which to spend an enforced holiday. Four weeks off and six weeks' pay, which could be construed as a bribe but then again.

'You'll let us know either way. We'll need the time to find . . . Of course if you decide to come back to us but feel you need another week or two . . . Up to you, just so long as you keep us in the picture.'

Tom had looked up finally, because of the silence. Meeting Keith's eyes. Which Keith hoped would reflect a kind of sneering pity instead of the growing panic within him.

He'd gone back to his office to clear his desk. So much rubbish collected in nine years, he'd had to ask Wendy to find him a carton. Four Jim Beam flasks in the back of the bottom drawer, two of them not quite empty; paper, dead ballpoints, sepia shaded clippings, a sock, four hundred and thirty-two paper clips . . .

He'd carried the carton back to the Hereford Guest House. He didn't want them at the office poking through his debris. His room at the Hereford was round the back. A smell of rubbish bins and a view of sheets flapping dry. Keith was Mrs Pemberton's third-longest-staying guest. He told her he had leave but would be back in a month near enough. Then because she had rules about toll calls he walked to the post office to ring the Shelleys. They were listed in the Auckland directory. Shelley . . . Mort J & Myra. Modern & relaxed.

He got Myra, Mort was still at work. 'Keith Muir.' Silence. 'From the *Star* remember?'

Myra was the editor's secretary at the *Star*. She used to wear clip-on earrings and read Ian Fleming. That was before Mort improved her mind.

From the post office he'd walked up Ludlow Street. His father had painted the picket fence fire-engine red and plucked the garden bare. Dry cracked soil edged the concrete path and the front of the house. The front door was open and the pushbike was leaning against the wall of the passage just inside. Keith stood for a few minutes across the street just looking, then he walked home.

The next day he caught the road services bus to Auckland. Where, even though Myra had said yes of course, the Shelleys seemed inconvenienced by his arrival. For a few uncomfortable moments on the doorstep Mort had great trouble placing him. Because—Myra said later—Keith had actually changed so little in twelve years, whereas they . . . She'd smiled to show it was over to Keith but he said nothing.

It went without saying that the Shelleys had changed immeasurably. Myra no longer wears pearl-finish earrings and knits fluffy blue sweaters; she's lost at least a stone, wears soft draped supercilious clothes and works in a marvellous little up-market boutique. Mort no longer dreams of starting an underground magazine tentatively titled *Outspoke*;

Mort is managing editor of *Wordsell,* a thriving publishing business that produces a number of trade magazines. The Shelleys' house is furnished with unobtrusive antiques and overbearing houseplants. The Shelleys' three children, unisexed and vocal, demand, dictate and condescend.

Episodically—in the spaces of evening left between sibling fights and wordy parental understanding—Keith told Mort and Myra about his suspension from the *Everton Times*. He knew almost as soon as he began that he shouldn't have bothered. Like telling Pope jokes to the Archbishop of Canterbury; comes the crunch they're both on the same side.

'Frankly,' said Mort when Keith had finished, 'I think you'd be advised to pull your head in and pretend the whole thing never happened. You know how things are at the moment. Well maybe you don't; some of the small towns may be getting off lightly. So listen when I say we advertised for a reporter, grade four or thereabouts, a few months back. Know how many applied? Forty-seven. Four tea sev en. We're talking about people with post grad qualifications, not the old bum boys like you and me. And experience. I'd think on that if I were you.

'After all,' said Mort with a fine smirk, 'what you were telling me, I mean let's face it, it wasn't exactly Watergate.'

It wasn't exactly. And even then Keith had given an expurgated version—no mention of his editor's counterattack.

'You're a pisshead Keith. Let's face it. You're an everyday pisshead who's on the way to becoming an incompetent pisshead. It's called, in polite circles, having a drink problem. You're gonna have to get yourself together.'

And he hasn't even thought to ask ...

Keith leans down towards a woman with Medusa hair whose head is level with his knees. 'Excuse me.'

She looks up. A brown face wearing red feather earrings; Africa rules OK. Her upturned eyes are bloodshot.

'Do you know, is there a pub on this island?'

Still February 4th

PARENGA IS AT the northern end of Motuwairua. The wharf is at Parenga, which is the island's main shopping centre. There is a post office, TAB, dairy, Four Square grocery, taxi office, hardware shop, TV and video shop, drapers, second hand shop, a small dress shop which also sells local handcrafts, and a pub.

Geoff is disappointed; 'I was expecting a couple of palm trees and a tin shed.'

But Josie is reassured. She knows that soon their breakfast will have worn off and she only has a half packet of cigarettes left. She tries to remember if and when she came here before but nothing stands out demanding recognition. Just another little seaside town over-run with the summer trade.

Outside the hardware shop people are boarding an old green bus.

'You wanta go . . . ?'

Geoff shrugs.

Josie calls up to the driver, 'Excuse me but where do you go to?'

'Where d'you wanta go?'

She looks at Geoff. He shakes his head. 'Never mind,' she tells the driver. 'Thanks.'

A small queue has formed behind her.

Josie and Geoff walk back towards the wharf and along the beach. They walk on the firm damp sand avoiding the golden bodies, the towels and cans and ice-block wrappings that litter the soft sand further up. The sun semi-shines like daylight through a net curtain. Geoff walks as if the world is watching and he wishes it wouldn't.

He complains, 'I feel like a tourist.'

'You are.'

'I'm not you know. You might be but I'm not. It's a state of mind.'

'There's nothing wrong with being a tourist,' Josie says, not really believing it. 'It's the height of ambition for many people.'

'Your kind.' He grins and takes her hand. She thinks, they have so many kinds of holding-hands, various as kisses. Their hands have a perfect understanding and are not easily misinterpreted. Unlike the messages of their mouths.

This a companionable hand-hold, a reassuring us-against-the-world clasp. It lets her feel the roughness of his calloused palm, patches of thickened dead skin like sandpaper.

She has a fantasy—these days not much used. Candles burning, an echoing building, a church or vault, and Josie spread on a low table, hugely naked. Her wrists are bound and lashed by ropes beneath the table, her shoulders pulled so sharply back her body arches. She is blindfold but has already seen the candles and the dark cloaked figures that stand silently surrounding her. Just before the calloused hands touch her flesh she hears the watchers murmur something hypnotic and probably Latin. As the creature mounts her their voices rise in a united chant. His flesh against hers is scaled, cold and definitely reptilian.

'*Rosemary's Baby*,' said Geoff when she'd described it for him.

She felt put out, a slight on her erotic imagination. 'I never saw *Rosemary's Baby*.' She might've, she can't remember for sure.

'Then someone must've described it to you.'

She's largely dropped it from her collection. It was one of the more selfish ones; Geoff complained that no matter how hard he tried, being a lizard didn't do much for him.

On Parenga beach in the clear and public light of day the hard-healed blisters on Geoff's hands seem mainly to proclaim a kind of integrity. Proving he is a working man. Despite her doubts.

So she squeezes his horned hand tight. Feeling a kind of joyful excitement she thought she'd long ago grown out of. Knowing that on a small adventure like this something remarkable or bizarre could happen to them; confident that it won't.

Parenga beach is a beach to suit all tastes. First, near the wharf, is a long clear stretch of sand backed by sandhills. Behind the sandhills runs the road and, this being the hub of the island, this section of road is sealed, at least around the potholes. Back from the road are houses, not in a tidy suburban row but scattered on large sections, separated by overgrown vacant lots. From the beach the houses are almost hidden by the sandhills. There are a few conventional post-war weatherboard places with wooden sundecks added, but most are simply baches that seem to have been built long ago and in haste from whatever materials drifted in on the tide. There is one A-frame and one stucco-finished thing with dwarf-sized Spanish arches.

Further along the beach there's a strip of sand piled high with driftwood, as if the sea has obeyed some council ordinance on the dumping of litter. And beyond the driftwood there's a clump of huge pohutukawa, their network of massive roots rearing and writhing above the sand.

After trying to squeeze themselves beneath and about these roots Geoff and Josie find a narrow track leading up and around them. On the other side is another, smaller, beach edged at either end with rocks. Not, as they'd hoped, deserted. Four naked bodies dished up on towels, degrees of succulent brown. Two wide city boys in jeans, jackets, boots even, tucked in the shade of the pohutukawa overhang sharing a can of beer.

Geoff and Josie sit on the dry sand a proper distance from both parties. Josie takes off her sandals and pulls her skirt up to mid thigh. She doesn't really mind being fat until she's sitting on a public beach. On public beaches she becomes a lump of lard, palely envious. She can't imagine why she agreed to come here; an island nothing but a circle of beaches, and beaches something she tries to avoid. She insists she burns easily, has a delicate skin. Yet in the privacy of a back lawn she can lie for hours without turning pink. As if her volume intimidates the sunrays.

Geoff takes off his shirt and rolls up his trousers with a gloomy precision. She feels the same discomfort, knows better than to reach out to him. Here among this company they are middle-aged. Assigned that role they are obliged to fill it. They sit side by side and separate, thinking their private over-forty thoughts.

One of the naked ones stands up, shakes her towel then fixes it around her waist. She walks past Geoff and Josie as if they aren't there. Flawless brown calves brushing the edge of the white towelling. Dark hair, damp and curling. A girl, categorises Josie from her currently aged perspective. A pretty girl.

It makes Josie think of Lake, who is twenty and beautiful. Or could be. But Lake slouches and scowls and seeks out cold climates and neon-lit libraries where she can hibernate in her matted jerseys and proletarian overalls.

Lake is Josie's oldest child. She was, to the best of Josie's calculations, conceived the weekend after Josie's first husband—a small time entrepreneur called Farley White—had finally decided he wasn't as bi as he'd thought and had moved in with his manfriend. Taking selected goods and chattels and leaving the small flat which he and Josie had shared largely empty yet thoroughly claustrophobic.

So Josie had emphatically volunteered to spend a couple of days in

Wanganui interviewing an ex-prisoner who had made the Sunday papers with tales of corruption in enclosed places. She booked in at a central hotel, located the man and taped their conversation, all on the first day. The man's name was Henry and his information was convincing but too libellous to be of use. Henry's boss, who believed in freedom of speech, lent them his office for the interview. In those days even ex-criminals could get jobs.

That night Henry came to the hotel where Josie was drinking alone in the private bar, to tell her of some detail which had earlier slipped his mind. She bought him a drink and he bought her one. She drank faster than he did. He told her she was the first real lady he'd ever known. Even though he must've been several years older than her he treated her with deference. And at the time this seemed to her only natural; she was educated and worked for the radio.

He followed the horses and had almost perfected a system which he explained in detail and she didn't understand at all. He'd done his military service before he went to prison and he thought shooting was too good for communists.

She didn't even bother to argue. He had very white teeth and long dark eyelashes. He had SANDRA tattooed on his wrist and told her, shyly, he would love to have JOSIE engraved on the other wrist. Willingly, unprofessionally, she took him off to bed. Where he was by progression timid, tender, unbridled. She allowed him the communists but refused his pleas to be permitted to stay there cuddled up till dawn. I love you, he'd said as she edged him furtively out onto a sidestreet.

It was generally assumed that Lake was Farley's child and Josie has never told anyone except Geoff that this might not be so. Not even Lake who would seem to have more right than anyone to know the variables. If Lake *is* Farley's child Josie thinks nature has a sardonic system of selection and reward. (And if she isn't at least Lake has squared things up with the communists.) Finding herself pregnant Josie reasoned that Farley had, however indirectly, caused it to happen and her baby was therefore entitled to whatever Farley might offer by way of emotional or material support.

In fact Farley offered nothing in either field. So when Lake was weaned at seven weeks Josie returned to work. Lake was cared for weekdays by a mother-of-four who loved, or pretended to love, cooing and wiping and hushing and feeding. In those days motherhood was still a sacred obligation, but Josie didn't feel altogether guilty of maternal neglect because she was after all a martyr to Farley's lack of conscience. She was a brave big wife-and-mother doing the best she could.

Nor did she feel bad at the time about the piddling amount she paid the mother-of-four. The woman told Josie how much she loved baby Lake and how wonderful it was to be able to earn a bit of money in her own home doing the job she was best at. Josie believed her. Josie had only been a full-time at-home mother for seven weeks and for the first four weeks had been too tired to want to do anything else.

Lake, as she grew, didn't resemble Farley. Neither, to the best of Josie's recall, did she resemble Brief Henry. She was a large featured child who only grew into her face in her middle teens which was perhaps too late. Lake had a pedantic and humourless intelligence and very little time for people who didn't measure up.

Josie ceased to measure up when she threw in a decent job – you even had a measure of *influence*, wailed Lake – and dragged her family up north to a run-down farm in the Hokianga so that she could be with her lover.

Lake. Josie had named her in a moment of romantic excess, imagining she was bestowing upon her daughter such elemental qualities as freedom, depth, fluidity and beauty. And Lake arguably had the first and last of those fairy wishes but they didn't seem to give her pleasure.

Josie has almost got over worrying whether Lake's personality was damaged in those first four years when she had two homes and two mothers. Or later, when she was a half-sister and therefore condemned to being different. Josie has almost stopped feeling to blame for whatever it was that has made Lake so judging and joyless. If life doesn't start at forty at least about then the guilt starts to disperse. Or takes on other forms. Josie now thinks that if she is the cause of Lake's unlakeishness then that's the way it goes. You can't unpick the past and take it in or let it out for a better fit.

And, to be honest, if Josie could remodel the past Lake wouldn't be her first concern. At forty-six Josie's only concrete regret is that Geoff, who alone deserved her youth, was too late for it.

One night when Geoff had made the four-hour drive to Auckland to visit her (in those early weeks when she still thought of it as a 'fling' she was having) Daryl had maliciously unearthed a shoe box of old family photos for Geoff's entertainment. Geoff had spread the photos over the carpet and knelt among them, shuffling and examining wildly as if the images would fade in the night light. He'd snatched up a picture of Josie aged about twenty at the wedding of her cousin Frank. Hair teased into a sleek fat beehive, a hideous navy blue lace dress. She's holding a wine glass and smiling at someone, not the photographer but someone unseen. She was slimmer in those days or at any rate firmer. Voluptuous, men used to say, greasing up. Big and fat was what she believed.

Geoff had looked at the photo for a long time, a little enraptured smile growing. 'Wow,' he'd said eventually. Causing Josie's past to take on a new perspective.

At the time of the photo Josie was going out with Farley White and in love with Terry Hackett whose desk at work faced hers and who was married. Neither Farley nor Terry had ever looked at Josie in a way that conveyed a wholehearted unambiguous wow.

Geoff is leaning back on his elbows looking out to sea, to a grey shadow of an island they'd thought, on the ferry trip, was this one. Josie takes a handful of sand and trickles it over his chest. Now they've been here a while it seems an allowable intimacy. The sand lodges among hairs and he brushes it away with mild exasperation but looks at her.

'I wish I was young for you,' she says. The moment is wrong and she's said it before but no matter. There will be other moments, and the fear of boring him has long since died.

He shrugs. 'I mightn't have liked you when you were young. You mightn't have liked me.'

And he's right. She's back there at cousin Frank's wedding in her navy blue lace. Underneath it she wears a boned contraption called, for Chrissake, a torsalette. (Or was it corsalette? Fancy remembering, whatever it was. No wonder she looked firmer.) She is cynical, already, about weddings and wouldn't be seen dead in an engagement ring. She has a job in broadcasting. Just saying so makes her feel a bit bohemian and outrageous, at least among her small-town relations with their provincial ambitions and bad honeymoon jokes.

She might notice Geoff hanging about in a corner. Being adolescent and a hayseed he'd have drunk too much. She would think, if she thought anything, that he had nice eyes. She might even feel that somehow he didn't *fit in* any more than she did. But if they talked she would think him ordinary. She was impressed in those days by wit and erudition; by men who drank dry red and recited Garcia Lorca to relieve life's boredom. If they talked Josie's eyes would be looking past Geoff in search of more appropriate company. That's the truth and tragedy of it.

29

She often thinks about the enormous odds against their having met. Now she must add to that the odds against their meeting when the time was right. Coincidence it may be, but thinking about it gives Josie a vague sense of obligation. Not so much towards Geoff as towards fate.

'There's a track behind us,' he says. 'Let's see where it goes.' Let's get away from here where we're only what other people see us as.

'Let's,' says Josie reaching for her sandals.

The track leads steadily up a hill. Once they've lost sight of the beach below it's hard to know where they are or where they're going because the track winds on through scrubby manuka. Geoff walks in front, holding himself back because he's fitter than she is. Still, she consoles herself, I'm not as unfit as I look; not as unfit as I was seven years ago.

They can't be too far from civilisation; cigarette packets and ice-cream wrappers and chippie packets mark out a trail. She thinks of Hansel and Gretel scattering crumbs.

Turning to wait for her Geoff says, 'They'll be there now. Sydney.'

Josie's ashamed it wasn't her thought. She'd forgotten. 'Oh god, I hadn't thought . . . what if they ring? If Dick's not there or something? We should've gone home.' Accusing him in her heart, thinking usurper.

'They'll be okay,' he says.

And she knows he's right. All three of her children have always been more capable of handling the world than she has ever been. Abandoned at Sydney airport they would ring their father, ring the police, ring the New Zealand Consulate if they have one over there. They would not ring their mother in Auckland.

'Goddam,' Sarah would say making a face, 'we can't drag her out of bed, not in the middle of the afternoon. Not when they've been waiting all these years to get us out of the way. That would be cruel.' Even an ocean away and by imaginative proxy Sarah can make Josie grin. On behalf of Sarah she slows her steps and lets Geoff get ahead. It's a kind of rebuke.

When she catches up with him they are out of the bush and at the top of the hill. He's sitting on the grass, his knees tucked up, grinning like a garden gnome. On one side, looking down, there are a succession of small bays, a few houses scattered here and there. On the other side is Parenga—beach, shops, wharf and houses spreading out behind. Beyond that, the sea with its small grey islands and the patterning of green and blue and grey.

He gives her a long time to take it in.

'Well?'

The way he's looking at her she assumes . . . 'Here?'

His laugh cracks out at her. 'I meant the place. Everything. What d'you think?'

'Terrific,' she says. 'Incredible. And any other superlatives you care to add.' But she's reading his face and her voice loses interest in her words.

'Josie, love, look at it. What more could we want? What more could you ask. This place is fucken paradise.'

Her face says, but . . . She's thinking of the little beach below them, the naked bodies, the hard-eyed city boys in their new boots. Yet she knows that's not where her doubts begin. She knows that if they lived here they could avoid or visit beaches on their own terms.

'What's wrong with it?' Already he's claimed the place and will take any criticism personally.

'An island.' *That's it.* Having said it she knows that this is precisely what bothers her. 'I don't think I want to live on an island. I think I'd feel trapped.'

'No you won't.'

'I suppose there's no harm in thinking about it, taking a look round.' It is, after all, Geoff's money.

'Horticulture,' he says tugging at a shoot of bracken. 'I've always fancied horticulture. Ten, twenty acres. We could even get a bit of a boat, do some fishing as a sideline.'

It's not ridiculous, she tells herself. It's perfectly plausible. Believe in him!

'Mmm,' she says. 'But we could do that on the mainland. A place along the coast somewhere.' She sits down beside him on the prickling grass. 'It's just . . . this feels like another country. Cut off. That's it. I think I'd feel cut off.'

He's hurt. 'With me?'

And now she knows exactly what the fear is. It's the knowing that if they split up—when they split up—she'll be stuck here on this bloody island with a pile of possessions and a handful of severed threads. Stepping back onto the mainland like some Rip Van Winkle, forgotten and outmoded.

Such thoughts are treacherous and possibly self-fulfilling. Shame makes her pretend to reconsider, to gaze around as if she's seeing through fresh eyes.

31

'It *is* beautiful. I guess it does seem very nearly perfect, and if the right place was on the market . . .'

It's his day for victories. He beams and spreads inviting arms. His lips smooch beneath her ear, his voice tickles. 'Mmm, let's . . .'

*   *   *

Motuwairua Island BussCos is painted in grimy white on the side of the green bus. The extra Ss are wobbly additions. In front where you'd expect to read the destination it simply says *wharf*, but people who have just got off the ferry are climbing onto the bus with confidence.

Keith has the idea that the island is small, the kind of place you could walk around in one fairly energetic afternoon. He's surprised to see not only the bus but also a taxi waiting and another departing. But then he remembers all those suitcases, children, cats in cardboard carriers, surf boards, portable stereos he'd had to navigate on board.

Keith will walk. He has only a backpack (a surprise donation from Mrs Pemberton) containing a few clothes and his portable typewriter. He needs to walk. The restlessness that fidgets within him is not just the old familiar restlessness that's calmed with the first glass, this is something more. A buoyant edginess. He can't remember having felt quite this way before yet he feels there was a time . . . he ought to remember. Something.

From Parenga a road runs behind the beach then moves inland and seems to curl up and over the hill. The signpost says *Whiripare Bay 8kms*. Past the shops another road – or the same road returning – heads past the shopping centre and straight inland rising up towards the hills where the flanking homes thin out. Keith finds a signpost. It has four broken arms and one intact. The surviving arm says *Kaimoana Beach 9kms*. The splintered remains of the other signs all point in the same direction. This road is busier – four moving vehicles and seven parked ones – but the bus, moving off, takes the beach road.

'Can you tell me, how do I get to Hoki Bay?'

She chews her gum thoughtfully. 'Should'a got the bus.'

'I thought I'd walk.'

'It don't come back this way you know. Goes straight through to Kaimoana. Still if you's to get there quick you might get to catch it.'

'I don't mind walking.'

'You should stick your thumb out. Someone's bound to stop.'

'Hoki Bay,' he reminds her.

32

'Well you go to Kaimoana, right? Then you turn off—facing this way it's your left. And it's . . . I dunno . . . maybe four miles something from there.'

'Thanks.'

When he's a few yards past her she yells, 'Hey, get that bloody thumb out.'

By the time the houses have started to thin out he knows why the islanders choose not to walk. Even though the sun is veiled by cloud the heat is oppressive. Halfway up the hill and the sweat is trickling into his eyes and where the pack rests on his back his shirt clings and wrinkles. Still he keeps to the righthand verge so they won't think he's wanting a lift. Walking does seem to calm the agitation.

He tries, again, to define that edginess. How strange if it was nothing more than excitement; if in thirty-four years he had forgotten such a commonplace emotion. When did he last feel . . .?

Crossing the road from Simon Street, pulling open the swing doors, squinting in the neon-lit dimness of windows painted on the lower panes, scarred varnished wood, Lynn with her sharp feral face smiling, reaching for a glass. (Excitement! he tells himself, oh very droll Keith, very funny I'm sure.)

Besides this feeling he has is more than excitement. There's something at stake between him and this island.

Round the bend at the top of the hill there's a sweeping view of Auckland poised at the sea's edge. From a safe distance it looks imposing, self-important, polished. From the top of the hill the road winds more steeply down to the sea. The houses are closer to the road and to each other.

Kaimoana beach is a stretch of small stones, broken shells and seafaring plastic fragments. There's a post office, a store, a garage and an undamaged signpost. Keith buys a packet of orange juice. He'd seen the pub in Parenga and walked right past. Big bay windows and a beer garden planted with umbrellas—not his kind of pub. And he'd thought in a vague way that if there was one pub there'd be others. Even Everton had three pubs.

Hoki Bay 7kms; Huri Bay 11 kms.

The road runs inland again. A bridge across a marshy estuary thick with mangroves then unsealed roadway winding through the bush. Keith walks on the brick-hard mud at the edge of the road. Above him trees join to make an arch, daylight shifts and flickers between leaves; a harsh chorus of cicadas rings in his ears.

A church in Napier; a vast, cold, echoing cathedral of a building close to the newspaper office. Where he'd gone for an interview for a job as cadet reporter. Taken her, out of pity or necessity. His brand new driving licence in the dashboard of the Vauxhall. Coming out to find her gone though he'd said, you will stay here, please. Then finding her, first shot, in the church. Perhaps because of the music. Someone in there playing the organ and her sitting there alone in the middle of the empty pews head bowed but her eyes skittering all around, only closing piously when she saw he'd found her.

The tunnel of trees opens out to bright sunlight and the first scattered homes of Hoki Bay. He can't yet see the beach, only a wide blue expanse of Pacific Ocean. Already he's reached the other side of the island. Small roads run off this road. He asks directions from an old woman (one of Myra's retired eccentrics) who's planting cuttings on the road bank. She points towards the sea. 'The next one, on your right. Only they aren't lot numbers any more. We've got proper street numbers and they're nowhere the same.'

'The place belongs to a guy called Veale.'

'I wouldn't know dear. But the Council people could tell you. Monday.'

'There's no one living there. You don't know if there's a place empty?'

She pinches her cheeks together. 'Not this time of year, love.'

But when he's thanked her and walked on she calls after him, 'Try the place with the old iron gate. On your right.'

The iron gate is open. It's been open for years, grass grows up to its middle. A track leads to the house which sags towards the bushes. There are towels on the clothesline and as he walks along the broken concrete path that runs up the side of the house he sees through the windows that the place is definitely lived in.

At the back of the house is an old-fashioned verandah covered with naked women. Only three of them and all a redeeming over-all brown shade, nevertheless it seems to Keith an overwhelming amount of flesh.

'Oh I'm sorry.' He takes a step back out of view and waits. He can hear the sea.

'What is it you want?'

'I was looking for a place . . . a bach . . .' It feels absurd, talking around a corner. 'It's supposed to be on this road. The owner's called Veale. Jerry Veale. An empty house.'

'Sorry.'

'You won't find any empty houses, not round here.'

'Best of British, anyway.' And they gurgle pleasurably among themselves.

On his way out Keith sees, behind the iron gate, the edge of a once white-painted board protruding from the long grass. He checks that no one is peering at him from front windows then kicks the board free of grass. It is in fact a small roughly painted sign which reads just visibly Lot 57.

Standing on the road Keith takes the key from his back pocket in case his memory is faulty. The attached label says Lot 57.

The sign could conceivably belong to another property. Jerry could've sent him to the wrong off-shore island. The Council could've sold the place to recover unpaid rates.

Back on the main road walking the easy distance to the Hoki Bay shop—*frozen bread film sunglasses* chalked on an outside blackboard—Keith wonders about the instinct that made him look closer at a piece of white-painted wood. And why he's feeling so jaunty when he may not even have a place to sleep tonight. So hug-himself smug as if he's finally stumbled into adolescence, though never his own.

Hoki Bay has, besides the store, a phone box and the Motuwairua Memorial Hall. Keith tries the store. He waits for the man at the counter to count out lollies—ten from each of three jars—and sort them into white paper bags for the five small children in crêpe paper hats.

'Veale you say? Lot fifty-seven?' The shopkeeper hasn't been here all that long, but he'll try and find out.

Keith waits among the paperbacks and occasional cards while the man makes a call in his tiny glassed-in office. The shopkeeper comes back with a smile lunging from a tight leash.

'You go back up and to the left, Agnes Road right? And along a bit you'll see these old iron gates pretty much off their hinges. Little place, not much more than a bach, back off the road a bit.'

'Someone seems to be living there.'

'That's right.' The shopkeeper's smile breaks free. It has sharp edges. 'Mizzz Glass.'

Keith doesn't smile back, 'But I've got the key.' He holds it up as evidence.

'Looks like the two of you'll have something to sort out then.' He pulls the smile back in.

The sun's gone behind substantial clouds and the women have put on some clothes. He'd coughed strategically before he turned the corner and tried to walk noisily in his canvas shoes, but all for nothing. He stands at the corner, at the bottom of the verandah steps and they look at him and wait. He has to clear his throat before any words come. 'Is one of you Miss Glass?'

This entertains them. '*Miss Glass,*' parrots the dark-haired one.

Keith waits.

'Me,' says the big one eventually and it seems by then an act of kindness.

'I came just before,' says Keith. 'I was looking for . . .'

'I thought you might be back.' She gets up slowly and moves a couple of steps towards Keith extending her hand. He's obliged to trot up the steps and shake it.

'Daphne Glass.' Firm and formal in her khaki shorts and torn T-shirt, bogglingly bra-less.

'I'm Keith Muir.' Never before has his name sounded so limp. 'We seem to have a problem.'

'We?'

'I've been told this is the place I was looking for. It belongs to Jerry Veale of Everton. Is that right?'

'Possibly,' concedes Daphne Glass. 'But you could equally say it's my place insofar as I'm the one who lives here.'

'But not legally.'

Daphne shrugs. 'Squatters' rights.'

'I'm afraid the owner's said I could use the place. I have the key.'

'How nice for you.' Ms Glass pauses long enough for her friends to smirk, then she smiles at Keith as if she means it. 'How long were you thinking of . . . ?'

'Three weeks . . . four. Maybe more.' He should probably offer to let her stay on for a few days until she finds somewhere else. He would rather not but it seems only fair.

Daphne is looking him up, down and across. 'That'll be all right,' she says. 'There's a spare bedroom, just needs a bit of clearing.'

Keith sighs a little too extravagantly. 'Look, I know the owner. We work together. I may not like him over-much but I know the guy. I have his permission. That makes me the legal tenant. I can't just let you. Anyway I want a place on my own.'

'You and everyone else,' says Daphne. 'You think I want to share?'

The red-haired woman says to Keith quite kindly, 'You do know we're in the grip of a chronic housing shortage. Everywhere, but here especially.'

'I realise,' says Keith. 'But that's not my fault. Not my problem either.'

Daphne settles herself on the windowledge as if they're in for a long debate. 'I suppose,' she asks, 'you've come equipped? Bed, pots, mattress, plates etcetera? All the stuff here's mine. If your mate thought the place was furnished you can tell him it walked out of here years ago. When I moved in it was bare. Even the stove, that's mine.'

Keith takes a long breath then a grin starts coming. He eases the pack off his shoulders and sits down on the steps. The women look at each other and smile a bit.

'Hennie and Kay,' says Daphne, 'meet my new flatmate. What's your name again?'

'Keith.'

'I suppose, Keith,' says Hennie from the old wicker chair, 'that after that boat ride you could manage a cup of tea.'

'I could manage a cup of tea,' agrees Keith gratefully.

Hennie is small and sun-browned. She has a dark, clever face. More like a bantam, Keith thinks fondly.

'Lemon balm, mint, or straight tea?' Hennie watches him intently but doesn't move from her chair.

'Whatever,' says Keith. Leaning against the verandah post, stretching out his weary legs and trying to hold in the idiotic grin of good fortune that wants to loll about his face.

No one moves. Keith looks across at Hennie. She moves a thumb towards the window. 'Kitchen's just through there.'

*   *   *

Maureen, Alan, Carly, Mickey and a damply snuffling Giggles have made it up the gangway, off the crowded wharf and across the street to the bus. They have made it onto the bus and off again—each movement an expedition fraught with hazard. In her anxiety Maureen herded them off the bus one stop too soon. She had the kids mustered in the aisle clutching things and when the driver said, Cashin Road, wasn't it love? You'd be better to hang on a stop . . . it all seemed unbearably difficult so she said, we'll walk thank you, we like to walk.

So they had to walk down the road watching the bus cruise on ahead of them and the cars, all going the same way, dispersing a boatload of travellers. They follow the track on the grass beside the toetoes which Carly must have one of so they try and break one stem. First Alan tries, then Maureen. They try another and another. The stalks bend and split but refuse to let go. The mauve-white plumage scatters with their efforts; fairy pony tails struck with mange. Carly snivels.

They turn up Cashin Road which is steep and unsealed. The air is fragrant with something unfamiliar and sweet. If Maureen knew what it was she'd point it out to the children as one of the wonders of their new world. Alan carries the birdcage so Maureen can have a free hand for Mickey. But past the first bend he pulls his fist from hers and stands with his legs braced against further progress. 'My little legs hurt,' he whines.

'So do mine,' says Maureen sharply. It's been a very long day. She tries to take his hand again but he resists.

'Okay.' She walks on. Alan and Carly scrunch ahead of her, Alan's jandals going plap plap against the soles of his feet. She got them a size too big, to last. Mickey whimpers and when Maureen looks back the kid's crouched in the middle of the road. But kind Carly has seen him and with a huge motherly sigh is going back for him.

Maureen wonders what they're feeling, Carly and Alan, behind their silence. The children haven't seen their new home. Maureen left them with Alice when she came over the first time to look at the place; and again the second time when she came over with Matthew. That time they'd driven down the coast from Auckland in Matthew's car with a trailer loaded with furniture—the old chest-of-drawers Alice had set aside to be dumped, and the other stuff bought from a junk shop in Mt Eden. She owed Matthew $250 for the stuff she bought. He'd said, no hurry, just whenever you can. It seems like a terrible lot of money considering the wormy, saggy old stuff it is.

Matthew is Maureen's brother-in-law. They'd come over with the car and the trailer on the vehicle barge which has its own separate wharf each side. Maureen would've liked, on that second visit, to scour the house and disinfect away its pervading old-man smell. But they had to catch the barge back in the late afternoon and that didn't leave time. Besides Matthew was being so desperately positive about the merits of the place it seemed impolite to draw attention to its ancient filth. And it would've been terrible if they'd missed the barge back and had to stay there together for a whole night. Maureen was very aware that Alice had only lent Matthew reluctantly and on the tacit understanding that furniture moving was to be the limit of his services.

As if she would! The last thing Maureen wanted to do was endanger her sister's marriage. Hadn't Alice—and Matthew of course—taken them in, the four of them, when they were broke and homeless. And put up with them, with the overcrowded house and all the strains and tensions that came with it, for almost two months while Maureen searched fruitlessly for a place they could afford on her solo parent's benefit.

Alice had done that even though she knew – for Maureen could tell that Alice knew – that a recently separated woman, all raw and emotionally quivering, was as appealing to a nice husband as a pile of warm offal to a passing blowfly. (The worst part was that Maureen, who had never before thought of Matthew as anything more than Alice's husband, had begun to notice his reliability, his consideration for others, his affection for his child . . . and to think that these were very, very attractive qualities.)

It was Matthew who found her the house by following up a bit of staffroom gossip. The old man who'd lived in the place had been dead four days when they found his body (sorry, said Matthew, I probably shouldn't have told you that). The son, who lived in Pakuranga, didn't want to sell the place until the island had realised its potential as a tourist resort. Nor did he want to risk an underdeveloped Motuwairuan as a tenant.

Maureen borrowed a dress from Alice (the label said *Peppertree*) when Matthew took her to see the son, who owned a restaurant called *Poppa's* but didn't look remotely Italian. The son acted as if his father had left him the house just to vex him by frittering away his valuable time. A bond, he said, and say $45 a week and I don't want to be bothered by complaints about what needs fixing; you don't like it, you don't take it. That way, he told Matthew as if Maureen had turned invisible, she gets a cheap house and I get to claim it as a tax loss.

Maureen knew before she even set foot on the island that she would take the house. The atmosphere at Alice's was growing more strained every day and $45 was an unbelievable bargain. The night after she went to see it she recited for the children, but most of all for Alice, its good points. 'The view . . . you wouldn't believe the view. From the living room you can see through the gap in the trees Auckland, the harbour, ships, everything. And it's a big section, absolutely private. You can't even see any neighbours. And fruit trees – all kinds of trees really. There's quite a big kitchen; sort of a country kitchen with an old wood stove, but there's a little gas cooker too. Oh and this funny old hip bath that might've come straight out of a cowboy movie. And the grapes . . . did I say about the grapes? . . . all over the outside of one of the bedrooms. And it's not far from the school and anyway I think there's a bus.'

There were other things it didn't seem right to mention: the water stains that spread from the blackened ceiling to the greyish walls, the ragged old wallpaper in the bedrooms. The bedrooms themselves, two tiny rooms—one with the daylight entirely blocked out by grapevine. One power point and in it one ominously blackened triple plug. The smell . . . which seemed to be of death and old fish heads. The bathroom. The tankstand which leant drunkenly against a bedroom wall and the tank with its rash of rusty holes towards the top. But most of all the toilet.

The children's pace has slowed to a dispirited creep. Maureen picks Mickey up and carries him for the last several metres, walking on ahead of the other two.

She waits for them outside the little wooden gate. Mickey has his arms wrapped round her neck. Right now she needs him there. Alan catches up with them. Then Carly. From here you can only see the tankstand.

'Is this it?' Alan's voice is unusually neutral.

'Mmmhmm, this is it.' She opens the gate. Unlatched it limps on one hinge and she has to put Mickey down and force it back against the over-grown mound of empty bottles. The grass is bleached and knee high, the path that leads to the house is simply a line where the grass had been trodden under and pushed aside. Around the sides and back of the section runs a high spiky hedge with scarlet flowers. It shows itself here and there behind or between the trees and shrubs that tilt and tangle. Beneath a huge old plum tree spreads a thick red and yellow stain of fallen fruit.

The children stand silent and wide-eyed. They are used to pavements and restrained parks. They trail their mother up the almost-track until they reach the house. Which isn't really a house, for a house is a substantial thing, solid and structured. This might pass as a bach or even a cottage, but coming upon it through the overgrowth it's hard to imagine it was even built. It looks to have grown there, an aberration of nature, tenaciously alive.

On her earlier visits Maureen, preoccupied by her purpose, had seen the heap of overgrown bottles, the ripe fruit, the silver beet persisting in a long abandoned garden and a home which despite its drawbacks didn't belong to Alice and Matthew. Now perhaps because she's picking up on the children's reactions, the place seems slightly magical, slightly menacing. Also a familiarity which has nothing to do with having been here before. Something shifting in her memory but not enough to . . .

Tendrils of fear taking hold. Telling herself it's only natural, *of course* she's afraid. She's an adult alone with sole and ultimate responsibility for three lives besides her own; she has a right to be afraid.

'Well what are we waiting for?' Dispelling the magic with her everyday voice.

Carly and Alan both talk at once and they all tumble in through the kitchen and take the place over. Their own things are there; clothes, toys and the wormy furniture – friendly talismen to ward off whatever it was that brushed against their minds as they stood outside.

Maureen stands in the living room explaining, justifying, telling half-truths. 'I know theirs is bigger Car, but ours'll get more sun. And they make more mess love, you know that.'

'It's not fair.'

'We'll make ours nice, you'll see. We'll paint it and get some curtains.'

'We gonna paint ours too?'

'Yes,' she tells him, watching Carly's bottom lip, 'but we'll do ours first.' She doesn't say, I put the boys in the bigger room because they don't have as I do an image of an old man's body lying there stiff while the flies settle and no one comes.

She wasn't told it was that room with the vine shrouded windows. And even before she had first visited the furniture had been removed and the place given a cursory sweep over. Yet the first time she'd opened the door to that bedroom she'd thought, *here*.

In any case she would have allotted the bedrooms this way; taking the smallest for herself just as she always makes do with the burnt toast and the gristly bits of meat. Apart from anything else it saves arguments. It was just bad luck for Carly that she was the only one Maureen felt she could share a room with and not break an ankle whenever she got out of bed.

'There's two windows broken,' says Alan, reporting.

'Just cracked,' says Maureen emptying the knapsack onto a mattress.

Carly and Maureen's room should get the morning sun but now it's dim, and very small. Two single beds and a chest-of-drawers and the door can just be opened enough to squeeze in. When she gets around to it Maureen will nail some wire across a corner of the room so they can hang their clothes from it. She tells Carly this. 'Then,' she says, 'we can hang a curtain in front to stop the dust.'

Carly looks at the corner in question. There's a calendar hanging there, it has a picture of a girl holding a bunch of daffodils. Above that it says *Kaimoana Beach Store for friendly personal service, 1963*. The wallpaper has faded into little pinkish blobs that must once have been flowers. Towards the ceiling there's a border line and above it the blobs are larger and more purplish. Carly takes her mother's hand and squeezes it in silent comfort.

No food in the house, not even the makings of a cup of tea. The Kaimoana Beach Store for friendly personal service is right down at the bottom of the hill, an expedition away. Maureen wonders about leaving them. Accidents. Strangers. Fear itself. The house itself not yet to be trusted. But taking them . . .

She keeps her voice casual. 'Look you guys I have to go down to the shop and get us some food. Best if I go on my own, quicker. And you stay here, okay, and keep a close eye on Mick.'

She sees the fear widening his eyes, the struggle to hold it back. The oldest, and most fearful. Always has been.

'Okay,' says Carly, off-handed. 'Only you won't be too long?'

'Quick as I can. Only . . . look. What say Alan comes with me to help me carry stuff and then I'll be even quicker? And you stay and play with Mickey.'

Alan's relief shines in his mindless grin. Carly's confidence wavers and Maureen starts moving before it's too late. 'You're a great kid you know. And I promise we won't be long.'

Back down the track and onto the road clutching her purse, thinking I shouldn't've . . . what if . . . Swallowing the sentences back down unfinished. Holding them down there with, what could *really* . . . and, other people leave their kids for hours. Alan bounding along beside her garrulous with relief, prattling about the sea and the ferry and which way is Auckland now. She points but even where the view from the road isn't blocked by bush or houses there's nothing to see but the low haze of soft rain that screens them from the mainland.

'I hope it's not coming this way.'

'Bet it starts to rain as we're just about home,' he says.

Home.

A part of Maureen still back there in the house, six years old and *in charge* among strange smells and alien noises. Trying her hardest to be a great kid.

Maureen worrying (again) about is she as fair as she ought to be. For instance; is it wrong of her to try and protect Alan—who seems to need protecting—at the expense of Carly who doesn't seem to need protecting? And is it fair to make use of Carly just because Carly is so amenable to being made use of?

The shop is open. It hadn't occurred to Maureen that it might not be but she learns from the card taped to the window that it only opens for two hours on Saturdays. In twenty minutes it would've been shut. She feels quite weak at the thought, an image of the mother bird returning empty-beaked. The pitiful cries of hunger. The accusing cavernous mouths.

She buys necessities, to eat and to clean with. Enough, she hopes, to last them until Monday. The woman at the shop says they do deliveries once a week, Fridays. Maureen thinks of the old man lying in the boys' room waiting for Fridays.

Alan wants to explore the beach. 'Later,' she says, 'first you're all gonna help me clean that place.'

'Looked clean enough to me.'

He dawdles so she goes on ahead. She's picked the heaviest bag of groceries; she's bigger than him still. She's worried about how long they've taken. A segment of her mind is listening for distant screams, watching for smoke.

If she had a car . . .

If she could drive . . . In Mangere Bruce took them once a week to buy groceries. That was one advantage of him working nights. Most weeks it was the only time they went anywhere together, at least after she had Mickey. They'd go to New World and Bruce would push the trolley with Mickey facing backwards in the little wire seat. Maureen would pick out the things they needed but Bruce always went too fast and she'd have to search down the aisles with her arms full of packets and tins. He hated the way she dithered over different brands, trying to work out which cost less or held more. He insisted on coming in, as if she couldn't be trusted to spend his money unsupervised, and then was angry all the way round the shelves, saying she pissed about like an old lady.

Alice said when Maureen left she should've taken the car. At least that way, she said, you'd've come out of it with something.

I would've if I could drive, said Maureen. Knowing it wasn't true. She hadn't even liked the car. She seemed to have spent at least a whole year of her married life sitting in the passenger seat in various stages of pregnancy while Bruce shouted at her from the bonnet to push the clutch pedal and shut up that bloody kid.

Bruce wasn't mechanically minded. He knew the names of the parts

43

that went wrong but not what they did or how to fix them. Maureen would sit helplessly watching the cars of the clever people roar past while Bruce cursed and crashed at the motor. She knew her helplessness enraged him, that what he wanted was to be sitting in the car like her while someone else wrestled with cross-threaded screws and malfunctioning solenoids. She'd learned that whenever some piece of the engine packed up she was to blame, for if he hadn't had her and the children to house and feed Bruce wouldn't have had to struggle along trying to keep an eighteen-year-old car on the road.

Carly says, 'You were a long time.' But her tone is perfunctory and while Maureen's been away she's organised Mickey into helping her sort the boys' clothes onto the shelves in the bedroom alcove which will serve them as a wardrobe.

Maureen lavishes praise, then remembers to also praise Alan for his grocery carrying services. She wonders, not for the first time, if her kids see through these conscientious efforts to hand out praise in regular doses like vitamin C.

At night, the children long in bed, she sits in the living room with the light off so she doesn't have to look at what has yet to be scrubbed or sorted. The sea mist has cleared and the lights of Auckland sparkle like fireworks. Cars weave tracks of light beneath flashing neon. The sea is bejewelled with reflection.

Maureen wishes she had a phone so she could ring Alice. Could ring someone. Anyone. The busy distant lights make her feel as if she's been flung off into space like a meteorite.

March

KEITH'S ROOM HAS a bed—a wire-wove base set on concrete blocks—a wooden school desk so old it has inkwell holes, a half-size set of drawers and a wall-size bookcase constructed from planks, beer crates and concrete blocks. One shelf contains books, the rest are crammed with magazines, newsletters, manila folders, press clippings, scissors, cardboard, pots of paste.

'What,' Keith had asked on his second day, 'd'you want me to do with all that stuff?'

Daphne rested her head in her hands and stared at him. She was sitting at the table with another manila folder. Eventually she said, 'You need the space?'

'Well, not at the moment. Not exactly. But it is my room.'

She considered that, then she smiled brightly. 'Yes,' she said, as if speaking to a backward child, 'so it is—your very own room. And if you can't cope with having all that stuff in there you better shift it in here.'

It looked like a big job. Instead he took down the posters from his wall. He took down *they've sent one man to the moon why not send them all.* And he took down *WOMEN WHO SEEK TO BE EQUAL TO MEN LACK AMBITION.* He left up *A woman without a man is like a fish without a bicycle* because he quite liked the fish's face and he didn't want to seem to be entirely without a sense of humour. He rolled the other two posters together and put them on the very top of the bookcase.

Three days later the posters had joined the others in the main room. (*Take the toys from the boys* and *SEXISM IS A SOCIAL DISEASE.*)

'I'm not unsympathetic,' said Keith, 'I'm glad women are making themselves heard.'

Daphne gave Hennie an oversized wink and Kay covered her mouth with her hand. Those two seemed to spend as much time at Daphne's house as they did at their own which was a couple of hundred yards up the road.

'I realise,' said Keith to Daphne some days later, 'that it gives you and your friends a great kick to have a representative enemy to shovel shit at. But don't you think it's a bit childish?'

'No,' said Daphne.

And Keith finally realised that despite all the amusement he caused none of them were joking. He said, for the pleasure of it and not because he'd come to a decision, 'I guess I should tell you I'm staying on. I'll be writing to Jerry to see about the rent.'

Daphne looked at him for several seconds, narrowing her round blue eyes. He stared back fixedly trying not to blink. 'Sure,' said Daphne softly, looking down at the folder, 'you do that.'

He was supposed to say next, so you'll have to leave, but somehow he couldn't. He'd never seen much point in winning. Besides he didn't want her to have the satisfaction of thinking she'd managed to goad him into taking revenge.

Ever since he came he'd been waiting for her to mellow. It didn't seem possible that she could go on treating him as some abstract enemy once they'd lived in the same house for a week or two. He underestimated her. The woman's manner is beginning to get very seriously up his nose.

In a way she has him cornered. If he said, look I'm not prepared to do battle; I don't care enough about the issues . . . well that would seem like arrogance – proof of male sins. Yet if he lets himself be constantly provoked into defensive arguments won't he just be confirming what she wants to believe?

Mostly he avoids her. Despite her best efforts Daphne isn't, for Keith, a major issue. He sees her as rarely as possible and thinks about her even less. Which gets easier – at first even when she'd gone across to the city or up the hill to Kay and Hennie's he was still a bit aware of her because the things he used in the house were unfamiliar and therefore *hers*. Her pan in which he fries up eggs. Her oven in which he grills toast for one. The routines of preparing food coming back to him after years of Mrs Pemberton's watery roasts and gluey casseroles.

What is it, she'd say, prodding with her fork. As if she couldn't see. Mutton. It was nearly always mutton or sometimes lamb. And very occasionally beef, when a steer had fallen down a cliff and broken a leg. See what those bloody butchers charge, his father would say. The middlemen are bleeding this country white.

Oh dear, mutton?

I asked you, I said did you want me to do you something . . .?

If you would. If it's no bother. I think an omelette.

Beating the eggs, drowning out the scrape, scrape of knife and fork from

46

the table, burp, newspaper raised up and rearranged. Never a thank you or new potatoes that's a nice change or even you're getting better with the gravy. But she must've felt this way so I shouldn't begrudge just beating eggs. But after all she married him.

More often he just buys food from the shop—apples or muesli bars or an ice-cream or biscuits—and eats it on the beach or carries it with him to one of the small bays that run on from Hoki Bay. These have no road access and now that the summer holidays are over and the boaties have gone home hardly anyone visits them. An occasional tramper or surfcasting fisherman, and once Keith came across the forest workmen boiling up their morning tea among the beach boulders. But such people understand the privacy of empty places and pass by with just a nod like an acquaintance on a busy street.

The days are still long and mostly fine and Keith spends them, like a child, exploring. He keeps to the east coast where the sea stretches out to the rest of the world. To the south of Hoki Bay you can follow the road as far as Huri Bay where it ends. Huri Bay has a store with post office services and fewer and newer houses than Hoki Bay. Beyond Huri Bay is forest reserve with signposted walking tracks. Keith's saving that for winter when the tourists have given up. Between Hoki and Huri bays the coast is scalloped with smaller bays. Crystal clear water magnifying stones and shingle, bush circled like cattle just above the water's edge. Perfect places where there's no reason to believe Daphne's information that this island is home for more than fifteen hundred permanent residents—at least half of which she'd be happy to see swept into the ocean.

Keith prefers these southern bays to the precipitous cliffs to the north. A disused farm track runs up over the hill to Whiripare. Gates at each end warn PRIVATE PROPERTY KEEP OUT but Keith, having a special relationship with the island, assumed dispensation and followed the road, picking blackberries and eating them by the handful, until it joined up with the Whiripare road. From the top of the closed-off road it felt as if he could see the whole island. One minute the road faced inland and he could see the toytown settlements and the next minute he would be looking down at distant jagged rocks and surging water.

From Whiripare Keith walked to Parenga and the pub where he drank two beers alone and didn't care about the second one. But could feel, as he sat in the corner furthest from the seascape windows, the edginess returning like a freeloader. Making him marvel at how he'd changed, how quickly his priorities had shuffled. For he knew the restlessness would settle when he got back to the parts of the island he felt to be his.

Away from the house and Daphne Keith feels curiously privileged. Almost *chosen*. He examines the feeling with a certain embarrassment and decides to allow it. Feeling chosen isn't the same as claiming you have been chosen. (By whom? For what? And anyway does it matter?)

As a child Keith believed himself to be chosen; a belief he was sensible enough not to broadcast. And the memory of it is still in him, reproachful, of a promise made but never kept.

Keith thinks now that he understands that childish self-delusion. Sees that it was fashioned from a sustaining logic. The boy Keith choosing to see his unhappiness as preparation for some undefined but dazzling future; giving sorrow the dignity of a purpose. Far easier to believe that than to believe that life deals out misery indiscriminately without cause or reason.

The boy Keith didn't *feel* chosen. Keith sees that now. The boy Keith felt owed. This time it's different. This time he feels lifted-up, lightheaded, in step with destiny.

He thinks now and again about the *Everton Times*. He thinks, the last mad rush to get the Tuesday edition to bed ... or, some poor bugger will be trying to unscramble the netball report. He wonders who Tom brought in to replace Keith or if he gave the job to Wendy who nearly ran the whole place anyway. He feels sorry for them all, dripping absolution like a parson.

Tom gave him four weeks' leave but wanted to know as early as possible if Keith would be coming back. They gave him six weeks pay but they may have owed him a couple of weeks. Holidays were a disruption Keith suffered unwillingly. When they were forced upon him he simply slept longer and spent more time in the Everton DB. That way it didn't seem like a holiday and so he could almost avoid thinking that he could've gone and seen her. Stayed at a motel and gone up every day. Maybe the last chance. Though he'd thought that last time, three years ago, and she was still hanging on.

He wasn't going back to Everton. Not because of Daphne, not even because there was some woolly principle at stake. He hadn't even sat down and thought about alternatives—once he was on the island there was simply no decision to be made. He woke up that first morning, his droopy wire-wove just touching the floor mid-centre, and knew in his heart he could never go back. He's tried to frighten himself a bit since then by running through the realities . . . Mort's forty-seven post-graduates, eighty staff laid off the *Auckland Star* only a couple of months back, one hundred and thirty thousand unemployed or on work schemes and he couldn't remember if those were only the registered ones.

It all seemed inconsequential. Ironic though. It'd been the job shortage that'd started the whole thing off; Keith Muir's last stand. Only stand. So far, he tells himself now he and destiny have a thing going between them; so far.

An everyday lunchtime at the DB, passing the time with a young guy called Doug who was a friend of Snort. And this Doug bitching away about his dole being cut off because he'd turned down a job.

'Two dollars fifty an hour. Two dollars and fifty cents a fucken hour. I mean what's the point, man? Whadda they think we are?'

'What was the job?'

'Gardening. Horticulture. I've done that stuff before, okay, two . . . three years ago and then THEN the award was four dollars something. These bastards offering two fifty.'

'You tell them what they were gonna pay? The social welfare people . . . did you say?'

'Sure I did. Two or three times. She looked right through me like I was the horizon.'

'The labour department . . . maybe you should tell them?'

'Well it's the same office. Shit everyone there must've heard me. Anyway it was the labour department bloke sent me to the job in the first place.'

'Yeah, but they can't know about the money. I mean if they're paying way below award . . . they're not allowed to do that.'

Doug laughed. Keith thought about how a few years ago you hardly ever heard that harsh inward kind of laughter in bars. Yet now it was sometimes the only kind of laughter going.

'Who was it? I mean the job, where?'

'Ashfords.'

'Ashfords! Shit.'

'Yeah, I know. Him with his fucken Mustang.'

'I thought he had quite a few people working there?'

'Does.'

'You know any of them?'

'There's Johnny Lucas . . .'

'Ah hah . . .'

'Pet Phillips? She's a Crawford. One'a that lot. Lives in one of those flats down Hika Street.'

Keith called at the flats after work. Pet Crawford had been in the same class as Keith at Everton High School. She was loud, brown, athletic and popular. Keith was quiet, white, bespectacled and largely ignored. Pet was never unkind to him. It made her different from most of the others. Nearly twenty years later when they passed each other in the street they would nod obliquely. Keith's being a reporter was bound to impress Pet more than it should. Pet had four kids and hoed onions to make ends meet.

Knocking on the door of flat three, a cluster of brown children watching him, Keith understood that even then, at school, both he and Pet had known that this was the way it would be. A knowledge that had hung like an invisible screen dividing the brown kids from all but a few of the white ones.

Pet told him she'd been working for Louis Ashford for nearly two years. She got the job through the labour department. She earned one hundred dollars a week for forty hours' work. 'But cash,' she said. 'We don't pay tax.

'I don't want you using my name or anything,' she said. 'I'd be down the road before I knew it. Hell a hundred bucks is better than a smack in the face. Better than nothing at all. No way we can manage anymore on what Joe gets. Most've them feel like me at work. You know, at least it's a job. We know it's a rip-off but for the young ones it's still more than they'd get on the dole.'

'It's illegal, you know that. He's taking advantage of people being desperate for jobs.'

'You telling me?'

'Sorry. I didn't mean . . . You think the people at the labour office aren't aware of what's going on?'

'Course they do. Any rate that Harry Henderson does.'

'You sure?'

'We-ell, it's not as though some of them haven't gone along there and said what about this pay.'

'Who has? Pet, I don't suppose you could get all the workers together one night? Here or somewhere. So I could talk to them.'

Pet sighed. 'Look they're all in the same boat as me. I told you. I mean what other work is there round here?'

'Ashford's still gonna need staff.'

'He can get others.'

'There must be some way of protecting your rights to first refusal.'

'Yeah? And how would they treat us after we'd . . .'

'You might be respected for standing up for your rights.'

'Look,' said Pet, 'you're a nice bloke but you dunno stuff all.'

'I know it's easy for me to say. I know that. But just think about it eh.'

'Yeah. Okay. I'll have a talk to Joe.'

'Have a talk to Joe. Then maybe you could ring me.'

Pet had organised a meeting of seven workers at her flat. They were prepared to be named and quoted, a couple were eager. Keith told Tom he had a lead story for the Friday edition. Tom said Keith had to be joking.

Keith said he would send the story elsewhere, one of the dailies. Tom said no one would want it – if Keith hadn't spent the last five years with his nose in a glass he'd know a so-what story when he fell over it.

Keith, suddenly dogged, said if the story didn't go in he would chuck the job. And Tom redistributed fault by bringing up Keith's drinking.

Wendy, having heard Keith's side of things, told him, 'You amaze me. Tom plays golf with Harry Henderson and that prick Ashford. You're so naive. What did you expect?'

Integrity. But he didn't say it, Wendy would've laughed. Not at the concept perhaps but at Keith's pomposity in using a city word too high powered for Everton.

Keith called on Pet before he left. 'You could still fight it,' he said. 'If you went as a group to the labour office . . .'

Pet smiled kindly. Keith got the feeling she'd known this was how it would turn out. Known it maybe as far back as when she won the sports trophies at Everton High.

'I could still try the dailies,' he offered.

Pet shrugged then shook her head, 'May as well not.' They both knew that coming from outside it wouldn't be the same. Everton people would see it as interfering. If they read it in a city paper Pet's neighbours wouldn't want to take her side.

'I'm going away for a while,' said Keith. 'I'll probably resign. I don't feel like working for Tom Brannigan after this.'

Pet looked embarrassed, as if she wanted to laugh at him but couldn't be so impolite. Which was much the way she'd treated him when they were at school. Keith was aware of that invisible screen tightening up like venetians.

He types his letter to Tom on a sheet of Daphne's blank paper. There's a stack of it beneath the pile of *Broadsheet* and *Circle* magazines. He's been helping himself, trying to write short stories but after the second page none of them have seemed worth going on with. The bits he's done sound like other people's stories; he wants one to come out sounding like him. He's not sure that he will recognise it if it does.

Dear Tom writes Keith. *You were right in thinking that time away from the place would give me a clearer perspective on things. It has. Please accept my resignation. Any money owing to me should be sent to the above address. Sincerely.*

And a PS. *Tell Jerry I'll be in touch about the bach.*

PPS I'm not drinking. Since I left I haven't needed to.

'My resignation,' he tells Daphne, sitting the envelope on the mantelpiece.

'You told me.'

'I hadn't written it then.'

'And the landlord?'

'I was gonna talk to you about it first. When it would be convenient for you to shift?'

'It won't. I'm settled here. It suits me very well.' She outgazes him.

'I thought if I offered forty a week,' he says, possibly to himself. 'That way, till you've found somewhere else, it'd be twenty each which doesn't seem a lot.'

'Seems bloody daft to me. Why not just tell him you've found another place? He'll never know—who's gonna tell him?'

'I am.'

Daphne goads him with her silent disgust, so he says, 'He owns the place for godsake. Pays rates. He's entitled to get rent if we live here. I suppose you don't believe in ownership? You'd think it was okay if I just packed up your stuff and walked out with it?'

She rolls her eyes—a cheap shot for an invisible audience. 'I just have more important things to spend my money on.'

'For all you know he might need the money desperately. To feed a wife and family.' He smirks at his own cunning but still feels Daphne is somehow ahead on points. 'It's a matter of principle really. If I'm gonna be ripping someone off I may as well've stayed where I was. There'd be no point in quitting.'

'So why did you?'

He'd been wanting her to ask but not quite in that tone.

She listens without much expression.

'I realise,' he finishes, 'my leaving won't achieve anything. I'm hardly irreplaceable, but still.'

'You've made your gesture?'

'Something like that.' He thinks she's loosening towards him, relaxing that dyke front.

'Wow,' she says, 'that must've taken a lot of guts. I mean someone in your position—male, middle-class, educated, white ... boy, you really stuck your neck out, eh.' She lets her mouth hang loose in a sloppy manic grin.

On a morning that feels like a Thursday a rainy squall drives him up from the little cove he's chosen as his own private place. Daphne went to the city the day before and usually stays at least a couple of days so he has no reason not to go home. On the way he calls at the store to buy eggs and bread and tomatoes. Lester at the store gives Keith the mail. The delivery man goes along Agnes Road but they haven't a letter box.

'Everything going all right up there?' asks Lester.

It's an interest Keith doesn't feel like encouraging. 'Fine,' he says, every time.

Two wrapped magazines and a letter for D. Glass. One letter for Keith, postmarked Everton. Jerry Veale. Who's written once already on a note of high dudgeon. Saying, come on bloke, I've had a gander at the property ads in the *Herald*. I could get $90 a week at least for that place but since you're a friend I'll knock it down to eighty.

Forty-five, Keith wrote back, at the most. If you'd seen the place recently you'd know why. It's very run down and nothing's been done on the section for years—as you rather suspected. And there wasn't a stick of furniture, nothing. Not even a stove. I've had to buy stuff. Fact is you need a tenant.

Seeing as you're a mate I'm prepared to settle for fifty. Cheers, Jerry. PS Wendy's got your job. A new and nubile young wench replacing Wendy.

Daphne is home, folding dough at the bench.

'That was a quick trip.' It costs nothing to be pleasant and he has an unconquerable instinct for peace.

She weaves and pounds. He puts her mail on the table. 'I got another letter about the rent. He'll settle for fifty. I guess twenty-five each isn't too bad.'

'I'm away a lot,' she says. 'I'm prepared to put in ten.'

53

'Your generosity bowls me over.'

That wins him a faint grin. 'I'd still be paying nothing,' she says, 'if you hadn't come along.'

'Twenty,' he says, encouraged by that bit of a smile, 'and you stay away as much as you want.'

'Fifteen,' she says, 'and you're allowed to eat my bread.' (They keep their food apart. Her cooking smells wonderful.)

'Okay,' he says, 'fifteen.'

'And,' she says, 'I'd like to borrow your typewriter for a while.'

'What for?'

'To type on.'

'It's quite good for that.'

'You can give us a hand,' she says graciously, 'if you want. I have to post out some badges.'

He sees them on the table, heaped pin-side-up in a shoe box. He turns one over.

we don't want a slice of the cake, we want the whole damn bakery.

*   *   *

Alan and Carly have settled in at the Motuwairua Area School.

Maureen hadn't thought of their passive acceptance of going to school each day in quite that way until she talked to Alice.

'And have they settled in at school?'

'Yes,' said Maureen, 'I think so.' Meaning, they don't seem much unhappier at this one than they were at their last school. But now she thinks of it that way; thinks, I hope they've truly settled in.

The school year began two days after they moved to the island. Maureen—and Mickey—went with them on that first day to do the enrolling. Maureen had planned to say something to their teachers or the headmaster in private; to say that the kids had been through a lot of emotional upheaval in the last few months and perhaps the school should know of this in case. But she didn't get to say anything like that; she couldn't. Not after she'd sat in the headmaster's office and filled in the forms.

Husband's occupation . . . Should she just put security guard and say nothing? They were still married and as far as she knew he was still at the same job.

But why did they want to know? To discuss, over cups of tea in the staffroom, the family income? Or so they could say, don't expect too much of Carly, her father's just a security guard?

'This one,' she said to the headmaster, '—I don't know what to put. You see I'm not living with their father, I'm a solo mother.' The first time she'd said it out loud to anyone except Alice. Maureen heard the words drift, brittle as crystal. Mickey stood beside her clutching her leg. Alan and Carly had already been led off like the little princes to the tower by two politely smiling teachers. She was glad they weren't there to hear.

'I see,' said the headmaster, heavily smiling. 'Well you're in good company—quite a few of our children come from solo parent homes. The island life seems to appeal to . . .' Talking with a doctor's transparent insincerity . . . anyone can contract VD, Mrs Harrison, you mustn't blame yourself . . .

But of course no headmaster would want a horde of solo parents who can't afford to sponsor cups and help pay for gymnasiums and computers and softball bats. It's nothing personal, Maureen tells herself. Nothing that the staff might in little ways take out on her children. Nothing like that.

So Carly and Alan go off each morning with their lunches and the books the school provides but Maureen has to pay for. And still hasn't but she will she must very soon or else the headmaster will be saying, it's what we've come to expect from that kind.

At least she has now got them uniforms—navy and white pinafore and white blouse for Carly and navy shorts and a grey shirt for Alan. Though they need another set each, for now she has to wash them after school on Wednesday and hope they dry. She paid for the uniforms before the books because she thought the kids must feel conspicuous in their everyday clothes while everyone else was blue and white and grey.

In winter they have to have a different uniform. 'They didn't have uniforms at their other school,' she told the headmaster. She didn't really mean it to sound like criticism; she said it because there was a gap in the conversation and she felt she was expected to fill it.

He took it as criticism. 'I do realise,' he said, 'that many schools these days are doing away with them. But at Motuwairua we feel a uniform has a levelling influence. As I'm sure you'll appreciate children can be rather unkind to their peers if they feel they are perhaps not as well dressed as they are.' His smile said, be grateful, we're doing this for *you*.

Alan and Carly walk to school because, even though the school bus goes past the bottom of Cashin Road, there's an education department ruling that only children who live more than a certain distance from school are entitled to ride on the free school buses. 'In winter,' the headmaster told Maureen, 'if they have their fare they'll be able to catch the bus if we have any spare seats. At the moment the bus is full and the laws won't allow us to take any more.'

Maureen and Alice used to walk to school. But things were different then. Everyone expected less, especially children. Winter storms will force rain down the necks of their coats and sting their bare legs. They'll sit all day damp and bronchial in their winter uniforms which being serge and viyella will be even more expensive.

She imagines these things even though winter seems so far off and fanciful. Maureen has never known so much sun. In Auckland, even in the middle of summer, it seemed to be spread a little thinly so there was enough to go round. Here it flows with melting extravagance day after sweltering day.

The real islanders—those who have lived here for more than one summer—take the sun for granted and don't mind spending time indoors, but Maureen feels she has a lifetime of lost summers to catch up on. She can never believe that tomorrow may be just as fine as today.

'I can't *believe* the weather here,' she tells Alice from the phone box down by the post office.

'It's been nice here too,' says Alice a bit sharply. 'You're only across a bit of sea you know.'

But Maureen sees the rain clouds that come down from the north and by-pass the island to hang around the city heavy with intent. And Maureen, who has begun already to feel the certain sense of superiority that infects those who belong by chance to some select minority, is tempted to say, it may seem like just a bit of sea but believe me we are a world away from where you are.

She doesn't say it. She doesn't want to sound smug. And anyway after sunset she would sooner be Alice. Instead she says, 'It hasn't rained since last Monday and that was just a shower. But you wouldn't believe the way things grow here. I pull out weeds and the next day honestly they're up again. It's weird when the ground seems so dry.'

'Mm, really,' says Alice through what sounds like a yawn. Alice always sounds, on the phone, as if she's being kept from doing something more interesting. But Maureen knows it's probably only watching TV or sweeping the concrete or doing the ironing. And Alice only has to walk into the kitchen and answer the phone with the high stool there waiting to be sat on. While Maureen has had to walk all the way to the phone booth at Mickey pace then fiddle around with coins and buttons. And will then have to walk all the way home again.

She wouldn't go to all that bother if she didn't *need* to ring. Surely Alice should understand that. Maureen wants to say to her, I won't keep doing this—it's just that I still feel a bit well I suppose insecure. And you are my sister. But don't worry I'll get over this need to know that you're still there and the places I'm used to are still there not even a toll call away. In time I will.

Once I've settled in.

On the hottest days she takes her togs when she goes to the shop or the phone booth. Mickey squats on the wet sand where the stones and shells aren't as many and as jagged, while his mother swims and coaxes. Mickey is afraid of the sea, though sometimes now he'll let her take him in until it's past his knees and even splash him a little. He still screams if she tries to carry him out further. He doesn't trust me, she thinks; not any more.

Kaimoana beach faces west, towards the mainland. Its waves slide and sigh and hardly ever break. They carry in souvenirs from the city— beer cans, detergent bottles, round tin tops with crinkled edges. Some days there's a grubby white foam that runs before the waves like a vast flock of sheep and forms a lacy tidemark on the sand, greasy to the touch.

'If you swim down here,' the woman at the shop told her, seeing Maureen's long hair wet and salty, 'you know to rinse off in clean water after? Because of the sea lice.'

Minute white creatures that lodge themselves in your swimming togs and cause a rash. Maureen's searched and found. 'Only on this side of the island,' the woman said, 'for some reason.'

At the second hand shop at Parenga ($1.60 return on the bus and half fare for Mickey) Maureen has bought a hammer, a garden spade and a hoe. When Alan and Carly leave for school Maureen does outdoor jobs while the weather lasts. She has pulled and piled up a mountain of weeds which she is afraid to burn with everything around so dry. Already her weed pile is taking root and spreading to places she has cleared. She planned a vegetable garden where the old one had been but the soil is rock hard and for her the spade will do no more than chip at the surface. So she works at clearing other places, finding that here there must have been, once, a flower garden and there, there used to be a cobbled path.

Sometimes she sees the place as it could be. If she had a mower and a saw and a rotary hoe. At other times she sees that the place will beat her no matter how hard she tries. The weeds are stronger than her and more determined. Big mother weeds urging on their offspring; saying, there's no such word as restraint. Insects the same. Maureen isn't squeamish about insects and Mickey is entirely enthusiastic, at least about these outdoor ones. But here they are so many and so big.

It's the country, she thinks. Maureen has never lived in the country though she grew up in a small town with country all around it. She knows that Motuwairua isn't really country but thinks, close as. Her kids will look back on it with love and pride the way country kids do.

Although they don't really show she's done some improvements to the house. She's nailed tight a few loose boards and covered two that were crumbling rotten with short driftwood planks she carried up from the beach. With her breadknife she hacked away at the grapevine so that more light gets into the boys' room and she pulled apart an old banana box and patched up the boards that the vine had split and gnawed.

There are things to be done which she will never be able to do. The toilet which stands out the back like a neglected sentry box will have to be moved to stand above a new hole that will have to be dug. And a smaller seat put on it so Mickey can't fall down into the depths. And the leaning tankstand will have to be straightened and reinforced and the holes in the tank plugged or maybe a new tank.

Matthew had mentioned those things when they brought over the furniture. 'You'll have to get a man,' he said, 'to come and do them.' Meaning hire one. How much does a man cost?

Maureen gets $156.45 a week. It's paid into her post office account by the government and when she sees it there—the figures appearing out of nowhere—it seems like a heap of money. It seems like enough for everything they need. It isn't.

It will be enough, Maureen tells herself, once they've got themselves established. Once they've paid for the basic things like the furniture money she owes Matthew and the washing machine she wants and the tankstand and the toilet and the school fees and the books and the winter uniforms and a saw and a scythe or a sickle and a fridge and perhaps a TV . . . then their money will last them through the week with even a bit left over to splurge or save.

'At least you know,' she says to Alan, 'that what you've got isn't gonna be taken away.' She tries not to say things like that, dragging Bruce into it, but Alan can drive her beyond discretion.

He wants a bike. Alan thinks the house is shameful and a testimony to his mother's inability to properly provide. If he had a pushbike with proud high handlebars and purring spokes the shame of his home would be easier to bear. A pushbike for Alan is something Maureen can't shrug off as an impossible luxury because Alan once owned a bike with gleaming paint and a selection of gears. He had it for three months before a man came in a van and took it away.

Bruce had got him that bike the Christmas before last. Maureen already had a calculator bought from the family benefit all wrapped with Happy Xmas from Mum and Dad, but Bruce arrived home on Christmas Eve with the bike.

Other men in other vehicles had come and repossessed things from the Harrisons. First there was the TV, then the stereo and the electric drill and the space heater. But the bike was different. Maureen had pleaded with the man to let her pay it off a few dollars a week out of the family benefit but it did no good. She couldn't bear to look at Alan's face she was so ashamed. She was his mother and she had let this thing happen.

In the bedroom with the door shut she'd cried for him and for herself. The world owes Alan a pushbike.

'You shouldn't go on about it,' says Carly to Alan. 'You know we're poor now.'

Maureen sets her straight: 'We're no poorer than we were before. Not really. It's just gonna take time to get us all set up that's all.'

Carly says in a hushed voice, 'Were we always poor then?'

'Yes. Not really poor but ... we had things we couldn't pay for. You know that.'

'But we weren't *poor*.' Alan's voice is scornful. Accusing her of defaming his father. Could his memory be so selective?

'We're not poor now,' she says crouching on the withered linoleum with an arm out for each of them but Alan steps back. 'We've got our own place, we've got each other. We've got dear old Giggles. That seems like rich to me.'

Even Carly is unconvinced and glances at Alan in rare conspiracy with her eyes rolled to the ceiling and a shadowy grin.

'You'll see.' Maureen stands up and begins to prick fork holes in floppy pink sausages. 'Someday you'll look back and know I was right.' She remembers that her father used those words, those very words time after time and she has never yet looked back and thought he was right, after all, about anything.

'At least I useda have a friend. And we had TV.' Alan will pick away at a grievance for hours keeping it raw and ugly.

'I'm sure you'll find a friend here love. It just takes time.' She ignores the TV part. There are times when she too thinks of their old living room, the TV, a certain reassuring solidity to those rented walls. Times of doubt and a kind of homesickness despite everything. Times when even her old powerlessness seems to have had advantages. We can't get one of those, she'd say, cos Daddy doesn't have enough money. Maybe, she'd say, if Daddy gets a rise ...

Daddy's fault. Daddy's responsibility. Now hers and hers alone.

'If I had a bike,' says Alan, 'then I'd get a friend.'

If I had a friend, thinks Maureen, I'd give her to you just to shut you up. Or him. But that thought is a dangerous one. She pushes it away cautiously and unopened.

Still, she does need a friend. When she goes to the shop or the beach, when she gets the bus to Parenga, she picks out faces of women around her age who could be, if somehow they got talking. Picks them out despite herself and the awful shame of being lonely.

Not that she had friends, real friends, in Mangere. She could've had, only it seemed better not to because friends would've called in any old time and she wouldn't have wanted to involve them like that.

Now she has nothing to hide. And no one to hide it from. People who are a long time lonely grow brittle. The skeletons of too many unsaid words drift like grey dust in their heads.

But Maureen has her kids. That makes her luckier than a lot of people. Kids should be enough. For a good mother her kids should be everything. And Maureen is going to be a good mother. Making up for what's gone before; her lack of judgement in choosing Bruce instead of someone like Matthew; for having taken so long to leave him. Me and the kids, she used to tell herself, watching the nightshapes of familiar things in her unlit bedroom. Me and the kids on our own together living like a family should. What more could you ask?

But by eight o'clock the kids are in bed and Maureen is alone with the transistor radio. Finding things to do. Alone with the announcer and the long-legged mosquitoes that fly in through the open windows, and the oversized spiders and the fleas that leap up through the floor, no matter how much she sprinkles and sprays, and move in on the children like fat little vampires.

60

Sometimes, still, she sits at the window and looks across at the lights. Sometimes she reads or re-reads the magazines she brought from Alice's. *On April 24 Angus Ogilvy and Princess Alexandra will celebrate their 21st wedding anniversary. What will he give her this year to wear on the delicate gold charm bracelet that encircles her wrist? ...*

To give a smooth finish to icing try covering it with greaseproof paper and something heavy like a chopping board. Then remove and PRESTO!

If Maureen had a hint they would pay her two dollars. If it was printed. Two dollars minus the cost of postage is still one dollar seventy cents, less the price of an envelope. But Maureen doesn't have any handy hints.

She could earn three dollars, less postage and cost of envelope, by sending a true original unpublished contribution describing a humorous or profound incident. If she sent sixteen true original unpublished contributions and they all got printed she could pay for Alan and Carly's school books.

Base your winter wardrobe on neutral shades. That way you can highlight basic items with the vibrant new season hues. Who has lives so safe and regular and unchipped that they can want to know about next season's vibrant hues and Princess Alexandra's royal bracelet? No one Maureen can think of ...

Not Maureen and Alice's mother who finds the bottles and puts them carefully at the bottom of the rubbish bag with newspaper between to stop the clink as she carries the bag out to the gate. Who sits through his performances with that swallowed-horror look as if a rat's walking over her and if she's absolutely still it'll go away. Who says you know he didn't mean it dear, it's just his way.

And not even Alice with her noiseless drapes and her new piano that no one can play but the children mustn't touch. Alice and Matthew with their darling this and sweetheart that but something somehow not quite the way it seems. So much civility and so little laughter. Or the way Alice says I can't be bothered with that women's lib nonsense, I'm happily married I'm pleased to say.

Happily married. Is there such a thing? Maybe a year or two until the novelty wears off, but after that? Twenty-one years on like Princess Alexandra?

People everywhere keeping up the pretence because what else is there to believe in.

Maureen looking across at the shining city. Maureen Harrison née Nesbitt, 28, female Caucasian mother-of-three ex-bank clerk ex-wife

61

beneficiary . . . feeling potentially strong and a bit scornful. Watching the diffuse glow thrown up into the sky by the myriad lights of suburbia. Thinking, you don't fool me . . . not any more.

*   *   *

Dear Mumsy and Whatsisname

'She's joking,' Josie tells him, and Geoff clutches at his head, miming the dazzle of enlightenment.

'I'm just,' she defends, 'trying to avoid misunderstandings. Which have happened often enough, god knows.'

'Most of them because you kept shoving yourself in the middle as self-appointed interpreter and negotiator.'

Josie's stunned, as she always is when he criticises. 'Then why,' she says, dragging the words out, 'was it that all of you did your moaning to me and expected me to pass the message on? You did. You all did.'

'Because if we moaned direct to each other you got upset and interfered. The minute we tried to get anything straightened out person-to-person you'd swoop down like the great white dove of peace and throw your feather around.' The image amuses him.

'You might've said so at the time. If I was stuffing up your inter-personal relationships you'd've thought that in eight years one of you would've been good enough to mention it.'

'I was waiting,' he says, still wrapped up in his amusement, 'for the right moment.'

She groans. 'Why do I even listen to you? You say anything, just for the sake of a reaction. Even hurtful things.'

'I have to don't you see? If you had your way we'd only talk about what's in the news or what other people say or what we've been reading.'

'What's wrong with that?'

'It's boring. Well not boring, but boo-ering. You know what I mean?'

'Not . . . precisely, no.'

'I just like sometimes for us to talk so it's you and me—that we are the only people in the world could be having that particular conversation, and only with each other. It's not what we say it's just . . . we're really talking to each other.'

'Nostalgia,' says Josie. 'The way we always used to talk to each other at the start . . .'

'When we were in love.'

She looks at him sharply. 'Aren't we, any more?'

'D'you think we are?'

'I don't suppose *in* love. Sometimes we are. Sometimes I am anyway.'

'Like now?'

She beams at him, 'Definitely.'

'There you are. That's what happens when we really talk to each other.'

'Of course,' she leans forward until she's looking up at him, her eyes wide and not entirely joking. 'You're amazing and wonderful. You tend the garden of our romance with unflagging care, and bring forth blossoms of great beauty.' She straightens. 'Whereas I have this habit of just picking the flowers and forgetting to even water the plants.'

'That's true,' he says. 'I have a natural romantic talent. You would be the envy of all women if only they knew.'

She frees the hand he has clasped between his. 'Something I find interesting is that all this began when I started to read you Sarah's letter. Even when they're that far away you're still competing with them.' She takes up the letter and holds it at arm's length so the words focus.

'You need glasses.' He's always saying that lately.

The last letter was just me being homesick. This will be a proper letter with even a paragraph on the weather.

Geoff gets up and walks away. 'I can read it for myself. If I want to.'

Hours later as they're bringing in the clothes from the washing line he asks, 'What did Sarah have to say?'

'Oh . . . that she's quite liking school, and that Dick's baby's nice but ugly and that Dick takes Daryl places and leaves her at home with Amy and the baby. Oh yes, and that I might be pleased to know that Dick is now rather bald and he wears tight jeans and a gold chain and his shirt unbuttoned . . . all that and a baby too, my god. And they have a spa pool.'

'And that's it?'

He'd wanted there to be something said for or about him. Josie had seen the flicker of satisfaction at the description of Dick. Geoff's hurt at being overlooked. Perhaps he has a right to be. The complexities of family life confound her.

Geoff picks the kiddie-coloured plastic pegs off the ground and puts them in the basket. She feels sorry for him trapped in the city house, its tiny section. Though he likes to go out at night the shops bore him. He follows her about the house like a toddler, wanting to help, getting in the way.

Josie has a routine and she has her work. I have to work this afternoon, she says as if the house chores were just a hobby. Her real work is pleasant but not exactly lucrative. She does a weekly recipe column for the Sunday paper, and book reviews for the same paper and sometimes for radio. It's when she works that Geoff paces and mutters and writes out lists and screws them up and brings her cups of coffee she forgets to drink.

'Never mind love,' she consoles. 'It won't be for much longer. Why don't you take Hogg for a walk?' Hogg's lying on the flagstones outside the french doors and can't have heard but he wags his tail hopefully. 'See,' she says, 'he's as bored as you are.'

But Geoff hates taking Hogg out for Hogg is a country dog who expects cars to slow or swerve and drivers to wind down their windows and personally curse him. Geoff refuses to submit Hogg to the prissy indignity of a leash.

Josie looks at Geoff and sighs. 'My god,' she says offensively, 'I won't be half glad when you're old enough for kindy.'

The house has a view of the harbour bridge and yachts sliding in and out of placid moorings. It's a large old house on a tiny high-fenced section. The view is only from upstairs. It's a gracious and well-appointed house but it isn't theirs and it doesn't feel like home. It's Carl and Edie's house.

Edie has been dead five years yet to Josie it still feels like Edie's house. As she vacuums the carpets and dusts the Chinese vases Josie sometimes feels that Edie is hovering and if Josie could turn her head fast enough she would glimpse something, maybe a thin white mist smelling faintly of brandy.

Josie and Edie worked for the same radio station in the smug and careless days before Vietnam, before television, before oil crises and delicatessens. Edie was the shopping reporter. She was working up to be a proper announcer, though not a newsreader because everyone knew that women's voices lacked the authority needed for reading the news. Even then Edie was living with Carl, who was a student, but Josie was one of the few people at the station who knew. Edie was risking her job by living with Carl—her listeners couldn't be expected to trust a shopping reporter who would shack up.

When Edie had her abortion, in the bathroom of a house no different from the houses on either side except that the address was passed on in whispers, it was Josie who took the day off work and went with her and took her home and stayed with her until Carl got back from a hard day's lectures. Edie couldn't have that baby because Carl had to get his degree.

After the abortion Edie's womb was so damaged she couldn't have any more babies and Carl didn't like the idea of adopting. They got married when Carl finished his degree and Josie, who was by then Mrs Farley White, was Matron of Honour. Edie had stopped working by then. She hadn't got to be a proper announcer and Carl didn't like the idea of being married to a shopping reporter. Besides he earned more than enough for just the two of them.

And Josie and Edie saw less and less of each other. Josie was still working and also reading her way through the library's psychology section to try and discover what was wrong with her, that Farley should prefer to talk about investments and inflation when they lay in bed together. Edie was buying drapes and Axminster and expensive Chinese bowls and vases and wall hangings and bottles of brandy.

When Josie moved south to make a fresh start she and Edie exchanged letters at Christmas. And when her second marriage went the way of the first and Josie fled north she began to see a bit more of her friend.

Josie had a new job, a house of her own (inherited from her mother) and three kids. Edie's life seemed not to have changed at all. She'd bought new drapes and a few more vases. She was thinner and a little more sardonic. And even if they just met for a quick lunch she insisted they went somewhere licensed.

When Josie left the city to go north she'd felt she was deserting Edie. Not in the way she was deserting her other female friends, who thought Josie was behaving pitiably; beneath the smart cracks Edie was, Josie sensed, both envious and proud of her.

'All I'm looking for,' Josie had protested, 'is what you've had for years—a stable, secure, uneventful relationship.' Edie made her feel like a butterfly; vivid, flapping and buffeted. A symbol of freedom or hope. Maybe just endurance. I have this friend, she imagined Edie saying, about my age and she's still trying to sort her life out. Things are still *happening* to her!

They wrote to each other. Edie's letters were rambling, funny and a touch desperate. You should get a typewriter, Josie wrote back, and sell this stuff. Wit is a talent you shouldn't just fritter away on friends.

Carl rang, it was a few days after Christmas. 'It seems she must've blacked out,' he said. 'Possibly the car stalled and . . .'

Edie sitting in her little Japanese car waiting for the train to pounce from behind the cutting. Thinking whatever it is people think when they're choosing to die.

Josie had wanted to blame Carl. She wanted to say, you began it the day you went off to your bloody lectures and she went off to have her insides scoured in someone's bathroom. You were her husband and it's all your fault.

But Josie was her friend who wasn't friend enough and had fluttered off.

At the funeral they murmured about a heart attack, about the need to change gear when approaching a rail crossing. Squeezing the guilt from their hearts and heaping it on the impassive shoulders of fate. But it seeped back.

Carl made visits up north to stay with Geoff and Josie. She'd never felt close to Carl yet now he'd drive for hours to stay a night or two. Alone. Bewildered and pathetic. As if, now it was too late, Josie could provide the clues that might explain Edie.

On Carl's last visit he brought with him his fiancée, Stephanie. Attractive, talkative and three years older than Lake. Edie was more than four years dead yet Josie had felt disloyal. Aiding and abetting, spreading fresh sheets on the twin beds. And observing Carl's sparkling new smile and his almost slavish devotion to the girl. Thinking, adulterer — you could've been like this for *her*.

He learned from his mistakes. You taught him Edie, if it's any consolation. Made him a better man. For Stephanie.

Carl offered them—Geoff, Josie, Daryl and Sarah—the use of his house when they had to shift from the farm. Rent free and for up to six months. Carl and Stephanie have gone on a six-month round-the-world honeymoon. And may the tower of Pisa topple on him thinks Josie, who always sees both sides to every question.

Carl and Edie didn't have a honeymoon. Carl said they knew each other well enough already. *On our wedding night—we'd just moved into that upstairs flat—Carl went round all the rooms making an inventory so the landlord couldn't accuse us of taking something that wasn't there. And I lay in bed and listened to* Highlights of the Goon Show. *When he reached the bedroom with his little pad and pen Carl said, you might've told me that was on.*

Josie thinks, oh the stories I've been told about what's been said in conjugal bedrooms! All those glimpses into other people's heads.

'Nearly finished?' Geoff brings her a cup of coffee.

She bares her teeth.

'It's all right,' he says. 'Won't bother you again. I'm just going out.'

'Where?'

He smirks.

'I'll be through in another couple of hours.'

'Fine,' he says. 'I'll probably be through about then too.'

The impulse to clutch at him . . . that demeaning panic of the heart, though she knows he's only playing games. Knows almost for certain.

She makes herself play along. 'Fine. See you later.'

Her fingers suspend themselves above the keys of her typewriter as she listens to the sounds of his leaving. Hogg watches through the window, hears the front door open and close, and sighs. 'Never mind,' Josie says to Hogg, to herself, 'we won't be here much longer.'

In her head seeing Hogg happy, as he always was. Sharing his new melancholy by letting herself think of what they've left. The big old house with its summer shade and winter damp, the sluggish flow of the estuary waters forested with mangroves, the silly stiff-legged jumping of lambs.

Her mind leads her up the familiar track towards the henhouse. Past the dog-kennels (Ken and Girlie gone now to new owners, only Hogg, ugliest, oldest, favourite, unfairly kept), the lemon tree, the peach tree, the overgrown axles and engines. She can smell it all; baked mud, pennyroyal, fermenting fallen fruit, dogs, grass, sea, wood, sheep, cows. And she thinks, if *I* miss it in such an aching way how must it be for him?

Should he have resisted . . . consulted lawyers? Should she have encouraged him to fight it? 'I don't think,' she'd said to Geoff cautiously, 'that an ex-wife has a claim on something that was inherited. Perhaps you should find out?'

'It was only leasehold,' he said. 'While she was there I was buying the freehold. The old man had signed the leasehold over to me a good few years before he died.' He sat there scratching his head, re-reading the letter, looking helpless. 'What d'you think I should do?'

And she had removed herself beyond the perimeter of his need. 'It's up to you.'

Before they changed the marital property laws to give wives, on divorce, an equal share of business and possessions Josie had researched for a documentary on divorce settlements. She'd talked to a lot of ex-wives, herself included. She'd never doubted that the change in law was necessary and that an equal share was a just division. She's never met Geoff's ex-wife. She has no reason to think Geoff's rueful stories about Michelle are exaggerations. Still—however selfish, spaced out or screwed up she may have been—there's something . . . a vague sense of loyalty . . . an obligation not to sabotage another woman's rights.

'If she was such a silly cow why did you marry her?'

'She wanted to, and I was used to her. Used to sleeping with her. The place wasn't so lonely. And she had such a nice accent.'

He'd picked her up when she was hitch-hiking and because it was late had offered her a bed for the night. Five years later she got a lift out with a man who came to see Geoff on 'business'. The last he heard she was still with that same man.

'What does he do? Her present bloke?'

'Wheels, deals. Bit of an operator . . . one of those.'

'So what was his business with you?'

That was how she found out that Geoff was growing dope. A side crop, just enough to help with the mortgage. He gave it up for Josie's sake; her kids were at the local school and would harvest the outrage if Geoff got caught. Still, she gave up her whole way of life and her job for him.

The farm was bought by an Auckland businessman for a staggering price. A tax write-off, everyone said, bitter and knowing. But Michelle would be rich.

'Not if she's still with that snake,' said Geoff. 'She'll be lucky to even get a smell of the money.'

'You don't mean that?' said Josie, shocked. 'Why didn't you say before?'

'What difference does it make,' he said gloomily.

But soon a fresh start. Three times they have gone back to Motuwairua and looked at properties. They've decided—Geoff has decided—on the place at Whiripare. Twenty hectares; five of them steep and bush-clad, the five around the house flat, the remainder what the agent called undulating. The house is weatherboard, pale yellow, characterless, set among a handful of scraggy bushes and a couple of unsteady outbuildings. The view is breathtaking.

Geoff has offered ten thousand less than the asking price. He's enjoying the power of disposable money. His enjoyment makes Josie nervous. He swaggers and jokes as if all that's at stake is a plaster-ofparis rabbit.

His enthusiasm for the island has swept aside Josie's fears. On their last visit she could almost share his compulsion to own some part of it. As if in buying the land they would also become shareholders in the ocean that rocked below and in the clear late summer skies above. *Our place*, she thinks. The words have a dreamy caramel flavour, a soft-focus shimmer. Some part of her is still sixteen and humble with faith and hope.

Yet having been twice married she regularly declines to marry Geoff on grounds of superstition. Besides, she can't be certain that the act of marriage doesn't in itself precipitate divorce.

April

WHEN THE RAIN begins in earnest Maureen is rethreading elastic in Mickey's pyjama pants. Pushing a safety pin through a limp greyish tunnel. One hand to push, one hand to hold while she frees the gathered fabric, the end of the elastic gripped between her teeth in case it disappears and she'll have to start all over again.

Through her tight teeth she's having a conversation with Mickey. 'Why?' he says.

'Why what?'

'But why?'

'I don't know what you mean love.'

'Why is Gigs?'

She takes the elastic from her mouth and holds it. 'Why is Giggles what?'

He stands there square and stubborn. He shrugs and looks at the paper on the floor with its crayon scrawls. Then looks back at his mother. 'Why?' he pleads.

Sometimes she thinks he may be backward. That what she gratefully took to be a placid personality might be just stupidity. He was slow to crawl, to walk, to talk.

'Why?' he says again, dogged and without anger. And then the rain comes. It hammers on the roof so sudden and furious that for a few seconds they're both afraid and Mickey runs to her, edging himself between her knees. Then they have to go to the window and look closer at the hurtling water, to prove to themselves; for there have been showers and dull brooding days but nothing to soften the ground and fill the tank. For the last two weeks Maureen has been washing their clothes in just enough water to wet and wring out again. And she has been taking the kids, after school, to the sea and urging them in—even Mickey—though the water's getting steadily colder; then making them rinse under the public tap because of the sea lice. When she tapped the water tank with a piece of wood, the way the old man down the road had told her to, the empty sound began somewhere in the bottom rim.

She might've guessed that, on this island, when it did rain it would do so immoderately. That her relief would turn to fear that the roof would cave in or the tankstand finally collapse.

She returns to the pyjamas. The elastic has run up into the tunnel; she'll have to edge out the safety pin and start again.

The pyjamas, once green, are a drab dishcloth grey. Most of their clothes are starting to look greyish. She tells herself it doesn't matter here on an island where people have worthier values. Yet the smiling ladies fondling automatic washer-driers leap out at her from the pages of Alice's dog-eared magazines crying *shame*.

Maureen would settle for her old agitator, but it had belonged to their landlord. She finds no pioneering pleasure in washing by hand. The demands of garments domineer her. She washes, hangs out, brings in, folds, sorts, mends, puts away, picks up, washes, hangs out, brings in. She knows with dreary intimacy the patterns, weave, shape, patches, darns, stains and defects. She knows which were bought at gala day stalls and which were bargains new from Farmers or McKenzies. And the ones with smarter labels, passed on by Alice. She could close her eyes and identify each one just by touch. If she kept a small square of every garment she has tended since she left the bank and stitched them together to make a bedspread she could look at it and say, there's my life.

She could say, that's Carly's pinafore I cut down from one of my old bank uniforms, and – those are the overalls I got from the bargain basement the day before I went in to have Mickey.

Clothes hector her into nervous rituals. She must *keep up* no matter what. If she gets behind the clothes will pile up and engulf her. She dreams, sometimes, about clothes. In one dream she was folding away the clean washing and all of it was stained with something fluorescently green and sticky. And when she rewashed the clothes it came off, but grew again as she pinned them on the line.

In another dream the children's clothes fell apart – split slowly down the seams. And when she looked close she could see they had been slit – not the stitches but the fabric – with something sharp . . . a razor blade, a knife.

The fact that she dreams about washing and mending depresses her. It makes her feel grey and reduced; wanting to mourn for herself without quite knowing why. Still, she prefers those dreams to the other one that repeats itself and sometimes hides in the shadows of her mind right through the day so she knows it's there yet can't confront it.

She doesn't dream, any more, of Bruce.

It's nearly twenty past three and the kids will be on their way home. Must have been already on their way when the rain began. So there's nothing Maureen can do but get towels ready and prepare herself for Alan's displeasure.

But at twenty to four she makes a dash to the gate and looks down the road. They're nearly home – drenched and coatless; jumping and splashing and shrieking in the middle of two small streams that used to be tyre tracks. Their arms fly, their bags thump and swing. Maureen stands at the gate and watches, the rain seeping through to her skin. *I did right*, she thinks. She could weep with relief at this flash of certainty.

When they see her there she waves. She turns back onto the dead yellow grass which is their lawn. She jumps, she spins, she tries a cartwheel and is surprised and proud to find she still can. When she straightens up, grinning, Carly and Alan are inside the gate. They stand very still watching their mother, their faces furtive with dismay.

'What's the matter?' she calls. 'Don't look like that.'

She sees they're not entirely reassured. 'Oh, for heaven's sake, aren't I allowed.'

They smile reassuringly in her direction then their eyes dart sideways to confer. And she understands. She's all they have. If she were to go quietly insane . . .

It has of course occurred to her. Not outright spectacular madness but a kind of mental dissipation that comes from too much worrying round and round in your own head. Or perhaps just from going too long without anything joyful or unexpected happening, so you get to dream of laundry.

She has an obligation not to go mad and an obligation not to die. She can see them standing at her graveside, almost orphans. Alan with his I-told-you-so look both smug and dolorous, being ostentatiously manful. Rather enjoying the gravity of the occasion though in private at a later date he may weep. Mickey too young to fully grasp the implications of nevermore. Carly struggling to put a brave face on her broken heart.

Who else would be at the graveside, come to claim them? Their father perhaps though that begins to seem more and more unlikely. It's nearly five months since they left and he could easily have traced them if he wanted to. She'd been afraid in the first few weeks; unable to predict what Bruce might do. Prepared for threats, abuse, maybe violence. Fearing she would be dragging in over Alice's glossy threshold something raw and unthinkably real; the obscenity of her marriage magnified because she would be seeing it already through Alice and Matthew's sheltered eyes.

He hadn't come. Not even a phone call. Of course she was relieved and it seemed like an endorsement of her leaving him. It also hurt a lot. On her own account, but mostly the kids. His own children! She still can't come to grips with such indifference. She'd been sure that at least when the social welfare people chased him up for maintenance . . . that then he'd be sufficiently enraged to make contact. His silence feels ominous. 'He sounds,' Matthew used to say in those first few days when she had to talk about it, 'a bit unhinged to me.'

Maureen privately disagreed. She thought Matthew just wanted to set Bruce apart so that no one could suggest normal men would behave as he did. It seemed to Maureen that Bruce behaved the way most of his friends did. Much as her own father had behaved, but Bruce could manage it sober. She didn't say this to Matthew because she was his guest.

Anyway would Matthew and Alice intervene, at Maureen's funeral, if Maureen's children were claimed by a father who was inadequately hinged? Place the children instead with (god forbid) Maureen's parents or Bruce's terrible mother? Or share them around like biscuits . . . Alice has always wanted a daughter so she'd take Carly . . . possibly Mickey as well . . .

When she left Bruce her worst fear had been that the kids might be split up. If he'd been willing to let her keep only one or possibly two of them who would she give up? Not Mickey her baby. Not Carly who was an extension of Maureen herself. But not Alan. Alan's the one she seems to have least love for which means he's the one who needs her the most.

She used to pray sometimes in her head like a child; let me keep them all and I'll never ask for anything else. A gentlemen's agreement which she doesn't feel bound to keep.

The rain hammers down all night and right through the next day which is Good Friday. After the first hour or two the cottage gives up the pretence of being waterproof. Drips and dribbles begin one after another. Two in the living room, three in the kitchen, another in the bathroom. Maureen arranges pots which plink and plonk in a hollow African sound. The children run from room to room listening for fresh leaks, fighting over the right to claim discovery. But no one finds the tiny discoloured creek that trickles down the corner of Maureen and Carly's room with a cargo of dead spiders and ants and daddy-long-legs. Not until Carly goes for her nightdress.

Wet blankets, wet sheets, wet mattress. Maureen arranges them over chairs beneath sections of ceiling that haven't yet succumbed. That night Carly shares her mother's single bed. Maureen lies awake for a long time listening to the rain. Carly tosses and wriggles. She has a warm sweet child smell.

The next morning Maureen readjusts the wet bedding to avoid the new leaks. Matthew, when they brought the furniture over, had legged himself up on the grapevine and pronounced the roof to be in pretty good shape considering. In the kitchen water trickles down the cord which holds the lightbulb and the white plastic shade. She warns the children not to turn on the light. She doesn't understand electricity, doesn't know if water on the light fittings can affect the wall plug, if it could give her a shock or even electrocute. She doesn't know if it really is dangerous or how long it might take to dry out when the rain's stopped. She marvels that in twelve years of schooling she learned none of the things that she needs, in adulthood, to know. She turns the power off at the mains in case. There's only the light and the single power point anyway.

'Right,' Maureen says in her leadership voice, 'we'll light the stove so this afternoon we can have a huge bath.'

Carly looks suitably grateful, Mickey gives a slightly vacuous smile. Alan gives a loud sigh, not looking at Maureen, picking at a scab on his knee.

'Look,' she says, sharp and weary. 'I know a bath isn't exactly Disneyland. But it's raining for godsake, what else can we do?'

He raises his head and stares at her. That long cold stare that she knows too well, arm-wrestling of the eyes. Always the lowering, the giving-in, is hers—it feels absurd to compete, and she hasn't the reserves of hatred the battle seems to demand. In ways such as this she sees in Alan, over and over, echoes of his father. The nervous pinching of nostrils . . . the clenched lifting of the shoulders . . . Is the child bound to grow into the man his mother couldn't bear to live with? (Just as Maureen stepped into a marriage as bad as her mother's.) What if you come to dislike your own child, not just now and again but irrevocably? What then?

'If we had a TV like everyone else,' says Alan to his bent knee.

'We'll have a game of cards,' she says, 'as soon as I've lit the fire.'

'Teachers expect you to have TV. Mrs Liston's always telling us things we gotta watch. I'm the only one that doesn't get to.'

'Must be others,' she says. 'I bet there are others.'

'Not in my class.'

'We have to watch it too,' says Carly. 'We're supposed to watch *After School*.'

'As soon as we can,' says Maureen. 'I promise. Just as soon as we can we'll get one.'

'Colour,' says Alan.

'We'll see.' Maureen revises the list in her head. TV before fridge. It makes sense now that winter's nearly here.

She's sent off the money she owed to Matthew and paid the school fees and the book money. She's started saving for the tankstand but she's not sure how much she'll need. And the toilet should really come first. It's full. She dug a bit of a hole behind the plum tree but the kids don't like using it. Neither, come to that, does she. Having to crouch there like a cat.

But now there's the roof to be done. And they're going to need more blankets with the nights getting colder. And next week's Mickey's birthday and she was going to buy the wind-up barking dog they've got down at the local shop. Each time they go in there he touches it so wistfully. And even though he's too young still to have many expectations she'll have to make a cake and get some candles and a few balloons and paper hats; which all mounts up.

She sorts them round and round in her head, these projects and priorities. There's a certain sense of achievement in getting by, satisfaction in a debt met, a bill paid. Yet sometimes she can't help thinking with hurt, childish dismay, *is this all there is?*

Before the rain started when she worked in the garden Mickey used to bring her insects clutched in his small sweaty palm. Once he brought her a large, perfect, transparent shell of what may once have been a cicada or a cricket. She told him, cruel and deadpan, that the thing he held was called a mother. See, she said, her children have eaten her all away.

Mostly she tries to be grateful; reminding herself that at least for her there was a choice. Her mother couldn't have fled with little Alice and Maureen—no support from the state in those days and women's labour paid at half a man's rate. Maureen's generation timing it right for equal pay and all those things they take for granted. Hard times belonging way back in the depression, now it's just that people want too much. Not honest poverty – just greed and carelessness and petulance.

Maureen would willingly put up with leaking roofs and gaping sneakers and no TV and even the squat-hole under the plum tree. It's just that she'd like something a bit better than that for her kids. She can't quite get rid of the feeling that they're being punished on her behalf; for marrying without due caution at nineteen; for having wanted so badly and injudiciously to belong to someone. (O Carly beware. There are crimes out there disguised as gingerbread houses.)

'Who's gonna bring in the wood? Alan, Carly, please.' Maureen scrapes the ashes through the grating. It's a long time since she lit the stove, she couldn't risk using water for baths and the little gas stove is quicker for cooking.

They come in with a few sticks each and drop them near her feet.

'And the rest.'

'That's all there is.'

'Rubbish, there's a whole pile.' She carried most of it up from the beach, smooth driftwood almost too pretty for burning.

'That's all that's out there,' says Alan. He looks at Carly.

'Where's the rest?'

'It was Car,' he blames. 'She wanted to make a house out the back.'

'You too,' hisses Carly.

He kicks her, swift and sideways with his eyes still on his mother. Carly wails.

'For that,' she tells him, 'you can go and get all the rest. You should've had more sense, both of you.'

'We didn't know it was gonna rain,' sniffs Carly.

'Oh come on,' Maureen says to the girl now Alan has gone, coatless, into the rain. 'I don't think he really hurt you.'

'He did.' She lifts up her leg. A small blushing patch of skin below the knee.

'Scarred for life,' says Maureen, then shame makes her hug the child. 'Never mind. Help me get this started then we'll play cards.' Carly slumps. 'Not cards? Well, what d'you suggest?'

'I could bake something. Once the oven's hot. Or make some fudge.'

'You could cook us all some lunch.'

'Not lunch Mum. Can't I make fudge?'

When she was six years old Maureen used to make fudge. Her mother would reluctantly allow: your-teeth'll-all-fall-out. Maureen doesn't want her daughter making fudge either. But not on account of teeth—she's thinking of the price of cocoa, the price of sugar. That's why they don't want to play cards, she thinks sourly; playing cards is free so it's no fun.

'Okay,' she decides, 'you can make fudge, but you're only allowed one piece each and we'll keep the rest till Mickey's birthday.'

The fudge doesn't set. Even when Maureen takes over and reboils and beats it it still doesn't set. She lets them eat it with spoons. Three whole cups of sugar. She says, I hope it makes you sick.

They play cards. Maureen plays Mickey's hand as well as her own. Carly keeps winning and Alan's eyes get pink with despair until he doesn't want to play any more.

Maureen reads them three stories which they've all heard before. Alan keeps edging towards Carly and jabbing at her with his bare toes. Just enough to make Carly squeak and Maureen look up and lose her place and say cut it out. To which he says either, di'in even touch her, or, servzer right.

For winning at cards.

The fire in the stove smokes and smoulders but finally burns. For a while the kids—all three of them—play a game of big-game hunters in which one of the still-damp blankets from Carly's bed is the tent. Alan invents the game. He is the big-game hunter and Carly is his assistant and Mickey is a lion cub whom they rescue when Alan shoots the mother and father lions. The scenario gets out of hand when Mickey arms himself with red plastic blocks and goes round shooting wild animals instead of being one. Alan, whose life is one long series of shattered expectations and misplayed scenarios, flies into a rage and knocks his brother down.

'What's *wrong* with you?' wails Maureen. 'Why do you *do* these things?'

The rain has lost impetus. It purrs softly on their roof. The pots on the floor no longer have to be watched and emptied. In the night the pots flooded. 'Ruined the shagpile,' Maureen said.

'The what?' said Carly.

'Never mind. It was a private joke.'

Now Maureen tests the water. It snarls and hisses from the kitchen tap. 'Who wants to be first?' she calls from the bathroom. She will be last and stay longest. She's been thinking about this bath for hours ... hot suds settling around her shoulders when she dares to lie back

. . . the luxury of that lazy weightlessness—even in this horrid little tin bath with the paint peeling and floating.

The water running from the tap turns orange and falters, runs again for a second or two then dries away. Maureen puts her finger in the bath, the water is scalding. There's just enough to cover the first knuckle of her finger.

Carly stands at the door. 'Alan's first. We tossed a coin.'

'Who tossed it?'

'Alan did.' Carly's wry grin. 'Was his idea too.' Carly's smile bothers Maureen. The girl assumes so readily a conspiracy between the two of them, a shared amused tolerance of Alan's little ways. Being patronised by a sister two years his junior could be part of what's wrong with Alan. She pretends not to have understood the grin, not this time.

'There mightn't be any bath. The water's stopped running. I think there might be rust blocking the pipes.'

Maureen unhooks the curtain wire from the living room windows. She's burnt the ragged curtains, thinking one day when there's a few dollars to spare . . . The kids stand watching as she pushes the wire up through the tap. She feeds in the whole length then pulls it out again.

They follow her to the porch and watch her tap the tank with a broomhandle. She starts halfway up and works down. Each rim clangs sharp and hollow.

'I'm sorry,' she says. 'I'm sorry. I was looking forward to it too.'

In case the wet-back explodes, being empty of water and the fire still hot with embers, she gets the kids to carry out the water-catching pots from inside while she stands on a chair and empties them into the top of the tank.

'I can get lots,' says Alan. 'I'm just waiting for the other pot to fill. It's running down off the roof by your room.'

She remembers Matthew saying, though off-handedly, that the guttering could do with a clean out. She'd thought it to be an observation, like saying the piles have gone or the plumbing's antiquated. She hadn't made the mental connection between guttering and their water supply.

Alan has a raincoat and isn't afraid of heights. She helps him onto the roof via the grapevine. When he's out of sight she moves back until he's in view again. Thinking, I should've gone up myself . . . as long as I didn't look down . . . it's not really high at all, not for an adult. 'Be careful,' she shrieks as he straightens and slides.

He looks down at her and waves, a small mountaineer. He

manoeuvres himself along the edge of the roof, leaning inwards, scooping handfuls of leaves, feather, mud and rust and dropping them over the side so that Maureen, standing ready to catch his falling body, has to jump aside. An echo of water trickles into the tank. 'Listen,' she calls to him.

His grinning face peers over the side.

'Don't do that, it's dangerous.'

He's round the corner when he calls down, 'Mum, look.' His hand wriggles at her through the cleared guttering. That large hole, then a sieve of smaller holes and the water already trickling through.

When he's done the whole guttering she helps him down. 'You were great. Very brave. I wouldn't have done it.'

He nods. 'You know, I reckon I could fix that hole. If you got me the stuff.' It pleases him to be manly. If there were just the two of them they'd get along famously.

'Let's get dry.' She follows him inside.

'I did it,' he tells Carly. 'We'll have some water soon.'

'I'm afraid,' says Maureen, 'we'll lose most of it through the hole. I should've checked while it was still fine. It was very stupid of me.'

'It's not your fault,' says Carly.

'I've had my bath anyway,' Alan says drying his face, 'out there. Who cares about a bath.'

Maureen does. In the bedroom she pulls off her wet clothes and thinks of warm water neck-high. Thinks; it wasn't as if I was just looking forward to a night out or a friend calling. Just a hot bath. It didn't seem like a lot to ask.

She puts on a nightdress and her dressing gown. It's still afternoon but what's the difference, who's going to see. And she lies on the bed with her head buried in her arms and cries. Because this—the long discordant day, the rotted guttering, the afternoon nightdress—does seem to be all there is.

She knows soon they'll come looking for her and will be, for a time, united in their concern. Worried and kind and eager to please her. And she'll feel guilty about having had to frighten them into it.

*   *   *

Josie grinds the cup hook into the huntsman's face. Chalky fragments erupt and drift past the horse and hounds to settle on the floor. The hook sags and, when she checks it, comes away in her fingers. 'It's

79

useless. Just goddam useless.'

'Whadda you expect?' says Geoff from the sofa. 'You have to tap along till you find the four-by-two. Anyone knows that.'

'But I want it here.'

'You can't have it there.'

She folds her arms and turns slowly to consider the whole dismal room. 'It really is hideous. Oh, I know the house isn't important – well not *as*. And I guess this is marginally better than the wobbly place over the hill. But look at it. They've wallpapered the kitchen bit and painted all the rest. Why would anyone ... Bloody huntsmen tallyhoing at me. And fuck-all cupboard space. You can tell it was designed by a man. And built by a man. Look at that gap there, waste space, you can't even reach in to clean. Compared to this the farmhouse was a palace.'

She pushes the chalky powder on the floor with her toe. 'It's probably asbestos, and I've breathed it.'

Geoff shifts his shoulders and gurgles. 'Blue,' he says. 'You should do all this deep blue with white bits around the windows.'

'I see. And what will you be doing all the while?'

'I'll watch and see you do it right.'

She waits for his smirk to die unattended. Too often, too easily he disarms her; making light of her honest worries until she can no longer be sure that, outside her own head, they have real substance. Yet here she is doing things and there he is reclining. There's reality in that; the way it seems to have been for much of their time together.

Perhaps she *is* a bit obsessive. She can see herself that there's something irrational about her need to begin at once on this house; to transform its featureless walls into something definitely hers, like a dog peeing out his territorial right. A dangerous nesting instinct.

But Josie has always been a doer of things. An only child of parents who kept themselves busy – who mended and built and grew and made and tended and altered and re-upholstered. The work ethic surging in McBride veins, at least until the latest diluted generation. Busy-ness was next to godliness but slightly higher up. Josie learnt at an early age to make the best use of her time and to finish whatever she started (married life excepted). Up until the day she began work she assumed that other people did the same.

In all her years as an employee she never quite got used to how little was expected of her. And she never ceased to be astonished at how little work her colleagues considered a sufficiency. Because the work she did was, in those days, more usually done by males and so she was surrounded by men who sat at their desks and told jokes and sold raffle tickets, she came to believe that most men were, by nature, lazy. And even when in later years she worked alongside women as often as men what she observed still seemed to support her earlier suspicions.

So she'd never expected Geoff to work his arse off. She had no knowledge of farming, no rule of thumb, no grounds for comparison. And of course she was eager, in those early days, to be a helpmate and would often go with him thereby halving the workload.

Workload?

Sometimes even she was impressed. Shearing and docking, when outsiders arrived and the place seethed with sweaty dawn-to-dusk action and Geoff fell asleep at the table and again in the bath.

But the other times. Hours he would spend propped against the tractor with the dogs patient at his feet while he yarned with a neighbour or a stock agent. Sometimes not even talking but both just leaning and gazing at the hills or out across the estuary while Josie watched, furtive and fascinated, from the house. And the lunch times which ran into tea times if someone called in, and almost always stayed. The rainy mornings when he coaxed her back to bed after the kids had left for school though there was always paperwork waiting for a wet day.

When she'd worried out loud he'd laughed and said she was talking like a townie. Or said, it's how we do things up here.

'Yeah, I can see that,' Josie would tell him. Meaning his farm, though the rest of the district was much the same. Fences at a lean, batons broken, strainer posts propped up forever in the meantime by iron bars, wires and buildings sagging. Behind the house like a spare vegetable garden a rusting crop of vehicle parts. The house itself not painted for so long it was almost entirely an old wood shade of silver-grey. The outbuilding leaning and creaking. Two kauri piles where the jetty used to be.

Josie enchanted by the untended timelessness of the place yet itching to restore, repair. No money for that, he'd say in the first years. And how could she argue; he was housing and feeding Josie and her three kids. The weekly rent from her Auckland house and the tiny bit of freelance work she'd been able to arrange only covered their extra expenses. And later Geoff would say, why should I do it up for her benefit; for by then he'd got the letter from Michelle's solicitor.

We get by, he'd say mildly. And they did. The grass kept growing, the lambs and the calves kept being born.

But this land they live on now has no reassuring pattern of performance. Too many owners have fragmented its purpose. Patches of gorse and blackberry sulk in the dips.

Geoff has a multitude of plans. He has money left over for development. It's the first time in his life he has money for more than his daily needs. Josie doubts that he will spend it wisely. There was already his suggestion that they should travel on it. He'd like to see New York. And Hamburg.

'Don't be daft,' said Josie. 'I'm not going on your money. Besides the kids might get to hate it over there with Dick. Any day they might want to come home and I can't be off tripping round the world.' For so long her children have anchored her against wild currents. What will she hold onto when they're really gone?

So Josie scrubs and scrapes and paints and Geoff takes Hogg on gentle walks around his property and gets back in time for morning tea or lunch. To tell her of some new discovery—the steep track down the cliff leading to a tiny beach, exclusively theirs almost, or a grand old totara in the bottom bush, or a nest of quails. 'Come and I'll show you.'

'Not now. I want to get the passage finished.'

'You can do that tomorrow.' Geoff's tomorrows are dew-damp leaves that fall when they're ready to. Josie's tomorrows are stern inquisitors asking what did you achieve yesterday?

He makes lists on the backs of envelopes, on fragments of disembodied hounds and huntsmen. He seeks her opinion on every option: 'I'm relying on you to provide the responsible viewpoint.'

'And what will you be providing?'

'The inspiration.'

They agree that diversification is important. They agree on hens and ducks and grapes on the north slopes and trial crops of strawberries and daffodils for next spring. They moot boarding kennels, a house cow, black sheep, a milking goat. She thinks animals are less risky, he leans more towards horticulture.

'But how much do you know about it?'

'Enough.'

All the options sound, to Josie, hazardous. Droughts, pests and gluts waiting up the sleeve of nature. Geoff himself another of nature's risks. 'Shouldn't you get this bore drilled before we make all these plans?

I mean what if there's no water down there?'

'There will be.'

She leaves the passage half done and lets him guide her down the precipice goat-track that winds and slides through scrub down to a crescent of rough sand. All the way down she thinks about the agony of climbing back up.

'I know I should be grateful,' she says, down on the sand. 'I know it's romantic and imaginative but it's a mite exposed.' She imagines how she'd look from a passing boat. A large smooth white thing washed up on shore. Her big white bum waving, his legs stretched beneath her; the two of them like some giant sea creature, eight limbs and a greedy pulsating body sucking at the world.

But now she is the world itself and no longer cares. She is land, sea and air—the indefinable moment where all three converge and the waves startle themselves with the sound of their arrival . . .

He pushes her hair out of his eyes and smiles up at her. She eases herself down beside him and doesn't yet feel the stones. 'Without you,' she says tenderly, 'my soul would wither away. You save me, you know, from my own brittle and busy inclinations.'

His finger brushes up and down her cheek. She thinks, he nurtures me in ways I don't fully appreciate. She feels eternally indebted.

'Tomorrow,' he says. 'I'll make a start on the henhouse. So stop worrying.'

She nods, ashamed. 'It's just that . . . well, we've had a holiday. We sat around all those weeks in the city.' She remembers the places they took Daryl and Sarah because they'd soon be gone. And the long drives to look at farms, prohibitively priced. Because she can sometimes read his mind she says, 'Well, there was all that time after the kids went.'

He shrugs. 'Everything was so . . . unsettled. You weren't in the right frame of mind.'

'I wasn't?'

'Neither of us were.'

'And now?'

He grins and shakes his head, meaning we'll talk about it another time. He sits up and reaches for their clothes.

'We picked the right place,' he says hopping to get a leg into his jeans. 'I can feel it.'

'Yes.' Josie's looking up at the track they have to scale. She makes herself turn towards the white-tipped sea, the shadow of an island on the horizon. 'It's almost frighteningly beautiful.'

She goes first up the track, though it's unlikely that Geoff could support her if she fell. It's not dangerous he says. It amuses him to watch the nervous, awkward way she negotiates her footholds. When she's edging past a clean face of rock with nothing to hold onto but a shoot of bracken he says from below, 'They get a lot of rich sods over here. Come for the summer. Rich . . . and bored . . . and decadent.'

He rolls the words out hardboiled and she daren't look down to see if it's a joke. She feels weak and precarious. But having got here she can only go on.

*   *   *

Daphne writes letters about rape on Keith's typewriter. There are the individual letters to publications whose letter columns are currently running letters on rape and there's the standard letter to publications who seem to be avoiding the issue. She types every letter though she could take them over to town and use a duplicator. She believes that duplicated letters will be automatically rejected no matter how important their content. She recognises that the media is the strong right arm of the oppressors and that even her laboriously typed efforts are unlikely to be printed.

In that all men condone it – if only by passive inaction – and all men benefit from the consequent intimidation of wimmin as a class it must be acknowledged that ALL MEN ARE RAPISTS, be they the perpetrators or the silent henchmen. Writes Daphne.

Four hundred and thirty seven thousand five hundred (437500) wimmin in this country have been sexually abused by the time they are eighteen years old. This fact has never made prominent headlines. Yet one white middle-class male is abducted and 'harassed' by a group of wimmin and it features as a headline sob and horror story. Over the last two months New Zealand wimmin have witnessed the astonishing spectacle of a male media bent double, hysterically protecting threatened testicles. Writes Daphne.

Because Hennie is in Auckland and Kay is curled up reading in Daphne's favourite chair, because it's still raining and Daphne has his typewriter and there's nothing in the house to read that doesn't accuse him, Keith hangs around.

Kay is, of the three women, the most approachable. With Daphne there's always that wall of contempt that forces Keith to weigh and limit his words. Hennie is unpredictable and not to be trusted. She plays games, pretending friendship then snatching it away for her own amusement – also Daphne's. But not, Keith thinks, Kay's.

The presence of Kay unaccompanied by Hennie makes Daphne less formidable. Keith stands at the table and reads one of the rape letters right through, even though Daphne stops poking away at the keys and watches him discouragingly. He puts the letter down. 'I don't think you should use *wimmin*.'

'You don't.'

'No, I don't. It's a kind of in-crowd affectation and you alienate half your readers the minute they see it.'

'You mean it would alienate you. The word offends you. You're threatened by it.'

'I don't feel threatened by it, I just think it's an affectation.'

'Because it's exclusive and a wimmin invention. Does the word menstruation also upset you?'

'Oh Jesus, forget it. I thought you were wanting to influence people, I didn't realise you just wanted to ponce about in print.' He smirks, confident Daphne won't give up on him this time, won't retreat – as she does when there's just the two of them – into superior silence. He senses that Daphne's need is not to convince or demolish Keith but to meet with Kay's approval.

'If we were reduced to seeking your opinion . . .' says Daphne a bit limply.

'As a journalist.'

She gives a here-we-go-again smile. 'So you're able to separate your professional personality from your sexual orientation and conditioning!'

'You're warped,' he says, 'd'you know that?' Daphne looks flattered and grins.

'Keith,' says Kay from the armchair, 'do you accept the argument that all men are rapists?'

'All except me.' He smiles jauntily and alone. 'Okay,' he amends, 'I accept that there's a certain logic to that argument, but it doesn't carry through. You could just as well claim that because murder can't be prevented all people are murderers.'

'No one benefits from murders,' says Daphne. 'Except perhaps the murderer.'

'I don't benefit from rape,' says Keith.

'Of course you do, indirectly. It means you can grope the office typist and feel entitled.'

'I don't want to,' he protests. 'I've never in my life groped the office typist.'

'I don't believe you,' says Daphne; her ace card, unbeatable.

Keith looks to Kay. 'You've benefited,' Kay says, not unsympathetically, 'from being in a socially privileged class.'

Keith has a quick thumb through his past. 'I suppose I might've,' he says humbly. 'I just wish I could remember when!'

'Haww,' says Daphne, behind Keith's back. Keith doesn't turn round. He talks to Kay, but loud enough:

'I find it strange. Daphne and I have shared this house for nearly three months yet all we've ever talked about is money and how she's going to change the world. She's never asked me one question about myself, my past, my beliefs . . .'

'Have you asked her about herself,' asks Kay. But is over-ridden by Daphne's voice saying, 'It hasn't occurred to you that I might find you of very little interest?'

He turns towards her. 'You're afraid to know anything about me. You can't afford to because it might stuff up your black and white sexist picture book of the world. *I* find you of interest, I find you really rather fascinating. Till I came here I'd never seen a fanatic close-up and in action.'

Daphne sighs. 'You're all the same. The thing you find fascinating, the thing that really upsets you, is my being a lesbian. The threat that implies. And you're quite right to feel threatened. I am a threat to you, so is Kay, we all are. We offer women an alternative. Choice means power. Now wimmin don't have to accept you on your terms or even on any terms. If the pedestal feels like its starting to wobble that's because it is, we have steadily undermined it.' She folds her arms and sits there triumphant.

Most of what she said has flooded over Keith. He says, blinking and defensive, 'I don't care about you being . . . I don't care who you sleep with, what you screw. I don't fancy you, so what's it to me?'

'He doesn't fancy us.' Daphne throws out her hands in limp horror. 'The *ultimate* put-down.'

'Being a lesbian,' says Kay patiently, 'isn't just to do with sex, Keith. It's to do with sexism. A political act. And therefore other people's response to it is in that same sense political.'

'Well, mine isn't,' he says after short consideration. 'My response is plain old indifference.' He leans across and pulls the paper from the typewriter carriage. He picks the machine up and clutches it to his chest. 'You can borrow it,' he says with some dignity, 'for the peace stuff.'

'Don't bother,' says Daphne, 'I'll get a loan of one from town.'

He feels foolish carrying the thing off. He wants to stop and say something friendly and liberal and placating – look, we're all adults, we can talk this thing through . . . but Daphne has the power to turn him into something petty and bullying and childish, substantiating all her assumptions.

'I have some writing to do,' he announces feebly from the door. Cringes to hear himself announce.

He sits at the little desk and taps the keys against the empty roller. PISSEDOFF he types. KEITH LAWRIE MUIR.

His mother was a Lawrie. Of English, French and Russian descent exotic blood mingling in her veins. In yours too, she would tell her sons; as if it was a treasure imparted. It was the Russian dollop that gave her her talent as a dancer. In her red album she had photos of her career. A dark-eyed young woman posed with her fingertips touching and her elbows out like roadsigns. Photos of her leaping in the air, photos of her standing smiling among foreigners. The dates and places underneath. Amsterdam, Los Angeles, London. Soft, respectful paper between the pages.

In the red dancing album Keith's mother is forever captured speaking with an accent and *esteemed*. Since that was a word no one else he knew had ever used Keith took it to mean blessed or magical. And no more real than movie stars or people in stories.

'Dance for us now,' they'd begged when they were still young enough. 'Stand like in this one. Plee-ease.' Prove to us that you are really Eve Lawrie esteemed and not Mrs Muir a bit peculiar.

'Here,' she would say. 'How can I dance here? Who would I dance for? Your father? You think he would appreciate my dancing?'

'For us,' one of them would say. Usually Howard.

'For you? For children? Some day when you're older, then I might. We shall see. If you grow up to show me you have the appreciation, the sensitivity . . . if you grow into men like that, then I'll dance for you. But not here. You understand that, I know you do. I will never dance in this house.'

She used to be beautiful. Even as Eve Muir, mother of Howard and Keith, she was still beautiful. Slim and dark and mysterious. Yet he can no longer assemble the features and assure himself it wasn't just a child's view of beauty. He remembers very well her face as he last saw it, and that may be more than enough. It seems to Keith she hadn't aged steadily, almost imperceptibly as other people do. It seems that for years she looked the same and then suddenly her face began to move; the eyes and lips were sucked in and the skin turned shiny and transparent like a petticoat.

He can remember when he was young enough to be enchanted by her. With her softly accented voice, the perfume that invited you in against her pale neck, the exotic red album, she wove spells that won her sons' unquestioning allegiance. Without her even hinting at parallels Keith understood the allegories of the stories she most liked to read them.

The princess and the pea, Rapunzel in her tower prison, the bird in the golden cage; Keith knew who they all were really. Jack and the beanstalk—even though Jack was slyly made out to be a man—made him tremble for her and brought him nightmares of a faceless ogre bent over their kitchen table mumbling and grunting and smelling of animals. Wearing his filthy boots on the floor she worked so hard at keeping clean.

Since he's been on the island memories like that have been homing in on him. Things he hadn't thought about almost since they happened, feelings he'd snubbed and shouldered aside. In all those years back at Everton, which was his hometown—the place, when he worked in Wellington, he told people he came from because you couldn't expect anyone to have heard of Lonewood Valley—he'd never once driven out to the valley and looked at the house. Someone he went to primary school with told him that the place had changed hands once again since the Muirs left; the new owners had put up high fences and were running deer.

He'd returned to Everton because he wanted to get out of the city and away from things connected with Ginny. And because there was the job going at the *Times* which he was sure to get because Everton employers would take on anyone rather than risk an outsider. If there were other reasons for returning he'd never got round to forking them over.

He'd never gone to look at the house and he'd never gone to visit his father. He would have if his father had asked him. In a place the size of Everton they couldn't avoid seeing each other from time to time. His father was always accompanied by his bicycle; in the middle of town he'd push it along the pavement in a straight line so people had to leap aside. He'd nod to his son the way he nodded to all the folk who had lived in the district long enough to look familiar.

Once Keith had stood in the path of that unswerving front wheel and his father had stopped. 'Hello,' said Keith. 'How are you?'

His father rubbed at the worn and crumbling leather of the bike's seat, watching his thumb moving back and forth. 'I'm fine,' he said eventually. 'How are you?'

'Good.'

His father raised his eyes and watched a couple cross the street, City people, dressed to impress, but wasting their time in Everton.

'I've been back a year or so now,' Keith tried.

His father gripped the handles and moved them so the wheel swung from side to side like a horse in barely restrained impatience. 'Yup,' he said.

'My wife left me,' said Keith. But the bike was now pawing the ground with the bit between its teeth. Keith could only move aside and let it past.

Later he thought he might have been tactless. That his last remark might've seemed like some grotesque attempt at establishing common ground between them. They went back to just nodding, and on reflection Keith felt it was the only dignified way. All that scrabbling through the ruins of the past in search of answers or absolution was far too popular and therefore open to question.

With his job and his friends at the DB, and being roped into the darts team and the occasional cricket or soccer match, not thinking about the past was a habit that was easy enough to maintain. Up until now.

Here there are too many spaces in his life and his head is too clear. Once the memories get in they may take over. He's safe out of doors; down by the beach or in the bush he's safe . . . he feels protected. When he has some corner of the island all to himself the pleasure makes him inviolable.

But winter is beginning. Even if he buys himself that heavy yellow rainwear that roadworkers stand about in he won't want to go visiting his favourite places all the time. He should think about a job, something he could do on the island, he would never commute to the city every day to work as a few uncommitted islanders do.

He doesn't as yet need money. While working for the *Times* he had a small part of his wages paid into a provident fund. Now he has that money and if he lives carefully and simply, if he keeps off the drink, he estimates he could live off it for a year. Longer if he could exchange his flatmate.

Sometimes he thinks, not altogether fancifully, that Daphne is the cause of his unbidden rememberings. Calling up his past for some malicious witchy purpose. He can think of no similarities between them, yet Daphne reminds Keith of his mother. He recognises in himself the same dual emotions of wanting to be approved of and wanting to strangle to death.

If it was possible he'd like to talk to Daphne about his mother. Daphne with her posters and petitions and statistics and statements is an expert on women whereas Keith in his thirty-four years has only known two women more than casually – his mother and his ex-wife, Ginny. And Ginny was never ambiguous; Ginny, wherever she may be, can look after herself and might even be a match for Daphne. But his mother . . .

Not dotty old Mrs Lawrie lying unvisited in the hospice, but dancing Eve Lawrie who married a Wairarapa farmer . . . if Keith dared risk the asking and Daphne deigned to answer she could tell him . . . Tell him whatever it is that a daughter would've known without ever having needed to ask.

In his head he has a whole conversation which will never be said because talking with Daphne is like trying to shake hands with a hedgehog. My mother (Keith would say) was a dancer. Not a ballet dancer but a kind of free-form dancer in the style of Isadora Whatsername. She travelled widely. She was born in France and later lived in England, then as a dancer she travelled throughout Europe, America, the Pacific. And in New Zealand she met my father and for some reason married him. She would've been in her late twenties. Perhaps she wanted security, perhaps she was afraid of being an old maid. Perhaps she even loved him or thought she did. She might've thought he was some kind of gentleman farmer, a bit of an aristocrat – the accent might've fooled her.

She was talented, beautiful, sensitive. Refined, I guess. And there she was stuck away in a farming community where a worthwhile woman is one who can grow healthy silverbeet. My father had no interests outside the farm – he'd played rugby of course when he was younger. She was completely out of her element and never did adjust.

Perhaps if she'd had a daughter . . . Anyway she didn't. And then my brother died in an accident and she felt my father was to blame – which in a way I guess he was – and she just . . . gave up. She became a kind of invalid, not entirely rational. Premature senility, they said.

My father just didn't want to know about it so I looked after her and I looked after the house. All my teenage years I'd get breakfast and see to her in the morning and I'd go on the bus to school and when I came home I'd get dinner and do the washing, all that. Feed her, feed him—they'd never eat together . . .

Keith wants to give Daphne his childhood so she can shake out the ambiguities, slice off the loose threads and return it to him cleancut, chronological and definitive. He'd be happy to accept Eve Muir as a victim, oppressed by male-oriented society, denied fulfilment, misunderstood, driven to despair, deprived of the friendship of her own kind (the interpretation he'd expect from Daphne—and not much different from Eve Muir's own version) if only it would stay the final, unquestionable version.

What Keith wants from Daphne—what Daphne has that Keith most fears and most desires—is certainty.

May

'HE STOOD AT the back of the hall and yelled pooh, bum and willies. They had to actually drag him out.'

'You're making this up.'

'I wish I was.'

'Willies?'

'Well it might've been wees, something like that. I was trying not to hear. I was standing there with my speech notes in a scrunched up ball . . .' Juliet gives up, for Josie has become all trembling flesh and dancing yellow hair.

'I'm sorry,' she says, pulling herself together. 'It must've been awful. You poor thing.' She splutters and turns away. 'I'm sorry Jule, but it is . . .'

Juliet waits with a patient smile for Josie to settle down. 'It isn't at all funny when you've had to listen to him try and glorify it as a moment of cute self-expression. It's pathetic . . . even a little creepy.'

'Did they know who he was?'

'The ones who didn't would've soon enough been told. Thank heavens a few of them also knew that we were living apart. At least they'd appreciate why.'

'You mean that was typical?'

'It was a bit over the top even for him. And it wasn't so funny, it was deliberate and malicious. He was trying to sabotage my chances of selection. Well, he succeeded.'

'You think it was . . .'

'He threw me off completely, I made a mess of it.'

'Well, I have to be honest, I don't trust that outfit at all. If you want to get into politics why pick on them.'

'It's not like that, the media distorts . . . and you know our defence policy—nuclear free, non-aligned.'

'I still don't trust them.'

Juliet's offended. 'But let's face it, Jose, you don't trust anything. You're the typical voter; the minute someone stands out, prepared to be positive, decisive, you get suspicious. No wonder the country's in a mess.'

Josie counts silently to five for friendship's sake. 'I used to be your friend,' she laments lightly. 'Now I'm your typical voter.'

'Oh love, of course you're my friend, first and last. Things go wrong, who do I run to? That's got to mean you're my best friend.'

Juliet is their first visitor from the world beyond. She arrived unheralded, having got a taxi from the Motuwairua airstrip. Naturally she wouldn't risk the ferry trip.

'Of course you can stay,' said Josie. 'Just as long as you want. It's lovely to have you.' Meaning it.

Juliet only plans to stay until Paul gets the message and stops pestering. Until he accepts that their marriage is really over. Josie doesn't ask how Juliet expects to know if Paul has stopped pestering her if she's not there to be pestered. Josie assumes, from her wealth of experience, that Juliet isn't yet altogether sure that she wants Paul to stop pestering her. It seems a bit soon for that stage. When Josie and Juliet last saw each other Juliet had still seemed fairly resigned to her marriage.

'Maybe,' says Josie by way of comfort, 'he's having his mid-life crisis and when he comes out of it you'll like him again.'

Juliet looks startled. 'You don't understand. I haven't liked him for years, I begin to wonder if I ever really did. I know he could be quite charming when we had company but when we were alone he was pretty boorish. Now he's gone public, that's all. He can't cope with my having done so well academically, so for him the political thing was the last straw. He's terrified that I might become a public figure while he's still a nonentity. His very words.

'The last three weeks – since he finally agreed to leave – would've been bliss if he hadn't kept making a pest of himself. It's brilliant not having him round. I love it. But he keeps doing these things – phone calls late at night and I know it must be him, and he comes round some nights and throws shoes at the front door. They're still lying there in the morning.'

'His shoes?'

'Women's shoes.'

'How d'you know it's him?'

'No one else in the street gets shoes thrown at their door.'

'They're not your shoes?'

'Course they're not mine. Last week I'd had enough, I took them round to his flat. He wasn't home which was probably a good thing but I could see in the window that he hadn't even properly unpacked. After two weeks.'

'Whose shoes are they?'

'How would I know? I think I'm supposed to believe they've been left behind by a multitude of womenfriends. Maybe he goes through rubbish bags or buys them at opp shops.' Juliet begins to giggle.

'What sort of shoes?'

Juliet grasps her belly with one hand and reaches for Josie with the other. 'What sort of shoes? What d'you mean, what sort of shoes? Old tacky sorts of shoes, ghastly shoes with great fat heels, and wedgies, and some unmentionable things with gold sparkle . . .' Juliet slapping at Josie and rolling about, forcing out the words with the effort of a drunk. '. . . shoes . . . you keep asking 'bout the bloody shoes . . . whose? . . . what sort of? . . . shoes, is it some kinda fetish with you?'

Josie goes with her. 'Oh Christ . . . shit . . . shoes . . .' Yet above their shrieks and gaspings she hears him at the door kicking off his gumboots. And she manages to turn and see him standing just inside the doorway watching them. Wearing the look she knows from Daryl and Sarah – the doorway look they wore when they caught her with Geoff's hand down her dress.

'Geoff,' says Juliet trying to rise from the sofa, staggering weakly.

'Juliet,' he says from the door. It sounds like mockery but his mouth smiles.

Josie worries that Juliet may see beneath the smile. Thinking, oh god, here we go again with me in the middle; just when I was getting around to having a few needs of my own.

Juliet has three weeks' holiday before tutorials resume. She has no need to return to the city before then. Josie picks this information up in the course of their unending conversation and so is able to pass it on to Geoff when he asks on the third night. And again on almost every night thereafter.

For the first few days they all expect Paul to arrive. The expectation begins from the time each ferry is due and fades after forty minutes.

'You know Paul,' says Juliet, 'he'd rather swim over than pay the air fare. We don't have to worry about the planes.'

'D'you think,' sniffs Josie, 'he'll bring his shoes.'

When they laugh like that in Geoff's presence he stiffens self-consciously and his mouth tightens.

'He's all right, Paul,' says Geoff, in bed, for where else do they get to talk these days. 'I always liked Paul.'

'You used to say he was a bit of a spoon.'

'Did I? Well you know me, I say anything that comes into my head. There's no reason to go remembering things I say.'

'I liked Paul too,' she says.

'It doesn't show.'

'Special circumstances.'

'He must be a bit of a spoon. When you leave me I shall go right after you and toss you across my shoulders and carry you home.'

'Would you?' Josie is ridiculously pleased.

'Or die,' he says with a grin, 'in the attempt.'

Which she ignores. 'Anyway it wasn't like that. She didn't run off. They agreed to separate.'

'I don't see why she should come here, involving us.'

'We're not involved.'

'You certainly are. You're on her side. You're as bad as one another the way you go on.'

'Well you're taking his side obviously.'

'What d'you expect?'

She slides an arm in under his shoulder. 'My love, it's not contagious. I'm not hatching plans to leave you.' She pauses. 'Not at the moment.'

'She'd like you to. Your women friends are all the same. They want to be in fashion, so when they screw up their own marriage they want all their friends to do the same. So if everyone's doing it it must be right.'

'I was the first,' she reminds him. 'I've, as you put it, screwed up two marriages. That must make me a veritable trendsetter.'

He shakes his head sadly. 'Don't try and pretend that her staying here is no kind of threat to me. Don't tell me that because it's shit. Like saying before that you liked Paul. I've heard the two of you cracking up about the guy, rubbishing him. There's a part of you that you save for your friends and you don't dare let me see it. When you're with her you look at me with picky eyes as if I'm the enemy.'

'Piggy eyes? Thank you. Thanks very much.'

'Picky. Pick-key. Picky eyes that crit-i-cise.'

She can think of nothing to say. It's true, that's all; she can't deny it, she can't explain it away. She tightens her arms around him and feels him resist. He wants words and she hasn't the right words to give him. She moves fractionally away.

'Hell,' she says lightly, 'why can't you just be the unobservant emotionally repressed clot you're supposed to be?'

She has to wait a long time before she feels his body give in.

Five days go by and Paul has not arrived. A man comes to reconnect the phone and give them a number. 'On the mainland,' he tells them, 'you'd've been waiting at least six months.' He has morning coffee and walnut loaf with Josie and Juliet. And when he goes they say things behind his back.

'I hope they don't give the number out to Paul,' says Juliet.

Geoff goes out every day. He marks out fence lines and does a few things on the henhouse which is almost ready for occupation. More often he takes the Land-Rover and goes off to do business. He has to see a man about the bore and to dismantle a shed he bought at auction for the demolition timber. He has to talk to the locals and get to know what crops or stock are raised successfully on the island and what has been tried and failed, and why. He brings home a bottle of wine or a few bottles of beer after thirsty afternoons devoted to research.

Sometimes he brings home a local or two as well. He brings home old Bill who has lived on Motuwairua all his life and travelled eleven times to the mainland. He brings home Leif and Helen and Peter who live on the way to Parenga and lease five hectares on which they'll be growing garlic because it's hard to go wrong with garlic, or so they've been told. And he brings home Harley who says he's eighteen but looks no more than fifteen and says with a nervous shift of the eyes that he's living in the bush out towards Kamakama. And he brings home Ben who isn't much older, and needs a good wash but asks only for a bed for the night because the road to the house he lives in is flooded.

Josie doesn't get to know much about any of them because Juliet is there wearing her worries closed-in yet dramatic like an astronaut's headwear. The last thing Juliet needs right now is chat about road repairs and export-oriented garlic. Juliet needs to sift and probe through the debris of her marriage until she has exorcised Paul in particular and men in general. To do that she needs a helpmate so the two of them can sniff, sample, jeer and discard together like a couple of cats in a rubbish bin.

Josie understands all this and doesn't mind helping her friend. In a way it's a kind of insurance; Josie will feel more entitled to run to Juliet for a return of the favour when that times comes. Josie and Juliet go back further than Josie and Geoff but not as far back as Josie and Edie. Josie has remembered, though she suspects Juliet hasn't, that when

Josie and Dick split up Juliet was no help at all. In fact she'd even talked of obligations and the little things a woman can do to keep a marriage alive. Josie remembers but bears no grudge. In those days Juliet simply didn't know any better.

If Juliet wasn't with them Josie would, when she had no work of her own, help Geoff mark out the fences or work on the henhouse or go with him to Tautoro to knock down the shed. But Geoff—on Paul's behalf and perhaps in his own defence—is acting as if Juliet is only visible in certain lights. Geoff wouldn't want her tagging along and Josie wouldn't think of leaving her behind. So they stay at home. But even a life-long friendship couldn't quite buy Josie's unoccupied attention. So they plant shrubs and make the beginnings of a garden around the house. Josie digs and Juliet leans on the rake and talks about her future.

And they make laying-boxes in the henhouse and fill them with hay shaken from the bale Geoff got from old Bill in exchange for the loan of Geoff's chainsaw. Josie hammers the boards together while Juliet looks out through the wire mesh at the far shadow of an island and says . . . 'even if he was prepared to be a peninsula . . .' Then as she helps Josie spread the hay into the boxes she says, 'You've got your own work. I'd've thought Geoff would do all this kind of stuff.'

'Men's work?' rebukes Josie archly. But after that she sticks to jobs in or around the house. She'd rather not have Juliet noticing how little evidence there is of farming in progress. What she doesn't want, not just now, is Juliet's pity.

Josie sets up old tables they bought from the second hand shop in Parenga in their third bedroom which is also her office and which she plans to use as a greenhouse as well. She spreads potting mix into seed trays. Juliet sits slumped in a corner with her knees high and wide, sitting the way Sarah used to sit. Seeing that, Josie feels dismal. Not just because she sometimes misses Sarah rather badly but because, no matter how girlishly they may sit, Juliet and Josie have reached their middle years and still haven't got life sorted out. She sighs.

Juliet looks up in question.

Josie grimaces. 'Just . . . feeling my age.'

'You filthy old thing. What does it feel like?'

'Ah . . . bland, flabby, a bit confused. I can't recommend it.'

'I wish you hadn't said that, I really do. I was sitting here feeling young. I was thinking about . . . it's funny you know, when we were young, our generation . . . well our mothers . . . we were conditioned into believing that it was a woman's duty, her purpose in life, to bolster up men's egos. Everything we did, even down to blinking, was designed to make men feel okay. Then along came feminism and we began to see that it was pretty degrading and we weren't obliged to behave like concubines. So we stopped all that. We stepped out from under, and what happened – the buggers collapsed all over the place. So in a way our mothers were right all along.'

Josie brushes the damp black soil from her hands. 'I must say it gives me satisfaction to see women walk out on their men. In a secret sort of way I'm not all that proud of. When I think of how it was in the sixties, husbands fleeing the suburbs in droves, their women left behind knee deep in nappies – don't know about you but I couldn't *afford* disposables. And now, that same generation of women – the ones who didn't quite get left to it – are saying sorry chum but the kids are grown up and you're neither use nor ornament, I'd rather be on my own. There's a kind of belated justice there.'

Juliet raises her arms then brings them down stiffly in front of her, palms pressed together. She breathes deeply. Josie finds these impromptu bouts of yoga stretching and hyperventilating mildly annoying. Too intimate to be performed in company. 'Right,' says Juliet after a long breath, 'I can think just off the top of my head of four . . . no five – at least five – women I know *personally*, all around our age, who've chucked it in the last couple of years.' She sags very slightly. 'Of course Paul claims I'm being influenced. He sees independent women as being some kind of Moonie set-up marching around the streets drumming up converts.'

Josie sees how, in offering up Paul's opinion, Juliet loses her edge of certainty; even now.

'Geoff too,' she reassures. 'He thinks there's a contagious disease called husband desertion. Well they're bound to see it that way, it absolves them from all possible blame.' She wants to believe it's that straightforward – silly masculine paranoia. Yet each time the marriage of one of her friends falls apart the margin of hope does seem to become narrower.

'Where are all the strong-minded men?' asks Juliet wistfully. 'All the women I know – all the women I like – marry Mister Weaks.'

Josie grins uncertainly. 'Is this where I should start defending Geoff?'

'You're not married to him so it doesn't really count.'

'Very tactful.' She ponders it, not prepared to deny on his behalf. 'Maybe that's the kind of man we prefer?'

Juliet knows better. 'They pretend to be what they're not. We don't learn the truth until it's too late.'

'Oh come on . . . I can think of some admirable men whose wives I've known and really liked. One or two.'

'Ah, they might have seemed admirable to you but I bet their wives know better.'

Josie laughs but she's beginning to feel uneasy. These conversations may reinforce Juliet but they erode Josie-and-Geoff. She says, cursed with the need to be fair, 'Maybe it's sex. No, what I mean is maybe once you've been to bed with a man and watched him come – all whimpering and defenceless . . . well, maybe that moment destroys a woman's confidence in his ability *ever* to be entirely in control of things.'

Juliet screws up her mouth. 'The only thing sex with Paul destroyed was my confidence in him as a sexual partner.'

'Oh,' says Josie. Her heart bounds in relief; different symptoms.

At night Josie prods at Geoff's implacable back. 'Stop scowling and turn over.'

'I'm not scowling.'

'Your back is.'

He doesn't move.

Tonight she feels lucky to have him, lucky enough to risk rebuff. She puts her arm around him and fiercely holds him. 'You're lovely,' she says against his back. 'It's an honour and a pleasure to share your bed.'

His chest heaves in a vast silent sigh. 'She could ring the bloody neighbours,' he says. 'If she wants to be sure. *Of course* he's not still hanging round. Probably never was.'

'She hasn't been here *that* long.' She keeps her arm around him anyway.

'I bet Paul thought good riddance.'

'You used to think she was sexy.'

'Well she's all right looking. Still got a good body.'

Josie's not sure if that was intended to hurt. She doesn't want to be oversensitive.

'Why?' he asks into the dark on his side of the bed. 'You think I should . . .'

'She's my friend,' says Josie primly. 'She'd send you packing.' Then again, maybe she wouldn't.

'Incidentally,' he says disengaging her arm and turning to lie on his back, 'we've been invited to a party next Saturday.'

'Where?'

'Peter and that lot. At their place.'

'The garlic ones?'

'Yeah.' The way he says it she knows there's more to come. 'Those three, they've got a thing going. A threesome.'

'How do you know?'

'He told me, Peter. They're into sharing . . . open relationships . . . all those wonderful things that went out of fashion before they filtered through to far-flung corners like mine.'

'Poor Geoff.' She sighs for him. 'So; a bunch of sweet old-fashioned hippies.'

'We'll go eh?'

'Okay.' She turns onto her back. His hand explores, like a solitary tramper, the hills and gullies.

'What will you wear?' His voice has gone rough at the edges.

So, she discovers, has hers. 'What d'you want me to wear?'

'Suspenders,' he says dreamily, 'net stockings, and that dress . . .you know the one.'

'I'd freeze.'

'So freeze; it's a good cause. And what would you do? Show me . . .'

After Dick, left with three children, Josie had worked for four impoverished years with a young and pretentious theatre company. She painted and moved scenery, took tickets, directed three dubious plays and acted in more. Had Geoff been her audience then she could have gone on to greatness. Geoff is the audience actors dream about, eager, attentive, roaring for encores.

'Go on,' he says hoarse with urgency. 'What then? What else would you do?'

But she's left him behind. She's beyond invention, beyond coherence. She hears herself cry out and wonders if two walls is enough to protect Juliet from such tactlessness. And she keeps her eyes open in case in the dark she is able to find some meaning in the moment when his eyes are white-ringed and his mouth gapes and trembles. Wanting to distil one pure emotion from within her peeping-tom heart; finding nothing that might account for loss of confidence despite her theory.

'What are you thinking?' He strokes her hair.

'This party. I'll bet they have chewy bean salads and wholemeal spaghetti.'

It's Friday and Juliet is going home to student essays that should've been marked, yoga classes, and possibly a pile of footwear. Josie had passed on Geoff's suggestion about ringing a neighbour but Juliet wasn't much taken with it. 'Would you ring a neighbour you barely know and ask if you husband's still throwing shoes at your door?'

Josie drives Juliet to the airstrip. Geoff and Hogg quietly disappeared early in the day and are probably hiding out until the Land-Rover returns; avoiding the insincerity of farewells. They're too early for the plane. Josie lives in fear of things that may leave without her and so allows time for flat tyres to be changed or old ladies to be helped into ambulances. Lacking mishaps they sit in the vehicle beside the deserted airstrip and wait.

Juliet talks about her future. 'He'll probably insist we sell the house, and I know it's a good house in the right kind of area but half the proceeds ... how far is that going to get me? At our age security's important; I really need security. Yet here I am with a not-quite doctorate and no prospects of a job at the end of it.'

'At least,' says Josie, trying to comfort by comparison, 'you'll have the evidence you're qualified in a rather exclusive field. I don't think I'd have a show in hell now of getting back into a decent job. In my field once you've been out of it for a few years all the young trendies've entrenched themselves and you don't get a look in.'

'But you've got half a farm. You'll never have to worry.'

Josie could so easily let it go, nod I-guess-you're-right. But her fingers tap sharply against the steering wheel and Juliet looks at her oddly, so she admits, too loud and hurried: 'But I don't. It's all Geoff's.' She fumbles in the dashboard for cigarettes.

'Well,' says Juliet, 'I'm sure legally it amounts to the same thing. De facto is the same as marriage after a year or so isn't it?'

'I don't know,' says Josie truthfully. 'I suppose I could find out easily enough. I suppose I should.' She imagines Geoff forced to sell up again, dividing, reduced to a quarter-acre section.

'But you must have some arrangement after all these years?'

'Not exactly. I've got the rent from my own house and I earn a little, a pittance actually, from my work. I contribute what I can and he provides the rest.'

'Don't you hate that after years of financial independence?'

'Yes. In lots of ways I do.'

'But you work on that place. Housework, other work . . . he should pay you a wage if he's not prepared to sign half the property over. Josie my dear he's taking advantage of you.'

'It's not like that,' says Josie winding down the top of the window to let her smoke drift out because Juliet is watching it and leaning aside. 'He intended to put the place into joint ownership only I wouldn't let him.'

'You fool.'

'It seemed . . . I dunno . . . a commitment. Something I couldn't walk away from.'

'Then he should pay you a salary. You'd agree to that?'

'I suppose . . . mm. But I can't ask him, Jule. He's generous with what he's got.'

'So he's generous. Then he'll agree.'

'I guess he would. But I can't ask because if it was the other way round he'd never ask it of me. He'd see it as . . . well as a lack of trust. He'd find it hurtful. Maybe unforgivably hurtful.'

Juliet's eyes are wrinkled up, gentle and full of concern. 'Josie, I can't believe . . . you, of all people, should know better. You're too old to be taken for a ride. When it's over what will you have to show for all your efforts?'

Josie leans back against the seat and closes her eyes. When she opens them the wind is still blowing the grass over and the red and yellow windsock still waves in a jerky idiot motion. 'He trusts me,' she says. There's a hint of wonder in her voice. 'He trusts me implicitly.'

'That's nice,' says Juliet. 'But do you trust him?'

Josie watches the windsock swipe at nothing. 'I must,' she says after a few seconds. 'Mustn't I?'

Juliet watches her steadily then gives a loving, enduring smile.

I do, thinks Josie. I do trust him. Of course I do. Except not really . . . not absolutely. I don't trust anyone absolutely. Not Geoff. Not Juliet. Perhaps not even myself. Apart from my children of course; I trust my kids. But that's something else—a different kind of trusting.

The kind Geoff has in me?

*   *   *

The week before school holidays began Giggles went missing. There was a hole in the bit of old net curtain they'd used for the top of his cage. 'We should've kept him in the birdcage,' said Alan accusingly.

'They need to eat grass. Anyway it wasn't big enough.' But she could've bought chicken mesh and made a proper cage.

'They can just live in the ground and around,' said Carly. 'The Wilsons had one that did.'

'There you are,' said Maureen. 'He's just gone for a walk. Have a look round, but he'll probably come back when he's ready.' The hole in the net curtain looked the right size to have been made by a dog.

'Why,' said Alan looking upwards, asking the universe, 'do all the rotten things have to happen to us?'

'You didn't seem all that interested in him when he was around. Only Mickey did.' But she knows that's unfair, it's only human to undervalue what's always there. And as a pet Giggle's charms were limited. He was short-haired and splodgy. He didn't nudge or nestle or companionably nibble. He existed. He produced copious turds and an occasional mournful whistle.

He was too rodent-like for Maureen to handle without suppressing a shudder. But he was given to the children by their cousin Simon who had an extended family of guineapigs and how could Maureen refuse. Simon had picked rattish Giggles from among all the sweet hairy ones and Maureen reminded herself that looks are only skin deep and don't count, even with guineapigs. As a pet he was better than no pet. He cost nothing and expected nothing.

About a year before Mickey was born a stray kitten had arrived and they kept her though Bruce kept saying, that thing's not staying, get rid of it or I will. They called her Lacey and she learned it was advisable to keep out of Bruce's way but she never quite learned not to jump on the bench and the table. The night Bruce killed Lacey Maureen heard, from the kitchen, some crashing and cursing. It woke her up enough to ask Bruce as he got into bed, what was that? Bloody cat, he'd said, into the butter you left on the table.

When Maureen got up a couple of hours later Lacey was in the corner by the door. Her legs were moving slowly walking on the air, her head was split and one eye hung out of its socket. Maureen just had time to take the cat outside and hit her head repeatedly with the spade, then bury her in the garden and wipe the blood off the kitchen door and the lino beneath before Alan woke and came looking for his breakfast. She cried all the while; killing the cat, burying her, cleaning away the evidence. But not really crying for Lacey, poor Lacey. Crying first because he had left her there not even caring if his kids had got up and found her like that. Crying second for herself who was married to him.

She told them Lacey must've wandered off and would surely have found a new home among people who loved her just as much. For months Carly peered through gates and trampled over gardens calling, Lacey. She put a saucer of milk outside the back door and filled it each night with fresh milk. If Bruce noticed the saucer he never mentioned it. Maureen didn't talk to him about the cat, there seemed no point.

When Giggles turns up it's Maureen who finds him. Who sees something round and quick scutter in the long grass near the clothesline post and is grateful for the socks pulled over the bottom of her jeans leaving no spaces. For they hear rats every night. Driven indoors by the colder weather they've turned the ceiling of Maureen's house into a fun parlour. At night there they fight and race and slide and play bowls. They scatter dust and rat droppings and dead insects down through the holes and gaps in the ceiling. They sound large and furry.

But this rat she sights in the grass is tan and grey and white and only Giggles. He lets her catch him. He seems glad to be caught. He's thin and muddy and one leg drags awkwardly to the side.

They fight over who gets to clean him, nurse him, feed him. 'He's crying,' says Carly. 'The poor hurt darling.'

'I think he's gonna die,' says Alan.

'Of course he won't,' Maureen automatically says, 'as long as we take good care of him.'

'Can he stay in our room?'

'No, mine.'

'I asked first.'

'He did,' says Maureen quickly. 'All right he can stay in your room just till he's better and we fix up a proper cage.'

Mickey asks, 'Why Gigs run away?'

'We don't know, love.'

'Was the rats gonna get him?' Mickey's big grey eyes seeking her for reassurance. Does he wake at night, this one, and lie waiting for the rats? She must get rid of them, but how? Place set traps up through the manhole and dispose daily of furry corpses? Touch them. Stretch her arm into that dark and inhabited space . . .

Poison? Which gives the rats an unendurable thirst and drives them out, dying, in search of water (so she's been told by the old man who advised her on tank-tapping). But which might just drive them down into the house, and she can't lay poison below the ceiling because Mickey might get into it.

'I think,' says Alan, 'he was just lonely. Poor Giggles doesn't have a friend.' Neither does poor Alan.

On their very bad days when he's forced her beyond threats into slaps and spiked words he'll wail at her, as if it's a reason; I don't have a friend. Leaving her disarmed, trying to comfort, saying, 'You'll just have to be patient.' Or, 'Maybe you try too hard to make friends. Maybe you should . . . well, pretend you like doing things on your own.'

On the worst days she says, 'I'm not bloody surprised, if you treat other kids the way you treat your family who'd want to be your friend?'

But if she could buy him a friend she'd put it at the top of her list. Even before the washing machine.

Carly has a friend called Lilly and a friend called Mahia though Maureen hasn't met them. Mickey has Giggles and is too young to notice his deficiencies as a friend. Even Maureen has a friend, at last. Her name is Shisha and they met the first time Maureen took Mickey to play centre. The other mothers—there was even a father there—were pleasant enough but Shisha was absolutely friendly; she came up straight away and introduced herself.

Shisha is her Christian name and her surname. She changed it by deedpoll from Raewyn Smith. Her daughter is called Leah and is six months older than Mickey. Shisha's another solo mother. She lives right down the end of the island near Kamakama which is as far as the road goes. Maureen has only been along that road as far as Tautoro where the barge wharf is. Shisha and Leah share a big house with some other people. You have to drive up a private road out of Kamakama and in winter, Shisha says, it sometimes gets too boggy for vehicles so they have to stay at home or walk the eight kilometres to Kamakama. That day they met at play centre was the first time Shisha'd been able to drive out for nearly a week.

Shisha drives an old van with hand-painted daisies and a rainbow chipping off the sides. She wears berets or old felt hats and slippery old fashioned dresses with droopy seams. She gets them from one particular opportunity shop in the city. She's offered to take Maureen there sometime, but Maureen tried on the dress Shisha was wearing one afternoon after play centre and it made her look like a librarian.

'The minute I saw you,' said Shisha that first day, 'I knew you were solo. So you can bet the others did too. It's not as though some of them aren't but they have their own little class system here. Those whose families come from the island think they're better than all the rest, and those who've got husbands think they're better than the ones who haven't. I can't be bothered with any of them. In fact I was on the point of chucking it in except you turned up.'

Shisha drove Maureen and Mickey home because it was only a little out of her way, and stayed for a cup of coffee. And, after that first time, she'd pick them up for play centre on Tuesdays and Thursdays and take them home afterwards. She always stayed for coffee and a couple of times she and Leah had stayed on until after dinner.

Maureen had begun to hope that Shisha might invite them all over to her place some time in the holidays but Shisha decided to take the van over to the mainland and go to the Coromandel with some of the people who lived with her. Her being away makes the two weeks of holiday seem that much longer. What if it rains most of the time? Failing a trip to Shisha's place Maureen has decided on picnics and bush explorations and a walk across to Hoki Bay where they can cook sausages on the public barbecue.

She'd invited Alice and all for a few days but they were going down south to see her parents. Flying there and back which must cost hundreds. 'Say hello from me,' said Maureen, 'if you like.' Not, give them my love. She hasn't seen her parents since she got married. They'd disliked Bruce, he'd disliked them.

Maureen's wedding day might have been the only day in her life she and her mother had told each other the truth. 'How can you stand there,' said Maureen, emboldened by fear, feeling trapped and ugly in a dress she'd been talked into, 'and tell me about men! Look at the life you've had . . . how he treats you . . . how mean he always was to Alice! You've never even had a life, he drank your life away.'

And her mother, looking hard yet sad in a bright red lipstick someone must've talked her into, puffed up in umbrage. 'You must be mad. That's your own father you're talking about. I never want to hear you talk like that again.'

Her mother had been right about Bruce. Maureen could end her side of the silence. Could write even if she can't afford to visit. 'But I couldn't,' she's told Alice, 'put up with all that awful pretence about *him*.'

'He's really not so bad,' said Alice. 'You just have to make allowances. He tries to be nice when he's sober.' Yet it was Alice he used to chivvy and taunt. Maureen, two years younger, would watch and hear and find small devious ways to flatter, pretend, deflect. It was Alice who used to drop tears into the dishwater while Maureen twisted the teatowel and whispered, don't cry – he wants to make you cry.

Has Alice forgotten? Is she down there right now, washing the dishes dry-eyed and making allowances? And is that, in the end, the best way for things to be? Alan, at sixty-nine, recalling his gloriously happy childhood . . .

In the meantime they walk the tree-tunnel road to Toki Bay with their faces turned up watching the patterns of daylight through the leaves. 'I wish we could go to Auckland,' says Alan. 'Nearly all the kids in my class are gonna go and see *Indiana Jones*.'

Maureen says nothing.

The rain holds off and when they reach Toki Bay she buys them each an ice-cream, then they gather driftwood though there isn't much of it around, and she lights a fire. There are a few other people on the beach.

Mickey makes friends with a child and a dog. Carly complains that her head aches. Lately she's complained of headaches quite a lot. Maureen tries to remember to cuddle her more in case that's all it is. The sausages take a long time to cook and the sand blows in their eyes.

But by the time they get home it feels like they've had a good day.

On the first really sunny morning they catch the bus to Huri Bay and walk into the bush where the sign says *scenic reserve*. When they've walked around the easy track – because Mickey's so slow – Maureen suggests the kids should collect up (quickly while no one's around to complain) pieces of moss and baby ferns and tiny seedlings and make, on the ground in a clearing, miniature gardens.

For fifteen minutes she gets to lie almost undisturbed on the grass and watch the clouds.

But they want to make it a competition; they clamour at her to be the judge. She doesn't want to. She walks around the creations and says they're all remarkable and artistic in their own individual ways and it simply isn't possible to compare them.

They insist. Carly, with reprehensible confidence, makes conditions: No saying they're all first-equal. None of that. We want a winner and a second and a last. Even Mickey in his agreeable stupidity demanding a 'tition'. So Maureen crouches over the exhibits and tries for a way out. She should say, just to serve them right, Mickey's. Which consists of a dollop of leaf mould, one askew fern and a few sentinel twigs. In all conscience she can't deem it best. So why not tell the truth?

'This one,' she says standing above it, 'is the winner.' Pretending she doesn't know whose.

Carly leers and preens. Alan gives a small aghast cry and blunders off into the bush. No one asks Maureen who came second.

Another day she takes them, never learning, to the creek. They go armed with plastic bowls, a bit of net curtain and a sieve. In the creek that ran behind town young Maureen and Alice used to catch cockabullies and fresh-water crayfish, then tip them back and watch them swim away. (Does Alice forget those things too?)

In the Kaimoana creek there is weed like slimy green cottonwool and even though they move the bigger stones there are no crayfish hiding away, and the one small fish that might've been a cockabully went so fast it was hard to say for sure. Alan loses the sieve, Carly gets a headache and Mickey slips into the water. Alan runs all the way home in mortification and Maureen has to carry Mickey who is dripping wet and making a small shivery humming noise of distress.

A happier day is spent at Parenga where they look at the shops and eat potato chips and an ice-block each. Maureen buys a metre of chicken netting for Giggles' cage though it's probably too late. Giggles reclines all day in a box in the boys' room and picks listlessly at chosen morsels while Maureen tries to pretend he's getting better. The Motuwairua vet has his surgery at his house in Whiripare. He's expensive (Maureen rang to see) and Whiripare is quite a distance from Kaimoana. She described Giggles' condition to the vet's wife who said it sounded like internal injuries.

If it wasn't for Carly's headaches Maureen might've been prepared to plunder the handyman fund so Giggles could be cured. But to pay the doctor and the vet could mean the tankstand would collapse before it gets attention. Then she'd need a new tank as well.

Maureen finds it hard to believe she is prepared to let the guineapig die. She feels angry about all the decisions life keeps asking of her.

Anger is something Shisha has lent her; anger to whet the sharp edges of self-pity. Not that Shisha would seem to have any great need of it herself – it seems to Maureen her new friend has things pretty much the way that suits her.

Shisha has given her the old magazines left lying round by the assorted residents of her communal house. The kind of stuff Maureen's seen on bookstands for years but couldn't afford even if she'd wanted. *Mushroom, New Outlook, Broadsheet*. It's the last she reads with a growing fascination. (Do more harm than good, says Alice, who meets quite a few of those kind of women on the staff of Matthew's school.)

The more she reads the magazine articles the more Maureen feels she's been peering at her life through a telescope she didn't know how to adjust. Now someone's turning the screw and it's all coming into focus; *of course*, she keeps thinking, of course! On a good day she can see herself having a future.

The doctor examines Carly and makes ponderously jovial conversation. Carly catches her mother's eye and gives the twitchy grin she gets when Alan's throwing one of his scenes. Maureen twitches back when the doctor's head is tuned to Carly's chest. The doctor sends Carly back to sit with the boys in the waiting room and concentrates on Maureen.

'Whereabouts does she come in the family?'

'Second. She's in the middle.'

'And she's a happy child? No problems?'

'No. No problems. Not really.'

'I can't find anything physically . . . It may well be her way of coping with something . . . some disharmony within the family. I don't want to pry, but if there was, say, parental discord . . .'

'I'm separated,' says Maureen. 'I had thought at first it was just . . . but now I'm sure they're real headaches.'

'Quite possibly. Very real. But let's try more cuddles, maybe a bit of special attention. And then, if they still continue, come back and see me and we'll see about a specialist.'

As they walk out into the street Carly says, 'What's wrong with me Mum? Did he tell you?'

'He doesn't know,' Maureen says. Nine dollars for nothing.

She buys two bags full of groceries because the specials are better in Parenga. There are balloons and liquorice allsorts among the groceries because next week is Alan's birthday. She thinks he won't miss paper hats, and there must be still enough candles left in the packet. She buys another tube of handyman's goo to patch up the bits of roof she and Alan missed in their last effort.

She looks, surreptitiously, at the watch in the glassed-off counter of the hardware shop, and she walks twice past the second hand shop window pretending not to be looking at anything in particular.

She borrows a pen from the woman at the hardware shop and writes out on a piece of cardboard the woman handed to her: HANDY-PERSON WANTED FOR TANKSTAND REPAIRS ETC. APPLY MAUREEN, 17 CASHIN RD, KAIMOANA.

Alan wants potato chips. Alan wants a comic book. Carly forces Mickey's fist open and finds a boiled lolly stuck with gritty bits; she throws it away. Mickey cries real tears. 'He's tired,' says Maureen. She pins her card among all the others on the Parenga noticeboard.

Carly wishes out loud that she had a pencil case with a zip that wasn't broken. Mickey stands looking down at the footpath and quietly pees his pants. Maureen still can't decide between the watch which would be sensible and the beaten-up old bike in the second hand shop. The bike costs more.

She asks Alan. Surprise isn't that important. He wants the bike. It's $20 more than the watch and it's rougher than it looked through the window.

Alan wants to ride it home but it doesn't look entirely trustworthy. The man in the shop seems to think the same. 'I can drop it off,' he says. 'Probably tomorrow.'

All the way home in the bus Alan wears a grin that won't lie down. He lets Mickey sit on his lap despite the dampness and the smell of ammonia. His joy wipes away Maureen's worries about the bike's condition and the handyperson's wage. She grins out the window at the faint daylight reflection of a cheerful woman. Straight brown hair loosely tied back and pointed little side teeth that sometimes catch on her bottom lip. Vampire mouth, they said at primary school. So she tried to keep a long upper lip.

Alan twists in his seat towards her. His smile engulfs her in a wave of unreserved love. Maureen looks back at the trace of her reflection. Who said money can't buy happiness?

*   *   *

The U.S., according to informed estimates, has 30,000 one-megaton bombs and Russia has 20,000. There's such a redundancy of bombs that 64 could be used on a city the size of New York. A nuclear war between the superpowers could be over in half an hour.

In half an hour Keith can walk three quarters of the way to Parenga. In half an hour, while they incinerate and poison the world, he could take the disused road to Whiripare and might even see from the top of the hills the glow of Armageddon in a midday sky.

And even then he wouldn't quite believe it.

Given such an over-supply of weapons New Zealanders have no foundation for the belief that this country would survive a global war. A city the size of Auckland is a logical and attractive target.

Nobody really believes this stuff, Keith thinks. We comprehend the possibility, even the probability. But no one—not even Daphne—believes it could happen. People don't have the capacity to envisage horror of such dimension. If the enormity of the situation wasn't too overwhelmingly, inconceivably appalling to be believed whole cities would be crippled, whole nations, while their citizens rioted in outrage or lay paralysed with fear.

'If you really believed it might happen,' he told Daphne, 'you wouldn't be marching around waving banners and tying bits of wool onto barricades and singing peace and let's-hold-hands songs.'

'What would I do then—if I really believed?'

'Don't quite know. Gun down Reagan. Burn down the Russian and American Embassies. More likely nothing. More likely if anyone really believed they'd be so shit-scared they'd scrape a hole in the ground and just lie there whimpering.'

'In your case,' says Daphne, 'that would be likely. But I believe in affirmative action. I happen to be convinced that we can and will prevent it.' When she says 'we' Daphne means womenkind. Men stand for war and women stand for peace. As soon as women hold the balance of power peace will be inevitable. Unfortunately, because the arms race looks as if it may get to the finishing tape before womenkind, it's necessary for women to temporarily divert their women-promoting energies into preventing a holocaust.

Daphne makes it all seem quite straightforward. To hear Daphne put it in perspective makes it seem as though she has copyright on the end of the world. 'I can see,' says Keith, 'that pertaining to the arms race you are chief shareholder, greatest living authority and our only hope of prevention.'

He's not altogether joking—one corner of their living room is stacked with information on warheads, fallout, underground tests, the Star Wars programme, nuclear-related diseases, Greenham Common, protest strategies and Mururoa. The most interesting bits are underlined with felt tip.

People were vaporised, some turned to charcoal; others were buried under falling buildings or speared by flying glass. Within five months 140,000

*had died from burning, radiation, related diseases or injuries. The
hibakusha—those who survived—are overly prone to leukemia and other
forms of cancer; their children show a high incidence of genetic
malformation.*

The information is repeated in different ways, under different
headlines. Daphne and her friends rework it into letters and newsletters
and banners and placards. Daphne believes nuclear arms are created
by ignorance. Once people know the *truth* they will demand
disarmament. But it's hard for the truth to get through to the people
without being warped or stifled by the male-controlled media.

Which, despite Tom Brannigan, Keith still feels obliged to defend.
'Where,' he asks her, 'do you imagine that mountain of clippings came
from?'

'Look for yourself,' she says. 'Most of it's from women's presses or
little independent outfits.'

'Well,' he says, 'there's such a thing as overkill. Readers get turned
off and there comes a point when you're defeating your own ends.'

'Dear Sir,' Daphne puts on the callow youth voice she affects for
the sake of argument, 'I'm heartily sick of reading all this boring end-
of-the-world stuff. Can't we have more tits and bums like we used to?'

'Droll,' says Keith. 'But all the same I think you and your mates
should take a close look at your motives.'

Daphne doesn't bother replying to stuff like that. She just stores
them away as affirmation and gets that 'exactly' look.

Someday she'll goad him into saying, 'You realise that I've paid taxes
all my working life so that your lot can sit around being paid while
you rearrange society!' It's a bit disturbing that such a thought should
even surface. He's always thought of himself as a liberal sort of bloke.
It must be a measure of how much she gets under his skin. Or perhaps
a testimony to her strength of conviction. He thinks he can feel himself
turning into what she believes him to be.

It's true, he does feel a certain satisfaction in the fact that he is still
living off his earnings while Daphne lives at the state's expense. It seems
like a moral advantage. He can appreciate the irony of his taxes funding
this agent of global salvation and male obsolescence.

Daphne considers unemployment her right. She doesn't want a paid
job, it would take up too much of her time. She and Hennie go out
to talk to other jobless people and urge them to give their time to
political action. They hand out leaflets that list things to do, groups
to join. *TIME CAN BE POWER* the leaflets say. *Remember this is*

election year.

Right now Daphne, Hennie and a raised fistful of sisters have gone on a peace march all their own. They're walking from Taupo to Wellington because change must come from the centre and flow outward to the seat of government. They're probably flowing, about now, in the vicinity of Everton. Tall patrons like Snort will see them through the unpainted top half of the public bar windows and whoop and choke. Short-arsed patrons will peer out the door or through scratched peep-holes in the lower windows.

Three inches, maybe, in the *Times* between the Women's Division AGM and the St Mary's white elephant proceeds. Depending on what else is happening. All kinds of curiosities pass through Everton on their way to the cities. The town doesn't take much notice beyond a gawp and a snigger.

If Daphne spent a few years in Everton she'd learn not to be so sure of herself.

The radio hasn't mentioned any peace marchers though they've been out there on the road for a few days now.

A relief to have the house to himself. This time he even has a decent pry in Daphne's room. She has a three-quarter bed with old wrought iron ends. It's more comfortable than his bed, but noisy. Lying there he thinks about Daphne being lesbian and wonders who she's lain here with. Daphne in sexual congress seems improbable.

The room is piled with books, papers, magazines. The drawers are tidy with neatly folded clothes. Trousers, shorts, shirts and sweaters. He's never seen her in anything else and that appears to be all that she has. There's one small mirror with a photo of a group of women sitting on some steps. Kay is among them. And there's a photo that has to be Daphne's family. She's the hefty one, but the family resemblance is certain. Two brothers and a sister and parents who look like teachers or maybe lawyers. Taken when Daphne was about seventeen. How many years ago? Five ... maybe ten? A family of open faces and comfortable incomes. The kind of family where the parents are called Daddy and Mummy, affectionately, by adult children.

Keith thinks, she would find nothing in my room to clarify me. It seems like a small advantage.

His replacement contact lens has come in the post. He's not sure, now it's here, that he'll go back to wearing them. After a few days of seeing through just one eye he left the other lens out and settled for wholehearted furry vision. It didn't detract from the charms of

113

the sea or the bush. His near sight is good enough for reading and there's been nothing further than an arm's length away that he's needed to see definitively. He's not even sure why he ordered the new lens, except for the vague feeling he'd had that if he could see precisely his mind might be correspondingly sharper.

Still, since the lens arrived he's been thinking it would be a good idea to have a car so he could get around the island. A car would take a large chunk out of his savings but it would improve the chances of finding a job.

He's beginning to think, too, that an old TV set wouldn't go amiss on these long evenings. Daphne is opposed to TV, which is a point in favour of getting one. For driving and watching TV he'll need his lenses. And with Daphne away he has the chance of wearing them in—a little longer each day until the optic nerves get reaccustomed—without having to justify them. He knows Daphne would see some deplorable significance in his wearing of such furtive accessories. Even he finds the implications of vanity bothersome.

He wore glasses through all the years that mattered. From the age of nine, when his teacher realised he was misreading the words on the blackboard, until he was twenty-four. He got himself fitted for contact lenses when he realised Ginny didn't intend to come back from the free press junket to Los Angeles. It was a consolation present to himself for having lost a wife. It was to be the first step in a course of self-improvement. His next step was to apply for the job on the *Everton Times*.

Lately he's been thinking more often about Everton. Not missing it and yet—

In some way—in some small way—the island has let him down. Leading him on at first with such promise ... such a sense of destiny. But now?

He took up fishing from the rocks, just hook and line and watching the slow shadows in the water and the clouds shuffling over the sky. No great catches—moki, herrings and the occasional undersized snapper. When he carried them home old men stopped to talk about how many there used to be out there, before the Japanese and the joint ventures.

But when the school holidays started he didn't feel like going out anymore, sharing the rocks. He hates the way the holiday people swarm over the island with loud voices and no real respect. Just *using* it, he thinks. As if his is a more meaningful relationship.

Even residents like Daphne lack a proper appreciation. Coming and going so casually. Taking the place for granted.

Alone in the house his thoughts are angular and awkward, they protrude and disturb like underfleshed bones. With a bottle of Jim Beam the hours would slide by and he would sleep more soundly. His survival budget doesn't allow for bottles of anything, but it's foolish to be inflexible.

He should be writing. If ever Keith is going to write anything this is the time. But how can he write with a head full of bones? And what can he write when eight thousand warheads and the hibakusha are waiting to upstage him?

Despite the tourists and their grizzling, clamouring kids Keith risks a trip to Parenga. Although he doesn't thumb he's only walked about three kilometres when a youngish man on an oldish motorbike stops and takes him all the way to the township. Neither of them wears a helmet. The man's long stringy hair blows into Keith's eyes. The traffic cop only visits the island once in a while.

'You don't want to sell this thing?' Keith shouts as the rider lets him off. The man grins and shakes his head. His up and down look says Keith's too small to handle the thing anyway.

There are no motorbikes listed for sale on the noticeboard outside the Parenga Hardware. There are three cars and one light truck advertised. The truck and one of the cars have Parenga addresses.

The car is an old Prefect wide awake with rust. Only an arthritic dog is home. Keith and the dog wait patiently at the doorstep but no one answers his knocking.

He walks back to the shops and past the pub and down the beach road to look at the truck. More like a utility; an old Holden station-wagon converted. A woman with a baby comes out and says she's selling it for a friend. She gives him the key.

It starts first try. Keith lets it idle and lifts the bonnet. Together they stare at the oil-soaked engine.

Keith's only owned one car in his life. He had it seven days before it was stolen. It was found four days later down a bank. The driver was still in it, very dead. There had been no passengers. The car was beyond repair so Keith drank the insurance money. He had the use of work cars and he didn't travel far in his social life.

Suddenly he wants this little truck very badly. He's thinking of it already, like an adolescent, as a *set of wheels*. Even though it's more than he intended to spend and the woman says she can't negotiate, it's not her vehicle you understand. Keith knows he should bluff a bit, bargain. It doesn't even feel as if she's telling the truth.

He takes the thing for a drive. The woman and child come with him in case he doesn't plan to bring it back. The dashboard's full of debris. When he tests the brakes an avalanche of rubbish falls into the lap of the woman and over the child then slides and shuffles to the floor. Keith apologises though it's not his rubbish.

The woman writes Keith a receipt and says the owner will fix up the papers and post them to Keith. It occurs to Keith this seems a very casual way to conduct such an important transaction but it's probably how things are done on an island. Distrust, he tells himself, breeds dishonesty, not the other way round as they would have you believe on the mainland.

He drives his truck to the garage to fill up. Parenga is full of shiny holiday vehicles. Keith's proud that his truck has sufficient dents and disabilities to prove he is a native.

Back at the noticeboard he looks through the rest of the ads. His extravagance has made the need for work more pressing. Someone wants a toddler minded during the week. People with experience as commercial machinists are asked to contact Lou of Tautoro with a view to setting up a clothing co-op. And a handyperson is wanted to do tankstand repairs.

Keith took woodwork in forms three and four and once helped an acquaintance build a garage. He thinks the notice must've been put there by one of Daphne's lot; handyperson another way of saying female preferred. He glances round to see he's not being watched, and prises out the drawing pins. He puts the notice in his pocket where the key to his truck, on its grubby leather key ring, lies snug and promising. Today he has to wear his lenses for four hours. Which means he has two and a half hours of driving time left.

He is almost halfway up Cashin Road which is steep so he can hear the motor straining and curses himself for not having had the elementary sense to try it on a hill. He's wearing his contacts (afterwards this seems important) and he's sober. The boy comes round the corner in a sideways skid and a shower of stones. There's an instant when Keith waits for the impact of body against metal. And when that's happened and he's switched off the motor and eased off the footbrake waiting to see if the handbrake will hold . . . there's a while when he sits there unable to move.

First there is his father, the morning sun just touching the old hat he wears tipped down so his eyes move soft-footed in a cave. Then the tractor. The old yellow caterpillar tractor like a big toy with its child's play gear stick and the chainmail clunk of its tracked wheels. Tossed so casually on its side and see-sawing in a ridge. Then the thing beside it—that pile of red clothing in the dip between ridge and hill—moving, reaching up in a blind sinuous way more like a caterpillar than the tractor could ever be. And then the noise begins.

Keith gets out, pushes the bike aside and bends over the boy. And of course it's only shock that makes him freeze for a second as he sees the boy's face—thinking, for a confused instant, this is only a dream and being just a dream the boy is allowed to resemble Howard.

The boy's eyes are open. Blood runs into one from a cut in his head. His mouth is open wide as if he's about to scream, but the sound is no more than a whimper.

'Can you move?' asks Keith. Remembering the injured shouldn't be moved. But the boy is trying to get up, yelping a bit and clutching his leg, so Keith lifts him and carries him to the passenger side and gets the boy to balance on his good leg while he opens the door.

'Your leg, your head ... anywhere else hurt?'

'My bike,' he says. Tears now.

'Don't worry about your bike, mate. What matters is you're okay.' He finds a cleanish cloth among the debris that was left in the dashboard and presses it against the boy's head where the blood is seeping.

'It's had it,' the boy says. 'It's stuffed. It's always the same for me.'

'Where d'you live?'

The boy weeps.

'What's your name mate?'

'My bike ... it was mine ... and before ...'

'I'll get your bike. Here hold this here. Okay, tight. I'll load the bike on and then we'll have to find your folks.'

Keith heaving the bent bicycle onto the back and climbing back into the cab. The boy's eyes are closed and there's a greenish shade to his skin. Keith turns his truck in the first driveway and heads back to Parenga.

At the doctor's rooms he says, 'He rode straight into me, just came skidding round a corner. I couldn't get his name and then he passed out.' He thinks they look at him with disbelief.

He stands around while the doctor and his nurse lay the child on the high white bed and probe at him with little gadgets. The boy wakes and seems bewildered. Keith says, from a distance, 'Do you remember me?'

The boy stares blankly and the doctor frowns. 'We may be some time,' he says to Keith. 'If you'd like to wait in the other room . . .'

Keith sits among the patients with appointments and turns the pages of a magazine. What To Do In A Civil Emergency, says the big print of a notice on the wall.

Lethal doses of radiation were generated at the time of the explosion and within half an hour black radioactive rain fell over an area of four hundred square kilometres. For two hours the black rain fell.

Eventually the nurse comes out to him. 'He's going to be fine. The leg's just a sprain. He's had a few stitches in his head. We don't really know him and he says they're not on the phone so . . .'

'You want me to take him home?'

'If you could. Doctor will have a word with you.'

The boy's talkative on the way home. Pleased with the importance of concussion and stitches. Until he remembers his bike.

'Mainly I think the wheel's buckled,' Keith tells him. 'It's probably possible to straighten it out. Your dad might be able to.'

The boy falls silent until Keith asks, 'What number Cashin?'

He has to think about it. 'Up the top. I think it's seventeen.'

Keith remembers why he was driving up Cashin Road. 'I think that's where I was going. Is your mother called Maureen?'

The boy nods. He doesn't ask why Keith was going there. 'That's her,' he says.

The mother is walking down the road towards them. She doesn't look inside the Holden until it pulls up beside her. Then she runs to the boy's door and they all begin talking at once and Keith tells the boy, move over so your mum can get in.

They show him which gate. There's no vehicle entrance so he goes past and turns and parks mainly in a shallow ditch. The woman keeps telling the boy, but without anger, that he *knew* he wasn't to ride it on the road, not yet. And she keeps thanking Keith. He can see she's not sure whether or how to ask him in until he gathers the boy up to carry him.

Inside, when the clamour from the other two kids has calmed down, she says to Keith, 'You look like you need something stronger than coffee, but I'm sorry that's all . . .'

He realises then that the shock is still tight inside him. He could've killed the boy. The moment of impact is preserved in his head ugly as a spider in perspex.

They drink coffee and talk about the accident. She tells Keith it was the boy's birthday present. It was his birthday yesterday. Keith remembers the doctor's instructions. Don't let him sleep or get too excited for a few hours, watch his colour. And take him back next week for a check.

She says, 'Oh, I must owe you money. Did you have to pay?'

'An accident,' Keith said. 'It's on ACC.'

'That means the next visit will be too?'

'I guess so.'

He sees the flicker of relief.

The house is run down but friendly. Keith likes the way this woman is with her children, as if everyone's equal and there's no mystery or status in being an adult. It's some time before he remembers why he was coming here in the first place.

'You had a notice up, for work? Have you got someone?'

'No one's come yet.'

'Well now I have. I'm not exactly an experienced handyman but I can do basic stuff.'

'I suppose it's basic. Shall I show you?'

It's getting dark. 'You have to keep him awake. What say I come back in the morning?'

'I think it's rather heavy work.'

'I'm not as feeble as I may look.'

She laughs quickly, embarrassed. 'About payment. I'll need a quote or something, so I know what I can or can't afford.'

'Tomorrow.'

It's on the way out, when he's given her the bike and is walking out to the road and turns and looks past her at the cottage tucked in among the trees, that he gets the sensation of ancient familiarity. It's the feeling he knew in his first days on the island and as reassuring as a hand taking his.

His eyes are sore and scratchy. He should've taken his lenses out about two hours ago. Still, it's nice to see someone clearly when you first meet.

June

MAUREEN HAS BOUGHT a washing machine. It squats fat and ungainly in the kitchen, for the cottage has no wash-house. She rinses the clothes in the sink. Her mother would have a fit. But the machine's too big for the bathroom. One of those square automatic things would go in, but this was a bargain. Besides the second hand shop man said automatics gulp through your water supply. Unless you've got a bore, he said, you'd be a fool; in all conscience I'd hate to sell you one of those.

The novelty will of course wear off but today's wash is only the third she'd done in her own washing machine. Watching the clothes slurp back and forth she feels a faint subversive glow of freedom. As she hangs out one load of clothes she can hear the next happening—the machine's glooping, reassuring heartbeat.

It's a fine windy Friday. As she pegs up the clothes Maureen admires her reconstituted out-house sitting firm on a hole that had reached Maureen's shoulder. They all tried it for size before the house was shifted on. A pile of loose clay lies beside the dunny. Keith had been going to shift it but by that time Mickey had excavated roads and established a gravel pit and gouged a dam. Since he so rarely executed anything recognisable she'd told Keith, leave it, why should I care when the owner doesn't give a damn about the place?

Keith charged her quite a bit less than she expected, which is why she got the washing machine. Shisha warned against Keith. She said Maureen was silly to take on the first person who applied—she ought to have got quotes and made comparisons.

'No one else even applied,' said Maureen, 'so how could I?'

Shisha said Ben would've done it for less, if he'd known. Ben is sort of Shisha's boyfriend. Maureen hasn't met him (she still hasn't been to Shisha's house) but she knows a few things . . . She knows Ben is only eighteen, that he plays the acoustic guitar *ad nauseam*, is self-centred, that his parents are THE Witterhagens, that he has a large prick and narrow hips but no imagination.

When Shisha tells about her sex life Maureen feels the way she felt at Christmases past when someone they hardly knew sent them a card. As if it had been sent just so she'd be obliged to send one back.

So Shisha now knows things about Bruce. How he was aroused by her tears, how he held her responsible for the dry-eyed times when he tried and tried but nothing happened. What Shisha can't be told is that such times were as good as Maureen ever knew it. Shisha, who describes and compares virility and technique as if her lovers were contesting some Olympic event, would find such an admission incomprehensible. Shisha's sexual standards are obviously very high for most of her lovers have failed to meet them. Their shortcomings confirm Shisha's belief in the uselessness of mankind.

Shisha, on the subject of men, is funny as well as shocking. She makes Maureen feel as she did at fourteen sitting round with schoolfriends trading put-downs on the boys; saying, Nigel, now there's a spunky dude, and falling about clutching their bellies in a lovely agony of irreverence.

Yet Maureen has seen the way Shisha changes when Keith's around. How when he was out there digging the loo hole Shisha insisted on bringing in Maureen's washing even though it was still half damp. And how she'd bring around her own packet of Earl Grey tea and make a fresh pot on the hour though normally she'd leave such things to Maureen.

Except once or twice when he came in and sat with them at the table, Keith would have his cup outside. And though Shisha would linger when she took it out to him Maureen watched and thought he wasn't impressed. When he did come in Maureen heard a transformed Shisha, soft voiced, with a just-perceptible lilting accent.

Sometimes, when Keith's around but Shisha isn't, Maureen tries to listen to herself in case she too has a different voice for men. And though it seems to sound just the same she wonders if that's just because her voice knows when she's listening.

As well as the toilet Keith has fixed the tankstand, making it steady with posts he brought from the small mill near Tautoro. For the first week Alan was home from school, hobbling after Keith like a maimed shadow, and maybe helping as Keith assured her. And when Alan went back to school he'd look for Keith the minute he got in the gate. At night she'd have to send him outside to search for the schoolbag he'd dropped casually in the grass.

She began to hope Keith would take a long time over the jobs. Having found a friend Alan was faced with losing him. Maureen, too, likes having Keith around. If he wasn't a man he'd feel more like a friend than Shisha does. She was angry when Shisha suggested he might rip Maureen off. Angry not just on Keith's behalf, but at the way you're

121

not supposed to trust anyone anymore. She doesn't want her kids to grow up into a world where survival depends on suspicion. Alan would probably feel right at home in that kind of world, but the others . . .

Sometimes she thinks she is handing on, to Carly and Mickey, outmoded values which will make them anachronisms in the twenty-first century; obsolete before adulthood. Perhaps Alan is right to resist.

But when Keith finished the tankstand and she'd paid him he talked about all the other things that badly needed doing. Sections of guttering replaced, patching the tank, patching up the worst of the walls (he'd laughed at her banana box repairs), sheets of corrugated iron to cover the major roof leaks. He'd looked at the gunk that Maureen and Alan had applied with such a glow of capability and sighed.

She'd said all that could wait. In fact she'd been watching the notice-board at Parenga for houses to rent and eventually one was bound to come up that she could afford—but not one of those where you had to get out in summer for the tourists to move in and pay fat rents. She'd said, so it doesn't seem worth it. And anyway I don't have the money. And there's the specialist.

Carly's headaches continue, cuddles notwithstanding, so this time the doctor has made an appointment for her to see a specialist in Auckland.

But Keith had said, hang on a bit, he didn't want to be paid. If he was going to be an odd-job man he'd need a bit more experience. He'd practise on her place. He'd noticed that lots of reasonably good stuff could be foraged from the dump. He'd get what he could from there and if it looked like some materials would still have to be bought they'd talk it over first.

So now he comes, not regularly but once or twice a week with some salvaged guttering or boards or roofing iron. Displaying it with triumph. And now it's not a business arrangement Maureen helps him or stands around chatting if there's only her and Mickey. But when Alan gets home she leaves the two of them together because she sees that Alan is jealous of this friendship and after all it was Alan who found him first.

Maureen hasn't yet told Shisha that Keith is now working for free. Shisha would jump to conclusions and, if Maureen denied, Shisha would want to know, why then—what's his motive? And Maureen honestly isn't sure, for the reason he gave doesn't quite seem like reason enough.

Already she recognises her own growing sense of obligation. From a woman such kindness would be okay. But, being male, Keith is bound to want something in return. *Something more.* The words reverberate in her head – a thin truth crying to get out of an inflated assumption. How can friendship be something less and sex something more when for so many years Maureen endured sex and yearned for friendship?

Might *something more* entail love? But love is by nature too short-lived to be *more.* Mankind's brilliance has given women long-life milk preserved in cartons yet no one's found the formula for long-life love. Maureen's reading confirms what she already suspected. After the first few foolish years there are only unhappy couples who admit it and unhappy couples who pretend otherwise. The conspiracy of pretence so vast . . . so much effort spent in perpetuating that myth of *something more.*

'It's as if,' says Maureen, 'the truth is just too depressing for them to face.'

'Too subversive,' says Shisha. Though she's not crazy about all those pushy radical feminists wanting to rule the roost.

All the same Maureen doesn't want to be a solo parent forever, until her children have grown up and left home. She has a hazy and comforting picture of an entirely suitable man who will one day become part of their family. Their relationship will be firmly based on friendship, preferably platonic in the interests of endurance.

This man will love and be loved by her children and will be in a financial position to support them all in the kind of modest luxury that would provide Alan with a reliable bicycle and Carly with the best medical and optical treatment around. In fact should such a man appear she would be virtually obliged to grab him even if he had rotten teeth and warts everywhere; her children's welfare is what counts.

'Maternal martyrdom,' says Shisha in disgust.

But Maureen seems to have no choice. How could she be happy if her kids were miserable? How could she fail to be happy if her kids were happy? It's the only criterion she knows.

There's the dream she has . . . at first, on waking, she could never quite remember it, only the fear was still there. Now she knows the dream too well, yet still the horror of it takes her by surprise. There are small insinuating variations on the dream but the version that stays with her is the one she first remembered clearly on waking.

She is with the children in a big old building, the kind where solicitors and civil servants walk about in white shirts with the sleeves held up by metal, stretchy bands. She opens the lift which has a heavy folding grill, then the panelled door inside, and she urges the children in. She remembers to close the grill first or the lift won't go.

Carly and Alan squabble over who will push the button. They're going up to the seventh floor. Alan wins and Maureen promises Carly she can push it on the way down. The lift begins to move. After the first floor the sides of the lift evaporate and the four of them are standing on a lift floor that is held up only by the heavy wire ropes attached to the centre and stretching away above and below. High above them the rope winds around a large pulley.

The lift floor tips and Maureen throws herself down to balance it with her body weight. She screams at Alan and Carly to grasp the centre rope, but carefully because there's also a down rope moving and they could catch their fingers. With one hand Maureen holds the rope and with the other she holds Mickey's arm. But as the other two grasp the rope the floor tips again and Mickey is over the edge. Only a few curls and his chubby arm can be seen. Maureen stretches to pull him up and the floor tilts further.

She can see down, right to the bottom. They are at least seven floors up now and the lift is still rising but she can see into every floor below. It's like one of those doll's houses with a wall removed so you can reach into every room. There are men sitting at desks and walking down corridors.

Maureen screams. She hears her screams echo in the cavernous emptiness that surrounds the lift as it tilts in space between the doll's-house offices. She edges Mickey up till his shoulders and chest are on the floor. She screams down for help. Some of the men look up then go back to writing or sorting papers at their desks.

She pulls Mickey further in and drags herself closer to the centre. Carly is crouching with her arms circled round the rope. Maureen sees that one of Carly's hands spurts blood where her fingers should be. She figures that if she lodged herself against the rope she would have two hands to offer. But as she tries to do this the floor tips once again. Maureen's left hand is clasped around Mickey's, she leans against the rope and reaches out her right hand. She knows neither Carly nor Alan can keep a hold of the rope any longer. She takes Carly's fingerless hand in hers and she shouts to Alan, 'My wrist. Hold my wrist.'

He tries to, but there's no strength in his fingers. He looks at Maureen as the floor tilts down and he begins to slide. There's a kind of resignation in his eyes as if he'd expected this . . .

When Alan falls the floor seesaws and Maureen pulls Carly and Mickey to try and redistribute their weight. She hears a distant soft sound that she knows is Alan landing.

The dream dogs her mind. She understands it to be a warning. Next time—if there is a next time—she must make a safe and prudent choice; on their behalf.

Shisha and Maureen often talk about finding a man with money. Only half joking. My R & B man, Shisha calls him: rich and besotted. After all, she says, they're the buggers that drew up the options. What other chances have women like us got of living in some kind of comfort? Shisha rates money even higher than sexual prowess. If he was rich enough, she says, she'd even settle for someone who asked May I kiss you there?

The way Maureen sees it Shisha's chances of finding a rich man are a whole lot better than Maureen's. Apart from shopkeepers Maureen hasn't met one man with a regular job since she came to the island. Again apart from the shopkeepers the only males she knows here are Keith, the old pensioner two houses down the road and the two solo fathers that go to play centre.

'You have to go to the city,' Shisha says. 'You have to look for them.'

It's easy for her to say! Maureen used to wonder how Shisha managed to run a vehicle and visit the city and take wine to parties and buy make-up and perfume even. Shisha, having only one child, should've been on a smaller benefit payment than Maureen. But Shisha explained it one day when Maureen was still talking about looking for another house and worrying about rents. That's no problem, Shisha said; you just go over and tell them at Social Welfare and they'll pay you extra to meet the difference in your rent. That's the way it works, she said— the higher your expectations the more respect they give you and the more they're willing to pay out.

Shisha had forged a receipt from her landlord to show that the rent on the old house at Kamakama was double what they actually pay, and she told them there was only her and Leah living there. The road's so bad, she said, they've never come to check.

'You have to use your wits,' said Shisha. 'In our situation you have to look out for yourself and get what you can how you can.'

Maureen is envious of what Shisha's wits have got her. She tells herself she disapproves, that a lie is a lie is a lie, but it's hard to be sure where the disapproval ends and the envy begins . . .

If Maureen did meet a rich man how could she besot him? Shisha smells constantly Eastern and sultry, but even the cheapest bottle of perfumed oil costs as much as a Little Golden Book or three treat ice-creams. Shisha uses creams to feed her skin and wears make-up every day, but modern make-up so only the lush blackness of her lashes or the brightness of her cheekbones let on.

Maureen has make-up; an old dried up bottle of foundation bought when she was still working, a tube of tangee natural lipstick the children found on a pavement, one brownish lipstick that she wore at the bank and an old mascara tube that leaves a faint brown smear if she spits on the brush. Maureen's make-up belongs to the 1970s and makes her look old-fashioned. Maureen belongs to the 1970s. It's as if she stopped living when the children began. She knows all the words to the Mercedes Benz song and the music she turns up on the radio is Joplin and John Lennon and Rod Stewart. The new music floats past her all sounding the same. And even though at night she handsews in the legs of her jeans and hacks fashionable jagged edges on her T-shirts she knows that it won't fool anyone. One look and you'd know that since seventy-four the world's moved on without her.

Shisha goes to parties on the island. Maureen could go with her if she got a babysitter. But she's never had a babysitter. Who could she trust? Besides, Shisha says the minimum babysitters ask now is ten dollars and you have to take wine or something to a party. For the same amount they could all take a trip to the city and back.

Shisha doesn't need to pay for babysitters. She leaves Leah with the people back at their house. At least she used to but recently Maureen had Leah for two nights because Shisha's flatmates had refused. Shisha was angry about that; they want the pleasure of having Leah round but none of the responsibility, she said.

Maureen didn't get a lot of pleasure out of having Leah around. The child kept undressing Mickey and grabbing at his loose parts. Then she'd screamed and kicked when Maureen tried to put her to bed. Shisha didn't pay Maureen for babysitting, but fair enough because Shisha drives them to play centre and also took Maureen to look at a couple of houses, before Keith offered to fix the cottage and it seemed she may as well stay put.

Anyway Maureen's not sure she can believe what Shisha said about the department paying your extra rent. If that was so surely someone over there would have told Maureen?

Sometimes Maureen gets the feeling that Shisha chose her for a friend because that was all she could get. If Maureen had spare cash, if she had a car and could afford to drive it, then she would find a real friend, someone she feels at ease with.

When she starts thinking like that she has to pull herself together. I sound like Alan—the way he used to sound.

Because of the wind and the clear winter sky, and because a wringer is so much more efficient than her waterlogged hands, the clothes are dry by early afternoon. She has time to bring them in and sort them and iron the ones that need to be ironed and fold the others and put them all away before Carly and Alan are even home from school.

It makes her feel smiled on by fate. What a good day. She wants someone to tell but it wouldn't mean anything to the kids and she'd be ashamed to say it to Shisha if she called round. Shisha never talks about housework. And it doesn't look as if Keith's coming round today. Anyway she couldn't tell him, a man wouldn't understand.

That's the kind of friend she wants; the kind who when you say 'today I got the washing dry and ironed and put away,' would smile and say, that's great. And mean exactly that, no more no less, no condescension.

*   *   *

At first light he's down on the beach pushing the heavy old clinker dinghy into the water. Hoping for an hour or two before the rain clouds reached the island.

It's not Keith's dinghy. It belongs to an old guy called Jimmy. Most times when Keith took his fishing line out on the rocks, Jimmy would row past and they'd nod a greeting. Keith's persistence out there in the face of little reward must've inspired trust or pity; last week Jimmy offered the use of his boat for two weeks while he went south to visit his granddaughter.

The boat gives the island a new dimension. Keith wishes now he'd got a boat instead of a TV. He could have taken the boy out in his next school holidays, camped in a bay, spent a few days doing nothing much. All the time he was working over at Kaimoana the kid hung around. An old man of a kid he seems to Keith, though he hasn't had much experience to make comparisons by. Really the boy reminds Keith of himself twenty something years back, burning away inside with a longing for the things he imagines everyone else has, the way

Keith used to long for parents who danced with each other at school break-up dances and joined committees and had the neighbours over for New Year drinks.

The kid misses the TV and Keith's had his set a couple of weeks and could've asked him over. But he suspects Maureen would rather he invited them all and he's seen how those kids can be when they're together and no thanks. Not in Keith's still blessedly solitary household.

He's been making a point of watching the news in case they interview Daphne's little troupe on the steps of Parliament Buildings. He's not sure if he hopes they will or hopes they won't. He might give that as his reason for getting the thing if Daphne objects too strongly. She's opposed to television which is even more of a tool of male oppression than the daily papers.

He's had no word on when Daphne can be expected to return. Her share of the rent is almost a month overdue. They should've reached the capital by now, perhaps unnoticed. As a publicity venture the walk was badly timed. First the media was preoccupied with pre-Olympic fervour and now even that's been upstaged by the announcement of a snap election to be held next month.

That prospect gives Keith only a sense of inevitability hastened. The Labour cause feels like Daphne's walk for peace—too worthy and boring to touch the country's blunted nerves. Removed by a few miles of sea Keith feels he has at last a true perspective on Godsown. There is, he has explained to Maureen, a prevailing mood of masochism. People have lost the sense of having any degree of influence over their own lives. This so-called snap election would prove to be no more than a government manoeuvre to assist its own ends.

When he talks to Maureen she actually listens. She gets her solemn attentive look and believes what he says. It's a bit unnerving, he's not used to people taking his words in; he gets self-conscious and begins to weigh each sentence and find it short on substance. He searches his head for thoughts that deserve such an audience. He feels inadequate but grateful. He likes the woman, enjoys going there, is pleased to be of help. She deserves a hand, that kind of life can't be easy. Her eyes have a wounded waiting look. Lonely. But who'd take on a woman with three kids?

Then again. The cottage has that significant signposted feel, like the silhouetted planes on the way to airports. Or does he just imagine these things?

Keith has never in his life propositioned a woman. He's just hung around available and gone to bed with the ones who directly or indirectly invited it. Forceful women and drunken women and some who were both.

His wife Ginny was forceful and occasionally drunken. She was drover-mouthed and capable. Keith worked on the morning paper and Ginny on the evening paper. In those days it was considered unwise or improper for couples to work in the same office. In the twenty-two months of their marriage they didn't see a great deal of each other. They hardly ever landed the same days off. They left notes on the table about essentials like whether the dog had been walked and whose turn to stock the liquor cabinet. Being Ginny's husband lent Keith a certain notoriety at the press club. Behind his back they called him Clark Kent. It was when he still wore glasses.

The dog was a Dobermann cross called Winston. It belonged to Ginny. When he realised Ginny wasn't coming back Keith removed Winston's collar and locked the dog out of their yard. When it continued to hang around he rang the SPCA and reported it as a stray to be removed. It's the only purely vindictive thing he's ever done.

Today there are no fish. The rain clouds come up faster than he expected and he's not long put down anchor when he has to haul it up and start back to shore.

He drags the boat up past the waterline and leaves it bottom up under the palms, one of several small boats, and he walks home with his fishing gear and an empty sack. There's no one else about, even the store not yet open. He loves the place so much more when it feels all his. He even likes Jerry's bach when there's only him living there.

He makes toast and coffee. He doesn't cook himself proper meals, just makes snacks, things on toast or crackers. It suits him that way and his health doesn't seem to mind. He could never go back to Mrs Pemberton's oily roasts and pale gravy, to the miniature saucers of morning marmalade and the clink of china making urban birdsong as the Hereford guests ate in their separate silences.

On his island real birds sing, the sea breathes and whispers, the rain taps on the roof determinedly like a Red Cross collector. It hurts to think of all the years he's wasted being somewhere else.

Because his house, like so many of the island homes, has no driveway Keith leaves the Holden parked on the side of the road. The doors don't lock but no one has yet borrowed his jack or the tools that lie round on the floor. Even in Everton you wouldn't risk leaving an unlocked vehicle overnight on a public road.

Nor is there any way of locking the house, despite Jerry's sturdy key. When Keith was young no one in the valley would've thought of locking up a house; but that must've changed by now.

The people of Motuwairua are proud of their innocence. Now he's a working man Keith's getting to meet a few of the locals and can recognise in himself already the same fears, the same parochial pride. They have a dogged belief that the stretch of water that divides them from the mainland is sufficient to insulate the island from the excesses of progress; that living a giant's stonethrow from urban insanity has made the islanders clear-sighted, forewarned and immune to temptation. Yet alongside that belief is the fear. The island is small and the islanders so few and the mainland is large and unscrupulous. Living so close to the largest of its cities is to invite contamination.

When the holidaymakers come the islanders keep to themselves. They watch the tourists with a distant and ancient suspicion and what they see too often confirms the dread none can properly define.

Keith drives to Parenga and studies the noticeboard. Nothing new. His own card is still there. *Odd Jobs Done; Anything Considered*. As yet no replies. If he got a phone it would help. But the cost.

Someone wants to sell a lawnmowing round. Which is worth thinking about. He would still need a phone.

Besides the work for Maureen he's got a few other small jobs from the noticeboard but by the time he'd bought the tools he needed and paid for gas he was out of pocket. Being self-employed is harder than he thought. Trouble is he's been treating it like a hobby, not a business. He doesn't want to be a businessman, he just wants to keep eating and paying his rent. Maybe Daphne had a point . . . if he'd said he'd left the house Jerry would never have known the difference.

He could try for the dole. It no longer seems such a come-down. He could live on the dole and write sensitive stories for small magazines. He'd have more time to spend on repairing Maureen's house and still do a few odd jobs on the side. News of Keith being on the dole would spread to the *Everton Times* and bring a chill draught of overdue fear. There but for the grace of—

Turning in at the Motuwairua dump Keith thinks suddenly of Pet Crawford and how he'd wanted to help. The memory makes him cringe. The island has changed him. Invaded his mind and sabotaged

130

his assumptions. Persuasion of a most subliminal kind. Daphne could take a lesson.

At the dump there's a dead dog, a set of drawers beyond reclamation and a cracked plastic bucket, all freshly deposited. Keith rummages further but the only things worth salvaging are a few strips of shiny new tin and a fair sized piece of plywood.

He was hoping for a pushbike wheel fifty centimetres in diameter. He has his measuring tape this time. Already he's taken three dump bike wheels up to Cashin Road but none the right size.

The rest of the day left. He could go to Cashin Road anyway and cover some decaying corner of the roof with these silver strips, but Maureen has said how offended Alan is if Keith leaves before the kid gets home and he doesn't want to face the boy until he's got hold of a wheel. It wasn't exactly a promise but the way Alan's face is—always braced up ready to be disappointed—there's no pleasure in proving him right.

He could go back home and watch the soap operas. Or take the boat out again, for the rain is only half-hearted. He could go down to one of his special bays where he hasn't been going much anymore. Because of his truck and now his handypersoning. And because . . .

So soon we take that which we love for granted.

'How did you meet him?' He'd always wanted to ask but you have to choose your time.

'How? How does anyone meet? We were introduced. At a supper the Mayor put on. He came along with some friends.'

'But where?'

'The capital.' She always called it that.

'The Mayor of Wellington?' Sometimes he almost thought she made things up. If it wasn't for the red album. 'What did you say to each other. When you met. I mean, how . . .'

But she moves her neck so it's all ropes and hollows and he knows there will never be a right time for finding out.

She says, looking up at the lightshade, 'We got married very suddenly. We only had known one another for two weeks.' Her lips tighten. It's as if she's just finished saying 'I won't speak ill of the dead', though he's alive in the kitchen thumbing through a National Geographic.

Keith tries to imagine those two weeks. His father eating in restaurants, wearing a suit, remembering to start with the fork on the outside. A man who'd caught himself a butterfly.

Then what? Brought her home to Lonewood Valley. But what looked

131

enchanting in the capital seemed perhaps a bit silly in a valley in the Wairarapa.

But why did she . . . ?

His best bay is as perfect as it was last time he saw it. Then he'd rowed round in the dinghy and looked at it in a new way like watching your wife at a party with the eyes of a stranger.

Keith settles on a large round stone up where the bush begins. The misty rain brushes against the parka he bought so he could get away from Daphne whatever the weather, before he got the Holden. He feels vaguely guilty about not coming here as often as he used to. As if between this place and him there was an understanding. He sits very still waiting for a sound or sense of rebuke, but the bay is serene. It enfolds him.

When he was young he had a place, not as magical as this but it had felt like his own. Bush, moss, summer mint and the smell of river stones. After Howard went off to boarding school Keith needed a place to turn to. When there were two of them they had enough substance to affect the balance of things but when Howard left Keith had felt himself diminishing. There was no one to distract him from the eternal undertones.

The river place got to feel like better company than Howard had ever been. The two of them went down there on Howard's last holiday, not by design but because a couple of beasts were missing and they'd been sent to search. Keith didn't mention he used the place to escape to. Howard had tripped on a fallen trunk and cursed; he always came home with the very latest in boarding school profanities. They found the cattle about half a mile up river.

After Howard died Keith stopped going to the place. He never got a chance to get away from the house for longer than it took him to do small chores like feeding the hens.

Keith stays in the bay until the wind gets up bringing a rain that stings his cheeks and hangs in the whiskers he no longer bothers to mow down. He walks back to the truck and heads home.

He sees first the pile of belongings in the middle of the floor overflowing from cardboard boxes. Then the glow of his TV and a figure sitting crosslegged on the sofa. Kay. She nods at him.

Keith sits down in Daphne's chair. Cartoon figures scuttle across the screen, their mouths slide open and closed soundlessly. Kay watches them.

'Are they back then?'

Kay looks across at him. She has reddish hair and a wide bony face scattered with freckles. If she was an actress she would always play those striding, intelligent, independent daughters of mildly aristocratic parents.

'That's Hennie's gear. To the best of my knowledge they're still over the other side.' She says it calmly enough but he knows something's up. He's getting better at nuances, he thinks with some surprise—a few months ago he wouldn't have noticed. But then pub society isn't long on shades and subtleties.

'So how did it go—the great walk?'

'They got there. It went.'

'Is Daphne coming over in the forseeable future? I only ask because I object to her paying rent only when it suits her.'

'I imagine she'll be over in the next few days.'

'What's wrong?'

'Nothing.' She smiles at him unconvincingly. 'Nothing at all.'

'So what's with Hennie's gear?'

'I expect she'll be needing it.'

'You two've . . . ?' He sees the way her eyes slide off. 'You mean Hennie and Daphne . . . ?'

Kay smiles faintly and not for him.

'So what about you?'

She turns back to him. 'What about me?'

Keith sits there fumbling then gets up. 'Cup of tea?'

'Got any wine . . . anything?'

'Sorry.'

'Okay, tea.'

From the safety of the kitchen corner he says, 'It's not on you know. Sharing with just Daphne, well that's one thing, but . . .'

'That's up to you.'

'You're gonna stay on, up there?'

'No. We had to be out soon anyway, the owners are moving back over.' She turns her face to the screen as if there's no more to be said.

He gives Kay the mug with Mean Mama glazed on the side. There are other mugs similarly inscribed. It's probably childish but Keith avoids using them. 'I thought,' he says a trifle smugly, 'that you lot had everything worked out. Some kind of superior system. I thought it was all consideration and sisterhood and no one got hurt.'

She humphs and sneers but he's not sure whether it's at him or on her own behalf. Then she says, settling her elbows, leaning towards him, 'I'll tell you about hurt. I have two kids, a boy and a girl. He's eight now and she's six. My ex-husband has custody. He was awarded it because his lawyer told the court I "had a relationship" with a woman. Hennie. We weren't even living together, her and me. My neighbour was called to give evidence – about the hours Hennie visited and having seen us holding hands.' She straightens her back, stares hard at Keith. 'I haven't seen my kids for two years. Their father's taken them to Canada. He has a housekeeper in to look after them because he travels a lot in his job. I don't have the money to go to Canada and visit them.'

Keith's instinct is to say I'm sorry but that might sound like an admission of guilt by association. So he says instead, 'So now it must seem like you lost them for nothing?'

She shakes her head in amazement. 'I did lose them for nothing,' she says. 'You miss the point entirely.' She shrugs. 'And anyway Hennie'll come back, she always does.'

He could like Kay. There's an accessibility there. She hasn't Daphne's sealed surface. And right now she seems awash with pain. He would ask her to stay but he doesn't want to be misinterpreted. It wasn't him who put up the barriers.

She sets down her empty mug and nods to him, standing to go. He says, 'You're gonna leave that stuff there?'

'I have,' she says from the doorway.

He hears her putting on the gumboots he hadn't even noticed on his way in. Once, he thinks, a few years ago, they could've kept each other company; where's the sense in all this sniping? Keith pitched into the enemy camp while other men go about their lives quite unaware that war has been declared. Still, he feels no obligation to men, no inbuilt fellowship.

He must guard against paranoia. He's landed among the lunatic fringe. Maureen – now there's an everyday woman. So why does it seem more important to try to disarm Daphne than to try to make love to Maureen? Daphne, who thinks all men are weak-minded appendages to unrestrainable lust. He finds the image flattering in a wistful way.

If he was the man of Daphne's imagination he'd throw Hennie's gear outside in the rain.

He fries up bacon and opens a can of mushrooms for his tea. He thinks of Kay in the house up the hill, without her kids, without Hennie. The rain's getting harder. If she'd stayed it would've seemed worth lighting a fire.

134

On TV a woman's face suddenly fills the screen. The camera draws back. The woman is being interviewed. She stands in someone's garden and the wind whips at her hair. The reporter wears a padded jacket, the garden must've been his idea for the woman hunches a little and wraps her cardigan tighter. Keith turns on the sound.

'Five generations,' the woman says. 'That's how long it takes for the effects of radiation to peak. As scientists we can predict with confidence that the grandchildren of kids now being born will suffer from gross genetic defects.'

The reporter cuts in, he's heard it all before. 'As New Zillanders,' he says, 'we tend to feel geographically insulated . . .'

She takes her cue. 'Contamination in the Southern Hemisphere is increasing at a faster rate than in the Northern Hemisphere. Research has shown that children exposed to radiation before birth are five times more likely to suffer from skin diseases, dysentery, asthma. I understand your country has an abnormally high rate of asthma sufferers.'

Her voice is American. The voice of soap operas and oversell, assisting disbelief. The sound cuts out a second or two before the picture fades and she is left stern and unheard until the magic leap back to the newsreader and the safety of the studio. If he was listening the newsreader has been left unperturbed. Industrial troubles at Marsden Point continue. And now to sport.

Sport gets ten minutes.

*   *   *

Josie waits at the post office part of the Whiripare store for Jackie Brodie to finish serving the shop customers and turn into a postmistress.

According to Harley, Jackie Brodie is a nark and she reads people's mail. Harley says it's common knowledge. A couple of weeks ago a young policeman from the city came to Josie and Geoff's place asking about Harley. Geoff said they knew no one of that name. The policeman gave a description of Harley but Geoff still couldn't help him. Josie had the feeling the cop was watching her too closely, but he just thanked them and went away.

She thought perhaps it was just Harley's parents, understandably worried, and they should've said. But Geoff doesn't believe in assisting authority. When Harley next called in he said his place had been searched when he was out. He said Jackie Brodie had been sniffing his letters.

135

'That one knows everything that's going on,' he said. 'You gotta watch out for her. You fart in bed and next morning the whole place knows.'

But Josie knows about country places and takes that kind of information with a pinch of salt. Besides the Whiripare store is hardly ever empty—when would the woman get time to read even the backs of postcards?

'Good morning,' says postmistress Brodie edging behind the counter and rifling unasked through the P pigeonhole. 'Nothing today I'm afraid. Oh, unless John's put it under M? Yes, he has. I keep telling him. These families with different surnames keep us on our toes.'

Josie hears the implication but just keeps smiling. 'Thank you.' The letters are bound together with a rubber band.

'Wet enough for you?'

'A good day,' says Josie looking Jackie Brodie in the eye, 'for going back to bed.'

The wind batters at Josie as she crosses the street to the Land-Rover. She puts the letters on the passenger seat and drives round the corner where the road runs for a little way alongside the beach and the crashing windswept sea. It's getting on for midday and thanks to the weather Geoff and Josie spent the morning in bed. She can remember promising, in the giddy moments after rationality fled, that she would spend a high-heeled night in Queen Street offering her considerable parts to strangers who wished, for a modest donation, to fuck her against an alley wall.

Josie looking down at her oilskin, now piddling rain onto the floor, at her gumboots and the knees above them in navy mansized overalls. Sensible everyday Josie disassociating herself from that other astonishing Josie who minces and grinds centre-stage through the final act then scuttles backstage as the applause fades. To look at her comfortable, decent self in the dressing room mirror, and see the funny side.

Josie, checking herself now in the rear-view mirror, looking for a glimpse of the slut within her, sees only a motherly face with a wide mouth and steady green eyes. An English complexion, as they say, still firm and smooth, and fine pale hair shadowing one eye, Veronica Lake-ish.

Josie, peering still into the narrow mirror, tries for a different face. She bites her lips and pouts them wetly, narrows her eyes. It's a long long time since she tried out faces, this feels like a new one. She thinks if she could douse the urge to grin she could almost get away with this one. 'Admit it,' she watches her sultry mouth whisper, 'you always had a taste for sleaze.' Making herself all warm and wanting.

'Christ,' says Josie reaching for the keys. Thinking, ten minutes to drive up the hill and down the driveway and it's a fair bet he'll still be in bed.

She takes a deep breath and pushes the impulse aside. Already they've wasted a whole morning. Enough is enough, as she'd told Geoff so often. We've already wasted half the day, she anguishes, squirming away from hands.

'Wasted?' he says. 'Wasted! What do you imagine we were put on this earth for?'

Josie edges the rubber band off their mail and stores it in the pocket of her coat. She shuffles through the collection. *Straight Furrow* readdressed, two bills (one with the amount owed—seventy-nine dollars and ninety-nine cents—showing through the cellophane window for Jackie Brodie's pleasure) and two letters. The bills addressed to Geoff, the letters to Josie.

First the one from Lake. Tiny tight handwriting scrawled over every centimetre of a page torn from an exercise book. PTO at the bottom with an arrow aiming for the right hand corner in case Josie is inconversant with the initials.

Lake is outraged over the deregistering of unions, but not surprised. *Just* (Lake writes) *the kind of fascist move we've come to expect.* Lake always writes of *we* and at first Josie had imagined her daughter in partnership with some earnest ink-smudged male. She has since realised that Lake's use of the plural is universal and non-specific. As in 'we the oppressed'.

'We,' says Lake in her letter, 'are in danger of being paralysed by hopelessness.' She urges Josie to fight deregistration in any way she can.

Lake still pretends her mother is a person of some modest influence. It's inconceivable to Lake that anyone could throw in a job as a current affairs researcher to become a helpmate and cookery columnist. Lake's initial disgust changed, on leaving home, into suspended disbelief at her mother's erosion of sanity.

Lake's letters make Josie feel pallid and trivial. Each time she delays replying and then has to screw up her first attempt. How can she send Lake, who is in last-ditch combat with oppression, frivolous pastoral tales of fowl husbandry or heart-wrenching sunsets?

At the end of her letter, crammed economically beneath the last blue line, Lake writes: *A letter from Daryl. Semi-incomprehensible burblings about the wrath of whatsisname and pious quotes from chapter whatever verse etc. What's happening to his head over there?*

Josie can't imagine. She reads this bit twice. Daryl hasn't written to her since he left but then Daryl has a strained relationship with the written word. It seems odd that he should write to Lake yet not to Josie. Sarah writes regularly and has mentioned that her brother is competing for king of the weirdos. Josie took no notice of that— Sarah exaggerates and, especially on the subject of Daryl, is not to be taken seriously.

He's sixteen, Josie reassures herself. It's only a phase. His father and his father's new wife belong to some Eastern religion. Presumably one of the more recent ones that annoints capitalism.

The second letter is from Juliet.

Dearest Josie she writes on paper circled with violets. *This is to let you know that after all I'm back with Paul. Hell I'm trying to pretend to myself it's what I want but I'm afraid the truth is I just hadn't the strength to hold out. I'm so ashamed.*

Please don't ring or anything, not for a while. Don't worry I'm not about to do anything drastic, but I can't bear to talk about it at the moment, it's all too depressing. Feel I've let the side down but most of all myself. I'll be in touch.

Josie sits and watches the waves battering their head against sand. So much quietly endured sorrow around, her own contentment seems at once fragile and obscenely robust. Not to be taken for granted. No more talk about wasted mornings.

Was it her fault then, the other times? Turning Farley queer, driving Dick to wild diversions? Never willing to waste time with them . . . So hard now to remember back beyond Geoff. Even the solo years lost in a blur of busy-ness.

Driving home Josie thinks of the party at Leif and Helen and Peter's place. A couple of dozen people and only Leif's mother, over on a visit, older than Josie and Geoff. Grace Jones on tape . . . island gossip and horticultural hints among those who congregated in the kitchen. The living room devoted to the intense listening and fragmented talk of the dedicated dope smokers. Assorted small kids in going-to-bed clothes refusing to go to bed and leaving chewed pizzas in ashtrays.

No evidence of domestic depravity and no perceptible undercurrents. Josie kept glancing at Geoff to see if he was disappointed. Until the hippie moved in on him, curling up beside his chair with her face tilted eagerly upwards.

Josie, listening to a young man who had crewed on a boat that had once gone to Marlon Brando's island, tried not to watch the woman. There was no need to, Josie knew the type. (Since she reached forty she's allowed herself to be judgemental.) Type was contrived orphan-annie look . . . limp dress with unstitched hem, carefully selected Corso cardigan, heavy bottle green stockings, sandals and a greasy beret. The spiritual look. Downcast eyes and a wispy voice. Calculated submissiveness. The head hunter syndrome . . . women who don't like other women.

Silly bitches. Josie can spot them a mile off. But men get taken in every time, their gullibility is boundless.

'Shisha,' he informed Josie on the way home. 'She-shah.'

'Figures,' said Josie sourly enough for Geoff to laugh.

'She lives down the bottom of the island. They have a whole bay to themselves. She invited us to go out there some time.'

'Us?'

'Well . . . whoever. They have ducks. She said I could have some.'

'Who's they?'

'A bunch of them live there.'

She heard the lightness in his voice, laughter held at bay. She knew he wanted to drag this out. So did she now it was just a game. Safe in the seat beside him she indulged her jealousy and he encouraged her. Like kids sticking needles into their own flesh to reassure them of the miraculous fact of their own existence. If it hurts you're alive.

Stopping at the top of their driveway to open the gate – they now have eight black sheep grazing on the front lawn – Josie invents a scene which features herself walking innocently into the house and finding Geoff and Shisha entwined. It hurts wonderfully.

In fact Geoff is on the phone saying he'll come and look at them on Friday. 'Look at what?' she asks as he hangs up.

'Ponies.'

'What?'

'Four of them. I'm going into Shetlands.'

'Why?'

'Whaddayou mean why? To breed, to sell.'

'There's a market?'

'Of course there's a market. Cute little hairy fuckers you can keep in your back yard. Everyone wants one.'

'Where'll you keep them?'

'Up the back.'

'The grape paddock.'

'Yeah, well I've gone off grapes. Too risky and too much work.' Josie stills her tongue.

'We could give pony rides,' he says. 'Summer. Down on the beach. That'd help sales.'

'I thought you'd had enough of kids to last you a lifetime.'

'On the beach. We wouldn't be living with them.'

'They have nasty natures,' she says. 'They bite.'

He sniggers. 'Only the ones from broken homes.'

She sighs. 'I thought you might still be in bed.'

'Old Bill came round.'

'What did he want?'

'Nothing. A chat. A cup of tea. Were you thinking of coming back to bed, if I was still there?'

She hesitates. 'Bit late now. Anyway it's clearing, and those blasted sheep have knocked down the shelter round my little oak. And we were going to do the seed potatoes remember. And maybe an asparagus bed.'

'Whatever would I do without you,' he says dismally.

'I'll make a cuppa before we start.' She feels like a nurse, kind but brisk, about to administer castor oil.

'I've been thinking,' Geoff says, watching her spoon in the tea leaves, 'that we should try a plot of barberasquas. They seem to be taking off. Quite a few growing them up north.'

Josie thinks, ideas ideas talk talk. 'Then do,' she says a little sharply. 'What are they anyway?'

'You know . . . those pinkish hairy things, distinctive taste. Sort of somewhere between a watermelon and a stoat.'

She tries to keep her smile in. He does this too often, too easily. Laughter his secret weapon. They'll go under laughing and screwing. If she told him that he'd say, what more could anyone want?

Well Josie wants more. She wants a sense of security. Even if it means less of the other. But there shouldn't have to be a choice—some people get the whole lot, don't they? No one Josie knows is quite that lucky, but that doesn't mean it's not possible.

She pours the tea. 'I got a letter from Juliet. She's back with Paul.'

'After all that!'

'It's not what she wants,' says Josie sharply.

Geoff says pointedly, 'None of us gets quite what we want.'

He's just trying to upset her, to pay her back for not laughing about the stoat. He seems to have succeeded. Josie's mind leafs through her dog-eared inventory of what Geoff really wants: Goldie Hawn. Edna O'Brien. Xaviera Hollander. A tropical beach and cricket on telly. All at once. 'And one from Lake,' she says. 'Daryl's apparently gone religious. He wrote to her.'

'Maybe we shouldn't have let them go.'

The *we* takes her by surprise. He hardly ever acknowledges a responsibility.

'I don't suppose it'll do him much harm,' she says without confidence.

Geoff asks, parodying her doubt, 'Why can't he settle for drugs and sex like a normal kid.' He counts off on his fingers. 'You realise they've been gone nearly five months?'

'And?'

'And here we are, just growing old together.'

She takes it as a reproach. When the kids are gone . . . they used to whisper to each other. Bedtime promises too lurid for daytime scrutiny.

'Did you mean that,' one of them would sometimes ask later.

'Did *you*?'

'I dunno. At the time but . . . You?'

'No. Yes. Maybe. I don't suppose so.'

Just growing old together. Sensible. Safe. Boring. A life like Edie's where nothing happened until she grew tired of waiting. For seven years Geoff patiently endured a life that revolved around Josie's children. She owes him this year, already half gone. And he's given her Shisha, seasoning to whet Josie's appetite.

She goes to him. 'I know. I know what you mean. And I've been thinking I should go over to Auckland and try to get a bit more work. Maybe some voice stuff now we're handy to the city. There must be something if I front up to enough places. Would you want to come?'

He considers, 'Where would you stay?'

'Motel?'

'You want me to come?'

'Up to you.'

'And if I don't come you'd . . . maybe do something . . . wicked?'

'I'd try.'

'Promise?'

'Promise,' she says. It's just a word; a shaping of the lips emitting sound. But at least it gives him something to look forward to.

July

'ANYWAY,' MAUREEN SAYS, 'it's so far I couldn't possibly.'

'Wouldn't they help? With the fares?'

'What with? All his money goes to the breweries.'

'That's more or less where mine used to go. Till I came here.'

'And you stopped. Why?'

'Not sure really.'

Mickey is standing with his arms raised waiting to be hoisted onto Keith's lap. It's difficult to refuse the kid, with his mother watching. Keith lifts him up and the boy beams and clings like a big toddler. He's astonishingly heavy.

Maureen looks at the child sitting there pushing his fingers into Keith's beard and her face becomes soft and unguarded. Dotes, Keith thinks as if he'd just invented the word. She dotes on this one. He doesn't much like the kid. Smug, he thinks, and a bit thick. Keith doesn't enjoy all the clutching and fondling. He much prefers the older brother's wary aloofness. He can see Mickey as an adult – brawny, sentimental and fearless with not even enough imagination to have nightmares.

'You just decided . . . like that?'

'Not even that. I . . . well for one thing I didn't have a wage coming in. And I didn't have the urge.' He grins to show it's a corny old cliché. 'I fell in love with the island. You know – these days I get high on life.'

She doesn't find it funny. She says heavily, 'I wish I did.'

She sounds so heartfelt he drags the conversation back to safer ground. 'So how long since you've seen her – your mother?'

She calculates. 'Nine years.'

'Her grandchildren – she's never seen them?'

'Not these ones.'

He shakes his head, but he really finds her answers reassuring. 'It's four years – no, more like five – since I saw mine.'

'She's still alive?'

He must have a motherless air. 'Sort of.'

She's waiting for an explanation. Mickey wriggles off Keith's lap and sidles out the door.

'She's in a home. She doesn't know where she is half the time. A kind of senility except she's been that way for years. I feel I ought to go and see her, there's no one else. Her family live somewhere in Europe—her parents would be dead by now—they didn't keep in touch. But then my going to see her can only make me feel a better person, or make the staff there think a bit better of me. It's not gonna help her.'

'Your father?'

'He's around. He's pretty crazy too. I suppose two crazy parents sound like a bit of an exaggeration, only it's not I swear. Anyway he'd hardly go and see her. Unless it was to gloat.' He worries that that was too harsh. 'I just said that. But if she had her head straight . . . all her faculties he'd be the last person she'd want to see.'

Mother, I'll miss the bus if I don't go now.'

Detaching her hand from the cuff of his grey school jersey. So she clutches instead at his fingers. Her nails are so long he thinks of hen's feet, claws.

'You'll get me a Vogue and the New Yorker?'

'Yes.' It means writing himself out a lunch pass and forging her signature so they'll let him down town.

'And tell me, is the murderer still in the kitchen?'

He pulls himself away from her, not answering. It's just another way of hanging onto him. She says it all the time, waiting to trap him into something. And she has him, in a way, believing it.

'Are you an only child then?'

'I had a brother. He died in an accident when he was sixteen.'

'What sort of accident?' As if she's digging for a prickle, poking about and watching him wince. No one's probed like this except Ginny when they were first together. Keith's used to people minding their own business. In Everton most people knew a version of the Muir story but wouldn't have dreamt of checking it out with Keith.

'A tractor. Rolled on him. Used to be a lot of kids killed that way on farms.' He hears himself making it commonplace. It doesn't seem fair to Howard—even he deserved something more. Keith tries again.

'Something happened. I don't really know . . . I must've been twelve at the time yet I still can't remember that morning, my memory seems to skirt around it. My mother blamed my father for the whole thing. Well of course if it hadn't been for my father Howard wouldn't have been out there, but she thought there was more . . . There'd always been this thing between them—she didn't want Howard growing up to be a farmer or something like that, she was set on his being a professor or a pianist . . . something *cultured*. It was as if her life depended on what Howard became.

'And of course my father thought she was turning him into a pansy. She wanted Howard to be entirely unlike his father, and the message there was clear enough. I always felt he disliked Howard. And Howard couldn't make close friends with him, she wouldn't have allowed it. It had to be a choice with her. That's the way she was.'

'Did they fight? Your parents?'

Fight? Loud voices hurling accusations, blows and tears. Ginny's parents fought like that, even once when Ginny and Keith were visiting. Afterwards the four of them went on a picnic and Ginny's parents held hands.

'Not fight. Cold war. Silences.'

'Mine fought. At least he did. Wild accusations and throwing things. Sometimes he'd hit her. And sometimes Alice, but not me. My mother would just hunch up and shake and cry. Next morning he'd be all jovial as if nothing'd happened.' She shrugs. 'They say the daughters of men like that choose the same kind of men. I did. That stupid. But no one tells you how you know which ones are going to turn out cruel. Once there are kids men seem to change, and once there are kids it's that much harder to get out of it.'

'My wife left me. I wasn't cruel or vicious. I drank less than she did in those days but she just went off and never came back.' He hears himself sounding querulous and pathetic.

Maureen says nothing but her mouth sets in a silence which says, that's your version.

Shit, he thinks, they all stick together. They're like the Mafia already and it's early days yet. Maybe Daphne's crowd are not the manic fringe. Mobilisation going on everywhere. Self righteous and vengeful – the most frightening kind of enemy. The revolution turning unsuspecting Everton on its ear.

'What's funny?' She sounds suspicious.

'Nothing.'

'Did you want children?'

He wonders if it's a leading question. 'Dunno ... I suppose.'

'Maybe your wife didn't.'

'We could've talked about it – leaving seems an extreme reaction to a moot point.'

'Maybe she just didn't like being married.'

Keith's becoming irritated. He laughs, 'Apparently she didn't. But if a man decides he doesn't much like being married and pisses off he's made out to be a monster.'

Maureen smiles at him. 'The monsters,' she says sweetly, 'are the ones that stay.'

'The men that stay?'

'In my experience, yes.'

She's chalking out the boundaries. Keith feels depressed. How can they be friends if already she's distrustful.

'Is that a hint that I should go?' He's half serious.

She grins, 'Of course not. Tell me more about your mother.'

But it's gone and there seems to be nothing to say. 'Like what?'

'Well, when you went to visit her, when you last went, did she know you?'

He thinks back. 'The time before last she didn't know me at all, she called me doctor. The last time she thought I was Howard.'

'Closer,' she said, 'I want to be able to touch you. Dearest you can kiss me.'

So he closed his eyes and made himself kiss her cheekbone.

'A real kiss.' Still that trace of an accent.

'Mother, it's Keith,' he said. 'Keith.' Holding his face right in front of hers.

'Don't tease,' she said. 'Don't tease me Howard I know who you are.' She grabbed at him with astonishing strength and pulled his face against hers. His instinct was to wrench free and his repulsion shamed him. He tasted the rough skin on her lips, the saliva that slid intermittently from one corner of her mouth, and smelt the old sourness of her breath. Then suddenly, disgustingly, her wet tongue pushed between his lips. He pulled away, wanting to retch.

She doesn't know what she's doing. Pity her.

She giggled then, like a schoolgirl. 'Silly boy,' she said. 'Now hold my hand.'

'Would you like some fruit?' He took the bag from the top of her locker and held it in both hands. 'Some grapes? Or an orange.'

'Not today, thank you.'

He opened the locker. The tin of assorted biscuits he'd brought last time, nearly eighteen months before, sat on the top shelf. He felt a glow of indignation, surely they would've reminded her it was there?

'Howard?' her voice grotesquely playful.

Keith slid the tin out, it was heavier than he expected. 'Didn't you eat your biscuits?' As if she would remember.

He tells Maureen, 'Then I took the tin out of her locker and opened it up. It was full of . . . she'd used it as a bed-pan.'

Maureen begins to laugh. 'What did you do?'

'I put the lid back on and put it back in the locker.'

She laughs more, then sees his face. 'It's funny,' she tells him. And Keith, for the first time, sees that it is. Dares to laugh at her, but a little apprehensively. As if, propped on her pillows at the Rosebank Hospice, she might know and exact some terrible penance. A few moments of bravado then his laughter deserts him. Like Ginny it goes and doesn't come back though he's expecting it.

Instead a small insistent squeaking sound approaches. Mickey, big eyed and whimpering, the guineapig in his arms. When he holds it up to his mother the animal looks half dead. One haunch is grossly swollen, the eyes half-closed, the mouth hanging open.

'Oh god.' Maureen takes it from the boy.

'Make him better,' he says.

'If we can, love.' She sits with the animal in her hands, not looking at it.

'It's my fault,' she tells Keith looking stricken. 'He was hurt weeks ago. I should've taken him to the vet but . . . well he seemed to be getting better, but not really. I knew not really but I didn't want to . . . I guess they could still . . .'

Keith says, softly so the boy doesn't hear, 'I think it's past it.'

For a minute she sits there looking helpless. Then she says to Mickey brightly, 'I think the kids should be home soon. Why don't you go to the gate and see if you can see them? Stay inside the gate though.'

He goes obligingly, so easily distracted. Maureen looks at Keith. 'We should put it out of its misery, shouldn't we?'

Keith nods, aware of the ominous *we*.

'Please,' she says, 'can you? I couldn't bear to. Once I had to kill a cat. I'll never forget it.'

Keith has never killed anything larger than an insect. His father used to set gin traps for opossums then club them to death. Once in Keith's presence his father made Howard do the clubbing. Keith stood well back watching Howard's face for signs of emotion, but all he could see was a cold anger that wasn't directed at the opossum.

'Would you mind?' she begs.

He wants to say, yes I would mind. Why don't you find one of those violent men you're so familiar with and ask him? You can't have it both ways.

But he says, 'I guess. But maybe we should wait until Alan gets home. It's his, isn't it? He seems to think it is.'

'Yes. But I thought it'd be easier . . . we could just say it died.'

'With a smashed in head?' He'd seen the opossums afterwards.

'If it was buried . . .'

'It seems a bit underhand. Just to announce . . .'

She draws back her lips as if she's in pain. Her eye teeth are sharply pointed. 'Look I don't think he'll be all that upset. I doubt if he'll be upset at all. The other two will, but not . . . If he's here he'll probably want to watch. He'd get a sort of thrill out of it and I couldn't handle that.'

'Okay.' He takes the creature from her hands. Limp body and brittle feet. Like holding a rat, he has to knock back the impulse to drop it.

Outside he lays it on the ground and grinds the heel of his sneaker into its head. Like standing on fishbones, but his stomach lurches. He takes the spade and digs a guineapig-sized grave, shovels up the body and drops it in. Covered, the grave seems to need some sign. Here lies . . . if the thing had a name he can't recall it.

'Giggles,' they tell him later.

'He was crying,' says the little one, complicating Maureen's explanation of a peaceful dying-in-his-sleep.

'Well, he was in pain,' she amends. 'And he was just about to die so Keith . . . just . . . put him to sleep.'

Keith feels framed. This, he thinks, is how it must feel to be a father.

'You killed him?' Alan sounds impressed. 'How?'

'Never mind how,' says Keith.

'Did you shoot him?'

'I don't have a gun.'

'Did you bury him?' Carly's face says, murderer.

'Yes. D'you want to see? I thought you could put something there with his name on.'

They all troop round to the back of the house and congregate beside the orange-tipped protea.

'Say something. You know, something proper,' Carly tells her mother.

Maureen wriggles a bit and clears her throat. 'We are gathered here to say goodbye to Giggles who was our friend.' A silence, so she adds. 'Goodbye Giggles.'

'Jesus Christ Amen,' says Carly.

Maureen glances at Keith and smiles. Keith smiles back. Fathers must also feel like this.

He accepts when she asks him to stay for tea, but before it's even ready he wishes he hadn't. He and Maureen don't get to exchange more than a couple of sentences without interruption. The kids are shrill, persistent and over-active. Alan, who talks sensibly and easily when he and Keith are alone, is sullen between bouts of vexed abuse, mainly directed at his sister. No one mentions Giggles.

'They're worse, I'm afraid, when someone's here,' says Maureen. Making it somehow Keith's fault.

When the other two have been put to bed Alan hangs on, usurping Keith, fetching from his bedroom a succession of broken clock innards and electrical and wind-up motors from abandoned toys. Keith's been shown most of them before.

'Where do you get all these?'

'Some I find. Some I get off kids at school.'

'He's the unofficial school rubbish collector. Anything that once turned or drove or sparked.' Maureen is collecting up toys and throwing them into a carton.

Alan glances at his mother contemptuously.

'Maybe he's a genius,' soothes Keith. The boy grins to himself.

There are things that go when you wind them or hold a battery against them. They don't do anything useful but Alan has repaired them to working order. He wants Keith's opinion on the ones he hasn't been able to fix. Keith peers and prods. 'You know more about it than I do. What's this wire here? Shouldn't it be ... ?'

Alan sighs. 'I know. I need a soldering iron. We don't have one.' He looks at Maureen.

She takes a deep breath. 'When Alan was tiny I showed him the moon. The first time he'd seen it. That's the moon, I said. Thinking about how amazing it was, you know ... the whole universe out there. Well, he looked at it for a while then he said, "Who drives it?" '

Keith laughs, but sees how Alan hates that story.

'And he never drew people. Even when he was little at play centre. All the other kids painted people, you know, mum, dad, my brother — sometimes animals. Alan drew *things*. Robots, guns, trucks, fighter planes. No people.'

'Well,' Keith watches Alan, 'he's a modern child.'

'Apparently,' says Maureen flatly.

Keith sees that it's not just the boy that bothers her but everything she feels the boy represents. He gives the boy a quick smile, they seem to be in the same boat.

'Women,' Keith says to Alan. 'They don't understand do they.'

Maureen sneers faintly and walks to the window. The boy grins at Keith. Keith feels hemmed in by the walls of their little triangle.

'You've got school tomorrow,' he says. 'Shouldn't you go to bed.'

'I'm not tired.'

'Perhaps Keith is,' says Maureen without turning her head.

'No he's not,' says Alan.

But Keith is. Tired of the whole thing. For a while there he'd thought, once the kids were out of the way . . . But maybe she wants the boy to stay. Maybe that's her way of telling Keith . . .

'Actually I am,' he says. 'And I've got a job in the morning.'

'Awww.'

'Next time I come I'll try and get hold of a soldering iron.'

The kid's getting expensive. Keith ended up ordering a bike wheel from Auckland, though it hasn't come yet.

'Promise?'

'No. But I'll try. Now you should take all this stuff back to your room.'

Alan doing as he's been told.

'There's a miracle,' says Maureen, following Keith into the kitchen.

Their moment alone. 'Keith,' she says lowering her eyes in a way that makes her look for a moment just like Alan, 'there's something I've been trying to get up the nerve to say all night.'

He stands still and tries to look casual.

'You know that you mentioned last time you were here, about having Alan round . . .'

'And you seemed a bit . . .'

'It was just, right then, it didn't seem . . .'

'I thought you had me figured as a child molester.' It's a joke but he sees her cheeks redden and her assurance comes too quickly. It feels like a kick in the gut.

'Don't be silly,' she says. 'It's just that when you asked . . .'

'You *know* me,' it feels like he's pleading. 'I've been round here a lot. Don't you feel like you know me?'

She looks at him for a long time. 'Not really,' she says.

'It was *Alan* who made friends with *me*,' he says.

'I know,' she says, dropping the pretence. 'I know. It's just that when it's your own kid you want to be a thousand per cent sure. And I know that even then it's the people you'd least suspect. Oh hell, now I can't say what I was going to say.'

'You may as well.'

'Well,' she gives a funny little smile, 'I was going to ask if it would be possible for Alan to go to your place on Thursday. After school.

149

I know it's a bit of a cheek to ask but Carly has her appointment and it'd mean a day off school for him. And me having three of them all day in the city . . .'

'Sure,' he says. 'No problem.'

'He could take the school bus to Toki Bay.'

'I'll meet him there. And bring him home . . . when . . . about six?'

'You sure? That would be wonderful. Thank you.'

'So now,' he says, 'you're a thousand per cent sure of me?'

She looks at him steadily. 'Perhaps I've just weighed up the awfulness of a wet day in town with three kids and decided what risk there is was worth it.'

Not what he was hoping for. The wind hits him as he opens the door. 'Well, thanks for the meal.'

'Thanks for everything,' she says holding the door. 'See you Thursday.' She closes the door.

If he was a real man, the kind she's used to, he'd still be in there. If he was a beater of wives, a casual killer of terminal pets, she'd never have suspected him of pederastic intent. Which seems to prove something.

But driving home the silence is reassuring, the solitude wonderful. The island knows best, he thinks.

There's a motorbike parked beside the road where he usually leaves his truck. A van right behind it. He has to drive further down and round the corner to find enough verge to park on.

Hennie's in the kitchen brewing tea. The rest of them—enough for a coven—are sitting in front of his TV.

'Hi,' says Hennie.

'How nice.' The batteries in Keith's torch were flat and he had to stumble down the road and along the path in darkness. 'I see we're having a hen party.' He smirks at the pun.

'Daphne's on,' says Hennie. 'So we came to watch.'

'On?'

'After the commercials. You've missed half of it.'

'I'll never forgive myself.'

Hennie grimaces. Keith feels suddenly wide awake and sparky. 'Have you moved in or is this just a visit?' He looks around the faces and doesn't see Kay. Or Daphne.

'I'm afraid it's just a visit.'

'But you intend to move in?'

'Sorry. But Daph should be back next week.'

'She owes two months' rent.'

Hennie rolls her eyes. 'There's an election come up, though I don't expect you care.'

But the others shush and settle and Hennie has to rush over. Someone turns up the sound. Keith from the far wall can see, thanks to the miracle of corrective focus, Daphne looking long-suffering and larger than usual. Next to her a prim spinster, a public servant and a car salesman if you can go by appearances.

'I was about to say,' close-up on the public servant, 'that we still lack an adequate definition of pornography.'

'You might,' says Daphne unseen, 'I don't.'

He turns towards her. 'But your definition, Miss Glass, is a purely subjective one, not shared by the wider population.'

'I wish,' says the car salesman, managing to look laid-back, 'that those who spearhead the feminist movement in this country would come right out and admit they'll only be satisfied when they have everybody celibate or homosexual.'

He goes on but the rest is drowned out by Keith's visitors. The groaning and hissing dies as Daphne is shown firing back. Something about sex which depends on the exploitation of one half of the human race. 'We know it's the thin end of the wedge,' she shouts as the salesman starts talking over her.

Keith goes to bed. He can still hear the heated TV voices, the partisan audience response. He doesn't care one way or the other but wonders if he should.

Keith's father kept magazines which exploited and degraded. Keith found them hidden in a corner of the woolshed loft. At high school the more sadistic kids had told him stories about his old man driving into town at night, paying Lizzie Hughes, and begging Marge McNeil.

No smoke without fire.

His father, leaning on a gate watching his best rams in tupping season and saying, almost as if Keith was an adult, 'No nonsense, you see. No nonsense. We should all be so lucky!'

Keith waited, embarrassed yet vaguely flattered, but that was it. He pretended not to watch the rams. It made him uncomfortable with his father there. This was at a time when he still thought his father went at nights to see his accountant.

By the time Keith was in the fifth form his father had found himself a regular girlfriend. After a while he didn't pretend about where he was going. Sometimes he'd be away a night and a day. Eventually he started bringing her out to the farm. Lee-Anne.

Trash, Keith's mother said. Water finds its own level.

By then his mother never went out of the sunporch except to use the bathroom. They called it a sunporch but it was just like a bedroom only pleasanter because of the big windows and the french doors. She'd slept there as far back as Keith could remember.

She stopped going into the other rooms of the house but once Keith got his licence she liked him to take her for drives. Now she would say, *adulterer*, as well as *murderer*. It made for a change.

As for Keith's father, the secret pornographer, he was besotted by Lee-Anne. He bought her a car and a chamois leather coat and a house in town so they could spend nights together. By then Keith had a job to go to and his mother was pretty much a full-time occupation. And his father was keen to sell the farm and start afresh with Lee-Anne, so they got Keith's mother into a 'home' though the only one that would take her was a long way away. It had to do. Keith was desperate to escape, it felt like his only chance.

When the farm was sold a fund was set aside to pay the home, or hospice as it later called itself. Luckily, as the rest of the money was disposed of rather rapidly by Lee-Anne. She talked Keith's father into a joint bank account and absconded with the last few thousand.

This Keith learnt from his father's solicitor when he returned to Everton. We could chase after her, the solicitor said. Your poor father's, well . . . rather lost heart.

What the hell, said Keith. It'll be spent by now.

Exploitation?

*   *   *

'Of course you have an agent?'

A small piece of something greyish—mushroom or possibly aubergine—hangs from Eric's moustache. It bounces when he chews.

'What for?'

'Commercials. TV. Whatever.'

'Oh, come on Eric. If you're female and over thirty or size twelve they won't have a bar of you.'

'Don't be so sure. You have a glorious face. I've always said that. Superb. I've told people, Josie McBride could model for the Madonna.'

Josie laughs. 'Perhaps you should be my agent.'

She's tempted to say, then how come it's not my face your little blue eyes keep goggling at? But that would open up dangerous avenues of conversation.

'Me?' he whines. 'I can't even keep myself afloat. Too old. No one wants to know. I admit to you we wouldn't survive if Nancy wasn't so bloody successful. It's all right for you women, you're on the crest. Times are right for you. But the likes of me . . . well someone's got to go under. The funny thing is I never expected it'd be me. What do you think? Did you have me figured for a failure?'

His self pity sours her salad. 'Come on,' she lies, 'you're no failure. Don't talk stupid.'

'I'm a kept man. At my age. Can you imagine how that feels?'

She loses patience. 'If you're a kept man what are we doing at a place like this? You can't afford it. I can't afford it.'

'Ah but we deserve it. The world owes it to us. Josie my love at our age most people have reached the top. We're the generation in power.' His hand flies across the table and lands heavily on hers. 'What's happened to us then?'

'Nothing's happened to me Eric. I'm happy with my life.' She slides her hand out and takes a sip of wine to give it an excuse. A large sip. What the hell's she doing here being dragged into depression? A meal, he'd said, let me buy you a meal—so long since I've seen you. And she hadn't been able to resist a meal.

She'd even been glad to run into him after a morning of dragging herself around offices where she used to feel at home. Waiting for someone to say, Josie how good to see you.

Solly had remembered her. Said there were still a few of her era round, off on a job or out at lunch. It was eleven o'clock. Said, I'll tell them you called in. They're all a bit fraught, he said, you know how it is with this sinking-lid policy.

No one anywhere who might feel inclined or obliged to do her a favour. Most of the new faces about Lake's age so she hated to exhume her past experience. *The Week*? On radio was it? Can't bring it to mind. And this theatre you talk of . . . folded, eh? Same old story! Bit before my time, I'm afraid. Besides (sigh) retrenchment everywhere. All running on a shoestring. Put you on our list if you like but . . . Auditions first Thursday of every month if you care to . . .

'Auditions,' she says to Eric, bringing the talk back to her ground. 'They told me to bloody audition.'

'Last proper part I had,' he says, ' was more than a year ago. Children's serial. I was the sea-lion. Bloody hot in a sea-lion suit.'

Josie giggles. 'How did you move?'

'Dreadfully. I shuffled about on my knees. And I had the most terrible rheumatism at the time. But it was a job.'

Josie frowns sympathetically. She'll have to pay, at least for her own meal. And the wine. He'd ordered, of course, something hideously expensive.

'Well,' she says running out of comforters, 'things might look up after the election.'

'You don't believe that. We're up to our necks. No one's gonna pull us out of this one.'

Josie's caught sight of the dessert trolley. Gâteau, whipped cream, apple strudel, something caramel topped with meringue.

'Something there you fancy?'

'Oh, I couldn't,' she lies, dragging her eyes away. 'I'm fully feasted.'

Eric's waving a finger at the waiter.

'Another bottle of your excellent . . .'

'Not for me, Eric. I still have some places to go this afternoon.'

The waiter waits. Josie smiles at him. 'Coffee would be great.'

He smiles back. He's gorgeous; big grey eyes and a humorous mouth, curls that loll across his forehead. Josie forgets all about dessert.

'We'll have a bottle anyway.' Eric showing off, being assertive. 'The lady may change her mind.'

The waiter's eyes slide towards Josie, he grins lopsided.

When he returns with the bottle she sees the little finger is missing from his right hand.

She takes her glass from Eric before he can refill it. 'As you like,' he says, put out.

'I live a good clean rural life now,' she tries to smoothe it over. 'I can't drink the way I used to. I'd be on my ear.'

Eric empties half his glass in one mouthful. 'Well, that'd be a start. I was hoping to get you on your back.'

Josie replays it in her head to be sure she heard right, even though the back of her mind had seen where this was leading. Then she thinks of Geoff and her wifely obligations. But Eric? Eric is surely quite beyond the pale of duty. She's allowed to draw the line at Eric.

'I hope,' she says, 'that was meant to be a joke.'

Eric shakes his head. At a glance he looks a little like David Niven. Josie mustn't let herself be made to pity him. Some women must fancy David Niven. Eric's Nancy for one.

'I think you'd enjoy yourself,' he offers humbly. 'There are a few things I'm still rather good at.'

Josie laughs. What else is there to do? Laughing with her mouth full of coffee so she chokes and whoops and becomes a minor spectacle. The waiter watches from across the room, ready to fly to her aid or throw her out the door. Josie recovers, dabs at her damp eyes.

'I'm sorry.' For laughing? For choking? 'Eric, this is ridiculous. I really must go. I'll fix them up for my share at the desk. No, really I'd rather. And I hope the job scene improves for you soon. It's bound to. Bye. Don't get up. You may as well stay and finish the bottle.'

She has to wait at the desk while they make up the docket. She lights a cigarette, keeps her back to Eric's table. She can't help feeling sorry for him, pathetic old sod. Must've thought it was worth a try.

'Here,' she mutters to the girl at the desk. 'That's for my meal and half a bottle of wine. He can pay for the rest.'

The girl grins at Josie, knowing and on-side.

'Josie— what are you doing in the big city?'

It's Paul, detouring in off the street and making her exit somehow less obvious. So she forgets that Paul and Juliet were the people she'd been determined not to meet up with. He gives her a peck on the cheek.

'I'm job hunting,' she tells him.

'Business lunch?'

'I ran into an old . . . acquaintance. I'm just over for the day.' In the city everyone tells lies.

'Any luck? With the job?'

'Not so far. Bit rough on the old self-esteem.'

'You and Geoff, you're not . . . ?'

'No, we're not . . .' she grins. 'I'm just hoping for a bit of casual work. Keep my hand in at something.'

'But you could stay over? You could. Geoff won't mind. Juliet'll never forgive you if you don't stay the night.'

'No, really Paul, I ought to get back.'

'Won't hear of it. We'll expect you for dinner.'

Goodbye motel room, goodbye unspecified intentions. 'I'm not sure it's a good idea, Paul.'

'I'll ring Geoff, if that's your worry.'

'That's not my worry. I don't need Geoff's permission to spend a night away from home.'

'You mean us? No worry there. Things have settled down. Guess we both had a touch of the old mid-life you-knows.'

Nevertheless Josie rings about five, when Juliet is almost sure to be home. Josie totters on asphalt-juddered legs to three public phone booths before finding a phone that functions.

'It's me,' she says wearily.

'Great,' says Juliet's estranged voice. 'Paul said he'd run into you. Are you on your way? Where are you? Shall I come and pick you up?'

'No. Don't worry. I'll get a cab or something. I just rang . . . look Jule, are you sure you want me coming round?'

'Stupid. We're dying to see you. Paul's making something special to please your professional palate.'

'A boiled egg and something to put my feet up on would do.'

Josie then teetering off again to look for a wine shop or a bottle store to buy something appropriate to go with Paul's something special. The city like a highwayman robbing you at every corner. Why is it phone boxes are always three blocks from a liquor shop and liquor shops are always three blocks from taxi ranks?

In the taxi—one eye on the sprinting meter while the cab twiddles its thumbs in front of red lights—Josie reflects on a day wasted. Nearly wasted. Lynn Harper, having got back from her eleven o'clock lunch, has promised to give her books to review for morning radio. Commercial radio.

'Culture for the masses, so it's kept short and pretty basic. No words over three syllables, that sort of thing.'

'What are you gonna send me? Harold Robbins?'

'The books'll be okay.'

Lynn has also put Josie on a list of possible free-lance contributors of news reports. Our Motuwairua correspondent? When Lynn joined broadcasting, straight from university, it was Josie who taught her short cuts to research, tricks of voice control and the questions not to ask civil servants.

This afternoon Lynn was indignant on Josie's behalf. 'No one with your expertise should be trudging the streets asking for work. I'll bet if you were a man . . .'

If Josie was a man she would never have left a job for a lover. She didn't really want Lynn's indignation. It felt precariously close to pity.

The taxi turns off Dominion Road. The trees are getting bigger and more numerous. Behind the trees houses grow old gracefully. Three blocks to prepare for a new and ambiguous Juliet. Happily reunited wife? Resentful prisoner, smiling lips and a scheming heart? Defeated woman, settling for the devil she knows? Maybe a bit of all three hopelessly intertwined. Josie could understand that. Consistency belongs to those whose vision is too narrow to enable them to see the other sides.

Four hours later and all she knows for sure is that Juliet is putting up a front. For Josie. Her friend. Josie tries to remember if she'd done or said something unforgivable. Was the letter saying don't ring don't visit really an urgent cry for help?

There was plenty of time while they sat with drinks in front of the fire and Paul clattered and hummed in the kitchen for Juliet to offer some kind of explanation . . . something. Yet she skated breezily around the recent past. The one time she mentioned her stay at Motuwairua she made it sound like a purely social visit.

They talked about Josie's day, about the plight of unemployed school leavers, about Daryl and Sarah and Juliet's daughter who is travelling in Europe (in the shadow of the BOMB) and Juliet's son who lives in a commune near Collingwood.

Then over dinner, when Josie has praised Paul's meal and Paul and Juliet have praised Josie's wine, Paul says to Juliet, wasn't there something on the box tonight?

'Election addresses,' says Josie. 'Tonight it must be . . .' She remembers, and it's a delicate area. She smiles at Juliet and says amiably, '. . . your friend.'

'Oh Christ,' says Paul, 'we're not gonna watch him are we? He turns my stomach. Josie doesn't want to watch him.'

'I don't mind,' says Josie honestly. 'He enrages me. I quite like all that adrenalin.'

'Forget it.' Juliet starts stacking plates noisily. 'You needn't think I'm gonna watch with you two sneering like Cheshire cats.'

'I won't sneer,' says Josie. 'I promise I won't. Only we are entitled to our views. Politics is about the only issue where I actually have convictions. We're all allowed to feel sure about one thing.'

'I wasn't entitled to my view,' says Juliet in flat voice. 'I was hassled and ridiculed.'

'I was trying to help,' says Paul. 'They want martyrs, that lot. They're all rich martyrs and self-appointed Christs.'

Josie grins unwisely.

Juliet sees and turns on her. 'I looked to you for support.' Her voice is heavy with betrayal.

'I tried to be supportive. It's just . . . well it would be easier if you'd

157

picked a cause I could believe in.'

'Then again,' says Juliet darkly, 'you never were exactly strong on sisterhood.'

Josie is stung into a moment's silence. 'What d'you mean?'

'Josie has a mind of her own. That's one of the things I've always admired about her.' Paul has no tact and less timing.

'What d'you mean?' Josie repeats.

'You know. Loyalty. I guess I'm talking about loyalty. I would think, after all these years, your first loyalty would be to your friends. Your women friends.'

That question's hung around in Josie's head for a long time awaiting a definite answer. Even now she sidesteps. 'Come on, Jule, that's like saying you should vote for Margaret Thatcher because she has a womb. I dunno. Maybe I don't even believe in loyalty. It feels like a word people use when they mean stick-up-for-me-even-though-it's-against-your-better-judgement.'

'And of course your judgement *is* so superior!'

'I'm not saying that. No, but it's mine. Look,' she says, needing to explain, 'you remember my mother? Lovely woman, right? Kind neighbour, good citizen and hard-line conservative. She believed in the terror of communism, the inbred superiority of the upper classes, the sanctity of the butter knife. I loved my mother but I had to remind myself of that very forcibly whenever she passed an opinion. We tried not to discuss politics but of course it's there in your attitudes to every little thing. In the end I simply convinced myself that she didn't know any better—that she'd led a sheltered life and wasn't capable of understanding the issues. Stupidity isn't in itself unlovable, but political selfishness and élitism is.

'You see,' she says, pleading. 'The price of my support would be my implicit belief that you're a fool who can't be expected to know any better.'

'But she's not,' says Paul quickly. 'Not entirely. Her main motive wasn't even political. Not in the usual sense. She was out to further my social castration.'

'I beg your pardon?' says Josie.

And Juliet hisses at Josie, 'You see!'

'Hell,' says Josie pushing back her chair. 'Let's clear these dishes and go and watch the self-made man.'

'No,' says Juliet. 'I've remembered what it was we'd thought of watching. There's a debate on pornography on the other channel.'

'Well,' says Josie, trying for a laugh, 'we seem to have a choice—one kind of obscenity or another.' It doesn't work. She realises that laughter's what seems to be lacking. When she and Geoff row it nearly always feels like entertainment.

'Ah, yes, the pornography debate.' Paul leans over and helps himself to one of Josie's cigarettes. Low tar, as a sop to her health. He taps it on the table the way people used to. 'Another milestone in the her-story of the emasculation of mankind. Soon nasty old heterosex will be a thing of the past.'

Juliet and Josie carry the dishes to the bench. 'I'll stack them in,' says Juliet. 'I remember the last time you did it.'

'I'm not used to those things.' Meaning the dishwasher.

'You should get Geoff to buy you one.' Juliet's tone makes Josie search for sharper meanings.

'Geoff,' says Paul sitting there talking to the empty chairs, 'now Geoff ought'a be watching this programme. There's a man who likes a bit of porn. I remember at the other place he had a stack of the stuff. Some of the most riveting filth I've ever clapped eyes on. Isn't that right, Josie.'

'I don't know, Paul.' Josie puts the salt-pig and the pepper grinder in the cupboard side by side. 'I suppose that would depend on the calibre of the filth you were familiar with.' She grins into the cupboard then glances at Juliet for some appreciation. Juliet is bowed over her machine rearranging cups on racks. Her mouth has a hard line.

'Last century,' says Paul, 'the feminists were taken up by the temperance people and it got to the point where they couldn't decide whether they were fighting for women or fighting against the demon grog. This time it's the puritans who have moved in, got them convinced that women'll be happier if they stamp out sex.'

'Exploitative sex,' says Juliet banging shut the dishwasher door. 'Manipulative sex. Unhealthy sex. No one wants to stamp out sex as a loving exchange between equals.'

'Great. So if you're eighteen and you're in love and you've both got UE you qualify for a bit of the old loving exchanges. What about the rest of us? Oh, sorry, I almost forgot—wanking has the seal of approval. Self gratification, as they say, is IN. But not, of course, if it's conducted with the aid of literature or cinematic material of a pornographic nature. Whadda y' think, Josie? I trust you've had a big bonfire of all Geoff's perverted magazines. You wouldn't renege, would you, on the movement? They'd put you on their list you know. Better have a check as soon as you get home. Get rid of anything they can use as evidence.'

Paul cups his hands into a loudhailer. 'Watch out over there Geoff old son.

'They'll be round to get you on a broomstick sonny
Better be ready bout half past eight
Hey Geoffrey don't be late
I gotta be there when they cut your thing off.'

Josie sliding the tablecloth out from beneath his drumming fingers, grinning at him. 'Is it the wine or are you normally this paranoid?'

'It's normal,' says Juliet coldly, marching off into the living room.

Paul looks at Josie and seems to be serious. 'All the signs are there. You think *I'm* joking, but is *she*? It's inevitable; but prophets are always accused of exaggeration. It's going to be a very dismal world – all asexual handholding and boring huis and general consensus. Sometimes I pray that the bomb'll get us first.' He watches Josie's widening smile. 'See. I guessed as much. You are a renegade at heart. Hold out, Josie, don't let them get you. I know what I'm saying. I'm not drunk. If I was drunk I'd hurl myself at your magnificent tits.'

'And I'd slap you around the ears.'

'Oooooooh,' he says on a sliding note. But Josie has folded the cloth and is heading towards the door.

'I bet you twenty dollars,' he says, getting up, 'that we don't get even a glimpse of what it is they're debating.'

'And of course you'd be happy to lose.' But Josie has a distanced look and Paul is rebuked.

Juliet's on her knees building up the fire. 'You're just in time.'

Josie chooses a chair on its own so she can be physically and philosophically non-aligned. 'Hey,' she says, 'that woman – the younger one – lives on the island. I think she does. The face looks familiar.'

'She's from the Women's Centre,' says Juliet as if Josie ought to have known. 'She's involved in a lot of the lesbian separatist stuff.' She says it so authoritatively and with such sombre respect that Josie is careful not to glance at Paul. Instinct tells her he's trying to catch her eye.

None of them talk through the rest of the programme. Tension drifts about the room so palpably that Josie half expects a small blue explosion whenever she strikes a match. When she looks at Juliet she sees her friend's head nodding adamantly or shaking angrily. When she risks a look at Paul she sees his half-closed eyes, the settled smirk. Josie guesses her own viewing expression would be, more than anything, vacuous. It feels like negligence to be forty-six and have no real opinion on filth.

Except perhaps by proxy. The only moment in the first half of the programme that has Josie sitting forward and frowning is the claim (made by the older woman, supported by the younger woman and fielded by no one) that men who perved over pictures of females 'upended, contorted and displaying themselves like mares on heat' did so with contempt and derisive delight.

Yet Josie has watched Geoff (spied on him in their early days when golden-thighed and spike-heeled paper women felt like opposition) gazing at those contrived and cloned pictures with rapt admiration. She's seen him stare at a close-up life-sized and maybe air-brushed vagina – a startlingly graceless and prehensile arrangement of hair and pubescent, glistening oyster flesh – with an expression that could only be described as reverential. She's observed him peering at studies of several women interwoven with the industrious dexterity of Japanese acrobats with a look that carried respect to the edge of awe.

Where, she'd like to know, do these so-called authorities get their information from? How many consumers of filth do they really know? And because she feels they fudged one salient point she loses interest and lies back and lets the words drift away unattended.

Will Geoff be watching? To hear himself be so off-handedly misrepresented. Or will he have gone to the pub? Or has someone dropped in with some new piece of island gossip or the latest election predictions?

Since she's been living with Geoff this is only the third night they've spent apart. Embarrassing; she'd hate her friends to know. That kind of togetherness is prehistoric.

Sillier still she misses him. If she doesn't keep her thoughts busy her whole being slides into a kind of soggy aching centre. Geoff, she says in her head in case he's alone and receptive, I'm sitting here like the big chunk of meat in a very unhappy sandwich. The more I see of other people's relationships the more I appreciate ours.

Yesterday – it seems longer ago, being away from home is disorienting – Josie and Geoff had a fight. It wasn't particularly consequential. On the face of it it was over the Shetland ponies getting through a hole in the fence and vandalising the strawberry plants. Really, it was about the same old things as always, her nagging too much and him lying about too much. It see-sawed through the day with them taking turns at who was contrite and who was still implacably sulking. They made up, conveniently, before bedtime.

The real issue was still there unresolved and maybe unresolvable but they'd frightened it off into a dark corner where it could be for a while comfortably ignored.

Their rows leave Josie finely-tuned and deliciously tremulous. It was quite distressing having to leave the next morning and forgo a day or two of romance. If she was Geoff she would've stayed and said what the hell I can go to the city any old time.

But we are what we are, Josie tells herself. It has a comforting ring.

If Geoff is, at the moment, thinking of Josie he will be thinking ... Oh hell! Something wicked, he said. Promise?

But he didn't really mean it. He knows she never would. Not actually.

On the ferry this morning, still tremulous, she'd got as far as deciding to book herself into a motel. If she hadn't run into Paul, if she hadn't gone to lunch with Eric, who knows?

Why couldn't she have fancied Eric? Why is attraction such an unreasonable and random thing?

Then there's Paul, who wasn't just joking. Paul she could fancy, on a good day and under different circumstances.

One day out on the loose and one and a half propositions. Not bad for a fat woman who won't see forty again. Josie grinning away to herself.

Would Juliet really not be jealous, as she has told Josie more than once? Even with Farley Josie had been jealous, imagining the two of them in silhouetted embrace flat chest pressed against flat chest.

Rule out men with wives. She has, at least, that kind of loyalty to her sisters. Though these days it probably doesn't count for much. That was sixties stuff when half the women in the world were straddled on top of other women's husbands trying to catch up on all those orgasms they'd just learnt they were entitled to. And the rest of the women were spread out on valium and mogadons and apologising to the world for being selfishly hung-up, still, on the idea of monogamy.

In the eighties no one seems to have affairs with other women's husbands. They have affairs with the other women instead. In the eighties it's okay to sleep with anyone you like as long as they're not of the other sex.

You're beginning to sound like Paul, Josie admonishes herself. She glances at Juliet. If I slept with Paul she'd probably pity me!

My trouble is I'm two decades behind the times. I sat out the sexual revolution, and now I've got around to thinking about its possibilities even adultery's out of fashion.

She eases herself forward in the chair, putting her stockinged feet on the floor. 'If you two don't mind I'll sneak off to bed. I had a hard day pounding the streets.'

They move and stretch and make concerned not-minding murmurs. And she can see they are both of them saddened and helpless, knowing it's because of them she's going to bed. She wishes there was something she could say. She wishes it was the way it used to be when she visited them and there wasn't a sense of having to choose sides. When they were Juliet and Paul and even if they disliked each other in private at least their friends could last out the evening.

She's tempted, even now, to say something blunt. Like, what the hell are you doing living together if this is how it is? But they've given no sign of wanting her honest opinion so she says, 'Good night.'

As Josie's about to close the door behind her Juliet says, 'Oh, by the way, you weren't planning to go back first thing were you?'

Josie is cautious, 'Why?'

'Well, Sandi called us after Paul got home, and I said you were coming round. So we tentatively arranged for us all to have lunch somewhere tomorrow.'

'I thought she was still in London.'

'No, it was just for a few months. She's been back a while now.'

'Sure. Be great to see Sandi. I'll get the afternoon ferry.'

But lying in her bed—unable to sleep because without Geoff she feels unanchored, her thoughts gusting in all directions—Josie sighs over lunch with Sandi. Which could still be wriggled out of if she came up with a plausible lie. The truth would be out of the question, it's far too pathetic. Of course she would like to see Sandi whom she hasn't seen for months, but she wants even more to be home with Geoff whom she's been parted from for a whole twenty-four hours.

She thinks, for a while, of Daryl and Sarah, giving it fierce maternal concentration so that maybe one small twinge of her thoughts will sneak into their dreams, day ones or night kind.

She thinks of Geoff again. In case she's too busy tomorrow she pushes her mind into reinventing the night that's shuffling away so slowly.

. . . to tell the truth I just went in to rest my feet . . . a quick brandy to get me through the rest of the afternoon . . . watching me, grey eyes, witty mouth . . . thirty? late twenties? I didn't ask . . . His name was Josh (an inspired name, just uncommon enough to be believable) . . . already rung to book . . . from my room you could see one end of the harbour bridge . . .

Get on with it, Geoff would say; though Josie herself liked a few extraneous details in the interest of authenticity.

. . . began to touch me, here . . . the little finger of his right hand was missing, it got caught in a car door when he was a child . . .

Get on with it, for godsake.

But why the waiter. Why not Eric, that story already half written? Just because he has a wife? But perhaps Nancy, whom Josie has never met, had that morning dispatched him to do something wicked? Had been waiting at home dry mouthed with nervous excitement . . . Poor Nancy. Poor Eric.

She hears Juliet and Paul going to bed, hears one then the other in the bathroom which is next door to her room. The light is switched off. Josie waits. She counts the cars that pass. By the time ten have gone they will be asleep. She's decided to ring Geoff; to offer up the kind of hints that will keep him awake, to get the reassurance of his voice so that she will sleep.

Creeping barefooted into the kitchen. Paul must pay a fortune in heating, no need for the blanket she'd dragged off the bed to drape round herself.

'Did I get you out of bed?' She hears her voice running sweet and thick as honey.

'No.'

'What were you doing?'

'Reading. Where are you?'

'Herne Bay. In a motel. (I can see the end of the harbour bridge) I just rang to say hello.'

'Are you alone?'

She pauses first. 'I am now.'

'You lying to me?'

'Uh-huh. Tell you tomorrow.'

A silence so long she considers retraction. Then, 'D'you miss me?'

'Of course I miss you. Do you miss me?'

'You know I do.'

The door from the passage opens slowly and Paul reaches for the light switch and stands blinking.

'Sweetheart,' she says, 'I have to go. I'll see you tomorrow.' She puts the receiver in its cradle, and smiles at Paul a bit shame-faced. 'I was just ringing Geoff.' (Who may be still holding onto the receiver, hearing hers thud down like a book closed.)

'I fancied a snack,' Paul says. 'I don't sleep much any more.' His legs beneath his bathrobe are spindly and white where Geoff's are solid and brown. Josie can't help making comparisons. 'Geoff, eh? Shouldn't've hung up, I would've had a word. How's the farm going anyway?'

'Fine,' says Josie, pulling the blanket round her even though it's warm enough. Wondering why it feels okay to discuss your man's failings with other women but not with other men.

Paul looks sly. 'But it wasn't really Geoff, was it?'

'It was Geoff.'

'Come on. You don't have to . . . You know I wouldn't breathe a word.'

'It was though.'

'And lunch today. I suppose that was Geoff too? You must think I'm dense.'

'Well, now you mention it . . .'

He grins weakly. 'Welsh rarebit and coffee for two?'

'No thanks,' she says. 'Not for me. I'm off to bed. And if you can't sleep maybe you should switch to cocoa. Good night again.'

Josie scuttling back to bed as fast as a large lady in a brushed cotton nightie can scuttle without harm. Pulling the bedclothes up to her ears.

Geoff my darling, my delicacy, I hope you enjoy the authorised version because it looks like that's all you'll ever get. One whiff, one wink of the real thing and I'm off thump thump with my ears flying out behind. To hide in the dark unembarrassing safety of this spare burrow.

*　　　*　　　*

'You'll definitely be back Thursday?'

'Don't worry.' But Shisha says this so easily, so breezily that Maureen feels anxiety sprouting.

'Her appointment's eleven on Friday.' She's said that already.

'Don't worry,' says Shisha. About the optician or her own reliability?

Shisha heaves the bag into the boys' room. 'She can top and tail with Mickey. She loves Mickey.'

Mickey and Leah. Shisha thinks they're so cute together, the way they cuddle and carry on. They're only four, for godsake, where's the harm, it's natural. But Maureen finds it hard to think of Leah as a four-year-old. She seems more like a well-proportioned dwarf. Cute isn't the word that comes to mind when Maureen sees Leah tweaking and licking away at her son's teddybear body. The minute Shisha's gone Maureen will swoop upon them with more traditional infant diversions.

But the mention of bed-sharing has reminded her, and who better to ask . . .

'Shisha,' she says, 'how does Leah . . . ? I mean is she maybe too young to react, you know, to you and Ben, or you and anyone if she knows you've spent the night . . . ?'

'Ha. Nothing escapes her. She's got it sussed all right, that one. Mind you,' Shisha looks wise, 'how Leah reacts and how your lot would react is a whole different bag.' She yawns, raising her arms high above her head. Today she is wearing layers of clothes like a desert nomad. A scarf round her neck and another round her head. 'Don't let that put you off,' she says when the yarn's completed. 'They get used to anything, kids. I'll just sneak out while she's not looking.'

At the door she pauses and says in a stage whisper, 'When I get back you'll have to tell me all about it.'

'Nothing to tell.'

'Well make sure there is by the time I get back.'

Leah doesn't cling or nestle (except with Mickey), and now on Maureen's lap she holds her body rigid as she screams. The tears fall onto Maureen's arm.

'Of course she's coming back,' prays Maureen, pressing her cheek against the child's taut neck. 'Won't be long and Shisha'll come and get you. She's gone to school for a few days to learn clever things. A kind of school. Soon she'll be back and take you home. Come on now, there's a good girl. Wouldn't you like to play with Mickey? It's clearing up now, we can find some trucks and you can play outside in the dirt. Come on, if you keep crying you'll make Mickey cry too.'

It's Sunday. Thursday isn't even a certainty on the horizon. Friday another trek into the city. Alan would love to go to Keith's again but the hint she dropped was left lying there. Maybe he didn't notice, but she doesn't like to ask straight out. He'll think it's going to be every second week.

What if Shisha misses the boat on Thursday?

The specialist didn't seem to do very much. They were in there for about twenty minutes. How much would a specialist make in an hour? The bill will come at the end of the month. And after that the optician's bill. Plus the cost of Friday's trip to Auckland. Goodbye TV. Just when she'd started reading the TV pages in the *Star*. Deirdre Barlow having an affair with Mike Baldwin. And Eddie Yates marrying a nice girl, which shows there's hope for everyone!

Not that she begrudges the cost of the specialist when it's for Carly. But if only they could've got her straight into the optician's that same afternoon. 'Friday two weeks,' the specialist's secretary said beaming as though she had done them a huge favour by making the appointment. The functioning world hasn't the faintest concept of how life is in the child-rearing belt.

When a Cabinet Minister has to travel he gets fifty-eight dollars a day. Over and above his salary. The salary is getting on for sixty thousand dollars a year. Imagine earning all that, and if you were single all of it just for you! Maureen has started buying the paper regularly. Alan has to cut out things and take them to school for current affairs. Maureen makes herself read the news stories as if she was part of a world where big things happened. She'd like to be better informed and to hold opinions that didn't start toppling the minute someone else leant on them. Though who is there to hear her opinions? Both Shisha and Keith seem more interested in having her listen to theirs.

Her children would listen. Carly would. Educate a girl, says Alice, and you educate a whole family.

When Alice was a girl she had a glory box. She started embroidering pillow cases to put away when she was in standard six. Alice has always known as much as she wants to know and no more. She has a tidy mind. When she's not envying her sister, Maureen fears for her but doesn't know why.

Shisha, lucky Shisha, over in the city doing a course in fabric art. Looking to her future, maybe a career if she doesn't manage to land her R&B man—and a hobby even if she does.

Maureen only willing to look ahead as far as Friday. When they will catch the morning ferry and Maureen will watch from an extra chair while Carly looks into lights and reads ZHPLKSM, and in due course Carly will have glasses and no more headaches.

Carly four-eyes. Fat, mousey bespectacled child. A teenaged Carly with dimpled white knees hanging round the grownups where it's safer. The one who does the washing-up at parties because it's better to be useful than to be nothing at all. No matter what they say it's worse for girls.

And Maureen, with her back against the bedroom door, has a brief but uninterrupted weep on behalf of Carly, sensible, kindhearted Carly who deserves at least the kind of average good looks her mother has. But gets, like a slap from God, landed with a disability. Which will draw attention to her other doubtful features.

Keith wears contact lenses. He took one out to show the kids then replaced it. A bit like a magician's trick. About seventy dollars each to replace if he loses them so what must glasses cost?

'I suppose it was vanity,' he said. 'Or depression. For years I'd been this little weed in glasses.'

'Did it make a difference?'

'To me it did. Instead of thinking of myself as a little weed in glasses I thought of myself as a little weed in contacts.'

Carly will make those kind of jokes when she grows up. When her children bleed Maureen haemorrhages. How can Shisha, also a mother, be detached from Leah to the point of indifference? Maureen didn't give birth to three small beings, she was sliced up like an earthworm and the raw edges have never healed. She exists in four independently moving parts, inviting pain. Did her own mother once feel this way? Is it normal? Do you grow out of it or does the vulnerability last forever? If you had ten children would the feeling be that much more intense or simply spread more thinly?

The magazine articles that have shown Maureen so much about herself answer none of these questions. Freedom, they say. Rights. Independence. Strength. And, motherhood. But they never explain how the last can fit together with the others. Don't the women who write remember how it was? Are they childless, or maybe Shisha kind of mothers who have evolved beyond being too fussed about their kids and so can't imagine how other mothers might feel?

Yet even Bruce understood that much. He had a sure instinct for vulnerability. As soon as Alan was old enough.

'See this,' Bruce would say under the guise of paternal discipline, producing a chocolate bar or a bag of jelly beans. 'I was going to give it to you son, but I don't much like the way you've been behaving.' And he'd slide it back into his pocket, holding in a smile, watching the mother from the corner of his eye.

Later, after Alan had greased and hovered for a hopeful hour or more, playing butterwouldn'tmelt, Bruce would dig out the confection, unwrap it and eat it slowly bite by savoured bite. Not watching the boy, watching Maureen again.

She soon learned the futility of objecting and would pretend instead not to notice. To take away that satisfaction. And sometimes he would relent and give Alan the last fragment or the last few lollies in the bottom of the bag. So Alan never learned; never quite abandoned hoping.

Neither did Maureen, so Carly was born, then Mickey. And when there were five of them – a real family – Bruce would sometimes agree when his night off fell in the weekend that they could all go to the beach, or the zoo. And once or twice they really did. But other times there would be preparation and excitement, she would have the children spruce, the bottles and napkins in the bag, her baby-stretched belly folded into her best trousers . . . Then Bruce would remember there was a test match on telly or he'd promised to help one of the guys from work shift house or the car wasn't really safe to use until they got a new brake cable. Watching Maureen with his held-in smile.

'Why,' she sometimes asked him through her trapped tears. 'Why do you do these things?'

'I don't know.'

No more did Maureen know. But when she thought back looking for signs and causes she saw – though there seemed to be no *why* – when it had begun. From the day she came home from the hospital with Alan, his cord still hanging from the knot like a dying twig, Bruce needed to hurt her.

He'd been so pleased about her being pregnant. He couldn't have known he was going to hate her for being a mother until she was one, and by then it was too late.

'We're hungry,' says Leah who always is. So Maureen halves an apple and gouges out the core.

'I'll make you some lunch soon so that's all you get till then, right?'

They nod and munch. If the other two see them they'll want one too.

'We want you to find something for us to do,' says Leah.

Maureen sighs but sees she has brought this on herself by not trusting them to their own devices. Or vices as the case may be. 'What d'you want to do? What sort of thing?'

'Shisha brought some toys for me.'

'Well go and get them then.'

'Can't open it.'

Maureen shakes the contents of Leah's bag onto the floor and Mickey grabs with one fist the doll with breasts and in the other a wind-up duck. Leah takes the doll from him, but when she wants the duck as well he hangs onto it grimly. Leah, cunning, picks up a worn old cloth pig and fondles it like a treasure. Mickey reaches out for the pig and Leah snatches away the duck. Mickey holds the pig in front of him and beams at it. Maureen has to restrain herself from sweeping the boy up in a hug. It's hard to resist an underdog, especially when he's yours.

She packs Leah's clothes back into the bag. They smell of damp and of Shisha's perfume. Elegant, adult kind of clothes with labels that say Sneeze and Candybell. Nothing from St Mark. If Maureen lied a little to the welfare people her children could also wear snappy little one-owner triple-stitched outfits. That being arguably just another brand of maternal devotion, and who's to say one kind is superior to another? Alan, if he had the choice would certainly prefer . . .

But things are going to get easier, so Keith says. 'It'll take a few weeks, even maybe months but then –'

He'd whistled and grinned all through the election results. Towards the end he couldn't even sit down and Maureen had wished she had more enthusiasm so they could be delighted together.

'I would've voted for them,' she said. 'I went down but I wasn't on the list.'

He was quite shocked. 'You should've checked.'

'I know, but I just kept forgetting. Anyway I still can't see it'll make much difference in the end, not to people like me. I voted for them last time. They seem to do better without my support.' She studied Keith for a while. 'I wouldn't have thought you'd be all that interested.'

He shrugged. 'Maybe it's a habit. No, it's the difference somehow between a door being shut and a door being open. I mean we may still not be able to afford to go anywhere but at least now we'll be able to look out.'

Maureen had felt a bit sorry for him, the way he was so pleased by every new result. She thought if he'd had a family or even plenty of friends he wouldn't have to care as much about things you couldn't change anyway, that happened or didn't happen. She tried to seem a bit more enthusiastic than she felt. It was the first time they'd been invited to someone's house since they'd been on the island.

And really it was a good night. The kids had behaved well considering it wasn't the kind of TV they'd been wanting to see. Keith's house isn't in much better condition than hers, but it can't matter so much when there aren't children. Still, you'd think he'd fix his own place up first.

Not really his own though, because of the lesbian. She thinks of

Daphne as the lesbian because that's about all she has to go on. Also because it's of interest. It has an authoritative ring, more like a career than a sexual preference. Maureen has reached twenty-eight without meeting an acknowledged lesbian. She can't even spot them in the street the way Bruce claimed he could. But then she can't even tell the Maoris from the Pacific Islanders the way everybody else seems to be able to.

She asked Keith, what's she like?

'Hitler,' he said.

'Down to the moustache?'

'No,' he said, 'just her personality. She looks like . . . let me see . . . like Benny Hill.'

'That's unkind.'

'She's unkind. All the time. Especially to me. And I imagine she wouldn't be terribly kind to you. She's not very impressed by women who go about with men.'

'It's hardly any of her business.'

'Everything is Daphne's business.' He said it without malice. Even with a kind of pride the way guard-dog owners describe their animal's viciousness. And for a moment a cloud of doubt drifted between Maureen and the political commentator who was confirming it was indeed a nationwide swing to Labour. Could Keith have just invented the lesbianism to throw off suspicion? She felt a twinge of something that could have been jealousy or just the ugly whisperings of distrust.

Silly, because there were all those posters on the walls and the issues of *Dyke News* and *Earthlinks* that Mickey had to be dragged away from before he caused a homosexual avalanche.

After that night at Keith's Maureen began to wonder if there couldn't be some better arrangement than her and Carly sharing a room. If she got bunks, she suggested, maybe Carly could go in with the boys. But neither Alan nor Carly wanted that.

'Why, Mum? Why can't I just stay in here with you?'

'Because,' said Maureen digging the girl in the ribs, 'you fart too much.'

'I do not.'

It probably doesn't matter anyway. So far she and Keith have got no closer than her academic viewing of his contact lens swimming in his eyeball. And that may be as near as they'll ever get. More would seem to require a degree of boldness neither of them possesses.

Then again there hasn't really been an opportunity. If she could get

Shisha to babysit for just one night . . .

Maureen doesn't even want to. Not particularly. And yet—

They're like a couple of polite shoppers jammed in the bottleneck of the checkout counter saying, after you, and, no, please you go first. And unless they both just back away and return to wandering the aisles one of them is going to have to shove on in. Even if it proves just to be embarrassing.

It would clear the air, Maureen tells herself. If nothing else it'd clear the air. Besides he's been so good to Alan, so kind to them all, he deserves something in return. At least to know just where he stands.

And if I don't someone else'll come along who will—and then I'll lose him as a friend.

Thinks Maureen, preparing to grin and bear it.

THE HANDWRITING IS astonishingly like her own. The letter—a laboured misspelt affair in black ballpoint—is an unremarkable communication concerned with the weather, a minor back injury incurred at soccer and the universal stupidity of the teaching profession.

The bit that has transfixed Josie, so that she now has to read it aloud to Geoff, is a kind of decorative addition that snakes around the edge of the page in green ink, heavily asterisked at beginning and end.

'Behold I come as a thief. Blessed is he that watches and keep his garments, lest he walk naked and they see his shame. D'you think we're supposed to take it personally?'

He says, 'You remembered the nails?'

'Yes.'

'The netting?'

'They only had five metres. Expecting some more Friday.'

'And that was all the mail?'

'Power bill.'

He grunts and lifts the chainsaw. It starts first pull, screaming and slicing through the timber. Josie goes to the Land-Rover and drags out the roll of netting. I could do with a hand, he'd said. But there was nothing he couldn't have done himself. Fetching and carrying so she feels like an errand boy. And then just standing around which he knows she hates when she could be doing something useful, even out here. But he never likes to explain a job so she can learn it.

If she complains he's liable to pass the saw over to her and walk off home. Leaving her with something to do. He only wants her round for the company. Likes to know that beyond the deafening wall of sound she is there. But company's a two way thing; Josie waits for the saw to stop.

'Why are you being like this?'

'Like what?'

'The way you're being. You know. I wanted an opinion before. About Daryl's letter. Some response. Some small person-to-person communication on a matter of some concern to me.'

He gives this a few moments' thought.

'Oh,' he says, beautifully rounded. And when she stands, waiting, getting angrier, he explains, 'That was it. That was my considered reply that I was, I admit, remiss in not giving you at the time.'

'Oh?'

'It means forget it. Let the kid be. Stop dangling your finger in his pie.'

Josie sags. 'Do I meddle?'

'Oh, I wouldn't exactly say meddle. More like you want to step into other people's lives and take over.' He sees he's hurting her feelings and says more gently, 'Just let people round you work out their own lives.'

'I can't,' she says with abject honesty. 'It feels like too great a risk.'

She lies awake trying to work out why her son should need the security of a god or congregation. As if by identifying the reason and apportioning blame she can plant a few seeds of doubt to temper this irrational faith of his. Will Sarah in turn embrace a cause, trade all doubts for the certain voice of dogma? At least, she reminds herself, Lake's intolerance is generalised and soundly based. Whatever happened to scepticism? Has it been swept out the door in this frightening new age of absolutes?

Josie lies in the dark and feels lonely. Old. A relic of times past. She tries to summon up her buoyancy-list of visible survivors: Tina Turner, stomping the screen in mini-skirt and haystack hair, Josie's age and a grandmother, out there proving a point, every grind and shimmy a salute to life after forty. And Mick Jagger and the rest of the Stones, still strutting, still preening and crowing and doing it right without concessions. Even Cliff Richard (unfortunate choice, she's trying to get away from God). There must be others. Surely there must be others still grinding and burning as if they've a right; bugger this growing old gracefully, what's the point of that?

Yet it seems to be what Josie's doing these days. She has her life wonderfully under control. Except she doesn't sleep very well; quite a few nights lately she's lain awake listening to Geoff breathing, to the sea below, to the occasional car winding down the road to Whiripare, to the moans and yelps of Hogg's dream soundtrack and the half-witted crowing of their new unsynchronised rooster.

Tonight all these sounds are upstaged by the wind and the tentative splashing of rain accompanied by distant thunder. A storm has hung in the air all afternoon so it will be a relief, thinks Josie, to have it over with.

But as the rain becomes more determined she starts to worry about the ponies who are in the boundary paddock without much shelter. Sneezie is expecting any day now which seems to place some special burden of responsibility on Josie. And she worries too about the sheep as if the weather is somehow also her responsibility. Too long a mother, she tells herself. It was the same up north—that wearying, helpless sense of concern for the animals known and unknown. She wishes this time they'd stuck with plants despite her preferences.

Soon there will be more animals. Geoff's latest brainwave is boarding kennels. His application for a permit has yet to be considered by the council but in characteristic confidence he's begun work on the runs. Hogg won't be happy if the scheme goes ahead. Even Josie is in two minds about it.

In the last few weeks the place has begun to look thoroughly utilised and feasibly productive. The bore is down and water, when they need it, will flow into troughs and down irrigation hoses. The small flock of black sheep are prospering. The hens produce enough eggs for Josie to sell four dozen a week to Jackie Brodie at the store. The garlic is sending out green stalks, the strawberries still show some signs of life and Josie's plants in her home greenhouse struggle on bravely despite her lack of expertise. The ponies—Grumpy, Happy, Sneezie and Dopey—loiter with intent around the fenceline. Together they're a vicious mob but individually they're docile enough.

The lean-to was to be converted into a piggery until Geoff got sidetracked into kennels. They've planted an orchard down beside the gully where the native bush grows.

Josie is beginning to fear they'll be over-extended. In the last few weeks Geoff has been working with abnormal energy and stamina, at least eight hours a day. His visitors call by and find the house empty, or only Josie at her typewriter and the cookery books from which she culls and adapts her recipes. At night he falls asleep too soon and sleeps too soundly so she doesn't like to wake him for what she tells her querulous body is only, after all, a habit.

They live like a normal couple. She suspects him of trickery. An ulterior motive which has to do with her. She's not used to being on the periphery of his life; it feels empty and joyless out there. She's beginning to ask herself, what's the point?

Of living with someone.

Of life.

She's beginning to think about what she could've achieved in the last seven years if—

The lightning has moved closer now, thunder booms above the hammering rain. Josie braces herself for the sound of something collapsing, thanks providence or Daryl's god that they live on high ground, wonders about the real facts on tidal waves.

Geoff wakes; the instant alert awakening of an easy sleeper. 'Christ. How long's this been going on?'

'An hour or two.'

'I'd better shift those horses.'

Already he's out of bed, dragging on trousers.

'I'll come too. But where'll we put them?'

'Should bring Sneezie up by the house. Storm might bring her on. Guess the others could go in the orchard.'

'Our trees!'

'They won't be worrying about food in this.'

They squelch across the paddock in their gumboots, taking the shortest route, climbing fences. The wires groan beneath Josie and she has problems trying to extricate the barbed wire from her trousers without losing her balance. Geoff waits but doesn't help. Hogg, having tested the rain for a couple of metres, has decided to give the outing a miss.

Despite her stinging face, the rain trickling down her neck and the rising damp in her boots Josie is enjoying herself. As they skirt around the strawberries she catches up with Geoff and takes his hand. He gives hers a squeeze which could mean anything or nothing at all.

The ponies are sardined together in the far corner of the paddock. Geoff runs his hands over Sneezie's swollen belly and looks beneath her tail and doesn't think anything will happen tonight.

'We'll leave her with the others,' he shouts at Josie, the wind whipping back his words. He puts the bridle on Sneezie and a halter rope on Dopey and hands the bridle reins to Josie.

The other two follow behind, heads jammed against rumps as if they are, altogether, only two articulated eight-legged ponies. Josie feels burdened by the animals' trust, by the terrible power of ownership.

When they let them go in the orchard paddock the ponies ignore the waiting shelter of bush and crowd hopefully against the gate. Geoff tries to shoo them off then gives up. 'Well fuck you lot. We've got ourselves drenched for you. Hope you all get struck by lightning.'

On the way back to the house they use the gates and Geoff takes Josie's hand. So after a hot bath and a pot of tea it seems all right to ask, 'What's wrong, love? Why have you been so . . . distant lately?'

'Distant? Have I? Guess I just got tied up with the work.'

'Well that's what I mean. All this efficiency, it's not like you.'

'Are you complaining? Do I hear you right? I thought that was exactly what you wanted?'

'Well, yes it is, but—'

'I was trying to please you.'

He sounds so genuine. Why is she not quite able to believe; because she puts so little into trying to please him?

It's over a month since she presented Geoff with three-fingered Josh of the lilting lips and childhood accident. Josh was well-received. He served his purpose and was summoned back for encores until his story became threadbare with inconsistencies showing through.

Josie's fault. She should've confined herself to action replays instead of trying for a touch of poetry, for ambiance, for conversational fragments. She couldn't resist revising and improving until she came up with a version *she* could believe in. By then Geoff was bored with suspending disbelief and Josh was banished as a fraud.

Yet tonight, when they have crawled back to bed and are warm and content and the rain on the roof is just as heavy but no longer threatening, he says: 'Tell me about . . . you know, whatever his name was.'

'The waiter?' she prompts, a bit surprised. 'Josh?'

'No,' he says disdainfully, 'the real one. Lake's father.'

'Him? Fleeting Henry?' And she feels a welling of sadness. Is that the best I have to offer him?

*   *   *

Maureen picks snowdrops from the roadside while she waits for Mickey to catch up. The stems smell of onions, she was expecting the spring fragrance of daffodils. By the time she gets home the flowers will be bruised and limp. She drops them one by one, silently apologising; sorry about that, I stole you for nothing.

With or without daffodils it is spring on Motuwairua. She can feel it in the air, in the sharp smell of the sea, in the unaccustomed buoyancy of her heart.

Maureen and Mickey are making the slow trek home from play centre. Shisha must be over in the city. Or perhaps their road was impassable after last week's storm. Perhaps she's just got bored with play centre. She and Leah weren't there Tuesday and again today.

The other parents are more friendly when Shisha isn't around. If

Shisha hadn't been so forward from the start Maureen might have other friends of a different kind.

Still, it's spring and they have survived. Nothing worse than common colds despite the drawbacks of the cottage and the big ones having to walk sometimes to school in bad weather when it was nearing benefit day and she didn't have the cash for bus fares.

Of course there was Alan's accident, but all kids have accidents and no real harm done.

No one can point a finger and say, you should never have left him, the kids have suffered, you made a bad decision. No one can say Maureen isn't as good as any mother can be. In her circumstances.

But Alan and Carly still aren't very happy at school. Carly dislikes her teacher, Alan sits alone at lunchtimes, still without friends. Maureen tells them, lots of people don't like school but you just have to put up with it. She has no alternatives to offer.

Maureen liked school. It was a whole lot better than being at home. She's offered to go and talk to their teachers but they say that would make things worse, that the teachers would take it out on them. She wonders if she should go anyway, but what should she say? Why don't you like my children? Why do you let them be unhappy?

They'd say, you have difficult children, Mrs Harrison. Like saying, you have bad breath, Mrs Harrison.

'But I clean my teeth regularly.'

'Nevertheless, Mrs Harrison . . .'

And in Alan's case perhaps they would be right.

On schooldays they both bring home with them a mood of restless misery and spread it about the cottage, but what can she do? It's the way things are, she tells them, so just try and make the best of it.

Do as I do.

At the bottom of their road the mail van pulls up alongside Maureen and Mickey and the mailwoman leans away from them sorting through her letters. Maureen walks on so the woman has to drive after them holding the two letters out the window. Maureen's surprised that the woman even knows who she is. It's reassuring to be known by the mailwoman. Especially considering Maureen hardly gets any mail.

One is a bill addressed, as most of them are, to Mr M. Harrison. She drops it unopened into her bag. The other is from Alice.

Maureen puts her bag, which is heavy with groceries, down in the midst of roadside honeysuckle and tears the letter open. A newspaper clipping flutters to the ground. Half of an advertisement for cut-price paint. She turns it over.

IMPRISONED FOR THEFT

A twenty-nine year old former security guard, Bruce Mervyn Harrison of Mangere, was sentenced to eight months' detention on joint charges of theft and false pretences.

Harrison was convicted of stealing a cheque book and subsequently passing off as his own cheques to the value of $5,735. His counsel, Mr W.B. Stanton, said that his client had been under considerable financial and emotional stress at the time of the offence. Late last year he was deserted by his wife who took their children with her. He was overcommitted to hire purchase companies and owed maintenance payments to the Department of Social Welfare.

Maureen reads it through twice, then she unfolds Alice's accompanying note.

We thought you might have missed this. The leopard finally displays his spots! Shows you're well out of it. We thought we might come over, Simon and I, in the holidays for a day or two if it's convenient. Perhaps you could ring and let us know if you have other plans. And what would we need to bring etc.

Flea powder, bedding, a port-a-loo, mosquito nets, mattresses, gumboots. But that would put Alice off completely. Why couldn't she have come last holidays when Maureen had needed the sound of an adult voice? Now it no longer seems such a good idea.

Scrunch, scrunch up the hill trying to find out what she thinks about Bruce in prison. Mickey dragging behind on her hand so she's taking his weight as well as the stuff in her bag. Wild roses beside the road showing new growth, glimpses of Auckland between the trees and over punga fronds. Her here. Him here. Trying to imagine—

An exercise yard. Men in ill-fitting clothes that never lose their institution smell. Tin plates, trestle tables, dour wardens, raging queens.

The images are borrowed from movies and don't convince. She ought to feel something definite. Satisfaction or even pity. But the thought that shoulders all else aside is *almost six thousand dollars*.

He could've. You'd really think he would've.

Managed to buy his kids Christmas presents. Or even birthday. He could've sent them care of Alice or even care of Maureen's mother come to that. No wonder he didn't come looking for them, he had better things to do.

At least for a few months she'll know where he is. No need to start at shadows or feel apprehensive in the moving dark. Relief is near

179

enough to a definite emotion.

She's home, waiting for the jug to boil before the other thought comes to her. If Bruce is a criminal maybe he's not such a representative male after all! It seems like a reason for tentative optimism about the world.

Maureen and Carly still sleep in the same room.

In the weekend Keith took them all for a drive. They went to the very end of the Kamakama road which stops just past the garage at a stony beach with a small jetty. Keith had brought fishing lines and they took turns but only caught a handful of sprats.

On the way back they stopped and walked through an old graveyard and climbed the Tautoro hill with its man-made terraces from the time when it was a pa site and the scene of a battle. But Alan, who was their source of information having been there on a school trip, was vague on details.

The boy trailed right behind Keith like a loose thread. Maureen let him ride in the cab with Keith while she and the other two sat out the back. She didn't want a tantrum to spoil their day. There was never a time when she and Keith were alone together.

When she was climbing the fence that led to the graveyard Keith had taken her hand to steady her. As a friend would, yet it hadn't felt as inconsequential as a friendly hand should seem. She'd worried about when to let go, not wanting to be first in case it seemed like a rejection. It felt to her that Keith was thinking the same thing. Then they'd both seen Alan watching as if he understood all that and more. Alan's face composed of neon-lit capital letters flashing DISMAY. So that their hands fell apart and Keith had asked her with his eyebrows up: 'Is it you he wants sole ownership of, or me?'

'I'm not sure,' she muttered back at him, 'but I think it might be you.'

They had dinner at her place. Mince and vegetables. She feels sorry for people who have to suffer her cooking. Keith went home not long after. They couldn't go to Keith's place because the lesbian was there with her lesbian friends.

Maureen unpacks the groceries from her bag and finds the bill from the specialist clinging damply to the defrosting sausages. Forty-six dollars. Which can't be exorbitant. But when you think about what it could buy. And the optician's bill still to come including the cost of the glasses.

Which arrived by registered mail almost two weeks ago. 'They make me look clever,' said Carly.

'My darling you *are* clever,' said Maureen, and remembered just in time. 'You're all clever, all three of you.'

Maybe times really have changed and these days looking clever counts. If she's teased at school Carly makes no mention of it. All the same Maureen is trying hard to discourage Carly's domestic bent for baking scones and little biscuits. Fat is another matter.

Every day those still-unpaid-for glasses are borne by Carly's small, slightly upturned nose into a hazardous world. And Maureen has said so often, you must take care of them I can't afford to replace them, that Carly wears them with the ostentatious dignity of diamonds. And now when Alan fights with his sister Maureen intervenes more quickly, less judiciously. So that Alan agonises to the universe: 'Why is it always her? Why couldn't it have been me that got to wear glasses?'

Next week Carly turns seven. She wants a party. She wants to invite Lilly and Mahia and her new and best friend Tanya. And she doesn't want Alan at her party spoiling things.

Keith would no doubt have Alan if Maureen asked him. But is it fair for Carly to have a proper party with friends when the boys only had family parties? Mickey wouldn't mind and Alan doesn't have friends his own age. All the same, would it be *fair*?

And what about the cost?

And what about the consequences for Carly? None of her friends have yet come to the house. They may be shocked by what they find. They may be accustomed to gleaming formica and flush toilets. Three supercilious seven-year-olds delivered by three impeccable mums; who may, god forbid, expect to stay for the party.

Yet Carly is plain and plump and bespectacled. She deserves a proper party, with friends.

'Mum,' says Carly, conscientious, with her head propped above her spelling list and her glasses sliding down her nose, 'you know my party . . .'

Maureen's heart groans. She says, 'Mmmm?'

'Well I've been thinking that Lilly's really stupid, and she's mostly Mahia's friend now, and really I only want Tanya to come because she's really my real friend.'

'If you're sure,' says Maureen. Strangling a whoop and a skip, so fortuitously reprieved.

And there's a knock on the door so she floats across to open it. Outside is a young man wearing an old herringbone tweed coat a few sizes too big for him. Jug handle ears and pale eyes with even paler lashes. He blinks at Maureen like a fledgling owl caught by a torch beam.

'I'm Bennie,' he says. 'Shisha's Bennie.'

'Has something happened?'

'I don't know,' he says morosely and shuffles a bit.

'D'you want to come in?'

Inside he looks around the kitchen and takes a seat at the table beside Carly. 'Is that your homework?'

Carly nods, looking him up and down.

Into the silence Maureen asks, 'Would you like a cup of tea?'

'I'd really appreciate a glass of water if that's all right.'

So Maureen fills a glass at the sink and takes it to him and Bennie sips away as if it's wine, and Alan and Mickey come through to have a look and Maureen says, 'This is Ben and this is Alan and Mickey and Carly beside you.'

Bennie nods at each of them in turn and takes a few more sips of water. Then he says to Maureen, 'I suppose Shisha's told you about me?'

Oh she has, indeed she has. In detail. 'She has mentioned you.'

'D'you know where she is by any chance?'

'Where?'

'Dunno. That's why I came here. She took off in the weekend, took the van like. Said she was gonna leave Leah with you for a couple of days. That was Saturday.'

'We were out all Saturday.'

'We still got the truck down there but no spare and the tyre was flat so I had to walk. Didn't get a lift till just past Tautoro and then only a bit of a one. Then I had to ask at all these places till I found someone who thought they knew where you lived.' He's saying all this as if it's Maureen's fault. 'I thought she must be here.'

'You can search,' says Maureen throwing out her palms in a kind of a joke.

Bennie, or Ben, shakes his head.

Carly taps out the silent seconds with her pencil. Her chin rests on one hand and she stares unblinkingly at Bennie. Maureen frowns across at her but can't catch the girl's eye.

'She relies on you,' says Bennie, still in his accusing voice. 'You can help her if you want to.'

'What d'you mean?'

'She was intending to leave the kid here.'

182

'You said.'

'She hates men. She's trying to work it through but she still does. That's why nothing I do will make any difference.'

'Leah, are you talking about?'

'You see how she treats her?'

Maureen feels she's in the rapids, nothing to hang on to. 'If you're looking for her, why don't you go over to the city?'

'You know, you're not what I expected. She doesn't have many friends, not really.'

Maureen is thinking there are no boats until morning and he's going to ask if he can sleep here the night. 'She might be on her way right now, on the last boat. Don't you think it'd be easier to just go home and wait. She's bound to turn up eventually.'

'She's got the van. The barge got in hours ago.' He stares at Maureen. 'I'm sorry. I know you don't want me here.' He stands up. The overcoat comes down to his ankles. He looks young and lost.

'It's not that,' she says.

'It's all right. Thank you for the glass of water.'

'If she comes here I'll tell her you were looking.'

Outside, his face in the dark, the kitchen light shining on his boots and the green socks drawn up over the bottom of his baggy trousers, he says, 'She's driving me crazy.'

Shisha turns up not the next morning but the one after. She's bought some new recycled clothes, including a dress which she doesn't want, it's not her style but it might do Maureen.

'It's nice, but I never wear dresses.'

'You should. Men find dresses sexy.'

'Ben came looking for you the other night.'

'Ben. What'd you think? Bit weird eh?' Shisha contorts her face into an owlish Bennie shape and Maureen can't help laughing. 'You can see why I need to get away whenever I can.'

'He said,' and Maureen grins a bit because Shisha is all charged up with city energy, and it's daylight, and Shisha has given Maureen an apricot coloured dress, 'that you're driving him crazy.'

'Me?' says Shisha. She flings out her arms and becomes Frank Sinatra. 'Me. I'm driving him crazy.

What can I do?

What can I do?

Because me, I'm driving Ben crazy.

But what can we do?

Cos I'm crazy too.'

Mickey and Leah watch her with delight and begin to bob about the floor in their version of song and dance.

'Okay,' says Shisha, 'that's enough. Knock it off now.'

The children stop self-consciously and slide off to Mickey's room.

'He seemed very unhappy,' says Maureen. 'Ben I mean. As if . . . well as if he needed some kind of help.'

Shisha's eyebrows flick the thought aside. 'You're not going away for the holidays?' she asks.

Maureen shakes her head.

'Ah, that's a relief. Look I've met these really neat people, a sort of travelling theatre troupe. They're off south in the holidays and they want me to go with them. Of course it'd be a drag for Leah. So you won't mind will you? Only a week or so?'

'I can't really,' says Maureen. 'My sister and her boy are coming to stay, there just wouldn't be room.'

'Nonsense. She can toss in with Mick. She's tiny, she don't take up much room you know.'

Maureen takes a large breath. 'I'm sorry, Shisha, but no. I just can't have her. Three kids and visitors is more than enough for the holidays.'

In a way Maureen can't quite figure she knows it's Bennie who gave her the courage.

*　　　*　　　*

'I suppose,' says Keith, 'you see it as some kind of personal victory?'

'Of course. It's our efforts that have contributed to the general change of attitude. Obviously if we weren't convinced of the power of persuasion we wouldn't've worked our arses off. None of us would.'

'So what now? You lie back and rest on your laurels?'

'We get back to wimmin's matters,' says Hennie.

'It's a very small triumph,' Daphne says, looking at Hennie sharply. 'Hell, we're just a pimple on the arse of the world, and now we're a nuisance pimple that they'll try and squeeze.'

'It's not gonna be easy,' says Kay. 'People seem to think it will be, that we can make our stand down here and the rest of the world will say bravo. But the States will see it as the thin end of the wedge, they won't just shrug it off. If we get complacent about it the Government'll start talking compromises.'

They're having a meal; a proper sit-down dinner with a sheet spread as a tablecloth and white wine from a cardboard clad bladder. And, perhaps because the occasion is so formal and a celebration, they were shamed or softened into inviting Keith to join them. It was Kay who asked him, perhaps having put in a few words on his behalf. Besides, none of them have transport and this afternoon they needed to go to the pub to get the wine.

So Keith and Hennie and Kay had gone for the wine and stayed a couple of hours because Hennie had wanted to. And Keith is not quite drunk but on the way. It feels good, a fond reunion after an inexplicable absence. He'd forgotten how good it could feel.

At the pub they sat at a round table in front of the panoramic windows. It's school holidays so the place was crowded with tourists but he didn't care. Hennie and Kay are tourists now. Their house has been retrieved by its owners. They're staying a few nights with Daphne.

Things seem to be back to normal with Daphne and Kay and Hennie. Though perhaps not quite, for at the pub Hennie seemed watchful and restless. She got herself into a pool game and left Kay and Keith to share the table. He probably has the right to ask how things were resolved, but he's squeamish about open wounds.

Kay talked about Mururoa. She has a sister living in Papeete. They don't keep in touch but still it makes it all more personal. In '81, said Kay, a cyclone hit the atoll and sealed plastic bags in drums, filled with nuclear waste, were swept out to sea. There have been no reports of them being found.

Eighteen years of French tests, and back before that the British and the Americans at Christmas Island. The islands of the Pacific so vulnerable in their scattered isolation . . . mankind committed to the acquisition of power, the expendability of the powerless . . . hard, given the lessons of history, not to just abandon hope . . .

Keith nodding and drinking and soon catching only those words that came in on the waves that survived the juke box. People all over the room chorusing with congregational familiarity *Outlook for Thursday—your guess as good as mi-hine* and Hennie's wrist extending, fine and brown below the sleeve of her jacket as she braced her fingers for a shot.

Keith half listening to Kay, the useless hopeless sadness of it all. But still surprised and somehow disappointed when she confided, almost guiltily, 'Sometimes it all seems so futile. I don't have Daphne's strength, her absolute conviction. Yet I can see if we were all like that . . . all

185

that determined . . . well then we'd have disarmament tomorrow. So the reason for despair lies in what we are.'

He'd felt slightly annoyed with Kay then. As if she was ignoring the rules. Doubt was his department. The alcohol had been lending his sense of doom a distant and ennobling quality. 'The only way to look at the nuclear question,' he told Kay, draining his glass, 'is drunkenly.'

She sniffed. She thought he was making a silly joke. But he wasn't.

Daphne was at home cooking the dinner. She had recently had a birthday and Kay's was coming up next week so the meal was a sort of joint celebration. They were having roast chicken because Daphne said the weight of her increasing age made her feel traditional. Keith has been invited to another birthday dinner tonight, but even when Maureen made the invitation he left himself a way out, saying he might have to go over to the city so not to expect him. He'd come if he could.

And he should've gone there where he was wanted. Gone and eaten the meal she thumped down on the table with the aggressive despair her own cooking seemed to produce, and listened to the kids bickering and shouting, and watched Carly cut a cake with the charcoal carefully scraped off the bottom and helped with the dishes. Instead of being here half-drunk and happy.

'You should have children,' he says across the table to Daphne.

Hennie groans. 'Sweet Jesus.'

'Why should I have children?' Daphne humours him, for reasons known only to herself.

'So they could give you grandchildren. And you'd be able to bore them with old war stories of your campaigns. You know, how-I-saved-the-world stuff. The times you went out in frail crafts to face the nuclear ships coming into your harbour. Hamilton 1981 when you got hit by a rugby supporter's beer can and thereby brought the South African Government to its knees . . .'

'Were you at Hamilton,' asks Hennie, 'for the match?'

'I went to Wellington,' he tells her truthfully. 'I didn't watch any match but I watched the protestors and what I saw frightened me. Moral righteousness is the most dangerous emotion ever invented.' He stares hard at Daphne, making a point.

'But were you for or against?' asks Kay.

'I didn't support the tour, but what I saw of the protestors got up my nose.'

'He who straddles barbed wire is in danger of losing his balls,' says Hennie.

'He who sits on the fence doesn't have any balls to begin with,' says Daphne.

Keith tells her, 'Some people don't know the difference between fanaticism and courage.'

'You trying to say something?' she says. 'Okay, maybe I'm a fanatic. So what?'

'Well,' he feels caught out. 'Well, it makes you dangerous. It makes your motives suspect and your aims questionable at the very least.'

'Nothing would change,' says Kay, 'if it wasn't for the fanatics. They're our only hope.'

'Our only hope of a fascist dictatorship perhaps?'

'Shit,' says Hennie. 'What is it with Kiwis? The minute anyone dares stand up for something you all point and shriek about underlying motives. The only emotion you want to exist is self-interest. Well I'd believe it of the males, but don't start trying to apply your standards to us. Are you so uncentred you need to try and undermine Daphne?'

'She undermines me, her mission in life is to undermine me.'

They laugh at this—a united sniggering. He waits it out, a chicken leg in his fingers, looking from face to grinning face. His looking makes them more amused.

'And we're the ones who get accused,' says Hennie eventually, nodding towards Keith's set face, 'of having no sense of humour!'

He won't give them the satisfaction of driving him from the table. He'll stay and finish his meal and drink some more of the wine which he helped pay for. Even children, he thinks—and the children he sees wear the grey and white uniform of Everton High—would have the grace, after ganging up on an outsider, to feel some shame or compassion.

'Are you afraid,' he says to Daphne, suddenly, loudly, 'to treat me as a human being? Would that be too much of a threat to your ideology?'

She takes a few seconds to compose a reply. 'Not at all,' she says. 'We treat you as we find you.' Even Kay smiles in applause.

They take the conversation out of his reach so he drinks and sulks and listens in.

Hennie contends that peace is basically a red herring diverting wimmin's energy from the real concerns facing the female race.

Daphne says they have to carry the peace momentum right on through. The crux will come when the ANZUS business comes to a head. Wimmin must still put in energy to demonstrate their supportive strength.

(Strength, energy, support. Supportive strength, energetic support. These words are plaited through their talk, flashing tinsel confidence each time they surface.)

Hennie says darkly that men are known to be actively encouraging the wimmin's peace movement because it keeps wimmin from putting energy into the real causes of female oppression.

There's not much point, says Kay, in being equal if we're all dead.

Hennie says supporting peace is respectable. Anyone can be for peace, it doesn't require any real commitment.

(Commitment. He'd overlooked that one. Energy, strength, support *and* commitment.)

Daphne says that they've been over all this and it's senselessly divisive, not to mention a negative waste of energy (again) that could be put to better use. And Kay says, almost at the same time, that some peace workers are one hundred percent committed.

Hennie says, yes, to peace—but not to wimmin.

Keith knows by the way they use the word that it's wimmin they're talking about and not the other kind. He's almost decided the use of the word is valid, referring only, selectively, to women who have the separatist seal of approval.

He takes his full glass and his empty plate and leaves the table. He rinses his plate and knife and fork under the tap though it's an extravagant use of their water. It seems important they have nothing to hold against him except an accident of birth.

Then he finds his torch—which he doesn't need after all because the sky is clear and the moon just a slice off full—and walks very fast down past the shop and onto the deserted moonlit beach.

For a silly moment back there at the table in his invisible silence he'd been eight years old and back in the farmhouse in the days when they still sometimes all sat in the same room. He'd been sitting there staring ahead of him, just feeling the silence. Howard with his nose in a book, not minding. But Keith badly needing to chip away at the nothingness with words. Lining them up in his head then rearranging them, then finally casting them aside unsaid because he knew that whatever the words he chose and however carefully he put them together she would make something different out of them, something bitter and devious.

It's his own fault really. He should've gone to Maureen's instead.

Or just spent the evening down here with the sea who is neither choosy nor acrimonious. Who has strength without support. Energy without commitment.

Somewhere out there in the breathing, sighing water there may be drums containing sealed plastic bags.

On Monday Keith buys a box of chocolates because what else do you buy for a sweet-toothed girl, and calls at Cashin Road. There he meets Maureen's sister who looks at the same time carefully cosmeticked and antiseptically scrubbed. She reminds him of Myra Shelley, but somehow Myra is better at being whatever it is this woman is trying to be.

Alice conducts the conversation which covers Keith's job, his past, his prospects. For Maureen's sake Keith feels obliged to imply that his being an odd-job man is a stop-gap, a kind of sabbatical. He feels that Alice is looking for reasons to disapprove of him, and her vaguely supercilious probing is, he finds, harder to take than Daphne's objective enmity.

Sometimes Maureen manages to catch his eye with a look of rueful sympathy but Keith finds it hard to look away from Alice because the sisters' resemblance is intriguing and admonitory. Alice is Maureen with short hair, a few extra pounds, permanent-press slacks, and a few lonely years older. They share the same anxious laugh, the same girlish habit of hugging knees to chest, the same edgy way of biting not their nails but the tips of their fingers, and the same South Island voice.

Sitting between them it feels uncanny. He thinks Alice may be a warning. He leaves as soon as politeness allows and pretends not to see whatever it is Maureen's face is trying to communicate to him over Alice's shoulder.

It was a visit unimpeded by children. He supposes the aunt is reason enough for the kids to stay well out of range. She deserves some credit for that.

The woman has unsettled him. He's not sure the meeting was significant, but maybe . . . The sense of destiny's steady hand which Maureen's cottage had for a time restored has faded again. Nothing has taken its place.

Keith fills up most of the week putting washers on taps and glass in window frames and cupboards under sinks. He gets more work now he has the phone on, and word-of-mouth recommendations among the oldies because he nods and listens and hasn't the heart to charge what he knows he should. He could survive on the cups of tea and scones and chocolate fingers and cinnamon biscuits pressed upon him. Along with the shoes, polished up for best, and the grey and green and the houndstooth trousers, and even a razor. Which belonged to his customers' late husbands ('he was sort of smallish, dear, like you') and now Keith must have them.

They sit in a box in his room. They're in fashion again but Keith would feel foolish wearing them. He's never been in fashion and sees no need to start.

The job *is* only a stop-gap. He's just not sure what comes after, but surely something must.

He starts calling in at the pub after work. He finds he doesn't really mind all those shining surfaces in the bar, all that space and light. It's better than going home where Daphne seems to always be spread in front of Keith's TV set wallowing in its transgressions. At the pub he parks his Holden in the corner right beside the fence. It's beginning to feel like his authorised space.

September

USUALLY ON BENEFIT payment Thursday Maureen and Mickey walk down to the Kaimoana Post Office and Maureen hands in her book. Then they wait among the patient group of pensioners and solo mothers while the woman at the desk rings through to get their savings books updated at an office that has a computer. And the old people chat among themselves about the prices going up every day, and the weather and whether or not it makes any difference which politicians you get. Some of them make a fuss of Mickey and sometimes slip him a lolly or two. And sometimes one of the old women will say, of Mickey, *he's going to break a few hearts*. And each time she hears it Maureen thinks to herself, now there's a weird compliment!

But because today began so badly that Maureen had to bribe herself out of bed nothing is usual this benefit Thursday. It began with Maureen being woken in the early dark by Alan shouting. And when she'd shaken him out of his nightmare he told her it was a dream of witches. 'Witches?' said Maureen, making startled eyes. 'Why would such a modern child dream of witches?'

She could see he thought she was dismissing it too lightly, and so she stayed beside his bed stroking his hair until he slept witch-free. After that she couldn't get back to sleep until just before the alarm went off to wake her and then she felt so weary that she promised herself a trip to Parenga and maybe a look at the price of a pair of cotton trousers for summer.

So after the others have left for school Maureen and Mickey catch the bus at the bottom of their road. And when their bus gets in they join the silent unfamiliar queue at the Parenga Post Office where they have a computer and no one can know for sure what the others are there for even though it is benefit day. It takes a long time for Maureen to reach the counter. Mickey has found himself a corner of a booth and is desecrating deposit forms. People keep going to the booth and borrowing back his pen-on-a-leash so they can do their business. Mickey smiles up at them. What a little angel, a woman says. The post office people can't see how fast he's getting through their forms.

The man at the counter takes Maureen's book and feeds it into the machine. An efficient sound of machine-gun fire. The man takes the book out and frowns over it. He puts the book back in and the computer fires off a few more rounds. More puzzled frowns. He goes off to consult with the woman at the back desk, they both look across at Maureen. The woman lifts her palms up and shrugs. The man comes back to Maureen.

'I'm afraid nothing's gone in this week,' he says across the counter. 'I've double checked.'

The people queueing behind Maureen feel large and impatient. She seems to be looking way up at the man behind the counter and her voice sounds in her own ears like the voice of a lost child. 'What am I going to do?'

'You better ring social welfare. They'll be able to check it out and tell you what's happened.'

Her last little lot of savings has gone to the optician. She has two dollars and thirteen cents in her post office book and ninety-seven cents in her purse. Ninety-one once she's pressed button A.

The woman who answers has to go and look for Maureen's file. It takes a long time. Maureen crouches while she waits. She keeps two fingers hitched in the waist of Mickey's pants because the door of the phone booth is missing and he has no traffic sense. Mickey thinks it's a game. He struggles to unhook her fingers and whines a bit when he can't. Then he throws himself flat on the concrete floor and she has to pull him up and balance the phone receiver between her head and shoulders while she picks off the chewing gum and mintie papers stuck to his front without letting go of his waistband.

'It would be much easier,' says the woman from welfare when she finally gets back to Maureen, 'if you kept a record of your file number for calls like this. Hello? Mrs Harrison, are you still there?'

'Yes,' says Maureen.

'Well according to your file your benefit has been suspended in the meantime.'

'Why?'

'It's . . . ah . . . we're going to reassess it.'

'When? I mean when will I get it again?'

'Someone'll be coming to see you. Probably next week. They'll explain . . .'

'What day next week?'

'I'm not sure when it'll be.'

'But what if they come and I'm out?'

'Well I think you should try not to be out. Have you a phone?'

'No.'

'Well there you are. You make it difficult you see.'

'But it will be next week?'

'Probably, but not definitely. You people who choose to live over there on your island you make things hard for yourselves and for us.'

Maureen takes the receiver from her ear and looks at it for a few seconds before she hangs up. She hopes it won't be held against her. *Hung up on me* scrawled across her file in red ink.

'I know I promised,' she tells Mickey as she drags him past the shops, 'but I'm breaking my promise. My money didn't come today. I can't go splashing out on ice-blocks, not now.'

Once they're out of town she piggy-backs him up the hill to try and make up. She has nothing else to carry. When she slides him off her back at the top of the hill his voice sounds weepy and his cheeks look flushed. She hoists him back up, it's down hill all the way to Kaimoana.

At the local store she asks if she can book some things up despite the notice above the counter saying NO CREDIT. 'My money hasn't come through,' she says. 'The computer's stuffed up or something.'

His look says he's heard that one too many times before. But he has a heart. 'Okay, love, but don't run it up too big will you.'

She knows she ought to resent being called love by a shopkeeper. When men call you love in that casual way it's a kind of put-down— one of the trillion subtle ways of eroding a woman's self-esteem. (And since her reading has alerted her to such things she notices it going on all the time.) But today *love* feels like kindness. Today the word makes her want to hurl herself into his comfortable middle-aged arms and weep.

She walks around the little shop selecting nothing on impulse, nothing that isn't basic, no pay-day after-dinner treat to make the kids' eyes light up.

What if they never put her back on a benefit? What if they look around her house and say this isn't a fit place for children, we must take them away and put them in a home?

She's decided it must have something to do with Bruce. Would they have cut off her money because he's been convicted? Shisha would know more about these things but she hasn't been around for ages. Not since before the school holidays when Maureen told her no, she wouldn't have Leah. (And thank heavens she did for what on earth would Alice have thought of Leah?)

On Friday she draws out her two dollars. What is the woman thinking, behind the post office counter, as she writes in the thirteen cents balance and hands over the book with the two-dollar note?

On Saturday morning, while Carly is busy arranging tiny flowers for the sandsaucer display, Maureen makes pikelets (the recipe that doesn't use butter) which of course turn out like scraps of mottled yellow leather. But they can't go empty-handed to the school gala when for days Alan and Carly have been bringing home newsletters requesting white elephants, used clothes, old home appliances, fresh vegetables, home baking. *A chance to help your school and get rid of all that junk that's piling up in the garage.*

'Only a dollar,' says Alan.

'Only a dollar! Only? A dollar for you, a dollar for Carly, fifty cents for Mickey and d'you know what's left for me? About thirty bloody cents. And that my boy is it. All the money we have till god alone knows when.'

'Thank you Mummy,' says Carlysmarmy.

When they leave the house Maureen thinks with a glimmer of pride that they all look very presentable. Until they reach the school gates and comparisons are to be made.

Here comes Mrs Harrison with her tatty kids and her gruesome pikelets. She gives the box in which her baking is safely hidden to Carly to dispose of at stall or kitchen or rubbish bin. And when Carly bustles back to join them she's hand-in-hand with dainty Tanya. Who came to the birthday dinner with a beautifully wrapped box containing three little china dogs and who didn't seem at all put out by the long drop toilet or the bits of ply Keith had nailed over the interior rat holes. And who was brought and later collected by a mother who said, what a charming little cottage. And when Maureen wrinkled her nose and said, not so charming to live in, Tanya's mother said she knew that feeling—they'd lived in a garage once for two whole years.

It's surprising how understanding some people turn out to be.

The Harrisons all stick together. A little group drifting from stall to stall even after the money's all gone. At the used-clothes stall they're selling garments for fifty cents each, some of them look hardly worn. If her money had come through Maureen could've clothed her kids for summer.

Just as they're leaving Maureen sees Shisha, in a new beret and an old scarf. But when Maureen waves out Shisha turns away, not seeing or pretending not to, and grabs the arm of a man who looks, from back view, a little like Bruce. Who certainly isn't Bennie. Not that it's any of Maureen's business.

Maybe Shisha feels bad about having come to the gala without calling in to offer them all a lift? The thought comes to Maureen that maybe the good times—when her money came in and Shisha dropped by and Keith called around with another bit of tin—are all over. If she'd known they were the good times and they were going to be so short-lived she would have made more effort to appreciate them.

On Sunday Mickey definitely has a temperature and throws up a bit on the bathroom floor so she keeps him in bed. Carly lets him borrow Jackson, who was Carly's birthday present. Jackson is fluffy and grey and chocolate-box perfect with two white paws. Even though Maureen got him free by following up a notice at the store he doesn't seem like a cheapskate gift. Besides there's the cost of feeding him as well as the promise Maureen made to herself that at the first sign of ill health she would take him to the vet. The promise she made before they stopped her money.

Jackson is not yet properly housetrained. It's hard to track down his mistakes because their smell gets intermingled with all the other damp and sour and ratty smells that hang about the cottage.

On Monday Mickey doesn't want food but doesn't throw up either. Maureen cleans the house especially thoroughly, but no one comes.

On Tuesday Mickey eats and then brings it all up again. She hopes it's just a bug going round. She can't possibly carry him all the way to Parenga and she can't ask the doctor to come all this way for a house call when she has nothing to pay him with. She stays home all day. She has no tea left but she's saved a bit of coffee powder so she can offer the welfare person a cup. No one comes on Tuesday.

On Wednesday she has to send Alan and Carly down to the shop when they get home from school with a short list and a note assuring the shop couple that she really will pay when her money comes through. She knows Alan will read the note on the way down and make Carly be the one to present it. Maureen could've gone herself because no one comes.

On Thursday no one comes. But Mickey is definitely getting better. She tries to look on the bright side—at least his sickness saved her a little on food. In the Thursday mail Maureen gets a letter inviting Mr M. Harrison to fill in the enclosed form and join the thousands of New Zealanders who swear by the convenience of being credit card holders. Also a donation envelope for the Save the Children Fund.

On Friday morning sometime after eleven when Maureen is scraping away with a knife underneath Alan's bed, removing the solidified evidence of Jackson's mistake, she hears a car stop on the road then do a bit of forward then reverse to try and get safely on the verge. So she knows this is it, for the locals park where it suits them and expect traffic to pass as best it can.

It takes him a long time to walk to the door. Somehow Maureen'd been expecting a woman. She watches her visitor from the corner of a window, he's craning around taking everything in. Maureen tries to calm her heart. They can't take away your kids because you don't own a lawnmower or because you harbour disorderly trees. That would be too silly.

He doesn't want coffee and she can't offer tea. Perhaps he's afraid of contamination. He stands in the middle of the kitchen not touching anything, not sitting down though all week she's made an effort to keep the table clear, supposing they would sit down together and she would be told . . .

'You'll be aware,' he's saying, 'that your benefit is being reviewed. We do these things from time to time.'

Mickey presses up against Maureen. His nose is running and Maureen hasn't a hanky. She can't use the edge of the kitchen towel, not with him standing there beady-eyed. She bends down and lifts Mickey, sweeping his head against her jersey in a fond gesture. Mickey's nose emerges damp but unadorned. Peering down her front Maureen can see the snot spread on the slope of her left breast. She holds Mickey over it though he's far too big to be held that way.

'I imagine,' he says conversationally, 'it could get quite lonely living here. You have a few friends?'

'One or two.' Mickey wriggles to be put down. She clamps his legs still.

'And perhaps one in particular—a male friend?'

For an instant she thinks he's about to chat her up. She looks at him more closely. He's nearly as old as her father, one eyelid droops in a permanent wink and his teeth look too big and too white, like borrowed dentures.

'Not so's you'd notice,' she says warily. Then in case it could be construed as an admission of availability, 'There's a man who's been doing some work on the house for me.'

'What kind of work would that be?'

'Repairs and stuff. Fixing up the tankstand.' It doesn't seem wise to

196

draw attention to the long-drop loo.

'Your landlord was employing him?'

'No. I did.'

'That must place quite a strain on your budget?'

She has a feeling she's being herded into a trap but she can't fathom how all this has anything to do with Bruce.

'Well, I paid him for some of the work. The rest he just did.'

'For no payment? As a favour?'

'Yes.'

'Why would he do that?'

'I don't know. Out of the kindness of his heart.' She looks at him hard. 'No other reason.'

'You see,' he goes now to the table and lays down his leather briefcase but doesn't sit down, 'we have had certain information about you having frequent visits from this . . . builder friend of yours. And while of course the department has no objection to your entertaining friends you have just said yourself that this chap has been doing work around the place as a . . . friendly gesture. You see, this could be construed as a way of his contributing to your household income. You do see my point?'

Maureen lets Mickey return to the floor. '*Who* gave you that information? Who did?' She wipes at her jersey with the towel, it doesn't seem to matter now, his seeing a goob of snot.

'You must realise we can't divulge . . .'

'You mean you stopped my payments because someone nailed up a few bits of tin to stop the rain getting in?'

'We have to look into these things.' He smiles placatingly. 'Look perhaps you'd like to show me round.'

She shrugs. 'You wouldn't exactly get lost on your own.' But she marches ahead of him through the living room to the boys' room in its unnatural state of tidiness. And now the barracks look of the room, the old water stains half-hidden by the indifferent art work of Mickey's play centre efforts, the austerity of their narrow and sagging beds feels like a moral victory for Maureen. She watches his face while he looks around him and he doesn't meet her eye when he looks her way.

'It's not easy,' she says, hands on hips, 'when you have to start from scratch—furniture, everything. This is where my sons sleep.'

She marches back through the living room and kitchen. She hurls open the bathroom door. 'This is the bathroom.' Together they look at the ancient tin bath with its traces of a futile paint job and its rusting bottom. And at the enamel bowl that serves as a handbasin.

Maureen presses on. 'And this is where my daughter and I sleep.'

For someone who ought to be abject with departmental self-reproach he takes a very long and careful look about the room. His gaze lingers on the clothes that hang from the suspended pole which is their wardrobe, then lowers to the jandals and sneakers beneath. Maureen has an angry urge to laugh, his unstated purpose is so transparent. How he must curse unisex fashions; standing there making a mental inventory even though Carly's bed with her old teddybear (legs wantonly raised and apart) is only an arm's length from Maureen's. Surely he couldn't suppose that ... with Carly right beside ... ?

'Thank you,' he says on the way back through the kitchen, gathering up his satchel. 'You've been very helpful. You shouldn't have any more worries on this matter. You can expect to be reimbursed for the suspended payments in due course.'

'What about the person who called you?'

'I'm afraid that's just one of those things.'

Maureen is watched! Vindictive eyes peering through the hedge, staring in at night through her uncurtained windows. Or seeing Keith's truck turn up Cashin Road; *there he goes again*.

Someone lonely, bitter, envious. Someone old. Kaimoana is full of old people. Half a dozen Maureen knows enough to say hello to. Most of the pensioners seemed so kind; now they're all suspect.

At least her money will come next week. Should come. You can expect, he'd said. You shouldn't have any more worries ... Still leaving her with that element of doubt.

Alan sulks off to his room the minute he gets home. Carly is several minutes behind him. Maureen knows by Alan's slumped and surly passage that she is required to respond but this afternoon she's low on compassion. Carly goes straight to the bread bin.

'Have a carrot,' suggests Maureen.

Carly screws up her nose. 'I'm starving and you say have a carrot.' She begins sawing into the bread. 'I don't mind being fat, Mum. I'd rather be fat than live on carrots.'

'Not too much butter,' says Maureen, 'because it has to last till next Thursday. And if you're gonna eat that in front of Mickey you better make one for him.' She bangs the iron down on the pocket of her jeans, it's one way of getting them dry. She bought the iron when she was a working girl, it was one of the few things she'd felt entitled to take from the house in Mangere. 'What's the matter with Alan? Something happen at school?'

Carly shrugs with her mouth full.

From the boys' room a steady thumping sound begins. Maureen hangs the jeans over the back of a chair and reaches for a pillowcase. Carly catches her mother's eye and jerks her head towards the sound. She rolls her eyes.

Maureen grins back at her. 'It's called body language,' she says. But she turns off the iron.

He's punching at the wall with his fist, but not hard enough to do damage to either. 'Come on,' she says, sitting on the end of his bed, 'what is it? You gonna tell me?'

The punching stops but he takes his time turning to look at her. His eyes brim with tears and melt her exasperation. She holds out her arms to him but he stays where he is, sprawled on the bed.

'So what's the matter?'

'Everything,' he says.

She waits.

'I hate it here. It's boring and horrible. I wanta go back to Mangere. I wish we'd never come here. It's a disgusting yukky house and we don't have any money and I hate it.'

'We can't go back. You know that.'

'You should never have taken us away. I could go back there. I miss my Dad.'

'Did something happen at school today?'

'Something always happens at school but you don't care. Nobody cares. I wanta go back to Auckland. I wanta live with Dad in Mangere.'

'Sweetheart he doesn't live there anymore.'

'How do you know?'

'I just know.'

'I could live with him anyway.'

She takes a deep breath. 'Okay. If that's what you really want. I'll try and track him down and you can go and live with him.'

His eyes flicker. He presses his lips together and looks down at the floor. 'I'd have to think about it,' he says.

She holds back her smile. 'You do that.'

He looks at her now. 'If I was in town I'd have somewhere decent to ride my bike.'

'Yes,' she says getting up, 'I guess you would.'

She goes back to her ironing. Too weary to stay there with him and dig for some kind of truth. Alan's discontent is like the kikuyu that infests the back garden. She wrenches out the shoots which appear from nowhere and pulls up the roots until they break and knows she's achieved nothing, that the roots will be back in a matter of days and she'll have to start again. It could go on like that for a lifetime.

Then again it's possible that his misery has no deep and central source. Not having somewhere decent to ride your bike could seem, to a male child, sufficient reason for tears and self-inflicted pain.

> I don't understand this child. He's an alien being I produced by mistake. I don't know how his mind works. I don't even love him as much as I should. How can I love unreservedly someone I don't begin to understand?

On Saturday morning Maureen is woken by Carly's screams and Alan's astonishing language. She waits for a few seconds in case it's just a difference of opinion happening out there. She can smell toast burning. She lies and listens until the anger seeps through to her fingers then she storms out to the kitchen.

'Don't ever,' she roars at the sight of Alan, feeling herself to be huge and formidable in her rage, 'call your sister that word again.'

The kitchen is filling with smoke.

'Bloody hell.' She pulls the charcoal squares from beneath the grill. 'Couldn't you see that? D'you want to burn the place down?'

Alan has shot off towards his bedroom. Carly stands with her glasses dangling from one hand. One lens is cracked in an inverted Y.

Alan packs his schoolbag prior to running away. Carly keeps Maureen informed. 'He's taking socks and two of his little engine things, and his pocketknife.' She smirks.

Maureen grunts in reply as she undoes Mickey's buttons and does them up in a synchronised fashion. The pathos of Alan's preparations is overshadowed by the pain of cracked glass. She couldn't trust herself to confront the boy right now.

'He's gone,' reports Carly. 'He took his bike. He says he hates us all but you most of all and he's never coming back.'

'I see,' says Maureen. 'Was he riding the bike?'

'He was pushing it.'

When Keith got the new wheel Maureen made a rule, no riding on the road. Which leaves Alan only the jungle that is their section or the tedious option of pushing it down to the stretch of grass between the Kaimoana store and the beach.

The bike hasn't turned out to be such a good idea. But now she's relieved to know he's taken it. It must mean he has no wild notions of sneaking onto a ferry and going to the city in search of Bruce.

In an hour or two hunger will drive him home shame-faced.

When nearly three hours have passed she thinks, he'll be at Keith's for sure.

She gives him another half hour. She's beginning to have pictures of him lying injured beside the road. She bundles Carly and Mickey into their jackets and does up Mickey's shoelaces. If she'd thought of it an hour earlier they could've got the bus to Toki Bay.

Except that her eyes leap round every bend searching for a mangled pushbike . . . and except for the silver lines that intercept in front of Carly's right eye . . . Maureen would enjoy this walk.

She's only seen Keith twice in the last three weeks. Once he brought round the new wheel and once when he drove by as Maureen and Mickey were on the way to play centre and stopped and gave them a lift. She looks forward even more to him coming round now that Shisha has stopped visiting and doesn't even turn up at play centre anymore. Now she has a legitimate reason to visit him.

Mickey and Carly are silly with excitement. Alan has brought them an adventure. Even Maureen feels sharp-edged and wildly alive. It's a feeling she used to know too well. The adrenalin rush of fear and unpredictability. She'd thought she hated it. Her dreams of escape glowed with the promise of sweet reason and absolute assuredness. That promise fulfilled now. Apart from her money getting stopped the only lightning-bolts in her life-after-Bruce have been caused by Alan. His accident, his running away.

She'd never imagined that reason and order could get to be so dull.

She hears the pecking of a typewriter as they file along the path beside Keith's house.

'What do you do all that time you have on your own?' she once asked him.

'I write stories. I try and write stories. One day I'll start one and it'll turn out to be the one I've been waiting for.' Like Bruce with his Golden Kiwi tickets.

'Someday,' Keith told her one time, 'my name'll mean something. You'll say you used to know me and people'll be impressed. Well, curious anyway. They'll know who I was.'

'Why do you think that?'

'I just know. I've always known it in my bones.' Then he'd laughed at himself. Or at her for seeming to take him seriously; though she knew he'd meant it.

But it's the lesbian who answers Maureen's knock. She doesn't really look like Benny Hill. Maureen remembers her name is Daphne but couldn't possibly use it. When she asks for Keith Maureen watches the lesbian carefully for signs of disapproval but it's hard to tell.

Daphne says Keith isn't home. She thinks he went out early. But yes, a kid came looking for him – that was well before midday. She'd told the boy she didn't know when Keith'd be back and he'd gone away. Daphne supposed he was one of the local kids.

She tells Maureen this in a brisk way as if she's being slightly inconvenienced. Then she stares at the kids for a few moments and says, 'You better come in.'

Inside Maureen feels ill at ease. Meeting a lesbian is like meeting a Red Indian or a sikh. There would seem to be certain rules or rituals which you ought to know but Maureen doesn't. In Daphne's presence Maureen feels naive and colonial.

'Have you any ideas about where he might be?' Daphne puts on the kettle.

'I just supposed he'd come here. If he'd been on his way home we would've passed him.'

'I'll ring the pub, Keith might be there.'

'The pub?'

'It's worth a try,' says Daphne. Maureen feels her surprise was noted and filed in that mannish head. Daphne picks the phone up from the floor.

How long's he had the phone on? He could've told me. We wouldn't have had to come all this way, probably for nothing.

'MUIR,' roars Daphne into the receiver. 'M U I R.' She holds it at arm's length and they can hear the seashell sound of a distant rave-up. 'See what we're missing,' she says to Maureen raising her eyebrows. Then she looks down at Carly who has edged close, eyeing a still-warm loaf of bread on the kitchen bench. 'You've gotta peace sign in your window,' she tells Carly. 'That has to be a good omen.'

Carly looks at her blankly then her eyes creep back to the bread.

Daphne talks to Keith briefly and hangs up. 'He's coming back. He says he thinks he knows where the boy'll be.'

While they wait Daphne distributes tea and milk and thick warm bread with butter sliding through. She moves the typewriter off the table where Mickey has just discovered it and shuts it away in her bedroom. 'I don't suppose you're a typist?' she asks as she returns.

'I can type,' says Maureen doubtfully. 'Or I used to be able to. Average sort of speed.'

'Ah.' Daphne studies her thoughtfully. 'You wouldn't have time on your hands some days? I can't offer payment or anything. I'm looking for a volunteer who can type half-way decently. It's in a good cause.'

'I wouldn't mind,' says Maureen. 'I'll give it a go. Except I've got the small one not at school yet, and I don't have any transport.'

'That's no problem. You can do it at home. I hope you weren't just being polite because it's too late now, you're hired.'

Maureen feels ridiculously pleased. Like a third former invited to sit with the senior heavies.

'One thing—the typewriter's on loan, I wouldn't like it damaged. You'd have to keep it out of your little girl's reach.'

Maureen nods. Thinking, well, she's entitled to say that—she's just being straight about it. All the same Maureen wishes Daphne hadn't said it.

'He's a boy,' she corrects. Is pleased to correct.

'Pity,' says Daphne.

*   *   *

On their way back Alan belatedly remembers to retrieve his bike and schoolbag from behind a clump of manuka. But Keith doesn't see the bike on his way down, doesn't even think to look for it. He's certain this is where the boy will be.

They went together to this bay the first time Alan came over after school, when the others were in the city. Keith believed the boy had sensed whatever it was that made this particular new-moon curve of sea and shore and bush different from all the others. 'Sometimes,' he told Alan, 'down here I've heard singing. Lots of voices, kind of like a choir. Singing or maybe some kind of chant. It's too faint to make out which. It's so faint you have to hold your breath to hear it at all.'

The boy turned and peered behind him into the trees as if he expected to see a chorus of eyes watching him. 'Who do you reckon it is?'

Keith shrugged. 'Could be just someone's record—the sound coming over the water from Hoki Bay and somehow bouncing off the hills. But the funny thing is once you get up the top past the bush it stops.

There's nothing, no matter how hard you listen.'

'What does it sound like exactly?'

'Exactly? Like nothing I've ever heard. It's hard to explain. It sounds like voices that have been singing since the beginning of time. They're getting a bit hoarse but nowhere near ready to stop.'

'You mean spooky.'

'Kind of spooky . . . but friendly too. It's more than something you just hear with your ears. If you could really know what they were singing I'm certain it would be friendly sort of things. Something like . . . hey, we're keeping an eye on you and don't worry . . . don't be unhappy . . . because everything's gonna be all right.'

'Like God?' Alan sounded dubious.

'In a way. Maybe it is God. Then again maybe it's just the wind coming in from a certain direction and causing the trees to sing. Then maybe that's what God is anyway – a bit of wind blowing through trees.'

'God sucks,' said the boy, but a little diffidently. When Keith didn't respond he added, 'When children are asleep God pulls out their fingernails.'

'Good grief. Who told you that?'

'Bruce Harrison. My father.'

'Well . . . maybe he's acquainted with a different God from everyone else. I'd say the God in this place does nothing much except sleep and smile and take deep breaths and generally lie around.'

The boy sat there hugging his knees and thinking, then he grinned and said, 'What a lazy bastard.'

Cattle have been using the foot track down to the bay. Water has seeped into the wells of their hoofprints. Keith keeps to the edge. He could've called in at home and got gumboots but Maureen might've wanted to come. It's Keith the boy has come all this way to look for – he can't help feeling a bit flattered by that.

Six Hereford cows stand goofily at the water's edge. Keith expected Alan to be down here on the shore. It's only as the cows make a short inquisitive lunge in Keith's direction that he remembers Alan is a city kid who'd feel menaced by that kind of overture. He's about to shout up into the bush when his eye catches sight of the motionless figure huddled out on the flat rock with the sea lapping just below him.

The flat rock sits on the eastern side of the little bay, part of a rocky outcrop, jagged with oyster shells, that you can walk to when the tide is out. From the flat rock you can see Hoki Bay, or at least the far end of it—the beach and above it the scattering of new pole houses blinking out through the bush of the sheltering hillside.

From the beach where Keith stands all you can see is the ocean and the distant silhouette of the Coromandel Peninsula. At high tide the flat rock is under water and it's coming on high tide.

Keith shouts and shoos at the cows and they blunder off towards the track. The boy has seen him now and waves.

'It won't be over your head,' Keith calls. 'Can you swim?' The water looks cold.

The boy waves yes and begins to edge himself off the rock. He swims straight towards Keith although he could've easier headed for the rocks. Long easy strokes—it wasn't a fear of water that had kept him crouching out there.

Keith takes off his jacket and puts it around Alan's sodden shoulders. 'They wouldn't've hurt you,' he says, 'the cows.'

'They chased me.'

'Yeah, well that would be their idea of being friendly.' He feels the boy's wrist. 'You're freezing. Let's get you home.'

'To your place?'

'Well, yeah. But your mum's there and the kids.'

'I'm not cold. We don't have to go yet.' Alan's lips are trembling and his face is splotched with pink and white and blueish shades of cold.

Keith crouches down. 'What's up?'

'I don't want to go home. Not ever.'

'Well, I tell you, it's gonna get bloody cold come nightfall.'

The boy hugs the jacket around him and stands there shivering. 'I done something really bad,' he says. His face crumples up. 'I cost her lots and lots of money. She really hates me now.'

'She'll get over it, whatever it was.'

Alan shakes his head. 'She doesn't want me. She said I could go and live in Auckland.' His eyes look right into Keith's eyes and his heart speaks. 'She likes the others more than me. I know she does. She tries to like me, I know she does but . . .' His stricken eyes clutch at Keith. 'Why can't she like me the same as them? Why doesn't she?'

Keith shuts his eyes to keep the boy out. 'She probably does,' he says. 'I'm sure she does. It's just the way you see it. That doesn't necessarily mean it's the way it is.' When he looks at the boy again he sees his teeth are chattering.

'But I *know*,' Alan whispers through his chilly lips. 'I *know* she doesn't.'

And Keith believes him. An unendurable truth—like the drums of plastic-sealed waste drifting in the currents, like there being more bombs than there is land to explode them on. And he sees in the boy's eyes that, having acknowledged the truth of it, Alan considers Keith accountable. He feels so helpless and a bit fearful, something's dragging at his soul and he senses there's an edge out there the boy could pull him over. He stands up, away from those eyes. 'I used to feel exactly the same way when I was your age,' he says too easily.

He puts his arm across Alan's shoulders. 'Come on. You're freezing to death here.'

They walk together as far as the track. 'And did she like you? Your mother?'

Keith decides to be truthful. 'She liked my brother better. But then my brother got killed in an accident, so she was stuck with just me, like it or lump it.'

Alan gives this a few steps' thought. 'I wish Carly and Mickey would get killed in an accident.' Then his eyes turn up sideways to look at Keith and he grins.

When they're halfway up the track, Alan in front, he says over his shoulder, 'Do you like your mother a whole lot?' And while Keith is still trying to find an answer he persists, 'Do you love her?'

'Of course I do,' he says. 'She's my mother.'

It's a very long drive,' she kept saying. 'Shouldn't we be starting for home?'

'Soon we will, soon.'

When they were nearly there he said, 'There's somewhere I want you to see. You'll like it Mother.'

'He would've wanted his luncheon,' she said, 'it's fair to presume.'

Good, he thought, good. Stay out there in the mist. But right away she was back with him. 'What is this place we're going to see?'

'It's an Arts Centre. An old building they've turned into a centre for the performing arts. And they've arranged this gathering of artists—retired artists—who were internationally known in their own fields.'

It didn't surprise her at all. 'Will I be required to address them? I sometimes have lapses of memory. Perhaps I should explain to them at the beginning—that the tragedy of my life has eaten away at the walls of my brain.'

'Yes, perhaps you should explain that to them.'

'Delightful,' she said as they turned into the circular driveway flanked by neatly bedded lushly blooming rose bushes. 'Wonderfully civilised surroundings.'

Any other day his heart would have winced over her indestructible snobbery.

As soon as she saw the stiff white uniform of the woman coming down the steps towards them she knew. Keith, watching his mother's face, knew that she had never been more lucid.

When she turned to him her eyes confirmed that all the indignity and loss she'd suffered at Lonewood Valley were nothing compared to this. The self-pity had run out, all she had left was loathing.

'I have to think about me,' he said. Perhaps aloud, perhaps just to himself.

When they're in the truck Keith leans to help the boy pull off his wet jacket. The left sleeve is stained pale red. Alan turns his arm away.

'Let's see. You've cut yourself.' Keith turns the wrist towards him. On the forearm, not deep yet more than just a scratch, the boy has carved a circle with three lines meeting in the centre.

'How the hell did you do that?'

'With my knife.' He's proud of it, in a way.

'Why? What for?'

'I got bored, waiting out there.'

Keith shakes his head. As he starts the truck he dares to say, now the moment has passed, something of what he might've said down there by the beach. 'I like you better than the other two. You know that, don't you?'

'Yes.' Alan smiles.

He gets the truck onto the road. 'But that's not the same is it?' He glances at Alan who looks at him gratefully and shakes his head.

Keith feels relief, the sense of danger wiped away. Yet beneath the relief a vague sense of loss.

'You've been drinking,' says Alan.

'How do you know?'

'You smell,' he says, 'like one of those cows. Hey, hang on, stop we forgot my bike.'

When the bike and the bag have been retrieved and they're on their way again Alan says, watching through the back window in case his bike shakes off, 'You haven't been to see us for ages.'

'Haven't I? I've been a bit busy. Anyway I kind of got the feeling you weren't too rapt about me hanging round your Mum.'

Alan straightens in his seat and grinds a wet sneaker among the tools that cover the floor. 'I don't mind,' he says. He doesn't look at Keith.

When they reach Keith's place he says, urgently, 'You know before, when I was there on my own all that time with those cows? Well

I heard those voices. It was after I'd done that on my arm. And you know what? I don't reckon it was the wind. I reckon it came from outa the ground.'

'It didn't scare you?'

'No.' He grins. 'Didn't scare the cows either.'

Keith watches the clumsiness of the boy and the mother together when they reach the house. She's angry and relieved and not sure which mood to believe in. When she hugs the kid her elbows jut out rigidly. The boy draws himself into a tight cocoon while she holds him.

When Alan's been dried and dressed clownishly in some of Keith's clothes and fed on Daphne's sustaining loaf Keith drives them all home. Maureen arranges the seating. Alan cannot sit in the cab with Keith because he is, after all, in disgrace. Keith says the grown ups should sit inside but she has other plans. It's not the first time Keith's watched her organising rituals which must somehow meet her private concept of fairness. To all but herself.

Carly and Mickey ride primly beside him.

'What happened to your glasses?'

'Alan broke them. That's why he ran away.'

'Ah. So that was it!'

'He didn't really mean to. It was just one of those things.'

Keith doesn't try to keep up the conversation, it's like talking to a thirty-five-year-old midget. At Kaimoana he stops and puts his head out the window? 'Who fancies fish 'n chips?'

Three in loud favour. Maureen's head comes round the side. 'Keith, I'm stony broke.'

'I'm not,' he says. 'Not quite.'

'But where?'

'There's a new place, just opened. Hang on, we're on our way.'

While they're waiting for the food he goes across to the pub and buys a carafe of Blenheimer. Holds it up to her outside the take-away. 'Okay?'

'We're costing you a fortune already.'

'I meant is it okay if I bring this and stay awhile.'

'Of course. We've already managed to ruin your afternoon.'

God, she can be depressing.

'Anyway,' she says, 'I'd like a chance to talk to you.' Her eyes slide towards Alan. 'He should crash early. He ought to be exhausted.'

She thinks he has some wisdom to impart regarding the boy. What will he say to her? Order her to produce a bit more love—like hectoring a cow in a desert to let down more milk.

'Shisha must be in there.' Maureen points to the pub carpark and the rainbow-gilded van.

'She goes there quite a bit.'

'Wonder what she does with Leah? Does she talk to you?'

'Not if I can help it.'

'She's not so bad really. She doesn't come round any more.'

'Should be a blessing.'

'At least she was company.' She looks wistful. 'What's it like in there?'

'Just your average tourist-type pub. You're not missing anything.'

She gives him a funny look. 'You reckon?'

The kids fight over who'll get to carry the dinner home. Maureen has Keith toss a coin. Mickey wins and Carly watches him all the way in case his fingers start burrowing in through the newspaper. The boy keeps pretending, just to tease. 'MICK-KEY!' she shrieks and Keith clenches his teeth the better to hold his tongue.

Imagine it, day after day. The aggravation, the complexity. Would you ever get used to it?

In the pub a couple of weeks ago Shisha glided up to Keith. She walked tilted back, her legs seemed to slide a little ahead of her body. She was wearing flat ballerina kind of shoes and flame-coloured stockings. She'd dyed one side of her hair black. She asked after Maureen, and Keith mumbled something.

'I hope you'll be good to her,' Shisha said. 'I certainly hope so because she deserves it. She's a very straight lady.'

'I know that,' Keith muttered.

'Of course you do. Not many guys would take on someone with three small kids.'

He blinked at her. 'I haven't taken on anything.'

'Then perhaps you'd like to buy me a drink?'

'Sorry,' he lied. 'I'm just on my way out.'

Keith and Maureen unload the bike and watch Alan ride it boastfully, not touching the seat, up the little track where the grass has died of footsteps. They look at each other and smile because he's so jaunty, ringing the rusty bell so Carly and Mickey will jump aside. Carly pretends to grab at the carrier, but keeps one hand on Mickey in case he falls over and flattens the chips.

Then Maureen sighs. 'He does it all the time. I let him get away with things. I think I'm too soft with him. It's because I don't know how he thinks. When he seems sorry or happy a part of me thinks it's just an act, the other part believes in him.' She looks directly at Keith, 'Is he so devious?'

'I don't think he's devious,' he says. But he sees her measure of disbelief. She's thinking, what else could he say?

'You see,' she says as if Keith hadn't spoken, 'if he is manipulating me and I keep giving him the benefit of the doubt he'll go on doing it. It'll just get worse and worse.' She reaches for a high clump of inkweed and viciously uproots it. 'I try and give him whatever it is ... attention, all that ... but you only have so much then you dry up. It's all gone. Sometimes,' her face is averted, her voice unsteady, 'I don't think I can go on. I don't have ... It feels that too much is being asked of me.'

He should do something, put his arm around her, take her hand, but he feels stiff and sober and slightly panic-stricken by her need. Then Alan, who has doubled back towards them, grates away at his bell and calls plaintively, 'Can we open them?'

'Wash your hands first,' she calls back then gives Keith a rueful smile as if it was just a moment's lapse and she's glad he knew better than to take it seriously.

He pours the kids a small glass of wine each, telling them it's good for the digestion, hoping it's also soporific. Keith and Maureen drink theirs from large plastic mugs which he regularly refills.

Keith and Alan light a fire because the nights are still cool. They burn the greasy fish and chip paper and they sit in a circle on the floor and play gin rummy, which Keith has to teach them. They make a couple of paper cards so they have a full pack. Mickey and Maureen share their hand. Keith keeps filling Maureen's mug and his own. Alan goes down at the start of the game and bites his lips to keep them from wobbling but then his luck improves and he wins by a fat margin.

'Bedtime,' says Maureen. 'Wonderful bloody bedtime.'

'Not us,' says Carly.

'All of you. Keith's just volunteered to read you a story.'

'I'll choose,' says Alan.

'Why should you?' demands Carly.

'In that case Keith can read to the boys and I'll read to Carly.'

'All right,' Carly is outmanoeuvred. 'I s'pose he can choose then.'

So Keith reads about the use of linear motors in railway engines. *The static part of the motor produces a magnetic field which seeps from one end to the other, the "rotor" portion of the motor being of steel or aluminium plate fixed permanently in position along the length of the track . . .*

After a few minutes tedium drives Carly off to her own bedroom but Alan listens entranced right through the future of magnetic suspension for the ultimate in frictionless movement. Then Keith puts the book down and says, 'Okay,' and the boy nods and grins and Keith has an impulse to put his arm around him but doesn't.

Mickey is sound asleep. 'I'll switch the light off, okay?'

'Okay. Are you going home now?'

'Not for a while. Goodnight.'

'Night.'

Maureen has stoked up the fire. She lies in front of it propped on a cushion. Her hair spread on the floor like octopus legs. He collects his mug and sits down almost beside her.

'Was this what marriage was like?'

'Mine?' she says. 'Hardly. What about yours?'

'We only met in passing.'

She holds her head to the side, studying his face. 'If it was,' she says, 'I wouldn't have left.'

'Thank you.' But he's not sure how to take that.

'Maybe I wouldn't have left,' she amends. 'You know this is the first time I've been drunk in years.'

'When I was first on the island I used to think that about being sober.'

'But you drink again. Why?'

'Dunno. It stops . . . the puzzles . . . the . . . melancholy.'

'Melancholy?' Her lips twitch.

'Well, maybe that was a bit over the top,' Keith laughs suddenly, at himself.

'No,' she says. 'I thought it was poetic. Very profound sounding.' He's not sure if she's teasing him.

'I suppose what I meant was it stops me worrying about the future. And smelling the bad breath of the past.'

'Why does the future worry you? What d'you want of it?'

'I want . . . to lie in the sun with my eyes closed and watch those changing colours you see on your eyelids.' He's not sure if he's trying to impress her, or simply reassure. What he *really* wants is a new edition of the world where he can look up the answers to this one. And he wants to be heroic. Eventually. 'What do you want?' he asks.

'I want . . . I want to be able to say I don't want anything. Just like everyone else. But at the moment I want so much I don't even know where to start.'

'With me?' His own voice, his drunken temerity, shocks him. When her eyes open wide they're slanted at the corners. Slightly Asian. She bears no resemblance at all to the sister.

'What do you mean?' She holds his glance for a while then turns her head away. 'I suppose this is where I should say that I'm not on the pill anymore.'

After a time she looks back at him as if he may have a solution. Keith wants to say there are ways around this problem, but he can't, he shouldn't need to. He can't even reach out and touch her, lying not even an arm's length away. He tells his body to move, to roll over once—casually—so there's no cold floor left between them, but his body is aghast.

She rests her head in her arms, and when she raises it again she says matter-of-factly, 'There would've been a kind of moral justice if we had.' And she tells him about them suspending her benefit, the visit from the welfare man. 'Imagine,' she says. 'Who would do a thing like that? I still can't know for sure the money'll come through next week. I'll never be able to feel sure about it again.'

He's thinking along other lines. 'If you weren't on the benefit . . . say if you were living with someone . . . your husband would have to pay you maintenance wouldn't he? For the kids?'

She gives a small laugh.

'By law he must,' Keith persists.

'Maybe, but how would I get it? When we lived with him it was hard enough to get him to support us. Not that he earned that much anyway, not to keep five of us. Anyway now he's not even earning. Now he's in jail.'

'I thought you didn't hear from him?'

'It was in the paper. I haven't told the kids,' she warns him.

'So,' he says, keeping it light, 'what you really need is a rich man.'

She looks him straight in the eye and nods. 'A rich man or a decent job. It's hard to know which is the more unlikely. It depresses me to think about it. It's like having to escape from a tenth floor window and having one shoe-lace to climb down.'

'That's nice,' he says. 'Nice imagery.'

'You like it? Then it's yours.' Suddenly she's angry. She gets to her knees and throws a piece of wood on the fire, then she sits with her legs drawn up, hugging her knees and he can see the anger dying down to a kind of smouldering acceptance. 'There's no other way but the way things are,' she says. 'So I'll just have to get better at it, not let it get on top of me. Today was good. I enjoyed today. My son runs away and we all have a good day! Thank you for finding him, and bringing us home and buying us dinner. And the wine though it seems to have worn off very quickly. It's a long time since I had such a nice day. Thank you, Keith.'

'You notice,' he ventures, 'that Alan's being good about us?' His hand reaches now, of its own accord, crosses the terrifying space and is met uncertainly by hers. Her eyes have got wide again. 'I could stay,' he says. 'We could just stay here and talk, just be together, whatever you want . . .'

She goes on looking at him with her wide eyes but he can feel her pulling back as if she's been caught in an undertow. She lets go of his hand. 'I can't risk it,' she says. 'I'm sorry, but suddenly I feel like we're being watched right now. I need that money. I can't, can't face even thinking that it might not come. Already the kids are afraid—they're starting to think I can't be relied on to provide. I'm sorry . . . but you do see?'

'If I had a real job? A steady income?'

'You wouldn't want to get stuck with three kids.'

'Alan's sort of attached to me.'

'We all are, in our own ways. I don't want you to stop coming round. I miss your not coming.'

'But in visiting hours? Daylight? And not too often?'

'It seems silly . . . but it would feel safer.'

He tries to understand her fear, to see it her way and not feel angry at the absurdity of it. He makes himself smile as he gets up. 'For however long they keep you in the observation ward,' he says, 'visiting will be between two and three pm.'

She doesn't bother to smile. 'You better take what's left of your wine.'

*　　　*　　　*

The pilot glances round at her. 'It's okay. We have an impeccable safety record.'

He thinks she's afraid of flying. Josie looks down at the coast of Motuwairua and feels like a stranger. Looking down at the tiny brave houses clutched to the hills and wondering what it would be like to live down there, to live on an island?

213

She has no fear of flying. Even in this absurd little plane with its ill-fitting doors and papier-mâché wings. Though what could be more dangerous, more unnatural than being transported at such height in something that looks less substantial than her washing machine?

Geoff's hand comes from behind and gropes for hers; a small blind friendly creature. 'We can just go to the movies,' he says softly to the back of her head. 'If you like?'

Losing his nerve? Or simply concerned about her? She squeezes his hand in hers. Geoff is afraid of flying.

Today they were going to plant out the tomatoes and weed the strawberries and trim the hooves of Grumpy and Dopey. She had reminded him of all that. A whole day lost! Two days in fact because nothing would get done tomorrow either.

'If everyone did this the country would be bankrupt.'

'The country is bankrupt.'

'Well there you are!' she said.

'I could go on my own,' he threatened nicely, 'if you prefer to stay and boost the national economy.'

All over the country at this very moment men in expensive suits sit in aeroplanes at someone else's expense trying to peel the wrapping from processed cheese slices and round crackers, while women are answering phones and updating files and writing invoices and making decisions and airline bookings for the men who sit on the planes.

Still, that's not really Geoff's fault.

Josie's thighs stick together damply above the tops of her stockings. One clasp of her suspender belt has worked loose, she can feel her right stocking sagging on the inside thigh. She wears the stupid belt for Geoff's sake, and feels silly. She could've left it off till later.

She imagines them at the movies, if that was what it came to. Being especially nice to each other when the lights are on, but separated in the dark by thoughts of IF.

Landing is the dangerous part. Yet the risk of a crash is minimal — more risk of injury any day in your own kitchen. Flying, an acceptable kind of danger . . .

'It's not as though it'd just be *anybody*,' he said. 'We'll have to use some judgement. You can be killed just crossing the road.'

Other objections. Naturally from Josie. 'It's people, love. Not blow-up dolls or pictures — people with feelings and egos and sensitivities . . .'

'And secret desires and curiosities. Do you imagine it's only us?'

'Why today? Why not next week? The week after?'

214

'Next week I'll be forty-two.' He sounded so desolate. 'It's already September. But if you'd rather not?'

'No. No. Come on. Strike while the iron's hot!'

The crazy fifteen-year-old irony of it all. Except then there was no ambivalence, not for Josie.

Her suburban period. Living with Dick, Lake and Daryl in an antique house in Wadestown. Hanging out nappies and polishing up the brass doorhandles. Penny-pinching because there was only Dick's scholarship – which was okay because they had prospects and there was a certain obscure satisfaction in saying that they were more hard-up than *even* shop assistants.

Sarah was well on the way though she didn't really show which was one advantage of being a big mother. Sarah-the-foetus would tap periodically on Josie's plumbing like any lonely prisoner trying to get a message through.

About two months since the drop-outs had moved in next door and painted nasturtiums over the front of the house. Dick popped over there most evenings. He said they kept telling him to bring his lady, but Josie wouldn't go over except to run across occasionally with phone messages for Dick. She said she wouldn't leave the kids alone in the house and she couldn't take them over there. It wasn't just the grubbiness, there were bottles all around the place containing uppers and downers and outers, in liquid, horticultural and pharmaceutical forms.

Dick would crawl home with a vacant grin and some new word to set him apart from the masses. He started referring to Frank Zappa as Mister Zee and he'd talk about John Lennon as if they'd shared a locker at Liverpool High.

The fragment that is caught, eternally preserved by that curiously selective process of memory, is probably a Saturday afternoon. Dick has just rolled out of bed, having arrived home in the morning hours. Josie is frying up onions for a casserole. Lake and Daryl kneel on kitchen chairs at the table trying to force wet bread down the mouth of a bird they've rescued from the cat. Josie knows from experience the bird will die in its cottonwool-lined box; that they will find it in a few hours rigid beside the rejected mush of bread and the jar lid of water.

Dick stands there, like a larger bird with pale legs dangling below the blue bathrobe, and tells her about last night. Remembering it she can still smell onions.

'You're joking?' She knows already that he's not.

'It wasn't at all the way you'd imagine. It was a . . . flowing sort of experience. It felt, I think, innocent more than anything. A kind of innocence.'

Life hasn't prepared Josie for this conversation. 'Well, if it's innocence you want there's quite a bit of it over this side of the fence.' Looking pointedly at the children.

She switches off the element and indicates he should follow her out of range of small ears. She's thinking about what *she* was doing last night – hemming up flannelette nightgowns, glueing new soles onto Dick's shoes, sorting out the laundry to be washed in the morning. While he was engaged in unimaginable group activities not ten yards away.

He reaches for her hand but she moves away. He looks dreadful; hollow-cheeked and rheumy-eyed. 'You should see yourself. Innocence seems to take a lot out of you.'

He glances in the mirror. 'That's just the cactus, takes a while to leave your system. They'll have some more on Friday. Sophie, I want you to come for that. We all want you to come.' He smiles. He's offering her a great gift.

He always called her Sophie. He thought Josie was a dowdy name and Josephine out of the question. She used to like being Sophie but now the name belongs with nappies and morning sickness and gooseberry fool.

On the Friday she said, please don't go – not sure if it was a plea or an ultimatum. He went. She locked the doors and barricaded them with the table, the bookcase and assorted chairs. When the back door wouldn't open at three o'clock in the morning he only hammered on it once and didn't even bother to try the front door. On the Sunday he called in to collect his clothes, his books and his Sergeant Pepper album. He was going to come back for the rest of his records but never did because about that time the power in the nasturtium house got disconnected.

Before Josie had organised herself and the children into their return north Dick and the cactus crowd had got themselves a bus, painted it with a whole frenzy of nasturtiums and headed off to a valley in Taranaki.

Geoff of course is familiar with this chapter of Josie's life. He's heard the traditional version with Josie cast as outraged wife and mother, and the wry up-dated version in which she plays the spoilsport. He's also enjoyed an improved version rich with voyeuristic detail and has participated in an imaginative improvisation of what might've taken place had she been bolder and less pregnant. ('Less selective', she corrects, striking aside 'bolder'. Timidity being an insult to all of her sex.)

The tiny plane bounces gingerly on tarmac and the passengers hold their breath. Then they are driving along the runway, pulling up as if this is a supermarket carpark, and the moment of fear is obliterated.

The motel is central and unremarkable. Geoff selected it from the yellow pages and booked by phone. Josie looks at the double bed with its candlewick spread, the Tretchekov print of a rose wilting on a step, the mirror with its fluted edges, and is reassured. Nothing devastatingly regrettable could happen in such anonymous and functional surroundings. Despite her suspenders.

Despite the cosmetics, the dress, the perfume, the foolish underwear crammed into the red canvas bag Geoff has tossed on the bed. Beside which he now lies looking at the ceiling which is scattered with grains of tinsel like tawdry stars. He's so familiar, so comfortingly solid and woolly, that she wants to scoop him up and run home with him.

Geoff spreads his arms. 'Pull the curtains, you gorgeous thing. We have hours and hours.'

Josie sits alone at a round glass table. She lights another cigarette. She's drinking gin and tonic. When she lifts her glass the ice clinks against the side but she can hardly hear it over other people's conversations.

Josie is Joan Collins. She is Mae West. She is Elsie Tanner. When she looks up her view is fringed by a feathering of eyelashes last worn by Lake to a standard five fancy dress party. When she looks down she sees a wonderful cleavage of pale flesh rimmed by black crepe, highlighted by a fine gold chain. The skirt of her dress falls open from a slit that begins just where her sheer black stockings darken at the top. This is the only dress she owns that doesn't billow and drape euphemistically; this dress proclaims every inch of Josie.

Dressing back at the motel, arranging her deceptively flimsy bra, refastening suspenders, she had felt at first too silly for words. But as her reflection changed she began to believe in it. Now her reservations are all burnt out. She's freewheeling on a fast highway. The sensation is familiar enough but this time she's on her own and there is no fond and certain climax.

This is the third bar they've tried. Josie has no wish to be recognised by incredulous ex-colleagues, there are certain pubs that must be avoided. The first place they looked in was packed with kids that looked no older than Daryl and Sarah. The second was so staid that Josie backed straight out again, jolted by the startled glances, the cold draught of reality. And Geoff had said, 'Shall we forget it? If you like we . . .'

But it was too late, for Josie, to turn back. And this bar was right. She could tell the minute she walked in. Expectations hang in this smoky air. The women smile and smile and never let their lipstick wear thin. The men wear pale trousers with the square outline of credit cards showing through their back pockets. Josie and Geoff came in separately, like strangers.

If she tilts her head back a little she can see him in the large mirror. He's at the end of the bar sitting on a high stool. Last time she looked he was talking to a couple, but now they've gone. She can see him laughing, looking up at someone beyond the mirror's frame. If they were strangers to each other she knows it would be him, among this room full of possibilities, that she would want to know better.

Briefly, this thought rattles her. What's she doing in here trying to prove a point that's beyond question? She thinks of just taking her drink and joining him. But now, when she tilts her head again, she sees that Geoff's face is partly obscured by a glorious mass of dark red hair.

Josie clenches her teeth. She looks across at the little pink man who has been gazing at her tits for the last ten minutes but can't bring herself to catch his eye. A part of her still wants to laugh at all this.

Three women walk past Josie's table. The nearest bumps against it with her thigh. Josie saves her glass. The woman glances down vaguely as if it was someone else's clumsiness. The place is becoming crowded. If Josie goes to the bar for a refill someone will steal her seat, her table.

'D'you mind?' he asks.

She hasn't seen him approach. When she smiles he slides rather awkwardly into the chair across from hers. His glass is half empty. He lays a hand beside it, a long pale hand with heavy knuckles. No rings. She can feel him looking at her but she doesn't suppose it to mean anything. Still, she's glad he's there. She imagines Geoff glancing over his shoulder and seeing the two of them reflected in the mirror.

She makes herself look at his face to confirm that first impression. A young man, perhaps even under thirty. A pale poetic face, clean-shaven, and a mass of light brown curls. She thinks he's beautiful. Too beautiful to be interested in women. It seems to be a rule of nature that men of such appealing features seek other men.

It's his mouth she wants to keep watching. In his still face the mouth seems small and nervously watchful. It reminds Josie of a sparrow, all that nervous energy perfectly still yet poised for flight.

'Are you waiting for someone?' A hint of Oxford english.

Josie's mouth twitches. 'You could say that.'

His eyes smile at her knowingly. He cups his chin in his hand. 'You had ... ah have ... someone in particular in mind?'

She shakes her head.

'Not even some kind of mental picture?'

'Nothing that definite.'

He shakes his curls about as if she's wonderfully beyond the pale. Josie laughs.

'And why are you here?'

'That depends,' he says, 'on the reason I choose to believe at the time.'

Josie's vaguely disappointed. Is he just one of those fools intent on boring people rigid with their coy obscurities? But she plays along anyway. 'So what is the reason you choose to believe right now?'

'Much the same as yours.' He waves aside her offer of a cigarette. 'As a matter of fact I come here every second Friday. And every other Friday I go wherever they have a decent band. I always come here alone. That makes it something of an adventure. Like fishing—you toss out a line and see what happens. Actually I've never been fishing but I imagine it feels something the same. Do you fish?'

Josie's laugh takes her by surprise. She chokes on her gin and coughs a bit before she can croak out the reply that came to her so quickly. 'This is my first time.'

He has to go back and get the sequence. Then he laughs.

'And do you have much luck?' She thinks, at least I'm enjoying myself. I've fallen in with good company.

'What do you think?'

'I think you'd do very well indeed.'

'Is that an invitation?'

'Me?' She can feel her mouth gaping. 'I had you figured as gay.'

'Oh. So it wasn't an invitation?'

'Do you want it to be?' She shouldn't let her surprise show like this.

He leans back in his chair and drains his glass. 'It's up to you.'

Josie panics. Her instinct is to say, don't be silly. She leans back a

219

little and looks in the mirror, as if just a glimpse of Geoff's wild grey hair will provide her with guidance. He's gone. Josie closes her eyes tight for a second. When she opens them her companion is leaning forward, waiting. She takes a breath. 'Okay. Yes, why not? But I need another drink. I'll shout you. What is it?'

'Vodka and lemonade.'

As he hands her his glass his fingers brush hers.

Josie shoves her way to the bar. She no longer feels like Joan Collins. When she glimpses her dark ankles in their high black shoes they don't look elegant, only middle-aged. She thinks that now he's seen her away from the camouflaging table he'll change his mind and who wouldn't.

Although she looks all around the tables and even pushes through to check the alcove she doesn't see Geoff. She doesn't see the owner of the wild auburn hair either. At the bar she pays for the drinks even though she's sure he'll have fled by the time she gets back. She's not sure if she's hoping he's gone or hoping he's stayed.

'Thank you,' he says, not touching the glass she sets in front of him.

Josie, seated again, looks everywhere but at his face. Now everything is awkward. She forces herself, 'Can I ask your name?'

He says something but she can't hear. For a weird moment she thinks he said Josh. She leans forward and cups her ear, deaf in her old age.

'John.'

She nods. 'Mine's Sophie.'

He smiles. 'It suits you.'

She watches him lift his glass and drink too much too fast. Nervous, or eager?

'I don't have a car,' he says.

'Nor do I.' Her eyes searching again among the crowd. Aware that this one's watching her and drawing his own conclusions. Part of her is still expecting Geoff to materialise at this table and extract her. Game well played but over.

He doesn't. She's on her own. Remembering, from the messy drawer of retrievable childhood memories, her first time on a two-wheeler. The bike too big for her—it belonged to her cousin Frank—so she had to give the pedals a furious downward thrust and wait for them to return. The ground miles below her and moving.

Frank, who was almost an adult, had given her a push. She clung on petrified, her feet catching the pedals, not able to stop. By some miracle of balance she was out the gate and heading downhill, knowing the silver lever beside her fingers was the brake yet unable to unclench her fist from the handlebars. Flying downhill towards the T intersection and the big memorial gateway to the park. Time, though, to work out that if there were no cars on the main road, and if she could aim the bike at that narrow, stone-arched entrance. If. If.

'You're waiting for someone,' he tells her.

'I saw someone before that I knew. I just wondered if they'd gone.'

'You don't want them to see us leaving? We can leave separately.'

'Have you got a busy schedule or something?'

A high apologetic laugh. 'I just don't like this place much.'

'Now it's served its purpose?'

He shrugs. 'Why pretend? It's easier if you're honest.'

If only he'd be consistent. One minute he's in control of the situation, the next he's being nervous and deferential.

She says, 'I can't drink that fast and I don't like to waste something I've paid for.'

He moves his head and hands—fair enough, whatever you say—then sits playing with her lighter. She takes small sips, deliberately delaying now. She looks at the people at other tables. Makes herself look at them so she can't see the tremor in his flighty lips.

The bike took her straight for the grey stone arch. She saw the pale marbling in the stone before she hit it. The bike came off worse. Josie got grazes, a fractured arm and a bump on her head the size of a bicycle bell. You must have a hard head, people told her. You must have nine lives . . . somebody up there must like you.

She finishes her drink, and they leave together. It's easier if you're honest. Josie stops in briefly at the bottle store. John pulls a handful of small change from his pocket and says he'd offer to contribute but.

He says he has a bedsitter, not far, they can walk if she doesn't mind. She can't offer the motel room which is presumably in use. It crosses her mind that this man could be cunning and crazy; he could have a knife in his top drawer, he could cut her up and put her dismembered parts in a suitcase. When they left the table she saw he limped—a dragging, ungainly walk that seemed to put weight on his shoulders. Out in the street she can see that he wears heavy shoes and one is built up. He sees her looking and says, 'I was born that way.'

Being crippled doesn't make it less likely that he'll harm her but it does make it too late, now she's seen his foot, to change her mind.

They're walking up the street. He's on the outside, probably by coincidence. Josie can remember way back to when men were instructed to walk on the outside. Being able to remember stuff like that makes her feel as if she's been plodding about the earth for aeons like a dinosaur.

Her feet ache in her silly high shoes but she can't complain of that. At least hers move in equal strides the way they're supposed to. Is it hard to keep that heavy foot in motion? As if he's reading her thoughts he says, 'I never know whether I should tell the people I meet. Whether to say, look I've got this ugly foot.'

She smiles at him because she doesn't know either. It depresses her to think of him coming out of pubs week after week with his foot weighing on his shoulders like an albatross.

His place is an old narrow house crammed between other old narrow houses, all with tiny verandahs and intricate rusting ironwork. The front door is open and leads to a passage with a high ceiling. His footsteps on the bare wooden floor sound sinister. Hers sound sharp and frivolous. Juliet and Sandi, who have taken courses in self-defence, know personally of dozens of instances where women have been brutally attacked. Innocent women, not half-way guilty ones like Josie.

His room is drab and damp. A double bed, low slung, and a couple of stools are all there is to sit on. Josie goes to the windows and lifts the yellowed net curtains. She sees more windows, long and high like these, more net curtains. The room is harshly lit by an unshaded bulb, too strong. There are books stacked in the corner. She looks at titles — thrillers, science fiction, popular psychology.

She can hear him opening and shutting cupboards in the kitchen alcove. The room has a smell she can't quite identify, neither pleasant nor unpleasant. He asks from the kitchen if she'd like some tea or coffee. She says she'll stick with gin. The bottle she bought at the bottle store, and the plastic bottle of tonic sit on the floor still in their paper bags. He says, from the kitchen, he's sorry she had to pay for it. If it'd been earlier in the week . . .

He told her on the way home that he was unemployed. Has been out of work for over two years. There comes a point, he'd said limping along the street, where you've been out of work so long no one will risk employing you. But he seemed vaguely irritated when she was sympathetic.

'I'm used to it,' he said briskly. 'I have a few friends. I manage to entertain myself.'

He comes out from the kitchen with a couple of candles stuck into saucers with the warm wax. He sets them on the floor and switches out the light.

'Sit down. Make yourself at home.' A small wry grin. 'I'll pour you a gin.'

He limps away for a glass. Josie sits on the bed. She keeps her legs over the side though the bed's too low to be comfortably used that way. It demands to be stretched out on.

He returns with the glass. Just one. 'Do you smoke? I have some excellent heads I've been saving for . . . a suitable occasion.' He sits on the bed facing her. She's relieved he's stopped walking about with that ominous tread. She watches him stick two cigarette papers together and carefully spread them with the contents of a matchbox. She's so sharply aware of the room, of his movements; an incredulous prying voice in her head squeaking, my god this is really happening.

'Sophie's not your real name is it? No. I thought not. They never give their real names.'

Fear again. Her heart screaming Geoff, Geoff. If anything happens to me this is your fault. Thinking of a knife, blood, her big body slumped and severed. (Her children would read the finer details after the inquest or maybe the trial.) The acceptable, calculated risks have already been taken into account by Geoff. In her handbag there is this small and slithery packet she accepted from him earlier, when the chemist shops were still open.

The harsh smoke makes her splutter and cough. He leans back, propped on his elbows. 'How do you want us to start?'

She coughs some more. Her eyes water. She passes it back to him. 'Talk to me,' she says. 'Tell me about . . . the other times.' Her lungs whimper in pain. They're black and sticky, encrusted with tar like burnt-on porridge. She's seen photos of lungs like hers. Poor lungs, she thinks. As if it's beyond her control.

He tells her about a woman whose friend was in a Singapore jail. 'She expected him to be executed. She kept saying, "I know they'll execute him". It made me start thinking about the word. If you execute a signature you make it exist, yet you execute a person and end his existence.'

'Did they execute him?'

'I don't know. She only came here that once.'

Then there was the teacher ('male,' he said, giving Josie a quizzical look) who'd run off with a fourth-former (female). Had left a wife and family behind in some country town and fled to Auckland with his prize. But after a couple of weeks he got sick of her. He got picked up by a club-footed man called John and stayed with him for four days. When he went back to see the girl she'd taken a handful of assorted pills.

'What happened then?'

'They pumped her out and shipped her home. He went away. I never saw him again.'

A wealthy woman took him to her home. She got him to dress up in her late husband's clothes before they made love. She asked him to go down to the basement where they had this big wooden tool box and drag it upstairs and lie down in it as if it was a coffin and then she threw herself on top of him in hysterical passion.

Josie thinking, as he tells her this, that his enthusiasm has a kind of innocence. He collects threads from other people's private lives as some people collect coloured bottles or butterflies. But she won't add a colourful splash to his collection. Although it is in Josie's nature to explain herself—to tell all and embroider a little so it has more substance and maybe gets a laugh or two—she will remain an enigma not worth relating to those who come after.

Josie is thinking too fast, too much. The gin and the joint have made her body slow and heavy and her mind nimble. It leaps from thought to thought with the effortless cunning of a flea.

John (she must ask, she must remember to ask, if that's his real name—he looks more like an Oliver) has got tired of talking. Or perhaps has just lost track of what he was saying. His slightly puzzled BBC voice fades off. There's a silence. It begins to feel to Josie like a very long silence. She tries to recall what it was she'd wanted to ask him. John sits looking down at the crocheted bedcover (made by his mother, a sister, the wealthy woman with the wood box?), his lashes are long and curly like his hair. Josie wishes he looked less like a pretty child.

'Would you like me to get into bed?' he asks.

It takes her a few seconds to grasp the words and assemble them and to remember that's what she's here for. 'If you want to.' She hears herself sounding like a mother and would like a second chance.

But he has stood up and is very slowly undressing. He takes off his heavy grey sweatshirt and slightly grubby net singlet. Josie looks at his ribs and the movement of his muscles. He's slightly built, hairless. Beside him Geoff would look like an old and furry piece of cheese. But she is not to start thinking of Geoff.

This man is very beautiful. Josie gazes, impressed at the indentation of his tilted buttocks and the gentle curve of flesh sliding away from his hip bones. He stands there naked with his eyes demurely downcast, waiting for something. His body pleases Josie, she could look at it for hours, but it doesn't arouse her. He's beginning to get gooseflesh. Josie turns and adjusts the bedding, folding it down at one side. She stands so he'll have room to get in and stretch out.

He sort of crawls and lunges into the bed. His eyes look glassy as if he's in a trance. In bed he throws out his arms and thrusts back his head, his legs thrash at the covers, kicking them away. He lies like a crucifix and waits.

Josie's head is cluttered with useless little blocks and she can't think. Dangerous laughter surges between the cracks where the blocks don't fit together. She remembers the small slithery packet in her bag, she considers the operation of getting herself undressed. Have to remember the tiny hook and eye at the top of the zip.

'Please,' he begs the wall above his bed. His voice is hoarse and desperate. 'Please. I'm your slave. Let me be your slave. You can do whatever you like with me. Be fierce. Be fierce and cruel. I know you have it in you.'

Josie tries to shake the blocks in her head into some kind of order. She tries to consider her situation. She bends and picks up her shoes which she slipped off when she sat on the bed.

He raises his head until he's looking at her. 'Yes,' he says. 'Yes.' He's looking at those sharp black heels.

Josie closes her eyes for a second. 'The bathroom,' she says. 'I have to use your bathroom.'

Irritation clouds his humility. 'First right at the end of the passage.'

She picks up her handbag. She's still clutching her shoes. 'I'm sorry,' she mutters. 'All that gin.'

He rolls his eyes impatiently, he can't bear her being sorry.

Josie is out his door, down the passage in her stockinged feet. Out the front door, across the street and running down a narrow sidestreet. Surely, surely he won't get dressed and follow her. She feels so bad, such a rotten cow—a mean bitch who could never have been mean enough or bitch enough to suit. Soon she'll stop and get her bearings, find a taxi stand, force her feet into her cruel shoes. She does want to use the bathroom, she did then and she still does.

She's back now at the motel. In the end she walked, in her stockinged feet, because when she'd worked out where she was it didn't seem that far, and she passed no taxi stands on the way. The bottoms of her stockings have worn through, pink toes stick out through fine black 15 denier.

There's no light showing in their unit and the key's not under the potted geranium where they'd agreed to leave it. She's afraid to knock, it's very silent in there, and what would she say?

Just a half block down the street is a nondescript pub where she used to go occasionally with a man who had a wife and a mistress and needed a friend to confide in. At the doorway of the hotel she leans against the wall and crams her feet into the shoes. A couple walk past hand in hand. The woman gives Josie an I-know-how-it-is smile that soothes her feet all the way to the Ladies Room where she sees herself in the mirror and is shocked to find she's still the tarted up version. She hoists her dress to cover a bit more in front, reapplies her lipstick and remembers her real need was to pee. And to sit there reflecting on what might have been, what nearly was, and what surely is happening for Geoff.

Then to teeter, with her hands still glowing from the free warm air, into the public bar and order a gin which she needs badly to dilute the pain that has just soaked through to her heart at the thought of Geoff and.

The small bearded man lined up at the bar beside her gives her a tentative don't-I-know-you-from-somewhere look. Josie thinks she does but doesn't want to be bothered about it just now. She lets her glance slide vaguely past him. The barman hands her her change.

'You're from the island,' he says. 'That's where I've seen you isn't it.'

So she has to turn to him.

'Your husband's the big fella with a mass of white hair. I sometimes see him at the pub.'

'That's right,' she says. 'We live at Whiripare. I know your face.' Absurd but she feels a wrench of homesickness, or something close, for the island. She's grateful now that he spoke to her, this stranger who feels at once like family because they share an island. They shop at the same shops and gaze at the same ocean. Already they have so much in common.

'Are you alone?' she asks. 'Shall we find a table?' Her feet are killing her.

He's not, it turns out, just a fellow islander, but also an ex-journalist. In a country where professional networks are tight and people drift from paper to paper to radio, TV, public relations, they have, of course, mutual acquaintances.

226

He's been over in the city for two days looking for a job. 'I was prepared to take anything,' he says, 'that paid a reasonable kind of wage.' But he found nothing at all.

'Two days isn't long,' she says.

'It's enough. I told myself if I didn't get something in two days that was it—obviously I wasn't meant to get a job over here.' He looks suddenly self-righteous. 'I was prepared even to stay over here during the week and just go back weekends.' The supreme sacrifice, his tone says. Josie doesn't smile even to herself. She can relate to that.

'All the same,' he says, 'the more places I tried the more I began to hope that I wouldn't find anything.' He smiles at her. 'I'm glad I saw you. I missed the boat tonight. That's two nights over here and I was starting to get homesick.'

'Me too,' she says.

He doesn't seem to notice she's disguised as a whore. And that, thinks Josie, is one of the virtues of the people over there. City standards count for nothing. When you think about it, it's a kind of subversion just living on an island. She must make that point when she next writes to Lake.

She explains to her new friend that she's locked out of their motel room. She says she and Geoff had different things to go to and he must've taken the key. But soon he's bound to be back. He asks her what it was she went to.

'Oh, just a movie.'

'What was it? Any good?'

'Bizarre,' she says, smiling, seeing bits of it purring soundlessly on a big screen. 'Rubbish really. Sort of soft porn. I wouldn't recommend it. Pretty tacky all round.'

October

DAPHNE HAD, OF course, known about it for ages. The information had been there, she said, for anyone who was interested.

Keith hadn't known about it, at least not in the certain way the programme told it with charts and maps and talking heads. Yet there was no surprise in what was told—except perhaps the wonder that anyone could've supposed otherwise. Watching the programme Keith saw that which he'd known in his bones being confirmed by people in a position to be believed.

Now it was a nightmare with a name. Nuclear winter. The name made it accessible, common currency. It tamed it. Having a name, nuclear winter could now go into circulation with all the other symbols of progress: technology, anti-ballistic, radiation, strategic . . .

Even here at the self-effacing bottom of the world the smoke from incinerated continents will choke the life from living things. *Even here.* That point had been made with a certain injured dismay. As if New Zealanders had rightfully believed that God would protect this, his own country, with some celestial polythene umbrella. And that here (where, they say, children do so well, though fewer of them are produced with each passing year) we would start afresh, populate the new world with an inchoate southern species.

Keith had felt compelled to ask Daphne, the expert, if New Zealanders had honestly believed in their immunity. And Daphne has said naturally, and the belief was still not without foundation. Some kind of mutant life form could well survive, adapt and reproduce.

It seemed to Keith that Daphne was in some secret way displeased by the screening of the programme. As if such a mass propagation of information undermined her standing as an authority. Or perhaps she was simply put out that a medium which enraged her with its gleeful, tacky sexism should pretend to have a conscience.

Although there was nothing in it that surprised him Keith has been unable to root the documentary from his mind. Since he watched it he has had dreams of a corrupted landscape. The first night was the surest dream. He was walking through the bush to his little bay. Everything was coloured in blaring distorted shades of purple and lime green—the kind of colour you get on a badly adjusted TV. There was a great silence. An absence of birds and not a whisper of the sea though he knew it was there just below him. The leaves of the ferns beside the track were spongy and moist. He didn't touch them. The leaves of the trees were fluorescent and pulpy but the branches, the trunks, though a purplish shade of brown, were scarred and knotted as they should be. Reassured, Keith reached out for a branch. It came away on his fingers, rotted flesh of tree, the consistency of yoghurt. He didn't dare go further.

When he woke from the dream it was still dark but he got up and dressed. He took his torch and walked up the hill and then down the track to his bay. He scrunched over the razor-edged rock oyster shells to the flat rock and sat there until the sun came up. There was a rasping pain in the back of his throat as if he needed to cry. It felt as if he was the only one who really knew. He wanted to take the world by the scruff of the neck and shake some sense into it.

For the next few days his brain was clogged by the horror of his nightly dreams. He went to work and dug and shovelled and carried the pipes and it felt effortless and timeless, as if he was watching himself working. He was laying sewerage pipes at a newly built holiday home at Huri Bay. The owner lived in Manukau. The house was empty. Keith dug the trench, laid the lengths of ceramic pipe fitted end to end, covered them over. The house was set on its own among the bush. It was the best job he'd had on the island. Maybe the best job he'd ever had.

When he drove home in the evenings he kept hoping Daphne would have gone to the city. He was finding her particularly hard to stomach. He couldn't get rid of the feeling that somehow Daphne and destruction went hand in hand. Even though she had, admittedly, done more than most to alert the world he'd decided her methods were suspect and her energy subversive. Like a clever child she could recite lists of missile bases, the latest warhead tallies and the fine print of the Limited Test Ban Treaty, the Anti-Ballistic Missile Treaty, the Outer Space Treaty. But her heart didn't comprehend.

Daphne's optimism was dangerous and her vision terribly flawed. She was riding fearlessly astride the world, charging into the twenty-first century in the assumption that effort was rewarded and sanity would prevail. Above her head she waved the muddled banner of collective feminist wisdom.

Whereas in Keith's vision of the future it was not, finally, the demise of the human race (flesh blown from bones by an unimaginable wind, the slow liquefying of the brain, the poisoning of the arteries, scavenging, starvation, cannibalism) that froze the heart and whined its high yellow note of certainty into the brain. The final horror was the sodden sound of leaves falling, mottled eggs lying forever in their nests, a silent sea thick as axle grease . . .

But now his anger at Daphne has softened somewhat. He makes allowances. He remembers the family photo in Daphne's room, those cheerful open faces, and he thinks he understands the source of her misguided confidence. She knows no better.

Keith does. He knows about madness; its guile, its moments of charming plausibility, its power. He knows the futility of trying to counter it with reason. The thing about insanity is you have to treat it on its own terms.

Night. Outside the opossums make their demented laughter. Keith doesn't, tonight, listen breathlessly for the sound that will tell him that this time, this time it's something else out there. He doesn't even have the blankets up over his head and held fast in case something shuffling and terrible should grope to his bed and wrench them free.

Howard is home for the holidays. He lies turning and breathing in the bed that, term time, is covered with Keith's books and socks and chess pieces. And although he's not quite the brother Keith would choose at least his presence keeps at bay the nameless night things. And when Howard is home their mother becomes Eve Lowrie and laughs and talks about when she was a young woman and a celebrity, and Keith can feel himself breathing right in and right out instead of stopping when there's still a bit of air that he doesn't dare use up.

Keith listens to Howard's breathing and is sure his brother's awake. 'Howard?'

'What?'

'I just thought, if I was you I'd want to sometimes bring a friend home for the holidays.' Silence. 'Why don't you?'

'Wouldn't have a bed.'

'He could have mine. I'd sleep on the sofa. If you wanted.'

'Well I don't.'

Keith looks at the ceiling, the shadows up there. An opossum chatters. 'Why not?'

'I don't, that's all.'

'Because you think they wouldn't like it here? They'd think it was sort of peculiar?'

'Don't be stupid.'

But Keith is determined to get to where he's been heading. 'You mean they'd think, if they came, it was just like their place? Just like anyone's place?'

Howard sighs impatiently.

'Do they tell you what their homes are like? About their families, things like that?'

'You ask some really stupid things.' But Howard likes to talk about boarding school, to be authoritative and worldly. 'Of course they talk about their families. And their people come and visit. I told you I went sailing one Sunday with McElrith's parents.'

'What were they like?'

'People. He let me steer the boat coming home.'

'Like our parents? Were they like that?'

'Everyone's different.'

'Why won't you ever say?'

'Say what? I don't know what you're on about.'

'You know. Them. Kids I know, none of their parents seem like ... you know.'

'What? D'you go round at school telling tales about your parents? Big blabbermouth, so all those kids go home and ...'

'I don't. I don't tell anyone.'

'You shouldn't either. Not that there's anything to tell that they'd be interested in.'

'Then why don't you bring your friends home?'

'Why don't you put a sock in it?'

'It's because she's a bit nuts, isn't it?'

'It's you that's nuts. You must be, going round saying things like that. If you don't know the difference between a great sadness and having a screw loose ... I bet he put you up to it. I bet he's been saying things. If anyone's crazy it's more likely him.'

'He never said. You don't see. She's different when you're here. Everything's different. But when you go. There's things. Honestly!'

'You shouldn't say stuff like that, Keith. It's bad to say things like that.'

'But she is. Sometimes I think she is. And it wouldn't be so bad if I knew she was. If someone else said. Then it'd be better, don't you see?'

'I told you not to say those things. She's our mother. There must be something wrong with you to make you say things like that.'

Those same holidays Howard was killed. At the time Keith felt very angry at Howard for having left him forever alone with his parents. It seemed all too typical of his brother. Eventually the anger had

231

dispersed; all his emotions seem to do that on him—give way to a kind of soggy grey futility. The end of the world will turn out to be just another frustrating eventuality in the life of Keith Muir.

How foolishly wistful the claims of historians that individuals have made a difference to the path of fate. As if destiny was open to negotiation. Of course there were always some who, by chance, would be in the right place at the right time and get carried high when fate changed direction. Daphne, for instance.

Daphne has moved in on Maureen. She has bought herself a pushbike and goes over to Kaimoana ostensibly to deliver more of her hand-written notes and collect the tidy typed sheets. But she's really recruiting, single-minded as a salvationist. Dragging Maureen in among the wimmin. Cutting Keith out.

He'd been prepared, even, to get a job and to support them—five mouths—if she'd lost her benefit again because of him. It seemed that might be the way things were supposed to happen. He spent two days in the city trying for anything that might pay a living wage. Two days trying to look keen, obsequious and confident. Two days losing his way in overheated office blocks and listening to city voices, strident with self-importance. When nothing came of it he was, on the whole, relieved.

The first night he'd stayed in a cheap bed-and-breakfast place. The only alternative was Mort and Myra's and he didn't feel up to a gawp at the good life. The second night he managed to miss the ferry and was stuck with his return ticket and not enough cash to buy a bed for the night. He was getting himself drunk enough to ring Mort when he met up with the big blonde woman from Whiripare, so he never got round to making the call because when he'd remembered about it it seemed too late to go ringing up.

He walked the woman called Josie back to her motel, because it was nearly closing time and because she'd seemed hobbled and helpless despite her size. He'd left her at the door, saying yes, he would call over and see them some time, he certainly would. Then for hours he'd wandered about the city. Right into the small hours when you could walk for blocks without seeing a living being. He could've been the last person left on earth. Or perhaps the first.

The people he did see were hardly more than kids. Moving in packs, huddled away in the dark corners of malls, tossing out glowing fag ends and scuffling in plastic bags. They made him think of rats. When he walked past them fear blew cool between his shoulder blades and

232

down his calves as if small sharp teeth might suddenly clamp there.

When he watched the programme on the nuclear winter he remembered those kids and thought, that's it—they'll be the survivors. If anyone gets through it'll be those scraps of life hiccuped out by the urban machine. The ironical justice of the thought pleased him.

Those kids, some of them must've been scarcely older than Alan. Keith hasn't seen the boy since the day he ran away. Three weeks, to Alan, may feel like desertion. Keith has this sense of unspecified obligation to the kid but he's avoided going round there because . . . Because he will feel compelled to say, I tried to find a job but I couldn't. And she would say (or at least think) that two days isn't a lot of trying. And he wouldn't be able to explain the inevitability in the way these things work.

Besides, she doesn't care enough or she would be prepared to take a bit of a risk.

And he doesn't care enough or he'd still be over on the mainland looking for work.

And Alan's one thing, but the other two would start to get on his wick. Things should've just stayed the way they were. Perhaps the most he can do for Alan now is to hope that Maureen gets sick of being a typist so the kid doesn't have to cope with Daphne on top of his other woes.

One afternoon last week Keith did drive, with good intent, up Cashin Road. But when he got to Maureen's gateway he didn't want to go in so he drove on up to the end of the road where there's a shabby piece of concrete and a sentinel rock with a plaque attached on behalf of the Motuwairua Citizens' Association 1951. Standing on the concrete you get an unimpeded view of Auckland.

Keith parked his truck and stood there for a long time though it was misty out on the gulf and all he could see was a vast grey shadow looming on the other side.

He stood propped against the labelled rock and thought about the manic brittle confusion that seemed to be city life, and how all the big decisions were getting made by people who lived like that.

Imagine cities three, four, five times as big as this one. People in them with concentrated power, with access to international secrets and exclusive smouldering phones. People who haven't, in years, heard a live bird singing or sat beneath an unplanned tree. Some not even seen the sun set in a clear sky. That kind of deprivation must in time mutate the mind and rust away the soul. The decision makers have environmentally impaired judgement. The proof is there but no one will admit.

There must be something wrong with you to make you say things like that.

For a while, as Keith stood there the mist cleared just enough for him to see a clear skyline, the reflection of the sun on towering mirror-glassed buildings. The city seemed to lean towards him. A great, glittering beast crouched at the water's edge about to pounce. Its cold eyes fixed on his island.

* * *

Josie folds dresses and lays them in her tattered cardboard suitcase. Each time she packs she's surprised to find she's not the owner of matching travel bags boasting international labels. Her potential harnessed by children, hobbled by lovers.

Even in her cold bright anger there's a softness in the way she handles her dresses. They go back, almost all of them, to the time before Geoff. They are Josie, unique and uncompromised. (She's too big to be intimidated by fashion. She wears, still, the loose soft cottons of the hippie era. Though now, more often, overalls befitting a country woman.)

She sorts through shared drawers, burrowing between matted socks and underpants with limp rubber exposed at the waist to find L-sized pantyhose and laddered knickers. She catches sight of herself in the mirror as she crosses to the suitcase. Even though her jaw is set and her cheeks are flushed the image is unconvincing.

Josie's seen herself play this part before. So even though this time she means it (her mind runs over and over the precise steps of logic that make leaving the only alternative) the spectator in her lies back blowsy and cynical, bored already by this latest repeat of the same old puffed-up melodrama. Having seen already the first act (pointed silences, sharp invective, tears) and the second act (politeness, terrible civility stretched between them like a perishing rubber band).

Almost always it's been Josie who has broken first. Well, someone has to, and Josie doesn't suffer the childish male affliction of pride. She would reach out to him, wearing her tears. He would pretend at first to be unmoved; she would draw back. Slowly, warily they would get back together. Make love wonderingly like a couple of old virgins. For the next few days he would watch her with a bemused young man's gaze and she would want to keep him always close enough to touch.

That was their pattern. In the past it had been complicated by her children's presence. So predictable. Yet not entirely. The element of risk has always been real. Without risk there'd be no beatitude in reprieve. Like a car journey—the assumption is you'll arrive intact yet you're aware of the road toll, you see the roadside evidence of other people's disasters; you know there is no certain immunity. If not this time—

Without the children leaving will be easy. She has friends. Despite her misused years with Geoff she still has friends. They are the people who love you regardless of your choice of partners. Guilty of gross neglect Josie can still expect her friends to stand by her.

The radio is on loud in the kitchen. The volume a kind of abuse being hurled at her through the wall. *Jailhouse Rock* as sung by someone new. They do that all the time—rework the old songs, as if Josie's generation never quite got things right.

She'd like to know if Geoff is still in the kitchen. She'd rather not meet him as she's lugging out her suitcase. She knows he won't be far away. When they're at war they circle endlessly around the same territory, keeping apart but unable to break right away.

So far.

There was a reason, a beginning to this fight although now it's hard to isolate it from the words that came later. From the time they went over to the city last month—right from then Josie has felt unsettled. Airy and apprehensive; she thought she was in for a dose of 'flu. After about a week of feeling that way she told Geoff she'd like to be paid a weekly wage for her labour on the farm and in the house.

He looked at her for a long time. So long that she got up from the table and stacked their dinner plates in the sink with a clatter of rage before he got around to replying.

'Tell me,' he said, 'how much for a fuck? Weekend rates? Overtime?'

She ignored that. 'I'll pay you rent and my half of the food. It's perfectly fair and reasonable. I want it like that. I'm beginning to feel too dependent. It's humiliating to be kept.'

'We could get married.'

She sighed. They'd been through all this. 'Marriage is also humiliating. I've tried it twice too often.'

'Well it would humiliate me to pay you to stay with me. Had you thought of that?'

'You're paying me for that anyway, only in a more devious fashion.

That allows you to feel generous, and makes me feel indebted.'

'Then we'll get a joint bank account. You can pay yourself wages—what's mine is yours. You know that.'

'I don't want a joint bank account. I'd still be obligated. I want to be earning a living. Can't you understand that?'

'Marry me?'

'For Christ's sake . . .'

'You'd feel trapped.'

Right.

'You are trapped, for godsake. You won't leave. You don't want me to leave. You're not going to get up and walk out.'

'What makes you so sure?'

'Not for good, you won't. You'd come back. Why would you want to leave me?'

'Because you won't pay me a wage.'

'You're starting to sound like Juliet.'

'Good.'

'She has such a happy life; no wonder you want to be like her.'

'You make me sick, you know that?'

Later he tried. Came in when she was typing out a description of groats and stood beside the desk. She went on typing.

'It was only one night,' he said. 'One night. One woman. It was for us.'

She'd folded her arms across the typewriter. She let her head fall till her forehead rested on her arms then turned her face slightly so her words would reach him.

'The issue was wages. Didn't you hear me properly. You must be obsessed.'

Josie's folding jerseys now. She avoids looking in the mirror when she passes. Her unseen self feels small and clenched, the voluminous sweater in her hands amazes her.

A vehicle turns in at the road gate. She hears Hogg bark as it comes up the drive, but the bedroom windows face south; only macrocarpa and their own little vegetable garden, she has no view of the driveway.

The radio is turned down just as the news begins. On the hour, every hour, which must make it two o'clock. A ferry leaves at three. She hears car doors slam and voices she can't identify. Geoff gruff in reply.

One jersey fills half a case. She'll have to unpack and eliminate the non-essentials. Some day she can make a dignified reappearance and claim the rest. He'll have moved another woman in for sure; he likes having something to wrap his arms around.

She can hear them all in the kitchen, chairs being drawn up by whoever they are. Geoff will be making tea. She thinks she hears him go out and toss the used tea leaves on her herb garden by the door. She wonders if he'll call her to join them or just pretend she's out.

They get too many visitors. People drifting in with a flagon of execrable red or small plastic bags of home-grown. Geoff feeds them her experimental baking. *Your* friends, she says. Her friends are different, durable. Her criterion is not congeniality so much as a long apprenticeship.

In the north Geoff's friends were people he'd grown up with. They wore boots and knee-length woollen shirts right through winter— men and women the same. They drank beer and talked grudgingly between long pauses or they laughed in wild guffaws over nothing in particular. Unless you'd been to the same school or played the same winter sport they'd never quite accept you and would leave you with little to say.

But Geoff's new island friends talk compulsively—of books read, movies seen, theories embraced or exploded, futures planned. They attach themselves like tumbleweed to anyone who comes near. Share their drugs and unwrap their relationships to expose their naked psyches in front of strangers. And they dress however the whim might take them, to please themselves, to draw attention, to brighten the world. No wonder Geoff's entranced.

The present visitors both confirm and confuse Josie's intentions. It seems important to know who they are, though she couldn't say why. In such circles vehicles are no real guideline. They are replaced frequently then left for dead on roadsides (by the people passionate about environmental protection). They are borrowed and swapped, written off and restored.

Josie carries her case out the front door which is never used except by the Mormon visitors. The car in the drive is a little old Austin splotched with primer. It seems familiar but she can't place an owner to it. Through the kitchen window she can see a curly black head and a thin wisp of smoke.

Geoff's friends, whoever they are, will be able to drive him to the wharf to collect the Land-Rover. She'll leave the key in the dashboard under the paper bag of nails.

But there is no key to use, to leave. Not in the ignition where it should be or the dashboard where it could be or under the seat where they used to leave it. He's deliberately taken it. He must've known she was packing. It's the very thing she would've done but she'd have expected him to be more mature.

She could ring a taxi but the phone is in the kitchen. She could hitch a ride to the wharf but he might have the pleasure of watching from the kitchen window as she lugs her case along the road. And someone they know might give her a lift. It's important to leave with a bit of dignity.

Josie feels weary. Her brain is limp with making decisions that only lead to more decisions having to be made. She can feel her resolve sliding away like sand. She has a dangerous longing to be held.

She needs more time to think things through. There'll be other boats to catch. What's one more night when you're on the brink of a new life?

She hauls the suitcase round the south side, past the bedroom, and stacks it in the lean-to they euphemistically call the implement shed. So it's there for when she needs it, is what she tells herself. Herself knows better and cries, *shame*. Reduced once again to bluff and gamesmanship. Wanting Geoff to find her clothes, her case, her person, is missing. Why are they so childish?

In her newest overalls and her best bush shirt and long-service leather boots (running away hadn't seemed an event to get too dressed up for) she walks across to the henhouse. Her fags are, reassuringly, still in her pocket. Lighter also. From the henhouse you can see the far end of their drive, though not much of the house, most of it being hidden by the big water tank and a scrubby stand of unproductive feijoas.

The hens see her coming and race towards her. They push and squabble just inside the netting and pierce Josie with their greedy little eyes. She upends an old petrol drum, saved for a thousand possible uses, and sits where she can see the hens, watch the driveway, watch the path that leads out this way from the house. Whatever happens, today will have been a workday wasted.

If she leaves him who will mind the chickens? Eighteen of them in their own movable A-frame pen. There were twenty, but two hatched late, in the hot-water cupboard where Josie transferred them, and when she put them in with their brothers and sisters and harassed mother they were embraced into the family group then methodically pecked to death. Josie didn't know until she found them next morning with holes gouged in their brains. She should've known better than to put them in there, Geoff said. What did she suppose *pecking order* meant. She said, I thought it was who got the most wheat.

Geoff wouldn't look after the chickens as well as she does, even though she hasn't quite forgiven them. He wouldn't move their pen as often, or clean their water bowl. And if she goes who will take carrots to the ponies and coddle them and scratch their shaggy chins? Who will commiserate with Sneezie about those last swollen weeks.

The hens lose hope of food and wander off, going about their twitchy poultry lives. They sidestep nervously when the rooster approaches. He's short-legged and heavy-necked with an orange mohawk and a splendid peacock-coloured tail. He swaggers among his hens with his wings hitched in his belt tabs. Josie loathes the rooster. She thought they would only have hens but old Bill brought the rooster one day in a sugar sack. Said he was a gift and that Josie and Geoff were his only chance of escaping the axe edge. Geoff had been effusive in his admiration of the bird.

'Need a rooster,' said old Bill. 'Keeps the hens happy.'

'Too right,' said Geoff.

But Josie has seen how the hens run and cringe when he saunters past. She's seen them trapped in corners, rammed against the netting like an old mat being shaken. Eyes closed, beaks open, thinking of Mother England. Happy?

Juliet would've appreciated the implications if only the rooster'd been here when she came.

Josie hasn't heard from Juliet since her night at their place. Geoff says, and swears it's true and not just his idea of a joke, that as he and the red-haired woman were waiting at the taxi stand Juliet and Sandi had walked past on the other side of the road.

'And they saw you?'

'Juliet waved. A bit . . . sort of furtively. And I sort of waved back. Then they had this excited little confab and glanced back a couple of times.'

'Oh no!'

'We were just standing there. Well I might've had my arm around her or something. I'm not sure.'

'You know what they'll think?'

'I was off with someone?'

'Mm.'

'Which I was.'

'Yes, but they'll think . . . and for them—for Juliet anyway—it'll be a kind of triumph. It'll confirm all the things she believes about men. And she'll feel so smug. She'll be lying in bed right now pitying me.

She'll be wondering if you've confessed or if I'm onto you and she'll be wringing her conscience over whether or not as a friend she should ring and tell me what you're up to.'

'You could get in first and explain.'

'Explain? Tell her . . . Don't be daft. Besides she'd never in a million years believe me.'

'At least she'd know you knew. About me.'

Oh yes, Josie knows. She knows what they talked about, what they did and didn't do. She knows details she didn't need to know. That the woman, for instance, had a head cold. She was all blocked up with it and couldn't breathe through her nose so that ruled out . . .

'But you *asked* her?' Whispering lonely in his tight arms, feeling his heart beating on while hers has stopped.

'Sort of.'

'What d'you mean, sort of?' She thought his heartbeat had quickened.

'You know. Not in so many words.' He buried his face in against her neck. His chin was rough with stubble. Unkempt, like his paddocks. He mumbled, 'Do you want me to show you?'

Her name was Lisa—the owner of the wild red hair. She had a head cold and two school-aged children. Her brother-in-law boarded with them and went to Polytech. He didn't mind babysitting. Her husband owned a sports supplies shop. Weekends he knocked off early and went sailing or diving with friends. She hated sailing, she was afraid of diving.

On the farm—the real farm—Josie would hang a cured leg of bacon in the pantry and slice off thick, wonderful chunks as required. Now she pares away slices of Geoff's woman as appetite demands. Soon there will be only bone and a lingering smell of resentment. She always takes bigger helpings than she ought to.

This Lisa is after a job but not just any old job. She'd like to do social work and meet with people whose problems are more interesting than her own. She'd never had an affair before, though she'd been thinking about it for ages.

'You mean she thought you were going to be a regular event?'

'I don't know what she thought.'

'But you let her think that? You didn't make it clear?'

'She knew I had someone. I think she just wanted something to break the monotony of her life.'

'But.'

'But . . . yeah . . . well my impression was that she was fairly unhappy and looking for a bit more than that.'

'You cared about that? About her being unhappy?'

'I felt a bit sad for her. Yes, sorry for her, of course I did. All that *and* a runny nose. Darling, what is it you're getting at?'

'Nothing I suppose. Nothing. I just want to know.'

Everything. The way your eyes moved, the exact words, if strands of her hair got caught in your mouth, in hers, what kind of hair? And afterwards did you hold each other, for how long, did she avoid your eyes then, did her fingertips trace the crinkled creekbeds of your face, did she . . .

Josie knows all that can be told. She doesn't know the things she needs to know. She and Geoff could grow old together and still she will never know, though she could ask him anything and he would answer to the best of his ability.

When Josie knocked on the motel door they were inside there in the dark, lying still. Geoff with his finger on Lisa's lips. He didn't know what to do.

Her outside, them inside. She thinks about that a lot. Her standing there in her wornout stockings. Them keeping quiet as mice.

She believes what Geoff has told her. It hangs together, she has to believe it. He gave her substance. She gave him only shadows in return.

She'd been unable to lie convincingly yet was reluctant to give him short measure. She'd elaborated wildly, she'd told the truth, she invented a whole impromptu scenario involving the ex-reporter from Hoki Bay who'd escorted her back to the motel the second time and whom Geoff had seen and recognised. Peering through a gap in the curtains after he'd heard their voices – above the pounding of his hyped-up heart.

Geoff saw her variety as deception. Though he had her expand the other stories, he knew right away which was the truth. He knows her too well. He wouldn't complain but she knows that, in a sense, she failed him. With just a little more fortitude she could've given him, as he'd given her, the agitating gift of uncertainty.

Josie has been sitting on the drum for what must surely be an hour. At least she has intermittently sat on the drum. In between she has moved the chickens to fresh grass, gathered some puha from the fenceline and fed it to the chooks, collected up a bottle, a couple of rusted tins, an old sheep skull, and a length of rusted wire and stored them tidily inside the drum.

She saw the afternoon plane circle for landing, then later heard it depart. The ferry must be sailing around about now. She's not leaving today.

She could, if it came to that, still get a room at the pub tonight and leave first thing in the morning. The chickens don't need her, nor do the ponies. She's invented commitments to weigh the balance.

> Dear Daryl and Sarah, wish you were here. Come home and anchor me. Without you I'm a large vessel floundering aimlessly round in ever-decreasing circles. One nervous eye cocked for icebergs.

Sarah, sharp and quizzical in her mind's eye, gives Josie advice. Just do what you want to do, old thing; it's that simple.

Nothing, Josie tells her, is ever that simple. You'll learn. Sarah smiles and knows better.

Josie hears Hogg barking. Then voices, car doors. She waits for the car to leave. The engine whines and dies. Again and again. She can pick Geoff's voice. It makes her heart twitch hopefully as if she had Hogg's ears transplanted in her chest.

The piebald Austin moves silently into view being pushed up the drive by Geoff and the owner of the black hair. Who, she remembers now, is Norman. Of Norman and Dave; twice met, bosom friends. The way it is here. The car shudders and splutters. The pushers stand aside and applaud as smoke pours from the exhaust pipe. Norman gets in the passenger seat. Geoff opens the gate and waves them off. They honk back.

He walks back towards the house slowly, looking about him. Josie's sure she's out of sight. Her heart pounds as if she's four years old and hiding in the hot-water cylinder when everyone else has been found. Then she hadn't been able to wait. Had called out, Here I am.

She's tempted to do it again.

He's walking around the house calling her name. There's an edge of panic in the way his gravelled voice holds onto the last note. He's not sure of finding her. This time she may have really gone. She has given him uncertainty.

She lets him call twice more.

'Here I am.'

*   *   *

Alan was right all along. She should've known he would be. Whether

242

or not he knows it the world's on Alan's wavelength. The men who care for machines and money are well on the way to inheriting the earth.

It was television he was so right about. She should've made it priority one from the outset. It's the most rewarding money she's ever spent. If you can't beat the world it obviously pays to try and join it. For hours at night their new possession takes the three of them off her hands, out of her head, shakes them away from her feet and elbows.

She doesn't watch it much herself. Though she knows she ought to watch it with them the way people say parents should. Point out what is fact and what is fantasy, what is hard sell and what is wishful thinking. As if there was always a difference.

And who is *she* to give her kids advice? She has only her own values to go by and they seem to be out of date. To have always been out of date, Alan and Carly go out among teachers and pupils each day, they are wiser than Maureen in the ways of the world.

Occasionally she has sat among the three of them – Mickey immediately scrambling upon her, settling his soft cheek against hers – and watched for a while. Never programmes of her own choosing, there'd be such an outcry. She's watched the screen and watched their faces. Even Carly sees no menace in tinfoil men, aluminium dogs as lovable as a petrol can, puppets with battery-lit eyes despatching sibilant missiles to annihilate an alien evening star.

And watching the images, the dreams that are being devoured by a generation, Maureen has thought that she's not the only one who's out of touch; in a different way Daphne, for all her knowledge and confidence, is just as far removed from the real world. Which isn't very real at all but has somehow been created by the tube in such a way that the old realities have been usurped.

At night when the kids are in bed Maureen could watch what she wants, but it makes her feel lonely to sit there staring at a world where people are hardly ever alone. So at night she takes Daphne's typewriter from its high shelf and types out handwritten letters, most but not all of them written in Daphne's tidy, rounded hand.

Ms or Mr, Unlike J. Tunbridge (issue of August) some of us have no difficulty differentiating between erotica and pornography. Erotica concerns itself with autonomous, responsible sexuality, pornography seeks to undermine and destroy it.

And she reads the magazines Daphne brings over for her, feeling like a junior student. Wanting to please, to measure up; though Daphne is probably younger than Maureen she seeks her approval. Maureen spends her days in the company of children; she feels, herself, childlike.

Her kids don't care for Daphne, and Daphne doesn't pretend to care for them. Daphne seems to see children as troublesome leeches, drawing from mothers energy that should be directed to more useful ends. When Maureen feels she knows Daphne well enough to talk about such trivial things she'll try and explain that while the leech view of kids is true enough, it's only one small truth among many conflicting truths about bringing up kids. She doubts, though, if Daphne would ever understand such bedraggled wisdom.

Daphne bothers Alan. Maureen sees this in the tilt of his head, in the way his eyes tiptoe and his movements become clumsy. Mickey has no such fear but Daphne brushes him away absently, sending him and his sticky affection back to his mother.

And Carly. Carly is a disappointment to Daphne in ways that reflect on Maureen's mothering. Carly cries too easily and tries too hard to please. Carly is a little mother, grating cheese, folding the washing and setting the table. She ingratiates, she's wimpish, she causes Daphne to roll her eyes despairingly.

She was born like that, Maureen has tried to explain. From the moment she first drew breath she's wanted to please. The way Mickey has wanted to hold and be held. But Alan – Alan was born tense. The first time I saw his eyes they accused me. I never knew why.

Daphne doesn't believe stuff like that. Old Wives' Tales, she said.

Some of Daphne's friends are compiling a book about old wives. Daphne has contributed a fulsome piece about her grandmother who died when Daphne was four. It was the first thing that Maureen typed out for her. The reason for the book is that the achievements and opinions of the old wives have been overlooked by historians.

Daphne believes it's conditioning that makes people what they are. With proper conditioning Carly could become aggressive and independent. At the same time Daphne doesn't hold out hopes that conditioning will do a lot for boys. As far as Maureen can understand Daphne's theory is that if you make all the girls assertive enough they'll be able to stomp on the boys and keep them in line.

It's not that Daphne visits all that often, or spends a lot of time with them when she does. She just drops in once in a while to pick up work or to bring a new lot. She'll stay for a cup of tea because it's a long hot haul up the hill, but she always has someone she's off to see or a boat to catch or a meeting to go to.

They have meetings on the island. A women's co-op. Thursdays at 7.30 pm. Daphne says Maureen should go along. There's all kinds go, she said—some are straight. They hold it at someone's home in Parenga.

'I'd need a babysitter,' said Maureen. 'Unless it's all right to take the kids.'

'No one does,' said Daphne rather quickly.

Daphne knows Shisha, though not very well (Daphne seems to know half the island and a quarter of Auckland). Shisha has problems relating to people, according to Daphne. 'She's had a lot of bad experiences with men and she's still trying to work through her feelings about women.

'When you think about it,' said Daphne, 'it's a wonder all women don't turn out like Shisha, given the way things are.'

Keith hasn't come round since that night. She probably offended him. Or maybe sex was what he'd been leading up to all along. The silly thing was she'd have gone along with it, at least that once, if it all hadn't been so awkward. She was quite prepared to be swept off her feet, at least until the wine started to wear off. Still if it had happened, where would they go from there? One night she could risk, but . . .

Daphne told her Keith went to Auckland for a couple of days looking for work. He didn't go back again so she gathered he hadn't found anything. Maureen doesn't like to ask Daphne questions about Keith straight out. She gets the feeling that Daphne thinks Maureen's liking for Keith makes her nearly as wimpish as her daughter.

Alan wonders sometimes, out loud and wistfully, why Keith's not been back to see him in so long a time. But the TV seems, for the time being anyway, to have replaced Keith as the main object of Alan's affections.

The way things turned out the suspension of Maureen's benefit was a grim couple of weeks that had a silver lining. When the payments were reinstated it was discovered that all along she'd been getting the wrong amount. Someone had boobed and she was only down as having two children. Human error, computer error? It hardly matters which. Their official letter said *the amount in arrears has now been credited to your POSB account.*

The day she got the letter Maureen floated down Cashin Road with Mickey wafting along behind, and the old man who lives on the corner and the little crippled woman further down (both under suspicion) said, how nice to see a happy girl. You must be in love, the old woman said slyly. And Maureen thought, better than that; much, much better!

She paid for Carly's glasses and the replacement lens all in one go and she went to the little part-time insurance booth in one corner of the taxi office and took out insurance on the glasses, and while she was at it, on the contents of the cottage because even if it didn't seem like much their stuff could cost a bit to replace if the house burnt down. Having done that she felt suddenly much more secure, as if all these months the thought of them losing everything in a fire had been gnawing away in her subconscious mind.

Still money to spare. Chicken for dinner two days running, and ox heart for Jackson whose habits are improving slowly but certainly. In the weekend not just ice-creams but Trumpets. Crisp notes giggling in her wallet whenever she opens it.

She got the TV the next week at a garage sale on the road to Tautoro. Colour set and good as new. So cheap she kept asking the young guy if he was sure there wasn't something wrong with it. He plugged it in and it looked fine.

Bennie was at the sale, still wearing his overcoat. Maureen said, hello. Then, because he didn't seem to recognise her, she asked after Shisha. Bennie blinked a few times and scratched his hip through layers of clothing. 'Your friend Shisha,' he said slowly, 'managed to rip us all off, more than somewhat.'

He nodded across at Maureen's television set with SOLD now written on the price ticket. 'We've had to sell some of our stuff because of Shisha. That was ours, and the sofa over there. We've put the word out,' he said darkly, 'so she'll stay off this island if she knows what's good for her.'

He had a bulging pimple just below his nose. Standing there between a box of old saucepans and a rusting deep freeze Maureen couldn't think of anything to say to him. He was disgusting and pitiful at the same time.

She arranged with the other young man for the set to be delivered. She and Mickey caught the bus home. By the time they brought the set—Bennie came too, she wished he hadn't said it was his—she'd convinced herself there must be a catch.

They delivered it that same day, just before the kids got home from school. Mickey met them at the gate babbling the news. Alan came in with a face like sunrise.

When Daphne next called she looked the set over. 'It's hot,' she said. 'You can bet your bum on that.' She saw Maureen's face, 'Don't worry,

246

they won't come looking here.'

'If they do what do you think they'd do?'

'Charge you with receiving. No. They'd probably just take the thing away.'

'We're used to that.'

Every day that no one comes to take it away it seems less likely that they ever will.

If the money had come in every week, the right amount, the way it was supposed to, it would never have given her so much pleasure. And if they hadn't 'reviewed' her benefit the mistake might never ever have been noticed. It's frightening to think of it that way. Any day they could make another mistake – misread a file, press a wrong button, listen to lies. They could come into her house and see that splendid TV set and draw conclusions about where so much money could've come from.

There's no certainty. Nothing can be relied on. The Harrison family is suspended on a very thin thread. Maureen remembers her lift dream, the tilting floor, the men in their offices, and Alan sliding from her grasp.

No. She doesn't need Keith coming round in his conspicuous truck. Alan can make do with TV. It's what he wanted. He can't expect to have everything.

Your father always wanted everything and look where it's got him.

Of course she doesn't say that. She still hasn't told them about Bruce. Rid of their father, she worries about inherited discontent, inherited avarice; the injustice of genes.

Alice wrote to Maureen saying, don't you think perhaps you ought to visit him – after all you're still his wife? Sometimes she can't figure Alice out at all.

Nearly three weeks and the TV is losing its grip. Already they begin to take it for granted and their eyes glaze. The images cavort and shriek, desperate to please, repeating the tricks that last week went down so well. The children sigh and wander off in search of food or Maureen. They switch channels and fight over who has the right to. They're even prepared to do a little homework. The TV is left performing its heart out to an empty room. The children think such unflagging homage is no more than they deserve.

'Ngaaa,' squeals Carly. 'Ngaaa muuum ngaaaaeee he's hurting me.'

'Alan!'

'You bitch,' he hisses at Carly. 'You bitch, you cow, you sissycock.' 'Ngaaee.'

The volume of the TV goes up. Sirens, squeal of brake lining, shatter of glass, crunch of steel.

'Mickey, turn that down.' Alan deflecting blame.

'Fuck you,' says Mickey, distinctly.

'Shut up, or I'll come in there with a stick.' Someday she really will.

It takes two years to recover from grief—the death of a loved one, a broken marriage, parental separation. Thirteen more months to go and then they'll be kind to each other. And Maureen will be strong. Thirteen more months and they'll all wake up in the mornings thinking, goody another day.

Over a year to go. But looked at the other way, she's almost halfway. And the first half is bound to be the hardest.

Daphne crashes in through the door, hands flying to cover her ears. 'I knocked,' she shouts above the sounds of Carly's bawling and the hillbilly music which has replaced the death rattle of motoring.

Maureen stalks among her hateful children and annihilates a grinning man in a ten-gallon hat. She stalks out again but Carly, still sniffing and blubbering, is trailing behind.

Daphne has brought a friend. She stands just behind Daphne, leaning against the closed door. Her hair is short-cropped like Daphne's. She's smiling faintly. Her eyes are an astonishing green.

Daphne looks down at snivelling Carly. 'Your brother beat you up again, huh?'

Carly looks to Maureen for help then nods unwillingly.

'And he's gonna keep beating you up until you learn to lam him back. I've told you. You make a good fist . . . so, and straight for his face, anywhere that's gonna hurt. You know where boys can get hurt a lot?'

Carly nods her tear-streaked face. Does she know, or does she want to just get away?

'Hit me, go on. Let's see you really punch.' Daphne defends herself, jiggling like a heavyweight. Carly looks miserably at her small clenched fist. There's a lot of Daphne to connect with but it all looks solid.

Daphne's friend has denim legs that disappear at one end beneath a long black sweater and at the other into softly concertina'd grey suede boots. Maureen can hardly take her eyes off the boots, she wants them so badly. She can't remember when she last felt lustful about a piece

248

of clothing. The emotion seems unworthy.

'Go on.' Daphne's still jiggling and waiting. Carly has her head lowered. She sways a bit as if in imitation of Daphne, then she makes a wild dash under Daphne's fending arms and through to the bedroom.

'No wonder he beats you up,' Daphne calls after her. 'I'd be tempted myself. Don't be a gutless wonder all your life.' She grins across at Maureen as though they're on the same side. 'Well,' she says, 'at least we seem to have solved the noise problem . . .'

Maureen can hear her own socked feet padding across the kitchen to put the jug on.

Daphne ducks out the door. Her friend smiles at Maureen over the washing machine. Maureen smiles back. Daphne returns with a plastic bag of things for Maureen to do, it's buckled from being under the carrier clasp.

'Did you double here?' asks Maureen. The woman in the boots nods and pulls a marvellously agonised face for only Maureen to see.

Daphne remembers. 'Hennie,' she points, 'and Maureen.' They smile all round.

'I think,' says Daphne to Maureen, 'I have the answer to your babysitting problems.'

November

SNEEZIE'S FOAL IS almost four weeks old and perfect. Josie wastes good work time just leaning and watching the foal. There can't be too much wrong with a world that can produce a creature so exquisite.

She's beginning to understand how standing and watching can be an essential part of a primary producer's job, a little more crucial than profit or loss. They've sold Grumpy, amazingly, for a good price. She hopes no one will want the other three. Not yet. Happy is due to foal in another few weeks. Her Happy event (groan) says Geoff.

Josie feels that between herself and the mothering mares there's a bond of exclusive understanding.

The ponies are Geoff's. The strawberry plants are Josie's, the small flock of black sheep is Josie's, so are the potted plants in her office greenhouse, and half the garlic crop. It's their new arrangement; an agreement carefully drafted on notepaper, witnessed by Leif and folded away in the drawer that holds receipts and bills and insurance policies and birth certificates.

Now that it's done they don't speak about it. She understands his disgust. A written agreement between lovers is, no matter how modern you are, a contradiction in terms. It proves a degree of suspicion, a meanness of spirit. She sees that and understands. What he refuses to see is that it was, nevertheless, necessary.

'Why?' he asked again.

'For my sense of security, for my own morale's sake. And because I'm entitled. Because, today, this is how things have to be done.'

Because, she thinks now, down among the ponies, it's proof in my terms that I'm valued.

      Yet I knew that already. His affection was never in doubt. Proof, then, for Juliet. A document to show that he loves me in the accountable fashion in which these days we all feel we have to be loved.

So why is she somehow ashamed of the contract, feeling guilty of emotional parsimony? Indebted as much as she was before, though this time she owes him not gratitude but recklessness. A day . . . an hour . . . of risk. Of faith. Of unmeasured generosity.

Already Josie's aware of her own inclination to spend more time on the projects they've specified as hers. She tries to do otherwise, imagining Geoff to be making mental notes to be held, some day, against her. (Right away, he'll say, you turned everything into yours or mine instead of ours.)

Considering the agreement was a personal victory for Josie it's brought very small satisfaction. I'll make it up to you, she promises Geoff in her head. But he mustn't ever know she has these reservations.

On her way back to the house she calls on the hens (which are his) and stands a while watching. The chickens have now graduated to the main coop. They're still getting a hard time from the hens who owned the place. Who terrorise the young ones the way they in turn are terrorised by the rooster. The chickens cower in an abject group. 'I'd have more sympathy,' Josie tells them, 'if I didn't know you were, all of you, murderers.'

She hears the phone ringing before she reaches the house. Which means Geoff is still not home. She doesn't run but neither does she stop to kick off her boots.

'Josie? Hello, is that Josie?'

It takes her a few seconds to place the voice. 'Paul. Sorry, I was outside.'

'I know. I've been ringing for ages. Look I'm on the island. I'm standing outside the post office. I wasn't sure which bus.'

'Hell, look Geoff's out in the Rover or I'd come and get you.' She stretches for a glimpse of the clock. 'I don't know when he'll be back. The next bus won't be for an hour or more. Do you want to wait somewhere or get a taxi?'

'I guess I'll get a taxi.'

Josie smiles to herself, hearing the pain. Paul's home has wall to wall tepid air and bouffant carpets but the small extravagances tear him apart.

'You have got our address?'

'Yes. Well I'll see you in a little while. It is okay, my just arriving on you?'

'Of course. I'll put the kettle on.'

Paul without Juliet, which means—

'Oh god,' she says out loud, kicking off her boots against the back doorstep, 'right now I think this is something I could do without.'

She goes out to meet him when the taxi comes. Peter—threesome Peter—is driving the taxi. He asks after Geoff and hands on the latest in island news (a break and entry at the takeaway shop last night).

Josie is aware of herself taking too much notice of Peter who's part of her present life and not enough notice of Paul who belongs to her past. She tries to introduce the two of them but they've done so already. Paul stands with his suitcase (reassuringly small) looking strained, and by the time Josie gives him her undivided attention it feels too late and they're both awkward.

Because they've got off on the wrong foot Josie isn't able to say to Paul, as she should, what's happened . . . you look dreadful . . . come inside and tell me all about it. Instead she asks about the ferry trip and avoids his eyes. And when they're inside she rattles about setting out mugs and a plate of biscuits as if it's a vicar who's called in.

Paul asks after Geoff, and Josie goes on at length about how he's helping someone build a garage . . . though why she doesn't really know with all that still needs doing around here. They sit at the table with the biscuits untouched between them and exchange a nervous super-fluity of words. It's a relief to hear the Land-Rover turning in at the drive.

Geoff and Paul shake hands. Geoff looks genuinely happy to see Paul. His eyes search the room for Juliet and Josie signals an almost imperceptible shake of the head.

Geoff and Paul aren't old friends. They're linked by the longstanding friendship of the women. It's apparently enough. Watching them so matey Josie's aware that Geoff, who is everybody's friend, has no close male friends.

Neither has Paul, or why would he come here?

Friends from Geoff's schooldays have no more status than friends he met yesterday. He doesn't grade friendships the way Josie does; merit points for long service or outstanding tenacity. Geoff has no expectations of his friends and feels no obligation to them.

By Josie's criteria she is the only real friend Geoff has. To float through life with such singular and perilous attachment to humanity . . . is that the secret of his imperturbable optimism?

Because there is no beer in the house Geoff takes Paul off for one. They feel obliged to invite Josie, she feels it prudent to decline. Three hours later Geoff rings from the pub and says don't worry about tea. We'll have it tomorrow, he says when she points out it's already in the oven. Remember, she warns him, that you're the driver. I love you, he says in a malt-flavoured voice.

In bed Geoff gives her details. Juliet has left. God knows where to,

Paul certainly doesn't. She took all her clothes and some of the furniture. Three weeks earlier she admitted to Paul she was having an affair with one of her students, a boy of twenty. But she hasn't run off with him. Paul went to see the student and believed him when he said he had no idea where Juliet had gone.

'Did he expect to find her here?'

'She'd hardly bring her furniture.'

'Does he want to find her? Make her go back with him?'

'Find her and strangle her I think. No, I reckon he knows in his heart that this is it and he's just gonna have to live with it.'

'Poor Paul.'

'I reckon he's better off. In the long run he'll be better off.'

'In the long run so will she.' Fairness demanded, but she knows he'll take it personally.

'I wouldn't be so sure. She might just get what she deserves.'

'She deserves happiness. We all do.' Why can't she just let it go? It's nothing to do with them.

Yet it is, and well they both know it. Juliet leaving Paul . . . Josie's insistence on an 'agreement' . . . ripples from the same current. New rights, new rules . . . No one promised it'd be easy, but who'd have thought it'd be so bloody paradoxical?

'She deserves shit,' says Geoff. 'She deserves the kind of misery she's causing him. That and more.'

'I don't doubt that right now she's got just that.' It sounds like an accusation, more than she'd intended.

Where's Juliet now, with her clothes and furniture? Did she take the dishwasher? She must've planned it, but not a word to Josie. Who has not proved friend enough in this time of Juliet's need?

'What about the university? Don't they know?'

'Seems she'd arranged for someone to take over till the end of term. Wasn't on an impulse.'

Josie trying to imagine what kind of house, what part of the country Juliet would've chosen. Ashamed because along with the sympathy she ought to be feeling is a resentment she ought not. Not at Juliet's leaving but at the way of her leaving. Like a cat that's messed on the carpet; someone has to clean up afterwards. Already Josie is bored and repelled by Paul's unspoken anguish.

And maybe she's a touch envious. Juliet and a student. In love, perhaps. Giddy of brain, limp of heart and obsessively, single-mindedly unclouded of vision. Because she was last, and most, in love with Geoff

Josie strokes him now and licks his salty skin.

'I haven't got a student on the side. I've got no plans of leaving. Their problems have nothing to do with us so please stop blaming me.'

He turns and searches for her lips. And her brain feels just a little giddy, her heart a little limp. Still.

Next day Paul helps Geoff clear the grass around the young fruit trees and nail a few more boards on the pig pens. Since his energetic phase ended the pig pens have been Geoff's concession to Josie's work ethic. The pens began as kennels, until Geoff learned the council chairman's daughter had also applied for a permit to run boarding kennels.

When he doesn't feel like working or defending his idleness Geoff takes his hammer and nails and staples and stands around among the recycled wood and pieces of wire and vague earth excavations he calls the pig pens. Occasionally a wild sound of hammering will break the long silences between. Whenever Josie strolls across the paddock to visit him or relay a phone message or announce a meal prepared she sees the nails clenched between his teeth, a symbol of industry.

He knows the nails don't fool her. She knows he knows. But in spring the spectre of bankruptcy seems less convincing. Besides, the pigs are listed as his concern; his loss if they never eventuate. Sometimes when she asks him what his plans are for the day he'll say, smirking, that he thought he might put in a few hours on the pig pens.

Josie can see the non-progressing pens from the window of her office. From the desk she types at she can see, now, the two of them leaning and gesturing. Talking about marriage? Women? Juliet? Josie? What do men say to other men in private?

Later they come and get her and the three of them scramble down the goat track to their own little beach, though on this still and shiny late afternoon their sense of ownership is shattered by the presence of a glossy launch anchored straight out from their small stretch of sand.

Geoff and Paul swap fantasies of launch-owning lifestyles. Paul pretending, for their sake, that he's just a struggling worker. They all test the water but only Geoff goes in. Watching him make a fast dolphin line for the boat Josie knows he's feeling obliged to perform because of Paul. And she thinks—amazed, because it's so obvious yet she's never figured it out before—that it's from those of the same sex that the pressures come. In the end women are most influenced by women, men by men.

Paul sits against the cliff rubbing at a small pink stone. A riverstone, he tells her. 'Imagine it having been washed all the way out to sea then ending up here.'

Josie's never thought of stones as having a home base. She suspects Paul knows no more about stones than she does. He has a way of casually dropping eclectic facts that she's always found a bit suspect. She tells him there's a creek runs into the next bay. It's true but unfair. He was ready to speculate about the secret currents of the universe.

So now he talks about Juliet instead. Checking that Geoff has apprised Josie of all the facts. 'I realise she's your best friend, but even you must've seen how she's changed over the last few years. She's got so hard . . . so self-seeking. No give there anymore. I tried, Josie, but I knew I wasn't reaching her.' He smashes his pink riverstone beneath a grey misplaced one. 'The stupid thing is the more she pulls away from me the more I want her.'

'Human nature,' says Josie. 'You should read more novels. We're all so predictable.'

'What d'you think I should do?'

'What everyone else has to do in your situation. Make a new life. Go out and do all the things you've secretly wanted to.'

Paul looks rueful. 'Would that I could.' He's looking at Geoff who's circled the boat and is swimming more slowly back to shore. 'We've been together since I was twenty,' he says helplessly. 'Too young. Too long. I don't know how to live on my own.'

'You'll learn.'

'That's what she kept saying.'

'You could grab onto someone else.'

'What's the point. Go through all this again? Relationships aren't built to last any more. Only a fool'd keep trying.'

'Thanks,' says Josie.

Back home they eat at sunset, their plates tinged red from the skies. Wine makes Geoff and Josie boastful. Our own vegetables, chemical free, lead free, so fresh they're still breathing. And crayfish—frozen admittedly, but only because we've been given so many we were getting sick of them. From sea to freezer, no preservatives, specified or unspecified. They may well live forever, Geoff and Josie. Except she smokes.

When the last of the red light has died away they sit on in the darkening room, having to grope for their glasses. Geoff uses his thumb as a measuring stick when he pours them refills.

They've all reached the stage where almost anything's funny. They

255

make plans for Paul to move to the island and live down the back beside the creek, among the ponies. He'll chuck accountancy and become a beachcomber, a carver of driftwood pelicans, a writer of tremulous verse and part-time astrologer. In lieu of rent he will help Geoff with the pig pens.

Mention of pig pens dissolves them completely. The table shakes and Josie sprawls helplessly over it. She's trying to make her words coherent. 'I never said . . . not all this time . . . not one single bloody word about . . .'

'Two words,' says Paul. 'Two . . . highly symbolic . . . encapsulating . . .'

'Fuck,' says Josie, aware that she's just knocked over someone's glass.

The laughter begins to dissolve and they sit there limp with exhaustion, yet feeling cheated by its unannounced departure. In the silence the sea sounds clear and infinite.

Paul goes sentimental on them. 'The two of you . . .' he says. 'The only two people in the world I can trust. The only real friends I have . . . I can turn to. I love you fuckers—you know that?'

Josie's heart wincing and willing him to stop. Wanting to hurry on past this, as if Paul is blind, disabled, begging in the street and no matter how many notes she may drag from her purse and stuff into his hand they will never be enough, so that the fact of his existence will go on reproaching her for days to come.

But Paul won't stop. 'You two really love each other. That's what gets me. In this phony fucken world you're the only people I know who really seem to love each other. I wish I knew how you did it. But promise me this . . . you look after what it is you've got there. You know what I'm saying? What I'm trying to tell you both?'

'Yeah,' says Geoff soft and gruff. 'Sure, Paul, we know.'

'Well I hope you do Geoff. Cos I know I'm drunk, but drunk words are words that come straight from the heart. And you know what, if you two don't make it together—if you bum out like all the rest of us—then we might as well all go home cos there's no fucken hope for the world. You know what I'm saying?'

'Yeah,' says Geoff placatingly. 'We know.'

'I wanta hear it from Josie.'

'We know what you're saying,' says Josie, hearing the schoolteacher tone that's crept into her voice. They sit for a time in silence. Josie sighs. 'I'll say this for you, Paul—you sure know how to ruin a party.' She knows if it wasn't so dark she'd see Geoff's cautionary frown.

'I'm sorry,' says Paul contritely. 'I'm sorry to have been boring and told the truth. It's just that I'm so bloody envious of Geoff.'

Josie reflects for a while on those words, on their possible implications, on the degrees of drunkenness among those present. And she thinks, here it is, everything falling into step of its own accord. It would be so easy, so almost natural. Slowly she reaches out her right hand in search of Paul. Her fingertips meet fabric, probably his thigh.

'Shit,' says Paul. 'I think I've spilled my drink.' He pushes his chair back and Geoff goes for the light switch.

They blink at each other in a blaze of light. Paul looks down at his crotch and then at his upright glass. 'Must've imagined it. Thought I felt something dripping.'

Geoff yawns and stretches. 'I'm for bed.'

'You know,' Josie tells him, her voice muffled by bedding. 'You know, there was a moment there tonight when I thought Paul . . . and me . . . and you . . .'

She can feel his body stiffen. 'You *what?*'

'Just a thought.'

Geoff sits up, as if for emphasis. 'Not a friend. A friend wouldn't do at all.'

She's rebuked into thoughtful silence. Then, 'But when I told you Paul'd been kind of chatting me up last time I was there . . . well that didn't bother you.'

'I thought you'd made it up.'

'I hadn't.'

Silence. 'He was probably only trying to boost your morale.'

Paul stays three more days. The morning they take him to the wharf there's a letter from Sarah.

Dear Josie,

You don't mind the familiarity? I feel that I've grown out of Mum. I may be able to handle it again when I'm properly mature.

Anyway this is to say that I'm putting on a brave front I'm much more miserable than I sound. There's to much praying around here. They even say grace or something in the spa pool Thank you God for giving us bubbles and such forfilling lives. So I've thought long and hard and decided for SURE that I want to come home. But not till after Xmas because they've made all these plans I cant just pull out of. But certainly before school starts. You havent said if theres a school on your desert island I could do correspondance. Daryl has more in common it's alright for him. Only maybe you and Geoff are having such a good time you won't want me back. I'm sure you wouldn't condemn me to a life of prayers and passermoney. Love to Geoff. Tell him I've finally seen an actuall aborigine and there was a definite resemblance I'll bring home a boomerang it may stir ancestral memories.

'She thinks,' says Josie, 'that you're of aboriginal descent.'

'Well, I can get some pretty amazing sounds when I use my didgeridoo.'

She whacks him with the back of her hand. 'She also says she wants to come home.'

'When?'

'After Christmas.'

'But she's just got there,' he says. Then he smiles, to show it was a joke.

*　　　*　　　*

Hennie and Maureen. Maureen, Hennie and the kids. It feels like a family. It feels more like a family than anything Maureen's known before.

Hennie makes Maureen believe in possibilities. You've had a bummer of a life so far, Hennie tells her, so from now on things can only get better. Maureen had never quite looked at it from that angle. Now she pictures a backlog of good times owed but never collected stuck away in some life deposit account accumulating interest.

Seems like she no longer imagines them than she's dipping in already. The good times since Hennie came.

Not so good perhaps for Hennie, who's only with them as a kind of fugitive. Hiding out not from the law or debt collectors but from Kay, the woman she used to live with. (Maureen was startled when this was explained to her that first afternoon when Daphne brought Hennie round. Because with Daphne you could see right away that she might be ... but Hennie with her wild green eyes and her dark hair and neat assured movements ... Hennie was beautiful, and you would've thought ...)

Hennie still likes Kay as a person. Sometimes she says she thinks she might even still love Kay. But she couldn't ever live with her again. The trouble with Kay was her possessiveness; she wanted to own Hennie, wanted to entrap and jealously guard her. Like a man. But of course, being a woman, Kay is aware of the destructiveness of that kind of behaviour. She knows in her woman's mind and from her woman's experiences that possession is a kind of death. She knows but is unable to change. And she won't allow her friends to give her support and help her work through those obsessive feelings. So Kay's problems are compounded by the conflict of her being aware of the need to change, wanting to change, yet not being prepared to help herself change.

Kay's friends (and of course Hennie too) have been terribly worried about Kay for the last few months. Ever since Hennie went off for a few weeks on a peace march when Kay didn't want her to go. Kay had even accused Hennie of not being sincere in her reasons for wanting to go. ('As if,' said Hennie, 'I was going on a peace march in order to promote war!') The thing about Kay is she'd had breakdowns twice already and been under treatment. The first time was while she was married and the second was after she and Hennie got together and Kay's husband went to court and got custody of her kids.

Knowing all this made it harder for Hennie to finally decide she'd have to get away. But their friends had been ready to surround Kay with their love and strength and support. Only Kay didn't want any of it. All Kay wanted was Hennie—she was that obsessed. She started behaving very badly. The things she did to her old friends weren't even civilised let alone sisterly. She made dementedly threatening phone calls to some of the women and when she found out who Hennie was staying with she put sugar in that sister's petrol tank and threw stones through her bedroom window.

That was when Daphne thought of Maureen's place as somewhere Kay would never find Hennie. Somewhere Hennie could wait things out without endangering her friends until Kay came to terms with her emotions.

Maureen, who has never encountered grand passion outside of the pages of the kind of books she used to read when she was fourteen, can only suppose that Hennie, having had that experience, knows best and that being the object of a jealous and exclusive passion could become very tiresome. All the same Maureen wouldn't mind if it happened to her. Just once, so she knew how it felt.

Because Kay and Hennie used to live on the island and there are lots of people over here Kay might come and visit and ask questions of (casual acquaintances the greatest risk, being liable to innocently say, oh I'm sure I saw Hennie the other day) for the first two weeks Hennie didn't even venture out as far as the Kaimoana store. Every few days Daphne would pedal over with the latest reports or rumours of Kay's whereabouts and activities (nothing spectacular now that Hennie was out of the scene) and the odd bit of typing.

Kay lent their life an air of excitement in those first weeks. When Maureen went to the store, to play centre and, once, to Parenga, she looked closely at strangers. But the only red-haired women she saw were either far too young or much too old. At Parenga she'd seen Shisha though. Maureen had just got onto the bus (gloriously untrammelled, Mickey being home with Hennie) when she saw Shisha coming out of the little dress and craft shop. She saw Maureen looking out the window and waved and shouted something that couldn't be heard. Maureen waved back but she'd thought, ha, if the bus door hadn't that second been closing Shisha would've looked right through Maureen. She'd wondered if Shisha knew that Bennie was out to get her. Maureen can understand now why Shisha stopped coming around; their friendship had been taking her nowhere. Maureen was a dead-end street.

And in those first two weeks, when Hennie stayed around the house, Alan and Carly would see red-haired women with bony freckled faces acting suspiciously all along the route between home and school. When they got home they'd report their sightings to Hennie, squabbling over the details and Hennie would interrogate them sternly, straightfaced, threatening torture for information withheld. Wonderfully macabre tortures that made Alan squirm with delight and Carly squeal with half-pretended terror.

Hennie can make a game of anything. No wonder the children love her. Mickey's her shadow, shoving himself up onto Hennie's lap whenever she sits down though more often than not she'll shove him away with a stream of interesting insults. Carly goes, now, much less often to visit her friend Tanya who lives in the street just past Cashin Road, and she eats carrots instead of bread because Hennie says carrots will give her bionic vision. Hennie never makes fun of Carly the way she does with the boys, but neither does she bully the girl the way Daphne does.

The first time Hennie saw Alan throw a tantrum she watched for a little while in silence then suddenly threw herself on the floor beside him screaming and writhing. Shouting, swearing, banging her head and fists on the floor. Then getting up and hurling herself about the room long after Alan had been startled into a rigid silence. Carly had been the first to laugh. She'd laughed until she was doubled up with cramp. Even Maureen had laughed although it felt a bit like treachery.

Alan hadn't even smiled. It made him, for a time, a bit more watchful, a little more sullen and clumsy than usual. But he seemed to get over it. Hennie's used the same technique on him since in various less dramatic ways. But not so often now. He no longer taunts Carly as constantly as he used to or throws the kind of wobblies he sometimes did. It's hard to tell exactly what Alan feels about Hennie.

Maureen of course loves Hennie; is bound to because Hennie, in so many ways, has made their lives better. For a start she does as much as Maureen does around the house. Between two of them the chores take hardly any time at all. They have hours left to just lie in the sun, keeping an eye on Mickey and turning themselves judiciously as if the future of the world hung on their getting an even tan. When the tourists flock in at the start of the holiday season Maureen and Hennie will be conspicuously advantaged.

Hennie also contributes more than her share of housekeeping money. These days they eat soft cheeses and sometimes gherkins from the delicatessen shelf, and drink real coffee and have puddings if they want not just for special occasions. Now Carly is allowed to bake just for fun, and Hennie has talked her out of fudge and scones and into bran muffins and carrot cake and apple turnover.

Sometimes when she sees how well Hennie handles the kids, how much the little ones love her, she feels pangs of jealousy. Then she has to remind herself of how it was before Hennie came. How they devoured and drained her. Hennie has prised them free. Some of Maureen is now left over for Maureen's own use. It's been so long since she had unclaimed resources she doesn't know what to do with them.

'Go over to the city,' Hennie urges. 'Take in a movie. Get drunk. Go to the Centre while Daph's over there and get her to show you around. Stay a night or two. Go visit your sister. Us lot'll be fine.'

'I should,' says Maureen. 'I know I should. Yes, maybe I will, sometime.'

'Be in while you can,' says Hennie, cautionary. Causing Maureen's heart to slump.

She enjoys herself more here with Hennie than she would in the city on her own.

When Hennie goes things will be as they were, only lonelier still. Maureen is afraid to ask right out what Hennie's plans are. Instead she sometimes talks in a casual but open-ended way about looking for a bigger, more comfortable, more respectable house, and how two adults sharing could just about afford a halfway decent sort of place. And how the trouble with that scheme is always that not many single people can cope with living with someone else's kids.

Hennie just puts on a dumb wide-eyed look and lisps, 'I wonder why?'

'What do you want,' tries Maureen one sunbathing afternoon, 'from life? What do you want most of all?'

Hennie looks at the sky for a while then smiles. 'I'm looking for Mrs Goodbar.' She looks at Maureen and sees she doesn't understand. 'Mrs Right,' she says. 'The woman of my dreams.'

'And Kay isn't?'

'Shit,' says Hennie swiping at Maureen with the book she has in her hand. 'It was a joke, my sweet. A joke. Where have you been while the world's been in motion?'

Maureen grabs the book and tosses it into the plum tree. Hennie pummels her, laughing, then goes to retrieve her paperback.

'If you go to the city,' says Hennie returning, 'you can wear my grey boots, my camouflage jacket . . . anything you fancy.'

When Hennie moved in she came in a taxi with a bulging knapsack. All the clothes she later dragged from it were boyishly fashionable and almost new. Maureen's tried most of them on one time or another but she's taller than Hennie and a couple of sizes bigger all round. Only their feet are the same size, though Hennie's are browner and neater and sometimes itchy.

Hennie travelled most of her early life. She was born in Australia but her father was in the computer business which was still in its infancy about the time Hennie was. The family travelled all over and Hennie knows a smattering of languages with which to dazzle Maureen's kids and has the confidence that comes with knowing that she's seen most of what there is to be seen.

At Maureen's Hennie sleeps in the living room and folds her bedding away each morning. Some nights when Hennie and Maureen sit watching TV or talking Carly stumbles in, still half asleep, to join them. Then they unroll Hennie's bedding and let Carly sleep there. And if, when it's late, Carly's too sound asleep to be easily woken and moved they just leave her there and Hennie sleeps in Carly's bed. Then they talk for a while before falling asleep, and Maureen's reminded of all the years that she shared a room with Alice and how they talked almost every night, yet still Maureen doesn't really know how her sister's mind works.

On a play centre Tuesday Maureen and Mickey get a lift right to their gate from a couple of early tourists. 'We only stopped because of the wee tot,' the woman says reproachfully. 'He's such a wee mite to have to walk.'

'Don't worry about him,' Maureen says, 'he does it all the time. Still I must say it's nicer to ride.'

So they're home, the two of them, more than half an hour earlier than usual. And Maureen thinks they'll surprise Hennie, creep up on her, and has Mickey tip-toeing behind her with his finger clamped to his lips.

Even before she's reached the half-open door Maureen hears Daphne's typewriter, the one Maureen uses, clacking away in a steady authoritative rhythm. Yet Hennie doesn't type. She's said so more than once. She's said, sometimes when I watch you I wish I'd learnt. My skills are all impractical.

Maureen stands listening to the keys strike and begins to grin. Typical Hennie, far too smart to let them enlist her as a voluntary secretarial service. She throws back the door and Hennie at the table, hunched over the typewriter, looks up so startled that Maureen claps in delight.

'Got you. Can't type, eh? Poor little Hennie who never learnt.'

Hennie's grin's a bit faint-hearted. 'I can't,' she says. 'Honest. I was just mucking about. Pretending.' She rips the paper from the carriage and lets it fall beneath the table. It lands the wrong side up.

Maureen bends to get it but Hennie stops her, flailing at Maureen's arms and laughing. 'You mustn't. It's in code. I'd feel too silly.' She grabs hold of Maureen, gets her in an armlock. Maureen tries to twist free and for a moment they're face to face, both laughing, but when Maureen catches Hennie's eyes they glaze and slide away.

Suddenly Hennie becomes Alan. 'Stop it,' she says in a high boy's voice. 'You bitch, you stink mean, indubitably stupid wankbottom person or I'll tell on you.'

Maureen can't help but laugh and leave the sheet of paper where it is. But before Hennie began to wrestle with her she saw clear enough right through the paper, that it was a letter. The first two words Maureen had recognised, even back to front. Dear Kay.

It's Hennie who retrieves the paper. But casually, scooping it up as she crouches in front of Mickey. 'All right Einstein, what did you achieve today? What dazzling intellectual concept did you distil into a few symbolic strokes of purple tempera, eh? What did you bring home to show Hennie?'

'Today,' says Maureen reaching for her bag, 'we made Father Christmases. But unfortunately we then accidentally sat on ours so the general effect is a bit dismal.'

'Father Christmas? Isn't it still a bit early?' Hennie slides the typewriter up on the high shelf where it's kept away from child damage. The letter has disappeared.

'The longer the preparation the more rewarding the event. I think that's the theory.' Maureen holds up the battered cardboard cylinder with its glued-on patches of red velour, its trailing cottonwool.

'I can see,' says Hennie gravely,' that before his accident befell him he was a most imposing figure. Well done, maestro. No paintings today?'

Mickey shakes his head.

'They're keeping his painting for the wall. It was that good.'

'Brilliant. Not merely an Einstein, but also a McCahon. What did you paint?'

'Cat,' says Mickey. 'A cat and a cat and another cat.'

'How many's that? Those cats?'

'Six.'

'Ah. I see. Was one of them Jackson?'

'All of them's Jackson.'

'You're gonna make those galleries yet, boy. You've got the art world sussed.'

Along with half their fellow countrypersons Hennie and Maureen watch the budget announcements on TV. (Since Hennie came she's decided which channel gets watched and the kids like it or lump it.) They watch the presenter, the leading economists, the new minister of finance. Maureen tries not to hope, personally, for anything, so that when it comes she'll be pleasantly surprised.

But her country has lived too long beyond its means and is, she's told, in imminent danger of repossession. The steady-eyed images impart this grave news in a manner that implies that Hennie and Maureen have knowingly, wantonly, contributed to the cause of this crisis. They have lived irresponsibly, are shiftless and self-indulgent. Now they must pay the price.

This causes Hennie to hoot and make foul fingers at the man on the screen, but Maureen's used to being held responsible. When the repossession men came it was always her who was home to receive their pitying or disdainful looks, their well-intentioned advice on better budgeting.

A plan is explained, a brand new scheme, to help low-income families. For some joyful minutes Maureen plans where she'll apportion an extra thirty dollars a week. But Hennie cautions her—they're talking about wage earners, I wouldn't get all excited. Not yet, not yet.

'You shouldn't take everything on face value,' Hennie lectures. 'It doesn't pay. Things are hardly ever the way they seem.'

Carly padding in to join them. The waking becoming a habit with her. They hear her broad bare feet crossing the kitchen floor. She's crumpled and child-smelling, owlish in the sudden light.

'You're never in bed,' she complains to her mother, curling up on the sofa with her head in Maureen's lap.

When she's asleep they lift her and ease her into Hennie's sleeping bag. 'I think,' whispers Maureen, 'she's getting lighter.'

And Hennie grins and rolls her eyes, meaning, you worry too much about these brats of yours.

So Hennie, once again, settles for Carly's bed, rather than trying to shift the kid. And in the bedroom dark long after they've said goodnight Hennie says, whispering in case Maureen is asleep, 'I bet you're lying there worrying about something?'

And Maureen grins against her pillow and admits, 'Sort of.'

'Which one?'

'It was nothing really.'

She can see her clothes where they hang from the pole in the corner of the room. Sometimes, daytime or night, their dark people-shapes will catch the corner of her eye and choke her with a startled fear.

Hennie says into the silence, 'No wonder the kid wakes at night. This bed is absolutely bloody uncomfortable.'

And Maureen, immediately guilty, says, 'Oh hell, why didn't you say so before?'

'I suffered in silence. I do that rather a lot. The trouble is, suffering in silence doesn't offer much by way of satisfaction. But you'd know all about that.'

Maureen giggles. 'Actually,' she says, 'it was you I was worrying about. Your leaving. I know you're bound to but I don't know how I'll stand being on my own again. I just wish there was some way of keeping you here.'

Waiting for Hennie to say something Maureen can hear the sea. She thinks that to Hennie it must sound like her real life calling to her. She can also hear a faint but ominous scuttling sound that seems to be coming from the kitchen ceiling. In winter Keith climbed up into the manhole and spread poison along the ceiling beams. The rats went almost overnight and apart from a couple of carcasses she'd seen beneath the trees she hadn't given them or their dehydrated, burning bellies another thought.

'Maybe there is,' whispers Hennie.

There's no such thing as frigidity, there are only unsuitable lovers and inexpert lovers. So said Shisha who surely ought to know.

Maureen's prepared to take Shisha's word for it. The strange and tender comfort of being held in Hennie's arms is enough in the meantime. It makes up for the lonely moments of trying to please and the guilty pretence of pleasure.

Now that she can compare it's the similarities that surprise her. Like Bruce, Hennie has set the ground rules. It seems to be enough for Maureen to oblige and allow. Maureen feels tender and dutiful. Much as she used to in the first few years of marriage before duty turned into a chore.

Because of the kids ('Not yet,' says Maureen. 'Later we could, but there's no point in complicating things by telling them yet.' And Hennie is disappointed with Maureen but holds her peace.) there's a furtiveness about what they do. And though Maureen watches Hennie closely and listens for clues she still doesn't know if her kind of loving is enough to make Hennie stay. She can't tell if Hennie is sharp enough to know that Maureen's need is only to please and to hold. Or if, knowing it, Hennie would care.

To please Hennie Maureen tells lies. 'Yes,' she says shyly. 'Yes, I suppose that's what it was. All along. But I wouldn't admit I guess, even to myself. Anyway how could I know?'

To please Hennie Maureen dredges her memory for times of significance. 'In the third form I was hopelessly in love with a student teacher called Miss Eider. When she leant over to look at my work I used to move a fraction so my shoulder was rubbing against her. I'd wait in the passage and invent stupid questions so I could get her to notice me outside of the classroom.'

It's clear to Maureen that, more than a lover, Hennie wants a convert. Hennie shuffles through the magazines left by Daphne and finds articles that Maureen, as a novice, should read. And she wants to take Maureen over to the Centre, when things are safer. When Daphne gets back from the city and can tell them the coast is clear. For Maureen's instruction and entertainment Hennie describes in complicated detail and with some wonderful mimicry the polemics, the power structure and the personalities of the sisters Maureen will meet when they go to the city.

Maureen looks at her reflection in a spotty and discoloured mirror. Sees her long straight out-of-fashion hair, her brown-green eyes, her narrow chin. Stands there staring although she knows Hennie has started on the vegetables and she should go out and help. Just staring, staring, in case her face has something to tell her before it's too late.

*　　　*　　　*

'A whisker from being down the cliff. From you to me – just that far. Another roll and they'da been splashed all over the fucken rocks. Whole family splattered. Kids, everything.'

The fisherman's unfocused eyes look through his companions and see carnage; dismembered bodies, the sea lapping blood from the rocks.

'They'd a never got down there with cameras, the news people wouldn't. They might'a got a dinghy but they wouldn't wanta put them big fancy cameras in some dirty old dinghy.' The fat youngster seems to be a friend of Harley's. He's a big blubbery young man in a leather jerkin, jeans dragged in under his bulging gut.

'Maybe,' says Harley with a bit of a grin, 'they'da brought in a chopper and lowered the cameraman down so he could get a decent view, some real nice close-ups of smashed-open skulls and a few goops of brain, still moving.'

'Brains don't move,' says Suzie.

The fisherman grins widely. 'Yours sure don't.'

They laugh and Suzie – who's known widely as Old Suzie, though she could be still under fifty, or Suzie the Floozie – screws up her face and mutters.

'It'd be a change anyway,' says the fat youngster, still back with the cameraman and his assignment, 'from all them starving kids. I reckon they shouldn't put them on the news alla time they way they do. You don wanta see stuff like that when you're eating your dinner.'

Pete, the taxi driver, shakes his head at the kid in commiseration. 'Yeah. I reckon it's too bad. Bloke like you, just tryna eat his dinner. What I say is they should line up all those kids and just put a bullet in their heads.'

The fat kid's eyes slide round the faces as if daring anyone to laugh.

'Wouldn't waste the bullets. They'd want us to pay for them. Best just bulldoze a big hole and bury the bastards.'

Keith, looking hard at this kid, has decided it's for real with him, all this talk.

Pete says, still deadpan, 'Could probably get Save the Children to sponsor the bulldozer.'

Keith adds, 'And get all these cameramen suspended on ropes from choppers to film them as the dirt goes over and suffocates them.' But he can't get just the right note the way the taxi driver does.

Suzie says in her rasping voice, always too loud, 'They don't show car accidents. Not these days. Not unless a few people die. There'd be too many. If they showed them people'd be just watching car accidents all day.'

'So they put 'em in the programmes now instead of the news,' says Pete.

'Bloody Yank shit,' says Suzie.

'There was a chopper,' the fisherman examines the damp end of his cigarette, pinching off soggy paper and threads of tobacco, 'Army one. Come and picked up the kids and their old man. Took 'em to hospital.'

'About four o'clock? I heard it,' says Pete. 'Thought they were coming to get me.'

'Same as me,' offers Harley. 'Hear a chopper and I think, cops.'

'Cops? Cops my arse.' The taxi driver opens his eyes wide, 'I thought it was ET.'

Keith could stay here forever, propped on this stiff little chair, his glass in front of him still half-full, the talk so familiar yet unpredictable—livelier than Everton pub talk, for sure. Nothing demanded here, nothing expected.

It's a weekday afternoon. Already the island has been infiltrated by the early holidaymakers. Outdoors they wear crisp sun hats and goo-smeared noses; indoors they are cleaner, merrier, louder than the locals. In the public bar in summer the islanders draw back into dim recess of the corner just beyond the bar. They abandon established territories and congregate in smug yet defensive solidarity. At the end of summer they'll disperse again into their own disparate groups.

A couple come in from the beer garden. Tourists. She pulls her jacket around her shoulders, acting out a shiver. At Keith's table they turn, one by one, to look. There's a perceptible drop in the level of conversation all around them. Locals exchange glances; get a load of these two. The kid in the jerkin sighs audibly, an old man's whimpering sigh of lust and longing. The fisherman elbows the cushion of flesh where the kid's ribs should be and chuckles.

'Butch Cassidy,' says the taxi driver, looking at the man, her escort, with his casually tailored suit, his white shoes, his white shirt open neck to nearly navel, his white, white teeth.

'Mr Ed, more like,' says Keith and is pleased to get a laugh.

The couple hesitate over their choice of a table, settle for one with a view of the sea unobstructed by sunshades. He draws back her chair.

The fisherman snickers. 'Poncy. Dead bloody poncy.'

They watch the man glide to the bar, his silky soft-soled walk. Keith tries to figure out what, exactly, it is about this couple . . . sensuality, or just an aura of money to heedlessly spend. Are they one and the same thing?

Harley kicks Keith beneath the table. The woman is coming their way. She's a tawny creature and the closer she gets the older she gets. All the same she walks like a young woman and though her face is a bit weathered it can hold its own. A hint of firm brown limbs through the Grecian folds of her yellow skirt. She looks straight at them, boldly around the faces—Keith, Harley, the fat kid, Suzie, Peter and Leon the fisherman—and walks on past to the juke box. She drapes herself against the machine and begins to read the record titles.

They grin at each other across the table—all except Suzie—and reach for their glasses.

'I say,' she leans towards them. 'Excuse me, fellas, but I seem to have a problem.'

The fisherman is first to his feet, lumbering towards her. 'Let's take a look at this for you.'

'Lady,' says Harley softly as she moves aside to let the fisherman see. '*Now* you've gotta problem.'

'Bloody Yank,' rasps Suzie, too loud.

'Now now Suzie.'

'Wouldn't give them the tim'a day,' she says.

'Shut up Suzie.'

'Have a drink Suzie.'

'Only speaking my mind. Think they own us, that lot. Think they gotta right to push us around. You lot are just gutless.'

'I know what you mean.' Keith's trying to be fair. When he'd heard the woman speak he'd felt disillusioned, the wrong associations leaping in.

Music rattles out through the doubtful speakers. *Don't know what they're doing but they laugh a lot behind the green door.* Why are the bad old songs never allowed to rest in peace?

Suzie claps along.

The man with the white shoes waits at the window table with two glasses. His trousers are carefully hitched at the knees. He wears grey socks with white stripes. He flashes his teeth at the woman as she weaves her way back to him.

'What a dork,' the fat kid drags his eyes scornfully back to his glass.

Pete waves to Geoff-from-Whiripare who has just walked in the door.

The fisherman slides into his chair looking smug.

'She choose this crap?' asks Harley. 'She's got no fucken taste but. Useless.'

'I did. She did the second one. She said, Ahm certahn we'd lahk the same theeungs.' The fisherman's pink with pleasure.

Geoff joins them. They readjust their circle and drag in another chair. 'You lot look like you've been here all day.'

'Day off,' says Pete self-righteously. 'What's your excuse?'

Geoff gestures with his head, 'Who are they?'

'Them. Americans. Bloody tourists. Whadda they look like?'

'Ask the Ancient Mariner here. Mates of his.'

'No, really. Leon here and that bit of sizzle . . . when I say close friends I mean CLOSE.'

'Ha bloody ha,' says the fisherman.

Sometime later they enlarge their circle again. This time to include Shisha, though Keith sees Suzie's barely contained displeasure. Only the young ones, Harley and his mate, seem pleased by Shisha's arrival. 'You should be over there,' Pete points, 'with the tourists.'

'Oh come on,' she wheedles. 'I may not live here now, but my heart still belongs. I can't keep away from the place.' Beneath the beret the hair that shows is today close-cropped as if it's been shaven and is growing back. Keith wants to touch it to see if it prickles. 'It's the people, of course, that make me keep wanting to come back.' Shisha smiles around at them all. Perhaps not at Suzie.

Now Shisha's there the circle is out of balance. The talk no longer hums between them, good-humoured and mindless. It wavers and eventually topples.

'Come on,' says Shisha. 'You guys been to a funeral? I came all this way for a good time. Goddam, doesn't anyone know any good jokes even?'

'I do,' says the fat kid. 'How do you turn a fruit into a vegetable?'

Pete groans. 'That's old. I heard that last year.'

Geoff raises a grey eyebrow at Keith and gets up and goes to the bar. Keith thinks of following him but the effort of standing and finding a pathway between chairs and legs seems too enormous. His head, or perhaps his stomach, is turning fluid and oily. Ridiculous, because Keith never gets drunk. Hardly ever. No matter how much he drinks he doesn't get drunk, just more and more relaxed. His relaxation right now is almost total.

Geoff, having refilled his glass, has calmly gone and introduced himself to that couple. Harley nudges Keith to look at him now, sitting there smiling and nodding as if they all grew up together. Keith has to grope about in his mind a bit to remember why the couple Geoff's with look familiar. It seems already that long ago.

He must be staring at Shisha too much. Her eyes seem to be catching his and drawing conclusions. Shisha's eyes are small and dark and hasty. Eve Lowie kind of eyes.

'You remind me of someone,' he says. 'Around the eyes.' But he can't remember who it was. He gropes for the dashboard to steady himself. The headlights pick out sharp stones on the road, kikuyu grass, power poles and honeysuckle. 'I could drive.'

'We're nearly there,' she says. 'Unless you've shifted. If you live where I think you live we're nearly there.'

'Where are we nearly?'

'Home,' she says. 'It's supposed to look familiar. Where do you usually park this thing?'

'Just there,' he says. 'On the verge. On the verge of.' He feels suddenly happy. 'We are on the verge.'

'I'll take that as a promise,' she says, switching off the motor.

'It's only mud,' she says. 'You tripped.'

'Who brought me home?'

'Your truck. Your trusty little truck. And misguided me.' She drops the keys on the floor beside his bed. 'I hope you're capable of sobering up a bit. Is there coffee?'

He nods once and the room slides. He closes his eyes and gropes on the floor for his keys. He's thinking about her wanting coffee and the joke forms in his head and it's so funny he starts already to laugh as he holds up the keys and jingles them from the keyring.

'What the fuck?' she says wearily.

He's forgotten what came next. He's stern with his rioting thoughts and they let him remember. 'I'm ringing for room service,' he says. 'For the coffee.' Now he's got there it's a bit flat.

'Very humorous.' She strides off to the kitchen and Keith drags his muddy legs up for their share of the bed. His own musty pillow lumpy beneath his head.

'Well she's not gonna come back tonight, is she? So she won't know. This thing isn't even a bed. Might as well be a ruddy camp stretcher. I wasn't exactly expecting a king sized waterbed with built-in FM sound. But I'm not gonna sleep in there with my bum scraping the ground when there's a perfectly good bed going to waste.' She touches his wrist, strokes it. 'Please,' she says. 'The little walk will do you good.'

Daphne's well-adjusted family watching them climb between Daphne's sheets.

'You're not going to be sick?'

'I don't think so.'

'The coffee helped. You're looking a bit more together. You sure you don't want to throw up?'

He manages a grin. 'It might depend on what you have in mind. Doing.'

'D'you often get yourself in this kinda state? What does little Maureen say?'

'What? Maureen . . . Maureen? She doesn't see me in this state. Or in any other.'

'That's all off?'

'Nothing was what you might call on.'

'That's not what she thought. She had plans to seduce you.'

'Someone rang the welfare and told them I was supporting her or screwing her or something.'

'And you weren't? Poor Keith, that was a bit of a bummer. Why are you looking at me like that?'

'You remind me of my mother. Your eyes. Something.'

'Oh Jesus, here we go. So you never got it on, you and Maureen?'

'Why do you wanta know?'

'Just curious. Who does she think it was? Who dobbed her in?' She's stroking his body with her own as if all these questions were endearments. There's a sense of danger about her that excites him and sickens him. She reaches for Daphne's light cord, her body arched, her neck stretched fine and faintly mottled where sunburn's peeled. In the sudden

272

blinding dark he sees a small, poised orange head, hard black eyes, a thin black tongue.

'Who does she think?' Shisha asked again. Her fingernails press hard into his back. She smells of incense. He'll get up early and wash Daphne's sheets and hope it's fine so they'll be dry if she comes back tomorrow.

'I knew I'd get you eventually,' she hisses in his ear.

Why, thinks Keith, daring now to feel the orange stubble on her skull, like fur on a stone ... Why is it always the alarming women I end up buried in?

December

CHRISTMAS CLAMOURS FOR attention. On TV clean white children, judiciously freckled, unwrap junior computers, dolls with high-heeled feet and ski outfits, fluorescent animals larger than life, commando suits with matching machine guns. Their perfect mothers in white dressing gowns and high-heeled feet hold hands with the perfect dads beside the sparkling, perfect, tree. The children's gratitude is not unbounded; they know that impeccable parents and appropriate gifts are no more than their birthright.

'The thing about clothes,' says Maureen, 'is they're a cop-out. No one wants presents they need—not kids anyway. Maybe Carly wouldn't mind. Something really nice. A dress or a tracksuit . . .'

'Not fair,' objects Hennie. 'You know it's not. Why should the boys mind getting clothes any more than Carly does?'

'They just do, that's all.'

'Or she has enough tact to cover up her disappointment.'

'They're my children,' says Maureen sharply. 'I should know.' Then tries to make amends. 'I know it seems like double standards, but really it's not. It's all right to have theories about treating them all exactly the same, but theories don't always work in practice. It's easy to have theories when you don't have to try and make them work.'

'How can you know they won't work if you've never tried?'

'I know. And I have tried. They don't fit. Kids are the way they are. You can't apply rules, because they're all different. They're all born different.'

Hennie's look says, hah. Says, it's mothers like you who perpetuate the myths.

'There's no point,' justifies Maureen, 'in me wasting money in buying them things they just won't like. Should I disappoint my kids for the sake of trying to apply some dumb theory?'

'There's worse things in life than a bit of disappointment.'

Maureen can think of no reply to that. She knows this matter of presents is just the tip of a bloody great iceberg. She doesn't like rowing with Hennie but sometimes it seems that the more Hennie gets her own way on things the more Maureen's kids miss out.

Maureen's cutting an order form from a mail order catalogue that came in the post. Just in case she decides . . .

'D'you think it'd be quite safe to send them off money? They have a proper address and everything?'

Hennie peers at the glossy brochure. 'Which one?'

Maureen points to the radio with a headset.

'Alan?'

'I know he wants one. They're dead expensive, but this is reduced, so I thought . . .'

'You plan to spend that much on the other two?'

Sometimes it feels as if Hennie's inside Maureen's head, echoing all her little reservations. 'Price,' she says primly, 'isn't the only thing. Anyway he's older.'

'And he expects more. And he demands more. And he plays on your guilts and gets duly rewarded.'

'I don't think it's like that. He's not that cunning. He's not that devious.'

'Of course he is. He's a male.'

'Well,' says Maureen limply, 'it doesn't seem to bring him a lot of satisfaction. The other two are more content within themselves. I think it's just the way it is.' He was born with a hollow space in his heart, he needs possessions to fill it. 'Some people just have greater needs than others.'

'Like you said,' says Hennie, 'they're your children.' Wiping her hands of them.

'Anyway,' says Maureen, injured and sly, 'if it's just because he's a male what about Mick?'

'Mickey, haven't you noticed, is on the way to being just the same.'

'Rubbish,' says Maureen with confidence.

She's dreading Christmas. It can never come up to expectations. It never has yet.

Alice has invited them over. Not including Hennie of course, she doesn't know about Hennie. And in a way the invitation is tempting. The ferry trip, a night or two in Auckland. It'd feel like an event.

But Christmas at Alice's; remembering how it was last year . . . Simon knee-deep in presents from Matthew's side of the family, her own kids opening the kind but impersonal nephew-and-niece gifts from Alice and Matthew. Maureen's shamefaced little presents to them all quickly and gratefully lost in the sea of Simon's discarded wrapping paper.

The kids would be bound to talk about Hennie.

—Hennie? Who's this Hennie when she's at home?

275

—Just a friend who stayed for a while.

Feeling Alan's steady, sardonic gaze. The boy knows. Despite their care and subterfuge, despite her steadfast refusal to have them told, she's sure he knows. Alan senses her deceptions as surely as she senses the depths of his unhappiness. They're bound together by a painful, jagged love.

Christmas without Hennie. Probably though not certainly, for Hennie has simply said, don't count me in on your plans, I think I'll go over and spend it with a few friends. (And Maureen didn't mind—had been surprised by how little she minded. But even if she had minded wouldn't have said so because she knows how Hennie hates the thought of being owned.) Already the kids have started asking—eyes drooling over the shrieking and glittering parade of TV ads—what are we doing for Christmas?

We'll see, she says.

And sometimes she shouts at them with sudden, irrational anger; I don't know—just don't keep asking me that, all right? And even Hennie gives her a reproaching look.

Maybe, Carly has said in a wistful, unguarded way (Carly, who of them all was always her chief support and ally)—maybe Daddy'll come this Christmas.

Maureen pretended she hadn't heard. Reminding herself that they still have Christmas, even in there. Plum pudding, maybe even turkey and a glass of beer. They tell you about it in the papers. He'll probably have a better meal than his wife and kids.

On a Saturday morning Daphne arrives. She's been in the city for nearly three weeks. No news of Kay, no one's seen or heard a thing. Seems she's gone underground. Some of them are seriously worried about her safety. She may of course have sought professional help to get herself sorted out. But that in itself is a worry, straight doctors or counsellors being liable to feed her so much negative, hostile crap and do untold damage.

Not much happening over in town, says Daphne, summarising. Some speculation about the motives behind the proposed new Ministry of Women's Affairs—a straight, white women's club, a Governmental sop for the female voters, or what? . . . Scare reports of AIDS groping its way across the Pacific, fuelling homophobic fears . . . ought lesbians to align themselves with male gays and lend their support or . . .

Maureen waits for the moment when Hennie will tell Daphne, and wonders how it will be phrased. *Maureen and I are lovers.* She wants Hennie to say it. She hopes Hennie will not. The words have no substance; are not strictly true. They're something less than lovers, she and Hennie. She's beginning to think they may even be something less than friends.

And the last seems more definite now that Daphne's with them. Watching Daphne and Hennie together Maureen knows she's still an outsider. They're so far ahead of her. They're so certain that they're part of things to come. By the coincidental timing of their birth and allotment of their hormones Daphne and Hennie are heading in the same direction as history.

But maybe it's not hormones at all, maybe it's just a matter of deciding definitely and determinedly what you want?

Maureen can still join them, make up the lost time, if she really tried . . . Perhaps it's the kids that make her so irresolute? Yet in the end it would be in their best interest. Besides there's not a lot of choice. When Maureen tries to envisage for herself a believable, endurable future, a loving woman and a backdrop of supportive women friends is the only course not strewn with monumental hurdles or else too dismal to contemplate.

'Hennie,' she says with the kids out of earshot, her voice sounding forced and foolish in her own ears, 'You can tell her, if you like.'

Hennie looks a touch uncomfortable. Then she says lightly, with a kind of shrug, 'I never tell tales out of school.'

Daphne looks from Hennie to Maureen and back again, raises her eyebrows and changes the subject. 'Who fancies a day at the beach?'

The day is brilliantly fine. They live on a perfect off-shore island in the Pacific. The state supports them. What more can anyone ask?

They walk the metalled road beneath the arched trees with their flickering dappled light. Daphne pushes her bike, keeping to the track worn smooth by car tyres. She takes passengers; first Mickey, then Carly, then Mickey again. She's being unusually indulgent with them. She doesn't offer Alan a ride. He doesn't ask.

His own bike has a flattie. Maureen bought a new inner tube at Parenga, but though she's tried and Hennie's tried there seems to be no way of easing the wretched tyre off the rim.

Alan mooches behind them, picking stones from the road and hurling them at trees. With them but not with them.

'How's Keith?' Maureen asks Daphne. She hears the mildly sardonic

277

inflection behind her words. It feels like progress.

Daphne scowls. 'I think he's had someone staying there. There's this Turkish brothel smell in my bedroom, incense or something.'

Hennie's dark green swimming togs are cut high at the legs and show the soft private curve of hip bones. Hennie is entirely tanned and perfect.

Maureen is also a presentable all-over shade of brown but her old blue togs are square legged and embarrasing. Hidden beneath their yielding stretch Maureen's belly is branded with the graffiti lines of childbearing. Maureen's breasts still sag with remembered exhaustion and there's a knobbled vein starting to show on her leg. Maureen can't believe that Hennie can find such a body attractive, given the perfection of her own.

Maureen wishes she could be like Daphne, sprawled to dry in her tattered khaki shorts and fisted feminist T-shirt. Daphne who doesn't give a damn. Or convincingly pretends not to. And whose (real or feigned) magnificent indifference makes minding seem so shallow and shameful.

Daphne and Hennie talk. Maureen watches Carly, who has found a girl her own size, maybe a schoolmate, and Mickey who has found a dog his own size. Alan has headed up the hill to Daphne's place in search of Keith though Daphne doubts that he'll be there.

'I don't really think you should,' Maureen had told him. She still has a vague sense of guilt about Keith, and it looms slightly larger now she's committed herself to the other side.

'I'd rather you didn't,' she'd said. Afraid to look the boy right in the eye in case she should see just how much he understood. Not wanting to forbid him outright though. Sure that if she did he'd go anyway.

Maureen's attention had wandered off after Alan. Now she looks up the beach and sees Carly running beside her new friend down by the water. She runs pink-legged and floppy like a rag doll. Maureen looks down the beach, and in towards the sandhill. Fear comes from nowhere to bunch in her throat. The water safety commercial where the parents lift, eternally, a small limp body from blue water . . . *Don't let it happen to you this summer.* Her eyes searching the sea.

She runs through the little hills of sand, as far as the road. She looks through the women's toilets, calls from outside the men's before cautiously venturing in. She starts towards the shops and sees the yellow dog, and Mickey close behind.

When she reaches him he's on the last dribbling lap of an ice-cream.

'Where did you get that?'

'Lady guv me.'

'Who?'

'A lady. She guv it to me.'

'You know you mustn't take things from people you don't know.' But he's here, not floating on blue water, and a lady sounds safe enough.

When she comes back down over the sandhills Hennie and Daphne look up to watch her, and she knows right away that Hennie has said. She stops right there, among the ice plants and the pampas grass, feeling shy and a bit foolish. Daphne gets up and walks towards her, her arms swinging at her sides.

There's the beach with its pale grey sand and the water stretching beyond and Daphne striding forward in her baggy shorts. And for a moment Maureen has the feeling that she's seen all this before in a movie, with a great swelling orchestral soundtrack overflowing with hope, and courage and awful inevitability. Daphne reaches Maureen and extends her hand and Maureen resists a wild urge to salute. She pushes out her arm and Daphne shakes her hand. In the movie still half playing in her head Daphne says, *good luck, and may God be with you*, and Maureen says, *I'll do my best Sir, no one wants to lick those blighters more than I do.*

'Mu-um!' Through the wall, tragically.

'Go to sleep,' Hennie calls back. 'Shut up and go to sleep. She's off duty.'

Maureen waits for him to call again, thinking, of Hennie, she has no right! 'He's tired,' she says.

'So are we all,' says Hennie. Her silence says but the rest of us don't make it an excuse to—

'He's disappointed, I guess,' says Maureen, 'about not finding Keith. For some reason he got very attached to him.'

The long day on the beach, the walking there and home again has left them bleached and brittle. They should've left earlier, Maureen had known just how it would be—the whining, the vitriol, the stoic suffering—had tried to say, but Daphne and Hennie were set on staying longer.

She hears his feet hit the floor and scuttle for the door.

He stands in front of them blinking. 'Mum, there's someone outside.'

Hennie gives a small irritated sound of disbelief.

'Was. At the window. I saw. Really.'

Maureen goes with him into the bedroom. They stand in the dark. The windows in here are small and curtainless, and only on one side of the room. Outside it's still a few shades off blackness the nights are getting so long. And there's a new moon, they saw it palely biding its time as they walked home. The grape vine that she cut back has grown again, clawing its way around the edge of the window. A cluster of young grapes the size of blackcurrants is pressed against the pane.

'There,' she says. 'That's what you saw.'

'No. It was someone's face. Looking in the window. It was.'

She believes him. Bruce, she thinks, sharp and cold. They've released him. He's escaped.

'It wasn't . . . not anyone you might know?'

He doesn't answer.

'Who was it?'

'Just someone. I dunno who.'

'How long was he there? If he was someone you knew would you have . . .'

He's pressed against her now, shaking his head.

'It's all right,' she soothes. 'It's all right love, they've gone now. It must've been just someone lost their way or maybe some stupid prowler.'

They go back to the living room, watching the windows, and she tells Hennie.

'Funny,' says Hennie, 'that we didn't hear anything.' She's looking up at the two of them. The boy pushed in beneath his mother's arm like a large chick. Maureen sees that Hennie still doesn't quite believe, because it's Alan.

'I'll go and have a look.' The fear she'd begun to feel in the bedroom has gone. She just wants to vindicate the kid, to see a retreating shadow, torchlight, something that would be evidence.

Hennie gives them both a lopsided smile.

But, so far as Maureen can see or hear there is nothing. No one waiting in the dark little porch or outside. An army could be lurking in the trees undetected, still, she has no feeling of being watched. She walks quietly on her bare feet to the corner of the house, past the feijoa tree, heading for the boys' room.

Something—a sound, a sixth sense?—makes her stop and turn her head. And there is a second or two when the fear is so icy and intense that her mind seems to step outside of her body as if to escape. She has time to think, absurdly, of the old man dying just through the wall beside her. Time to think of a ghost . . . of supernatural forces.

Then she is fighting, scratching, screaming (someone is screaming if not her). She fights to wrench away the arm that's dragging at her throat. At first she thinks there are two people, she feels surrounded, her head is held back so chokingly tight. She kicks and struggles, then something hard and sharp is jabbed down against her cheek, her arms. She realises it is one person, but taller and stronger than she is.

Suddenly her assailant stops, pushes her to the ground and runs. In the semi-dark second before she sprints for the door Maureen sees what looks very much like a ghost. Something pale and indefinite and rapidly disappearing.

Hennie helps her in the door and sits her down in the kitchen then Hennie and Alan drag the table across to barricade the door—the only door there is to the cottage. Maureen feels her face and sees blood on her fingers. Hennie gets a bowl and a cloth and disinfectant and wipes at the cuts on Maureen's face and on her upper arm where her shirt's been ripped.

'They're not deep. This one here's the worst, but I wouldn't think it'd need stitches. What was it she used?'

'She?'

Hennie looks down at her sadly. 'It was Kay,' she says. 'Didn't you know?'

'Are you sure?'

'I just got a glimpse, but I'm sure enough. Who else?'

Maureen tries to think it through again. Kay seems better than a violent apparition.

Alan is draping the kitchen windows with towels. Did Hennie tell him to? Anyway it makes Maureen feel better—them not being looked in at.

'D'you think she's still out there?'

Hennie gestures who-knows?

If she tried to get through a window they would hear the glass. All the same Maureen says, 'D'you think we should bring the others in here?'

'Let them sleep,' Hennie sounds unsure. 'There's no point in frightening them if . . . I'm not hurting, am I?'

'No.' Maureen feels the sticking plaster. There's no pain anywhere but her teeth are beginning to chatter. Her mind keeps dragging her back to that cold, shrill moment of pure fear before anything happened.

'It's shock,' says Hennie looking at Maureen's jibbering teeth. 'I'm sorry. I'm so sorry, honey.' She puts her arms around Maureen, her head on Maureen's shoulder.

Maureen looks at Alan. His eyes accuse her of nothing, he gives her an almost comical smile.

'It's not your fault,' Maureen tells Hennie.

Alan comes to stand beside them. They're all waiting and listening. But there's only the sea and a distant car going further and further.

'She's waiting,' says Hennie. 'She's just waiting.'

'I don't suppose . . . if you called to her . . . if you talked to her?' It's beginning to feel a bit silly to Maureen. One woman, and three of them cowering in here in the kitchen. She has a feeling there must be something more than she knows, some key that would make sense of it.

'It wouldn't help,' says Hennie. Her cheeks are flushed and she has a nervous, childish smile.

Maureen feels suddenly very alone and threatened. She's spread, unprotected, through three rooms of the house.

'Would you be brave enough,' she asks Alan, 'to run and check on Carly and Mick?'

'Don't wake them though,' says Hennie.

'You sure we couldn't reason with her?' Now her teeth have settled Maureen's beginning to think they're over-dramatising.

'She hit you *with* something,' Hennie reminds her as if she's reading Maureen's thought. 'Can you tell me exactly what happened, what you saw?'

Maureen tells her. Hennie's eyes look glittery. 'I think she may be schizophrenic,' she says.

A noise begins beneath the kitchen window. A steady deliberate thumping. It brings Alan rushing back from Carly's room. They all watch the wall as if it might suddenly crumble. Slowly the blows move in the direction of the door. Maureen tries to tell herself, it's only Kay— if I looked out beneath the towel Alan's hung at the window all I would see is a poor, unhappy woman. But she's unable to move. The knocking sound has a disembodied, manic air.

Maureen whispers, 'What'll she do?'

'She'd never hurt the children,' says Hennie. 'I know she wouldn't. She loves kids.'

'There are two of us,' says Maureen. 'Two against one . . .' Her voice dies on her, choked by a terrible, crazy thought: *which two against which one?* 'You think she'll go away?' But why would she—having tracked Hennie down and come all this way to terrorise them, why would she then just quietly give up and go away?

Hennie has her hands clasped over her ears as if she's blocking out the sound of the thumping. 'I don't know what she'll do. She's never gone this far before. Nothing like this. But then I've never stayed away from her this long before.'

Maureen's noticed already the way Hennie talks as if Kay's excessive passion for her is regrettable but not at all surprising.

The banging stops. They wait a while. 'So what are we going to do?' says Maureen. 'Just go to bed?' She's beginning to blame Hennie in her heart for causing it all. 'We can't just sit here all night waiting for a mad woman to make up her mind.'

Hennie takes offence. 'It's not her fault. She's had a wretched life. Her husband was a turd. And how would you like to lose your children?'

'Maybe it's your fault,' says Maureen. She's beginning to feel on Kay's side. Thinking of her out there crouched beside the drain with its choking strands of hair and grey cotton threads and slivers of yellow soap. Angry and crumpled and clumsy and desperate. Maybe she should get what she wants. That kind of love almost seems to deserve to get its own way.

'I could get out the window and get a policeman,' says Alan.

Hennie says sarcastically, 'A cop, yeah, that's just what we need now.' But it's the first constructive idea anyone's had.

They decide he could go to the phone box by the store, or maybe to a house with a phone and ring Daphne who could borrow Keith's vehicle. Maureen would go herself but somehow it doesn't feel right to leave Hennie here alone with the kids.

So Hennie peeks beneath the towel to see that Kay's still there, but doesn't clear the window so they could look at each other face to face. Maureen can understand why Hennie can't do that. Somehow Kay has become something more than just a person out there; their fear has made her half-apparition and half-maniac, something beyond confrontation.

While Hennie keeps watch Maureen bundles Alan, the torch and Daphne's phone number out her bedroom window, waking Carly in the process. Alan waves before he gets to the hole their games have made through the hedge. Climbing out the window he could hardly

283

contain his excitement. A mission of such importance.

Maureen, watching until he flashes the torch briefly to show he's through the hedge, imagines him blundering, obscurely impelled, through enemy fire and minefields. Are the heroes, all of them, hollow-hearted boys.

'Oh look at them,' the woman says crouching in front of Carly and Mickey. 'Nearly asleep on their feet. Let's get them settled down somewhere.'

They're all standing in her kitchen, a crowd of them looking around uncertainly like in-passengers at an unknown airport. The woman's husband seeming just as bewildered. Siddown, he'd said, make yourselves ... this is Josie ... these are our refugees ...

Alan wants to stay with the grownups, having earned that right. Maureen gathers up Carly and Mickey and follows the woman down a passage to a room with twin beds. This house is bright with fresh paint and has the smell of fresh ground coffee and cinnamon. It's so long since Maureen has been into a house other than their own (except for Keith and Daphne's which isn't much different) that she's shocked by the comparison. The cottage is like a shudder in her mind, especially after tonight. She must find them somewhere else. A place like this.

'One each, or together?' says the woman. 'What about the little boy? You can all stay the night. There's the sofa. Someone might be left with the floor—we can sort it out later.'

Maureen puts the kids together in the one bed.

'Is this one a boy or a girl?'

'Boy.' Mickey's asleep already. Maureen's just remembered where she's seen this woman. 'You've met him before. The day we moved to the island he hid under your dress.' She sees the big woman really doesn't remember. 'It seems terrible to land on you like this. It's been such a crazy night.'

The woman waves it aside. 'Makes life interesting.' She stands there in a shiny black robe and bare feet. She seems uncertain whether to stay or go. 'I think they're asleep already. There's some coffee on.'

'They had a very long day,' says Maureen, remembering back to the morning which seems so long ago. 'We went to the beach.'

She turns from the bed but Carly murmurs, Mum, and flings out an anchoring hand. 'You go,' she tells the woman, 'I'll just get her ... Thank you, for all of this.'

Carly fights to keep awake and keep Maureen beside her in this house of strangers, on this extraordinary night.

After Alan went Maureen and Hennie had waited, checking now and then to see that Kay was still out there, hunched beside the drain. Occasionally she would thump against the wall but it had begun to sound sorrowful rather than menacing. Every little while Maureen would wander off to check on Carly, who had gone back to sleep and Mickey who still hadn't stirred. She'd remembered at one point that her axe was out there, only a few metres away from Kay, leaning against the porch wall. They'd whispered about it but by then Kay was beginning to seem a lot less fearsome. Still, Maureen remembered the sharp thing—which she now supposes was just a bit of stick—being jammed at her and thought, if it had been instead . . .

Neither of them was prepared to go out there. Hennie tried talking to Kay a couple of times through the wall but got no reply. A voice to go with the huddled figure would have made her seem more definitely human. Hennie had begun to talk about the importance of her not giving in, not this time. And Maureen sensed that Hennie's will was wavering. Hennie was telling Maureen this in an effort to convince herself.

And for a while there Hennie—all flushed and taut and anguished, but more than that, *exhilarated*—had reminded Maureen of her last few years with Bruce. Of the moments amid all that vacillation and despair and rage when she had felt so fiercely, exquisitely *alive*.

It took maybe three quarters of an hour before they heard the vehicle come. When they knew it was stopping at Maureen's place Hennie checked the window and saw Kay running into the trees. No one saw her after that, though Hennie and Daphne called a few times. It seemed better that they all just leave.

Daphne had come with the man, Geoff, who looked like a Mexican or one of those Norwegian troll dolls with a rubbery smiling face and a mad mop of hair. What had happened was that Alan had rung Daphne from the phone box down by the store, but Keith wasn't home and Daphne didn't want to come on her bike, so she rang the pub and was told Keith had gone home with Geoff. Someone at the pub had given her Geoff's number—an advantage of living in a small place. Daphne had rung Geoff's to get Keith, but because Keith had been taken from the pub in an unfit state for driving, Geoff had obligingly, and because Daphne was sounding so urgent, offered to come over himself. So he had gone first all the way to Toki Bay to collect Daphne, then they'd returned to Kaimoana where Alan was waiting to be rescued, beside the phone box, and the three of them had arrived at the cottage and frightened Kay away.

It was agreed it would be better if they didn't spend the night in the cottage. And in the confusion it was decided (who by?) that Daphne's place might be risky, so Geoff had volunteered his place, at least for the meantime. By the time they got to Geoff's house Keith's truck had gone. Geoff's wife said he'd just got up and taken the keys from the table and left. 'Still drunk,' she said, giving Geoff an oddly intense look, 'but not *as* drunk.'

While she's in the bedroom with Carly Maureen hears the Land-Rover start up and drive off. Now that the drama's over she'd like to be out there with the others reliving it. It seems a long time before Carly's fingers slacken their grip on her hand and she can slide it out and tuck the covers up.

When she gets back to the kitchen there's only the woman sitting alone at the table and Alan on the sofa, curled asleep beneath a rug.

The woman gets up when she sees Maureen. 'It's still hot. You do drink coffee? I wondered if I should bring it down to you. I'll have one too. And a dash of brandy, how about, for medicinal purposes? Geoff's driving your friends back to Toki Bay. See if Keith got home safely. I think they're worried about the other one, that something might happen.'

'Are they coming back?'

'I'm not sure. They didn't say, but don't worry you're fine here. We can take you home tomorrow or whenever.'

'I don't think she'd do anything—Kay, the one they're worried about.'

The woman sets the mugs on the table and gives Maureen a careful kind of look. 'Well, they seemed to think there must be someone else. The one that grabbed you. That there might be someone dangerous, some wild man, hanging about.'

'What?'

'Well maybe I didn't quite get the hang of it, but the way I understood is, once they sat down and thought about it, it didn't seem that this other person—Kay—would have done something physically violent so it seemed . . . Are you hungry? There are some biscuits?'

Maureen shaking her head, as much to clear it as anything. Daphne and Hennie covering up in front of these kind, straight people. Looking out for the image. Men the night prowlers and crazed attackers. Women no threat, at least not to other women. Least of all a *sister*.

'You don't think there was someone else?'

Maureen is suddenly cautious. Hennie and Daphne may be back any minute. She feels nothing for Kay, now that she's safe in this big bright room, but a kind of awed pity. She must decide now which side she's really on.

She shrugs and doesn't quite meet the woman's eye. 'I couldn't be certain. It could've been anyone.'

The woman is watching her knowingly, as if she's measuring up the differences between them, then putting them aside. 'Tell me about your kids,' she says.

Maureen's surprised and grateful. She struggles to find a right place to begin. Nobody's ever asked her that before.

*   *   *

His pyjamas are rolled up at the ankles, Howard's cast-offs and still too big. The sleeves flap halfway to his fingers. He'd always been too small. As if his body was holding back, afraid to grow.

Yet the elastic round his waist is tight, pressing a narrow red-ribbed line into his flesh. She always does the elastic too tight but he doesn't dare complain. She'll be wild enough about him getting the fat rolled bottoms of his pyjamas wet. He'll try and dry them along the window sill where she might not see.

He notices each single drop of dew on the grass before his feet stamp down. His new glasses have black hooks that pinch his ears; in a few more weeks they'll be looser or else he'll just be used to the feel of his ears being pushed forward.

He skims over the grass and his feet are silent, his legs are driven by a soundless motor, and he hears the screaming begin, but can't be sure, it could just be the extended bleat of a worried ewe. He thinks, did I hear it before? And why am I running?

It seems a great distance, yet he knows it can't be. The house paddock isn't so big. There's the flat then a steepish slope down to the river flat below. A clump of totara stands, blocking the view of the horse-shoe bend in the river, at the point where the slope is easiest and pitted with sheep and wheel tracks. He's among the totaras now, seeing with magnified clarity the intricate husky weave of the bark. And he hears again the ambiguous bleating screaming sound from below.

Godlike now, he can see everything. The toppled tractor, precariously balanced, Howard below and slightly thrown to the side—his legs at odd angles and facing uphill. And making that sound; then he lifts his head and shoulders and something flaps down, part of his face falling loose like a disconnected jaw. (And Keith thinking, I can't really see this at all. It's not possible. Not from this distance.) His father's favourite dog, Maisie (I haven't remembered her name, Keith thinks, not in years) in a wary half crouch watching that torn and moving flesh.

And his father standing still and gaunt as a scarecrow with his eternal stick, crumpled greasy hat and old torn jacket. His father willing the tractor to roll once more and finish it all. Or simply paralysed by shock? Then Maisie, the silent eye-dog beginning to yelp in a high, disused, puppy voice.

Keith, not quite awake—still clutching onto his place at the edge of the totara trees and the gentle, lonely smell of paddocks—hears the puppy that has come with the holiday family next door. And lies there with half the day gone—the late morning sun splashed all over his blankets—marvelling at the sly flexibility of the sleeping mind which can weave reality so cunningly into the fabric of dreams.

Only a dream? He can't be certain. The morning of Howard's death left no clear memory, except for one small moment among the confusion. When Keith had stood in the doorway between the passage and the kitchen, and his father was on the phone and the muddy marks of his bootprints on the lino led straight to the back door. His father was shouting into the phone, saying they'd have to hang up, this was an emergency. (They were on a party line. Their ring was short-long-short, but the only people who rang were stock agents and farm supply salesmen.) And Keith's mother was standing beside the table in a slippery white nightie looking tiny and almost naked. She was watching him make the phone call, but then she'd turned her head and seen Keith in the doorway and had gasped. A terrible indrawn sound of pain. Keith knew then that his father hadn't told her—not which son. She'd thought it was Keith out there. And had stood waiting, dry-eyed.

Of the rest, does it matter after so many years which was real and which is only nightmare? The margin between has never seemed distinct. And does it matter if his father had, in the end, put his weight against the tractor so it rolled once more? There were nineteen miles of bad road between the farm and Everton. The doctor couldn't have made it in less than forty minutes.

After the funeral her insanity began to show, but it was years before the doctor confirmed it. Brought on, he said, by the shock of Howard's unfortunate accident. The doctor hadn't lived with her and was entitled to his opinion. Insanity absolved her, she couldn't be held responsible. All through his secondary school years he'd waited on her, humoured her, endured her complaints and listened to her accusations. And remembered her standing calmly by the table in her nightie, without tears.

Keith has no excuse for sleeping so late, and no one to make excuses to. Since that very strange night when Josie drove him home from the pub Keith hasn't been drinking. It's not just that he's uncomfortable about the idea of running into Geoff at the pub . . . not sure about whether his own stance should be a rueful leer or moral outrage . . . The morning after he'd felt so hopelessly, desperately ill and it had occurred to him as he lay there parched and shivering with his skull wanting to crack open that his death would be lamented by no one (except, just possibly, and no longer deservedly by the boy Alan) and would be advantageous to Daphne who could return to being a solitary squatter.

He forces himself out of bed and pulls on his trousers. He goes through the big room to the bathroom. Daphne's sprawled on the floor talking on the phone. Probably to Hennie who rang last night from a call box but only Keith was home.

In the bathroom Keith peers at himself in the small shaving mirror which is the only mirror in the house. He's looked at it often in the last few weeks, trying to detect a certain slackness of the lips or heaviness of the eye-lids which might suggest . . .

He smiles at himself. Well, something resembling a smile. Perhaps Shisha had put it about that, drunk, he was easy. Keith hasn't seen Shisha since. She left while he was still sleeping. He doesn't want to see her again. Keith, that night, had got the feeling that Shisha in her own convoluted way hated him more single-mindedly and impersonally than Daphne ever has.

Right now in the other room Daphne is raising her voice, getting worked up. Keith listens.

'It's not possible, Hennie, it's a contradiction in terms. No one can love someone who's got them . . . Pity, okay then. Pity I understand . . . Be surprised then, but pity is, okay, and love is something else altogether . . .

'Maybe you do, maybe to some extent you do provoke these situations but . . .

'Listen to me a minute . . . Love *is* feeling safe, all the rest is just hetero shit that's spilled over. Okay don't listen.'

He hears the receiver clatter into its cradle.

When Daphne's home now she spends half her life on the phone. Keith paid for the installation and pays for the rental because he's the one that wanted the thing. Daphne had always managed perfectly well without one. Keith thought having a phone would get him more work, but it hardly ever rings on his behalf. When Daphne lies for ages with the receiver clamped to her ear Keith imagines all the little old ladies with cracked windows and blocked drains who are desperately trying to get through to him.

His bout as a drinker has lost him a few customers. Besides, it's a bad time of year, everyone hoarding for Christmas extravagances, and the pensioners thinking that if maybe they wait a grandson or nephew will turn up and oblige with a few repair jobs.

Last Wednesday, having taken sober stock of his circumstances, Keith went across to the city and registered as being jobless. His idea was to get the dole, but they offered him a job on a weekly hand-out paper in Hamilton. 'The job market's freeing up,' the woman said, 'but all the same you won't find anything in the central city area and certainly not on that island of yours.'

'But I live there,' said Keith.

She looked at the form he'd just filled in. 'You're single,' she said. 'Unattached. Mohammed may just have to consider moving himself to where the mountains are. Nothing to keep you where you are now.'

Just the thought of leaving the island had made his heart stumble. He told the woman it was out of the question. 'I'd rather be dead than live in this city,' he said to get the message across. She looked at him as if he'd kicked her dog. He hadn't meant to upset her. 'Really,' he explained, 'all I want is to get on the dole.'

The woman shook her head, trying to pretend this wasn't giving her any satisfaction. 'We don't pay benefits to people on the island,' she said. 'Not to single people who choose to live where there isn't any work.'

He was about to accuse her of lying and cite Daphne in evidence. But of course Daphne would've given them an Auckland address, they wouldn't trap her so easily.

Having to wait for the last ferry he climbed the stairs to Mort Shelley's office. The receptionist's face made Keith aware of looking shabby. He saw there was even dirt beneath the skin that rimmed his nails. He couldn't think what had induced him to come to a place where he'd be made to notice his own fingernails.

Mort gave him ten minutes and a cup of metallic coffee. He said

Keith was looking well, beachcombing must agree with him. He said he, Mort, was seriously thinking of packing it all in and clearing off to somewhere simple. Having run out of affable lies he sat there folding an envelope into a single strip of mud-coloured paper until Keith said he had a boat to catch and better go.

On the way down the stairs Keith realised he hadn't even asked after Myra. He seemed to have lost the knack of those kinds of things.

The boat home was crammed with sturdy young foreigners with bare legs and windbreakers that crackled like new cellophane. The school holidays hadn't yet started but already each day brought a fresh platoon of tourists to flood the beaches as if it was coming up D Day.

At Parenga Keith stopped and made a new notice. *GET THOSE FIX-IT CLEAR-IT JOBS DONE BEFORE XMAS* and his name and phone number. So far nobody's rung.

Old Mrs Twiss, hunchbacked and squinty-eyed, invited him to her place for Christmas. He told her he was going away. He should've accepted. It would've been a kindness. But sitting the day away in her matchbox cottage where everything's so neatly in its place, so carefully patched and matched and glued to keep on being useful, would've seemed too much like defeat.

Keith has replaced the most conspicuously rotting boards on the dark south side of Mrs Twiss's house. He's seen the decay within and covered it swiftly, wordlessly – like a doctor drawing the sheet briskly over naked and terminal flesh. He hopes the house will outlive the old lady, she hasn't the money for the kind of repairing it needs.

Over in the city the shop windows were jammed with toys, tents, cassette players, fishing rods, electronic devices. He'd thought of Alan. Keith turning up there Christmas Eve with some present so magnificent, so thoroughly *choice* . . . But he would have to buy for them all, the whole production. And he's left it too long to just turn up. Daphne goes in his place. Maureen will be by now one of Daphne's stormtroopers.

It gets harder all the time to get outside of himself long enough to take some kind of overview. He can still bring back a semblance of that heady sense of destiny he had last summer – a faint and far-fetched feeling. Sometimes it seems that all the island has done for him is scrape away at his surface, leaving him flawed and floundering.

The pub was a salve but no solution. The kind of living he knows best, but not the income to sustain it. The last time he was there they'd talked for an hour on dogs. The loyalty of. Keith had thought of

Winston. He'd just listened. I read . . . that reminds me . . . that's nothing I . . . we useda have . . . you ever heard about . . . (Is that why he'd remembered Maisie?)

Then ghosts. Ghosts are always favoured in public bars. The island's haunted houses . . . rocking beds and lipless whispers. This time Keith could contribute; in this bay, a singing, a kind of singing. Several times I've heard it, maybe more.

Of course they'd laughed. Except for Leon the fisherman who's lived here all his life. Who said beneath the laughter, I know that place; I've heard them voices, they been there for years.

Geoff then jumping off about people exploding. It's true, it's true . . . spontaneous combustion. You could be digging the garden, making love, cleaning your teeth, and suddenly WHOOF.

Vietnam, Josie had brought up. Remember then, a kind of fashion — all those monks, dousing themselves and setting light. Self-immolation — the ultimate protest. Not only monks. She saw a man try it once, right at the end of a demonstration.

A cooking demonstration, Harley'd said. Keith would like to be that quick.

They wanted to know the rest of the story. Not a lot, Josie told them. The guy was wearing a caftan, quite radical in those days. It didn't catch so well but it caught. People moved back. What else should they do? He had a right — he was an adult. But someone'd moved in with a blanket.

'He'd be scarred to buggery,' said the fisherman. And Geoff said, funny you never really got to know the end of stories — the papers, now, they never tell you the end.

There isn't an end, Harley insisted. Even death, you can't ever say something ended here or there, there's always more.

There was more for Keith that day, but most of it gone beyond memory. A moment or two of clarity when he found himself watching his own truck winding ahead of him on the beam of their lights. Josie beside him at the controls of a four-wheel-drive, over-riding his objections, saying it wasn't the drunks she cared about but all those other innocent drivers.

He remembers being put to bed, shoelaces undone, jeans peeled off. A large soft bed and their voices rising and dipping somewhere above him. A brown voice and a golden voice dancing together.

And when he awoke again the voices were still there but cautious and separate in the dark. Fingers ran over his shoulder then jumped away. Keith could feel her weight, the mattress drawing him into the gully where she seemed to be kneeling. He kept his eyes closed. It seemed advisable.

Her voice, a whisper but not for him. 'I feel bloody ridiculous.'
Geoff's voice, further away, soothing.
'You're never ridiculous.'
'I can't.'
'He won't mind. Men don't.'
'He's out to it. I feel like a necrophiliac.'
When she giggled the bed shook.
'Keith,' she said very softly, 'Keith, wake up. Are you awake?'
He made his eyelids flicker then cautiously open.
'Oh god,' she said, 'oh hell.'
'Please,' said Geoff.
'I dunno what to do?'
Keith felt her hair against his cheek, her big breasts like cushions against his chest. Her lips chewing at his neck. He lay perfectly still.
The brown voice out in the dark whispered, 'That's right. I love you.'
She smelt of soap and shampoo. Her fingers moved in small uncertain jumps, her tobacco breath was warm through his whiskers. Keith had a sudden repugnant vision of his mother's mouth and jerked his head aside. The phone began ringing in another room. He felt Josie take her body away.
'Australia,' she said sharply.
'Don't be silly,' Geoff said and sighed. 'I'll get it.'
Josie sat for a few seconds on the edge of the bed. Then she got up and went after Geoff, closing the door behind her. He didn't fall back to sleep. After a while he heard a vehicle start up and he thought with sudden panic that someone had taken the Holden. He found the lightswitch and got himself dressed. He followed the passage through to the main room which was both kitchen and living room. Josie was there alone. She said Keith's flatmate had called, there was some kind of emergency. They hadn't liked to wake Keith so Geoff had gone instead. She didn't once look him right in the eye. She gave him his keys when he asked, and he thanked her for driving him home. She laughed but still didn't look at his face.

He drove home very slowly. Somewhere he'd lost his contact lenses. He may have removed them himself but he couldn't remember. He couldn't go back and search through their sheets; not then or since.

When he got home the house was empty. That night he'd dreamt of Howard, one of those half-removed, documentary dreams that cut too close for comfort.

He's waking from a tender dream he hates to let go of. But his father's voice is tugging at him and now, although it's not quite daylight, he can see his father filling the doorway. He's dressed for work; the tattered sportscoat and the lumpy hat.

'Come on,' he's saying. 'We haven't got all day.' He sounds the way he usually sounds—mournful and irritable. (The dreaming Keith notes this to himself as if it's of importance. 'He sounded normal, for him.')

Howard humps up his bedclothes and makes a faint whining sound of protest.

'Come on. Shake a leg.' (Still normal.)

Howard puts one leg out between the edges of his sheets and thumps his head against the pillow. 'Wish you'd told us last night,' he mutters to the wall.

'Weather's cleared. Won't take more'n an hour or two.' (If anything more cheerful than usual.)

'I'll do it,' says Keith, pushing back his bedding. 'I'm ready just about.' Not wanting to be left in the house alone with her.

'I want him. You stay where you are. We don't need you.'

'I could just come anyway.'

'No. (Are there special signs of agitation now?) It's him I want. You get back in there and stay there.'

He must be angry. To put so many words together in one go he has to be angry. Keith gets himself back into bed and pretends to close his eyes, but enough gap left to see Howard pulling on his clothes. Outside the birds are starting up. Inside the air is heavy with silence. Keith hears his father leave, his boots on the bare boards. Once he's gone Howard swears softly to himself. Howard curses the way Keith plays rugby—ineptly but always hoping to improve for the sake of popularity.

When his spying eyes watch Howard leaving Keith (the Keith who is dreaming and knows he's dreaming) thinks, I'm seeing him for the last time.

He owes her nothing, but she can't just let him be. She lies bedridden, hundreds of miles away, sending him dreams.

Yesterday he visited the little bay and found people camped there. A bright orange tent and one with green and purple stripes. Clothes were hung over the guy ropes drying, more were spread over bushes.

A woman was sitting on Keith's flat rock. She had a pad on her knees and seemed to be sketching the hills above Hoki Bay.

He made himself walk past the tents, the flippers and goggles piled together, the pile of broken kina shells. He wanted to order the woman to leave, to hurl rocks at the tents, to grind her face into the kinas, but he just walked as far as the rocks then turned and walked back again to leave through the bush the way he'd come. After all they were probably allowed to be there.

Allowed? What does that mean except that no one cares enough to prevent it.

Daphne believes in the domino theory of social change. One small, well-aimed blow against the existing social order will eventually ripple its way right around the globe. She thinks there's that much time left.

Among the curled yellow clippings that Daphne has pinned to the wall is a newspaper photograph of a soldier standing proudly smiling beside, and dwarfed by, a bomb. The caption doesn't identify the soldier but it does identify the bomb which is called Corpus Christi 11.

*   *   *

'They've just connected the phone. You're my first call. My very first.'

'I'm honoured,' says Josie. 'Can you wait a sec while I grab my smokes?' She has to run to the bedroom and keep out of reach of Geoff's lunging arms. 'It's a toll call. You may as well get up.'

'I can wait.'

'I'm sorry,' Josie says to Juliet, breathing smoke, 'but I was desperate for a fag. Taupo. Why on earth Taupo?'

'The way it happened. And I've got a job here. Only a desk job but with prospects, my dear, with prospects. I would've written, only I wanted to wait till I was properly settled. I was staying with my brother and his wife but now I've got my own place. It's small but kind of nice. Not too bad. Feels like a bachelor pad.'

Juliet gurgles hopefully. Her voice is small and brave. Already Josie feels incumbent and afraid of what's to come.

'Sounds as if you've got it all together.'

There's a silence. Was she too obviously hoping. She pitches her voice more carefully to a note of friendship. 'It's great to hear from you.'

'Well, I presumed Paul would've been in touch.'

'Yes,' says Josie, hearing Juliet's grin and now her own, 'regularly.' Paul rings at least once a week, usually on a Friday or Saturday night.

He makes depressing jokes about his failure to have 'found anyone'. And in her heart Josie holds Juliet responsible. She knows the feeling is unfair and the reasoning repressive, but all the same . . . The trouble with principles is that in real life they tend just to redistribute the burden. Husbands are like dirty clothes, if you leave them lying there long enough someone else will feel compelled to deal with them. They won't get up of their own accord and leap into the washing machine.

'How's things with you? How's the island?'

'Fine,' says Josie. 'Busy,' she adds, trying to forestall what she senses is coming. 'Some of the crops have startled us by actually producing. And of course we have to be in time for the Christmas market, catch the good prices. Oh, and we've got one stunning little Shetland foal and another expected any day.' She hears herself and cringes a bit. Does she sound boastful? Insensitive at least – parading out the trivial concerns of those who must resort to inventing their worries.

'Jose, I wish you could come down and visit. Just for a few days even.'

If only Juliet's words hadn't come bursting through in an urgent voice, no longer brave. If only Josie could've been allowed to believe it was just a casual invitation. 'Oh god,' she says fast before she weakens, 'I can't Jule, not just now. We've got all this bloody produce to get rid of. Maybe in a couple of weeks, after . . .'

. . . Christmas. She stops herself just in time. You can't say Christmas to a woman in a bachelor flat who's facing it, probably for the first time in her whole life, alone.

'. . . after the rush,' she says lamely. It's less than true. They are, at least by Geoff's standards busy, but not so busy that she couldn't be spared for a few days. She just doesn't want to go. She doesn't want to sit in a little flat being bolshy about men. She doesn't want to go to restaurants and talk about male oppression, global peace and the symptoms of menopause.

It would be lovely to see Juliet again. Juliet needs her support; deserves it. But at the moment Josie and Geoff are devoted, tender, inseparable. Josie hears her voice melt when they talk and smiles at herself out of mirrors. Eight years on! Every second must be treasured, it may never happen again.

If she told the truth Juliet wouldn't believe her. She'd wonder at the nature of the heartbreak Josie was covering up with such wild tales.

Right now Juliet's silence is saying, well if you can't come down, why not invite me up? *Why don't you come for Christmas?* Juliet's silence is willing Josie to say those words. Her need is sucking the words to the tip of Josie's tongue. At Christmas people who watch out of windows get an urge to jump. Christmas kills. Remember Edie.

Paul, too, has been probably hoping they'll ask. Why can't the two of them just spend it together? Go and visit their Collingwood son and draw up a divorce agreement between roast lamb and trifle?

'I'm sorry,' says Josie. 'I'm sorry, love, it's just that right now . . .'

'It's all right for heaven's sake. Don't start apologising. It's no big thing. If you're busy, you're busy.' Juliet's mouth is away from the receiver, her voice comes through with distant indifference.

'What's your number down there. Hang on, I'll grab a pen.' Josie scoops three ballpoints from the jar on the kitchen windowsill. The first two are always empty. She salvages an envelope from the waste paper basket and smoothes it out. Relief makes her grab a cigarette forgetting she has one going.

She held out. The important thing now is not to go soft and reconsider. Keep the conversation buoyant and no mention of X M A S.

Rationalising: We've never had a Christmas on our own, just him and me. This year we can, even Lake has other plans. We may never get another Christmas on our own. This may be our last Christmas together. One of us might die, one of us might leave. I may get fed up with his idleness, he may get repulsed by my thighs. On all sides our love is threatened by variables forseen and unforseen. Yet we feel obliged to disguise and disavow it because it may cause offence.

When you're over forty passionate love must be either fresh or furtive. Prolonged lust is a social embarrassment. It has the pathos and tacky desperation of scarlet lipstick drawn wider and deeper than the edges of an old and narrow mouth.

When Josie replaces the receiver she doesn't hurry back to Geoff but goes to stand at the window that gives the most expansive view of sea. Having chosen in his favour she now holds it against him. Juliet, drowning, stretched out her hand to Josie, who turned her back.

Didn't Juliet do just that to Paul? Who has first claim—friend or lover? For the first time in her life Josie seems to have made her choice. If it was the right one why does she feel so lousy?

When she does go back to the bedroom (why not, having decreed that his company is so precious to her?) he looks up and says, 'Juliet?'

'How did you know?'

'You have your Juliet look. She's not coming for Christmas?'

'I think she would've liked to. I didn't offer.'

He glows with relief. His delight annoys her.

'You know that woman with the three kids who spent the night here—Maureen. I think she's lonely. Maybe we should . . .'

'Not Christmas.'

'It's just a day like any other day.'

'It won't be. I've made plans for us.'

'What plans?'

'A surprise. I'm working on it. That's the most I'm gonna tell you.'

'Your kind of surprise I don't trust. You have a bent streak.'

'Everyone has. I admit to mine is all.'

'Look at the trouble it gets us into.'

She holds him responsible for the night with Keith. He says it was her idea and she can't be sure it wasn't. She was marginally drunk and may have been joking. That's what comes, she warns, of mind games. You begin to believe . . . When the fantasies start taking flesh it's time to pull back.

Then again, he says, you can look at it this way . . . Boredom kills. Proof of that wherever you look. Diversions are the price of sustained emotion. What happened with you and Farley, you and Dick, even maybe me and Michelle? Someone got bored, that's what.

But he *shuddered*, remembers Josie. I'm sure I saw that poor little guy actually shudder.

Happy, the little yellow mare, gives birth ten days before Christmas. They'd begun to think she would hold out until Christmas day. It would've been nice, said Josie. It would've been a bloody nuisance, said Geoff.

On her way to check the trough Josie discovered the mare struggling to her feet with two bagged black feet protruding from beneath her high-held tail. She ran for Geoff, not because anything seemed wrong, just not wanting him to miss out on the arrival.

Nature is letting Happy down. She snorts and heaves, now, white-eyed. Geoff has fastened a rope around the foal's slippery fetlocks. There's nothing for Josie to do but squat on the grass and watch. When she tried to offer the pony comfort the mare thrashed and Geoff told Josie to get away. So she watches helplessly; the miracle she ran breathlessly to announce has turned back into a small yellow horse racked with pain.

Hogg crouches beside Josie. She strokes his brittle old hair. Geoff is talking to the mare in a steady tender fashion. Josie feels limp with love for this man who is kind and usefully occupied. Strong too, as he braces his legs and heaves at the rope, shaking his head at Josie as she motions an offer to help.

At first the foal's progress is torturously slow. Josie remembers Lake, the longest and loneliest of her labours. She recalls the sharp hospital sounds and despotic hospital faces. Better to have been a Shetland pony on the grass among friends. (Times have changed, she promises herself. Giving birth in hospitals is no longer a punishable offence. She needs to believe this, she has daughters.)

In a watery rush the foal comes free. It and Geoff fall at the same time. Josie squeals with relief and delight. Then hears Geoff.

'Oh god,' he says. 'Oh Christ.'

He's bent over the foal. Josie can see the damp legs kicking. Geoff looks up at her, his eyes bunched and injured. He moves back so she can see the foal. Which isn't quite a foal at all. The perfect hind legs, the shiny black rump and scraggy tail lead to a terrible joke of a single stunted hoof mid-chest and a head so big it could almost be Happy's own head. A disproportionate head with big eager eyes, struggling now to raise itself up as Geoff automatically strips back the membrane.

Josie steps back, afraid those eyes will focus on her, that she might be the only thing the creature sees in its blink of a lifetime. Happy has got to her knees and is stretching round, her nostrils tremble anxiously.

Geoff takes the thing by its hind legs and carries it towards the macrocarpas. Josie puts her body between Happy and the creature that swings from Geoff's hand. By the time the mare has got to her feet, swaying unsteadily, Geoff is hidden by trees.

Happy hobbles stiff-legged to sniff the afterbirth. Josie imagines Geoff prising a rock from the ground. Josie weeps; for the foal, for the foal's executioner, for Happy with her swollen teats and cheated instincts. The mare now lets Josie stroke her dusty cheeks and fondle her ears. Happy's eyes are like bronze cauliflowers preserved in glass. They have nothing to say, no pin-hole ducts to shed her tears.

'I'm crying for you,' sniffs Josie, bending to press her cheek against the neck still patched dark gold with sweat.

Geoff brings back the body and lays it beside the afterbirth. 'It seemed better,' he spreads his hands, 'than nothing at all.'

'Yes,' says Josie damply.

When Josie's friend Sandi was many years younger she had a stillborn baby. They refused, at the hospital, to let her see him. They said it would upset her. Sandi still wonders out loud what her baby looked like. It was the only one she had. Nowadays, Sandi says, they believe a woman is entitled to look at her own child, dead or alive.

'We'll leave them for a bit,' says Geoff. He reaches for Josie's hand and holds it very tight. He's about to brush away her tears with his free hand when they both see it's smeared with slime and blood. Josie smiles at him, a damp brave smile that makes her feel wonderfully tiny and fragile and cared for. She squeezes his hand and they walk together.

It's times like this, when she feels tragic and small and dependent when she loves him most of all. And it's times like this, when she's tragic and tearful and dependent, that he loves her most of all.

Behind them Happy swings her dumbfounded head from the still black creature to the sky and gets no answer.

Christmas Day

THERE ARE NO words to suit this or any occasion. All the words have been worn out. They no longer add to the picture, simply diminish and defuse.

The world has developed an immunity to words; they no longer work.

It doesn't feel like enough, so beneath this Keith draws an uneven circle divided in the peace symbol. Then he feeds the paper back into his typewriter and puts, at the bottom.

You can keep the typewriter.

He leaves the paper in there, rolled back so it'll be seen. He puts the typewriter on Daphne's bed, right in the middle. He expects the significance of the gift, the wider irony, will escape her. She won't understand that he had outmanoeuvred her. From now on even her best efforts will be insignificant.

He's borrowed a pair of Daphne's cotton trousers. She left them hanging in the bathroom and will probably never miss them. He's had to roll them up around the ankles because they flapped down over his feet. And they billow out around the hips. He's had to pull out a bit of the elastic and knot it, a bit too tight now, to stop them sliding down.

The Holden is parked in its usual place at the side of the road. He hasn't been able to get it started for a week or more. The battery's flat but it seems to be something more than that. The can he keeps full, because the petrol gauge no longer works, is wedged in behind the passenger seat. The driver's door doesn't lock and in holiday time things walk if they're not well hidden. In the winter he could leave his tools lying on the back even and no one would touch them. When the holidays started he began keeping his tools in the house, even though they're of no great value.

It's lucky he never bought the lawn mowing business. He'd seriously thought about it, but come summer he would've bummed out. Already the lawns are dry and brittle and dead, only the daisies hanging on in there.

'Morning,' says Jimmy who owns the dinghy, sitting out on his front steps among a bunch of cats. 'Another dry summer.'

'Looks like it,' says Keith crunching on up the road. The wire handle of the can cuts into his fingers. He sits it on the road and changes hands. The house just below him has cottonwool snow on the front window and HAPPY XMAS in a half circle of large red letters, wished to the world.

A car passes Keith—a Toyota, churning up dust. The kids wave out the back window in an extravagance of goodwill. He spits out dust and doesn't wave back though he turns to watch them. Only the visitors drive Toyotas.

He turns off the road up towards the top of the hill, past the houses. It feels like late morning. A breeze blows sweetly from the sea.

The tents are gone from the bay as he expected. The campers have come and used and gone. There's not even a broken bottle or stray can left as evidence of defilement. Either they took their rubbish with them or threw it in the sea so it could float back incognito.

The tide is almost full out. Among the driftwood lie the usual washed up relics; a rack from a fridge or clothes dryer, giant crumbs of polystyrene, clotted membranes of polythene, half a tin opener.

Keith sits for a while on the dry sand. He listens for the voices. He felt sure that today he would hear them again, but there's only the buzz of a jet boat and the seagull-sharp sounds of children, carried across the water from Toki Bay.

Keith is content and, for the first time in his life, absolutely certain. He can see the inevitability of today. When he looks back his life has a pattern and a purpose. Everything was bringing him steadily to this day, this place.

He's awed by his own intention, by the unrestrained magnificence of it. The ultimate act of love. A man's act; that will be implicitly understood.

He wants to touch everything—the sand, the stones, leaves, bark, grass, water, rocks. The new stillness inside him makes him believe that his touch would bestow on things a kind of blessing, he has that power. But there's also a sense of urgency, a longing to get it done.

He carries the can across the damp sand to the flat rock. When the tide's out like this the rock becomes a natural platform. Having clambered up with the awkward can he looks down at his own footprints, forever one-way.

From the rock he can see part of Toki beach. A couple of swimmers close to the shore, a few kids running about clutching bright objects unwrapped at dawn, a cluster of adults around the barbecue, a small dark dog with legs so short it seems to roll from the water's edge up to the sandhills and back again. He can see all that though he has no lenses. Yet he's not surprised.

A tiny sailboat glides towards the beach. Out of Keith's range of vision the jet boat makes circles of sound. He pats the pocket of his shirt and feels the lighter still there. He found it on the mantelpiece left over from winter fires. In white lettering it says RONALD WHO? He knew that was beyond coincidence.

What would it be like to sit all day in an office thinking up new slogans for car stickers and cigarette lighters and joke cards? To drive a Toyota on the motorway five days a week and find the world a bit crappy but comfortable?

It's like looking in a cow's eye in search of a soul.

Keith turns away from the tiny people on the beach. He faces inward. Manuka, pungas, cabbage trees, bush lawyer and up towards the skyline a tarty splash of pohutukawa. The tide turning. Water below so clear it seems to pull him right down there among the stones. Keith unscrews the cap of his standard five-litre tin which is blue and white with a circle of red on either side making the O in Mobil.

*   *   *

She would feel calmer if Geoff would move aside from the mirror. This concern with his appearance is quite out of character and making her feel slightly hysterical. He's knotting a peacock blue scarf around his neck. A silk scarf. Edie gave it to Josie maybe fifteen years ago. Josie never remembers to wear things like scarves but she keeps them in case.

'Whada y' think?' His mirror eyes shifting anxiously.

She sighs. 'To be honest I think it's a bit much. It's okay, but it looks like you've tried. You know?' Josie never wants her appearance to suggest she's tried in case others may conclude she failed. Better to convey a casual disinterest.

He undoes the knot. 'Is that better?'

She giggles, mainly from nervousness.

'Looks silly?'

'I suppose,' she says, 'it all depends on what you're trying to convey.'

He removes the scarf and tosses it on the bed. 'If I knew that I'd know what to wear.'

'What about me? You think I'm all right like this?' She's wearing one of her Indian dresses. Cotton so fine and soft you scarcely feel it, gathered at the yoke like a little girl's dress; a voluminous grey and blue disguise.

'Fine,' he says unconvincingly. 'You look fine. Except it might get a bit hot out there.'

Meaning straps and cleavage. She'd thought about that and decided the loose and sometimes shuddering flesh on her upper arms would cancel out any advantage.

'Cold more likely,' she argues. 'In my experience boats are always cold. We'll need to take jackets.' She's trying not to sound unenthusiastic. She's spent a few afternoons on people's boats and never enjoyed herself, can remember only feeling cold and bored, watching others get drunk in a cramped space.

'You don't want to go.' It's not quite an accusation.

'I don't mind. No, of course I want to go. Anyway we can't pull out now, it's all arranged.' She catches hold of his hand, smiling, promising, 'It'll be all right.'

She doesn't want them not to go. Not now. Christmas alone together was proving to be a more protracted business than she'd imagined. They'd woken early and exchanged presents. He'd given her a wildly improper nightdress which despite her predictions turned out to be large enough to contain if not cover her flesh. She was amazed that anyone would produce such a garment in her size range. The manufacturing decision must've been made by a man—any woman would've been too conscious of the absurdity implied.

Josie had felt very faintly resentful at the gift. It was more a present for him than her. She'd got him a lavishly illustrated, meticulously indexed book on Shetland ponies. She could tell that he too was marginally disappointed.

Then there had been Lake's present to them both, which had been sitting on the sideboard unopened since it arrived the week before. A paperback featuring news photographs of the more celebrated politicians, national and international. Little white bubbles of extemporised speech had been added. Lake being so poor it was the thought that counted.

Geoff had grabbed the book first and thumbed through it with periodic guffaws. The glossy volume on Shetland ponies slid off the bed, having been barely skimmed through.

'I bet someone gave this to Lake,' he said, 'and she couldn't get the point of any of them so she sent it to us.'

Josie doesn't like it when he makes fun of her kids. Besides she's secretly proud of Lake's incorruptible dedication, humourless or not.

Geoff let her look at the book while he went off to make them tea and toast. Then he got Josie to try on his present to her. And after she'd modelled it standing, with and without high heels, and oozed back to bed where they capitalised on his investment, the day would've stretched rather limply ahead of them if it hadn't been for Geoff's arrangements. Josie might've sat around all afternoon fretting over whether Sarah and Daryl's gifts had reached them in time, and whether or not she'd chosen well. (In any case her efforts were bound to be overshadowed by Dick's superior offerings.) Sarah has sent a card, saying she'll bring their presents when she comes in January. Nothing from Daryl who is always late and has, anyway, more pressing concerns.

It wasn't possible for Geoff to keep his secret plans a secret. Josie needed a few details or how could she be prepared. Even though he'd assured her she wasn't expected to take provisions—he had some booze set aside and these people were filthy rich—she'd got together a basket of baking and strawberries (their own) and chocolates because you can't go somewhere empty-handed, especially not on Christmas Day.

Will I like them, she'd asked.

He said, you're not required to like them.

Geoff had said eleven but nervousness makes them early. Much longer in the house and they might have changed their minds.

So they're parked just off the road that runs beside the Whiripare beach and the boat is out there looking worldly, queening it over a couple of other, inferior, boats also moored in the bay. The tide is well out and the beach is almost deserted. All at home, thinks Josie, basting turkeys and beating cream and tripping over toys. She's glad she hadn't said it aloud in case it sounded wistful.

Someone comes out on deck and waves. Geoff gets out of the Rover and waves back. They watch while the figure draws in the dinghy, lowers himself into it and pushes off with an oar levered against the hull. Then they gather up the basket, the bottles and their jackets and are careful to lock the Land-Rover because of the tourists.

He rows towards them; a squeaky clean, athletic type in dazzling white summer trousers rolled to the knee. When he turns the dinghy to land he smiles at them over sparkling white teeth. Josie pokes Geoff with the basket and says, 'You should'a worn the scarf.' He grins back, his eyes are hidden behind dark glasses. All three of them wear them but the man in the dinghy has blue-tinted mirror glasses with stainless steel frames. He has sun-bleached hair and a clean shaven, anonymous, deodorant-advertising face. Seeing him properly Josie relaxes a bit. He's too blandly unflawed to be taken seriously.

His name is Robert, his manners are charming and slightly formal. He stands in the water to steady the little boat while Josie climbs in. The dinghy immediately plunges and settles itself with a gravelled crunch.

'Don't worry,' says Robert. 'A little push.'

But Geoff, who knows all of what's hidden by the billowing Indian cotton, says, 'Think you better get out love, till we're in a bit deeper.'

When they're all of them afloat, and Robert smiling and trying to pretend rowing is no effort at all, Josie sees how he glances every few seconds at the inch of aluminium that separates them from lapping water.

Geoff sits facing her, their knees overlap. He keeps craning round to look at the boat they're heading for. Geoff has the country habit of despising and coveting luxury in equal measure. When he's turned back to her and she guesses his shaded eyes are offering her slightly doubtful reassurance she leans forward until Geoff's head blocks her view of Robert and whispers, 'I'm not climbing up first.' He gets her point and when they're alongside the boat he stands to grasp a railing and says to Robert, on behalf of them both, 'After you.'

The woman is an American. She glides up from below as they come on board. There's a purr to the way she walks towards them, her heels don't seem to touch the deck. She wears very short white shorts and a black halter top with a white blazer slung across her shoulders. Her body has a tightly sprung look and her skin is darker than Geoff's and of a more expensively acquired shade. Her name is Brenda. Her voice is low-pitched and furry and she has the aggressively intimate style of American women.

At first sight she's twenty-five, but close up she may even be over forty. If you look hard enough you can see that her face has the pigmented mottled shine of peeling varnish and her thighs have the loose fleshed quiver of muscles that are losing their grip. Josie looks hard and begins to feel slightly happier.

Brenda and Robert usher their visitors below deck out of the breeze. Inside is all padded bottle-green leather and cool dark woodgrain. Everything is deceptive, folding away, sliding back, closing up. Geoff shows interest so Robert demonstrates. He slides back a door and the bed, at least, seems to be a fixture. It's custom made, vastly wide at one end sloping away to become much narrower at the other so heads could be close or maybe feet. Josie glances in from the doorway to see Robert pushing aside bedclothes to display the air mattress made to fit. 'Unfortunately,' he says, 'none of it's ours. We're simply leasing it for the summer.'

Robert, too, has an accent. Flattened vowels and prissily clipped consonants. Josie doesn't want to know where he comes from in case it's South Africa. Geoff wouldn't understand such specialised squeamishness, but then men seem more adept at compartmentalising their attitudes. If only Josie had the same ability this could be a truly memorable Christmas.

She must be looking half-hearted because as Brenda hands out glasses of, of course, champagne, she says, 'To break the . . . ice.' And in the perceptible pause she glances at Josie with a big American smile. After seeing that she'd almost downed half a glass in the first needy gulp Josie rations herself to refined sips.

Both Brenda and Robert seem eager to be liked but not sure how best to go about it. Josie begins to feel as if she and Geoff are exotic species of marine life accidentally fished up and now flopping about looking rare and inscrutable while their captors feverishly try to discover the secret of keeping them alive. Josie senses that, beneath their indulgent charm, she makes them uneasy.

Brenda enthuses over the contents of Josie's basket in just the way Josie's mother overdid her praise for Josie's schoolgirl efforts at pottery. All items highly acclaimed but never ever put to use. 'You're gonna take them right home again.' Brenda waves a definite brown finger and begins to restack the basket. Josie takes them out again. 'Keep them for tomorrow . . . the next day.' Threatens, 'I'll be offended.' And wins.

Brenda has everything prepared. 'This one,' says Robert, 'is efficiency disguised as a woman.' Brenda smiles at him and for a moment they link hands and Josie, who still can't quite believe in them has the feeling that all this is happening within the confines of a TV screen. Which could explain why, although she's never before met them, these two seem so naggingly familiar.

Would Geoff and Josie like to have a sail before they eat? (Brenda uses their names in every sentence as though repetition will hasten familiarity.)

Geoff would, and Josie has resolved in her heart to agree to anything. Robert apologises that it's not *real* sailing. He spread his hands tragically and looks paternal and boyish at the same time. Josie estimates him to be ten years younger than Brenda, but it's hard to be sure. The rich have a different way of aging.

They motor out of the bay. Geoff points out their house as it comes into view above the cliff. Josie wishes he hadn't, the place looks so vapidly lemon and uninspired. From this distance you can't see the trees that will make it, someday, a home she might want to acknowledge. She thinks having seen the place their hosts will be a shade more patronising.

Geoff's getting carried away, inviting them round sometime. Next thing he'll be planning joint holidays. He's too far away for Josie to remove her glasses and catch his eye.

They turn towards the south end of the bay. If they kept going in a straight line, says Robert, they'd land at Equador. Having had to dodge a few islands on the way.

'Which islands,' Josie wants to know. Off-shore islands are the nearest she's been to overseas. She's never learnt to see the world in her mind's eye and say this is Africa and in relation to Africa this bit over here is Italy.

'Tahiti, Pitcairn, Mururoa atoll . . .'

'I *should* know,' she says, ashamed.

Geoff grunts. 'We only noticed they were our neighbours in the last ten years. Up to then we thought we were somewhere off the coast of Britain going ra ra for the Commonwealth.'

Josie wonders if she and Geoff seem utterly provincial. The trouble with not having travelled is you begin to feel deferential to any idiot who has set foot in a Boeing.

As they round the point the breeze hits them. Watching the clouds Josie sees a dark haze spreading above Toki Bay. She points.

'Someone's charred their Christmas dinner,' says Robert.

'Bloody . . . irresponsible,' says Geoff. Josie smiles because she knows he was on the point of saying bloodytourists which is the catchcry of Motuwairuans all through summer. 'There's a fire ban. Already the grass just snaps in your fingers. If that gets away . . .'

'It's miles from us,' says Josie, pragmatic to go with her new environment. 'It'd have to sweep through those houses, right over the ridge . . .'

'Shall we go and take a look?' Robert turns to Geoff. 'You wanta take the wheel?' He steps aside.

The smoke doesn't come from Toki Bay, they see this as they get nearer. It comes from the little cove tucked in behind the point. Like a huge chimney the stand of bush above the waterline pours smoke into the sky. The flames sneak and flicker among the trees. 'What a shame,' says Brenda. She sounds dismissive, meaning let's go.

On Toki beach people are clustered at the far end where they can see the fire. They move back as a helicopter in their midst begins to blow up a storm of sand. The breeze delays the sound of the chopper until it's well above ground.

'That's what they need,' says Geoff. 'Up home they carry great buckets of water. Put it out no sweat.' *Up home* thinks Josie, surprised. It feels as if they left the north years ago.

The chopper sound fades as the thing disappears over the hill. It's replaced by the faint asthmatic wheeze of the island's fire engine. The firemen are all volunteers but there's never a shortage. Young Harley and his disgusting fat friend have joined the fire brigade. When you're that age it's about all the island has to offer by way of excitement.

'They'll never get down there,' worries Josie. 'And what about water?'

'So long as they contain it,' says Geoff. 'It's hardly an inferno.' Perversely he sounds disappointed.

'We can look in on the way back and check it out,' says Robert. 'That is, if you want to go on.'

'Yeah, let's.' Geoff's eager to get on with playing skipper. Enjoying that so much that even if the rest of the day turns out to be regrettable he won't feel entirely robbed. Hopes Josie.

Robert sees her shivering and suggests they go downstairs. Her hesitation is so laudably brief he doesn't seem to notice. As he takes her hand to steady her down the steps she sees Brenda snuggle herself beneath Geoff's arm like a waif coming in from the cold. Efficient all right, Josie gives due credit—these two work together like a military operation.

Which is just the way it needs to be—with all that's asked of Geoff and Josie being their compliance. In the long view surrender has many advantages. Take Japan.

Yet in the cabin she instinctively fends him off with questions he's too courteous not to answer. Brenda, she learns, has two grown children. Robert is her second husband and yes, indeed, they are really married, have been for four years. They met in Trinidad. ('I was what you would call a beachcomber,' Robert says and snaps his white teeth together.) He comes from South Africa (she didn't ask) but—he says this hastily, his eyes looking down at the colourless contents of his glass—he hasn't been back for years. His discomfort gives Josie some abstract satisfaction.

She can see he's not really enjoying this personal interview. She knows she's ignoring the rules of the game; that the whole scenario is being jeopardised by this leap of hers into improvisation. But nervousness makes her persist until he begins to look hopefully out a porthole and suggest it's time for a swim.

Robert's swimwear is as white as his teeth and not much bigger. His haunches are all slim curves and glorious concaves.

Geoff is sturdy and hairy and shapelessly solid like a wharf pillar wafting seaweed. His swimwear is Jockey nylon with exposed elastic. Josie knows he's straining to keep his belly jammed against his backbone.

Geoff dives from the deck. Robert dives from the top of the railing. Brenda spreads a thick black towel on deck and offers herself to the sky. Her togs are belligerent purple with cutaway legs and a slash to the naval. Josie sits on deck propped against some nautical protuberance like an invalid, tucked up in acres of demure blue and grey diaphanousness.

A cliff stretches ahead and high above them, patterned by tenacious plant life. To the right a cluster of imperious rocks throw the waves into turmoil. To the left the cliff softens into native forest. The place is entirely perfect. Apart from this boat, these four people, there is nothing as far as Josie's eye can see to suggest human habitation.

Gazing about her Josie is reassured. Her thighs, her hips, her upper arms shrink back into defensible proportions. She watches the men. They've swum to the bottom of the cliff face and are pushing off for return. Robert bobs silently in effortless breaststroke. Geoff splashes and heaves violently in overarm and doesn't quite keep up. Josie wishes he didn't feel compelled to. Comparisons are out of the question. Brenda and Robert aren't ordinary people, they're images created by technology. Their existence is whimsical and episodic. Their bodies consume matter gracefully but never discharge it, they were designed to specifications based on extensive consumer research.

Alongside that Josie and Geoff can't help but look shabby and ill conceived, flawed by superfluous hair, sloppy flesh and stunted fingernails.

'If it suits the two of you,' says Robert towelling his hair, 'we'll eat at the Little Tasman bay which is just around the corner. You know it, either of you? No, I thought probably not. It's very popular you understand but there's no road access, so it's only the boaties go there. What do you think?'

Geoff shrugs. 'What's wrong with here? Places can't come much more beautiful than this.'

Josie squirms inwardly at his patriotism, though she was thinking the very same thing. But she supposes that in some circles a bay all to yourself is a bit like a Saturday night at home watching telly.

And around the corner they find a place just as lovely. A beach as pale and delicately curved as a fingernail clipping. One single boat at anchor, a dinghy drawn up as far as the yellowed grass leaving a straight indented line between footprints. Not a person in sight.

Brenda says to Josie woman-to-woman, 'He's missed out. Hah. There are a couple of gold-digging lovelies, not much more than kids, have been hanging around this place, oozing over Robert. That was the reason we came here.' Brenda's been-around eyes say you-know-how-it-is. But Josie isn't certain that she does, even though she tries to give Brenda an appropriate kind of smile.

'Well,' says Brenda announcing dinner, 'let's eat and drink and— best of all—be merry.'

Robert wipes his mouth with a scarlet napkin and clears his throat significantly. He reaches for the tape deck with its forest of knobs and switches and lowers the volume of a singer mourning away in a subterranean growl. Josie feels some relief, the singer was conspiring with the wine and reducing her brain to churning sludge.

Robert stands as authoritatively as possible in the limited space available to him. 'We're all adults,' he says, looking at each of them in turn, 'so in the interests of your reassurance, and so there should be no offence taken, I wish to say that we should all be most careful in the matter of precautions and hygiene. We would not, any of us, wish to risk any kind of infections.'

Josie keeps her eyes fixed on the cheeseboard, the little cleft knife lying among crumbled blue-vein. She can feel sweat on her inner thighs. She tells herself she would feel reassured by Robert's speech, not insulted and not terrified. 'We should do the dishes,' she says into the silence. And they laugh as if she's a sweet but silly child.

With the little curtains drawn and the door closed on the dishes and the table (not even cleared), it's dim but not quite dark. The bed is indeed large though not quite large enough and the danger is of being bruised or winded by a stray heel or elbow.

Robert's mouth feels cool and palely fleshy like raw filleted fish. Josie tries without being too obvious about it to keep his mouth away from hers. She wants to be able to turn her head and see what else is going on. It seems to her the arrangements have been rather arbitrary, that when Robert was being so practical and up-front they could well have gone on to discuss preferences and expectations. Perhaps had a show of hands if consensus couldn't be reached. Instead she is stuck with Robert, and a view.

Naked, Brenda is taut and tawny as an old lioness. She has Geoff by the haunches, biting and mauling. No signs of being prepared to share, and there may be nothing left of him when she's finished.

Robert is a talker, murmuring soft words in the tongue of the Broederbond, of Danie Craven. 'Milk,' he whispers, 'milky breasts. Skin like milk, so soft. Beautiful, beautiful skin.' Burrowing between belly and breasts and now urging her on top so he can lie half-smothered. 'Magnificent. Enormous. They hang so wonderfully.' (Geoff, are you listening?)

Her belly hangs too, perhaps as magnificently, but she can't see that far to judge. Robert has ushered both her nipples into his cool mouth and Josie can feel her objectivity slipping away.

Geoff are you watching?

But Geoff is otherwise occupied. His mouth and Brenda's mouth are clamped together tight as a plumbing joint. Josie feels rage and dismay. Not *that*. Kissing is betrayal. The mouth leads straight to the soul.

She wants to object but Robert is rearranging them again. She closes her eyes. Robert's hair is soft and fluffy, it feels like Farley's hair—how odd to remember Farley right now. Robert is using her body much as a frightened rabbit might use the nearest, softest hill. Brenda is making noises, whimpering and groaning in an American accent.

Suddenly Josie's brain quits. Like going to sleep and taking your dreams as they come. Like being feverish and somebody puts you to bed saying, don't worry I'll see to everything, and you know they will. So, suddenly, Josie is comfortable and carefree, though certainly feverish, and everything's okay and nothing can really harm her. 'That's right,' says the man in her dream, 'enjoy.'

'The wonderful thing,' says Robert, accepting a cigarette, 'is that it's always different.' Josie smiles and pats his leg and almost forgives him his nationality. Geoff is sitting right beside her, holding her other hand tightly.

Brenda has fallen asleep with her head stretched over the bottom of the bed. Josie has drawn the bedspread over her. Brenda's mouth is open showing a mass of black fillings. Josie thinks she looks unwell, like a brittle twig with the sap dried away. 'Should we move her?' she wonders, but Robert doesn't seem concerned.

They eat leftovers from the table then Josie clears and stacks the dishes while the men pull up the anchor and start the engine. Geoff is eager to get home despite Robert's protests. It's already coming on evening. Josie remembers that she promised herself she would ring Juliet before the day was gone.

On the way back they detour briefly in to look at the result of the fire. Some burnt-off soil and blackened bush but just in that one small cove. People stroll along the beach without even glancing across the water to the little charred bay.

'You'll thank Brenda for us when she wakes? For the wonderful meal, and . . . You don't think we ought to wake her?'

'No, no,' he says, 'please don't. I'll convey your thanks to her.'

Josie kisses his smooth cheek. She feels rather fond of him, he could almost be an everyday person. Besides, she's grateful. Geoff's eyes are stricken with love for her. He keeps one arm proprietorially around her shoulders as he shakes Robert's hand. It's a cursory handshake on both sides. Does Robert also suffer jealousy?

They performed all their farewells forgetting they still had to get to shore. The dinghy seems to ride a fraction higher in the water now the basket's empty. Geoff grows suddenly sentimentally talkative. 'Nine years,' he exaggerates, 'we've been together now. And I swear I'd cut my balls off rather than do anything to damage what we've got. But sometimes you have to risk a bit. It's only human to start taking people for granted. Complacency—that's what you have to watch out for.'

Robert listens or doesn't listen and the oars dip and soar. So that when they've reached the shore and have clambered out to stand with the tepid water lapping mid-calf Geoff says, uncomfortably, 'Look mate, I understand how you must be feeling about me right now. I feel just the same. I mean the jealousy . . . it's just there. Brenda's your woman and . . .'

Robert is adjusting the rowlocks to the middle seat.

'Don't be a clown,' he says to Geoff. He gives him a quizzical pitying smile. 'I can't stand the woman. She's a slaggy, self-centred old crow. She'd fuck anything that was still breathing and maybe if it wasn't. I'm delighted you could oblige and spare me the repulsion. I'd leave her tomorrow but I rather like the fringe benefits.'

A few metres out he gives them a small ironic wave.

'My god,' says Josie.

Geoff gives a subdued grin and puts his arm around her. 'Oh, well,' he says, 'Merry Christmas.'

*　　*　　*

Tinted, simulated crystal boasts the little gold label. The bowl, watery red imitation cut-glass has stood so long on the top shelf of the Kaimoana store that its angles are clogged with dust. Maureen keeps gazing at the thing in a flood of bemused tenderness. Tinted, simulated crystal—is that the way they see her? Impoverished, feminine, genteel. Or did they simply think it was pretty?

They'd crowded her bed as she carefully peeled off the cellotape so the garish green and red paper could be saved for next year. She'd felt cowed by their eager pride; how could anyone's delight fulfil such boundless expectations?

So far, a good Christmas. The agony of choosing their presents, the fear of seeing the shadow of someone's disappointment ... all that dispersed now, a silly little cloud of worry gone until next year. And the Christmas tree, though it's not a pine even but a branch she hacked from the macrocarpa pushing its way through the back hedge, is looped with twisted crêpe paper and hung with decorations laboriously fashioned out of cardboard and pine cones and sticky tape and crayon. (*Which is the best, Mum—oh, go on we just wanta know?*) And Jackson looks splendid in his red Christmas ribbon.

They've opened the heavy parcel that came in the post two days ago. From Alice and Matthew and Simon, a big tin of biscuits. Well, it gets harder and harder to shop for personal sorts of presents and biscuits are still a luxury item. All the same, Maureen can't help wondering if the present meant that Alice was upset with her because they hadn't accepted her invitation to go over there for Christmas. She's supposed that Alice was just being kind and would've been relieved not to have four extra mouths.

The mother of Carly's friend Tanya had also invited them for

Christmas, being kind. And of course Carly had been set on going. Since Hennie left Carly and Tanya have become almost inseparable.

At Tanya's place the kids could've jumped on the trampoline and splashed about in the plastic pool. Maureen could've sat on the balcony with Tanya's parents and drunk lager or maybe gin. Tanya's mother knits Tanya jerseys from wool she's spun from fleeces and has a Greenpeace sticker on the back window of her car. Tanya's father commutes to the city to work as an architect.

When Maureen said, thank you but they'd made plans for Christmas, Carly wanted Tanya to be included. Maureen said no, Christmas was for being with your own family. She could imagine Tanya reporting back, surprised, that they'd only gone to the beach. Maureen can do without comparisons. She wishes Carly had found a friend with improvident and imperfect parents.

Maureen has packed their Christmas feast into a carton. Ham (thin sliced, vacuum packed), sausages (pre-boiled), chippies, hard-boiled eggs, tomatoes, chocolate, liquorice allsorts, jelly beans, bread, butter, pepper and salt, knife, paper plates, a fork for cooking the sausages, teatowels for a tablecloth and a packet of paper tissues. Into a bag she has crammed towels and togs and sandfly repellent and jerseys and a book lent by Daphne weeks ago and still unread called *Images of Women in Antiquity*, and sun hats.

Her wallet is in the pocket of her jeans and the taxi which she booked yesterday by phone is ordered for ten o'clock. That's a treat in itself. Apart from that astonishing night when they rode in Geoff's Land-Rover and home again next morning, the kids haven't been for a drive since Keith.

Hennie never came back. You'd think at least she could've written. It was left to Daphne to try and explain.

'I really thought this time she meant it,' said Daphne bleakly. 'I'm beginning to think I don't understand either of them. How can they pretend that something so destructive, so angry and negative, qualifies as love?'

After Geoff had dropped them back at Daphne's Hennie had insisted she and Daphne walk all the way back to Maureen's place in the middle of the night. They found Kay crying, sitting among Hennie's clothes in the empty house. Daphne spent the night in Alan's bed because she didn't want to walk home alone. She left early in the morning when they were both asleep. They must've caught the first boat over. They were gone by the time Maureen and the kids got home.

'There's something between them,' said Daphne, 'but I wouldn't call it love.' And for the first time Maureen had seen Daphne as a frail person blown up large and fierce to scare off enemies. She was ashamed, seeing that Daphne loved Hennie while Maureen had simply become afraid of being without her.

'Besides,' said Daphne with a kind of resignation, 'Hennie likes a bit of drama, especially when it's centred around herself.'

Maureen had thought, though without resentment, that Daphne might have warned her about that weeks ago.

'Looks like you're gonna have a party,' jollies the taxi driver as he packs their carton in the boot. 'All right for some,' he says ducking his face towards Alan. Behind his back Carly smirks at Maureen. There are some adults who, the minute they see a child, feel compelled to turn into Crunchie the Clown.

'Do you have to work all day then,' Maureen asks sympathetically, even though he must be getting double time at least. He seems to be driving very fast considering the bends and the loose metal. But then the island buses seem also to travel very fast, so it may just be that she's got out of the habit of locomotion.

'Knock off at four. Not that it matters to me. All said and done it's just another day.'

'So people keep telling me,' says Maureen and sighs so he won't take it the wrong way. Liar, she thinks, what people? Only Daphne who didn't quite say that, just that she didn't believe in Christmas, it being one of those occasions dedicated to reinforcing male supremacy. (Had she meant Father Xmas or Jesus of Nazareth?) Daphne therefore abstained from Christmas, setting an example that other women would do well to follow.

(Living with Hennie has taught Maureen there's no point in disputing such theories. She's confident that, in the final analysis, children will always prove to be the fly in the doctrine.)

The taxi driver drops them at the north end of the beach, but when they've walked from the road to the beach itself the breeze is persistent enough for Maureen to make them trek, with their provisions and their carry-bag, to the south end where the curl of the hill offers some shelter. The shop is at the north end—another good reason for not staying in that vicinity. It closes at eleven and re-opens at two. The kids checked it out on the way. Alan is wearing his Christmas watch. Maureen got it by mail order, it was cheaper than a head-set radio from the same firm. When it arrived it looked much less imposing than the photo in the brochure; it didn't seem such a great bargain. But Alan's happy with it. She hopes it won't pack up before he manages to lose it.

There's a public barbecue at each end of the beach. Every week or two people from the Forestry or maybe the Parks Committee come along and make a pile of firewood beside the concrete blocks. They do it, so Hennie said, to discourage people from hacking down trees to cook their chops with. The piles of wood disappear so fast the locals suspect each other of sneaking down at night and hoarding the stuff for their winter fires. Some think the tourists take it home with them when they leave. It's threatened that, because of misuse, the supply will be stopped. Today, though, there's wood. Maureen explains to her kids how it's put there for free. She finds the gift of wood a wonder—a defiant kindness pushing against the tide.

Maureen thinks they should eat later but Alan worries that the barbecues will be in use by then. Hordes of strangers will appear on the almost deserted beach and monopolise the fireplaces. As always his fears infect. They stake their claim and she sends the kids foraging for kindling. There's a ban on open fires. The Kaimoana store has carried a notice all week. But if it included barbecues they wouldn't have left the wood.

'We'll have the sausages,' she says, accepting Carly's handful of skinny sticks, 'and keep the rest for later.' She kneels beside the grate looking out to sea and thinking about the infinite curve of the horizon and how soon you grow beyond a sense of wonder at such things.

She's happy. The thought sneaks in to take her by surprise. She'd been afraid of this day with just them and her rattling around in an empty world. But the beach was a fine idea. It pleases the kids and leaves the day wide open for anything. Someone who will love her enough to weep among her clothes may at any minute come along. She's earned the right to that kind of daydream—they've survived a year, two Christmases, pretty much unaided. She's allowed to admit now, if only to herself, that kids aren't necessarily enough to stop the heart from feeling short-changed.

Folded away neatly in the section of her wallet designed for credit cards is the letter from Bruce. It came three days ago, readdressed by Alice. Later Maureen will take it out and read it once again and perhaps her mood of hope and the sea's sighing sympathy will settle her thoughts into some kind of consensus.

The letter was written from prison, but said he would be out by Christmas. A contrite and constrained letter, quite unlike Bruce, yet definitely his writing. Cunning, was her first thought, yet ... How much can a person change in a year? In ten? Perhaps it was dictated, or at least influenced, by someone else. Girlfriend? Cellmate? Some authorised counsellor with a bent for human restoration. *All this man needs in order to become a stable, contributing member of society is the support of a caring wife and family.*

Such a tentative and inoffensive letter, concentrating on the kids. Regrets that he hadn't the funds to send them presents (nothing left out of six thousand? nothing?) and hopes that after his release he'll be able to see them. A humble bit about how he knows he hasn't earned the right to their affections but a belated father is surely better than none. *As you can imagine I've had plenty of time to think about things.* (Could he be trying to impress whoever reads the outgoing mail before it leaves the building?) He gives a Westmere address and a phone number where he can be contacted as from Christmas Eve.

But she has nothing to say to him, not in her head, nor in her heart. Except perhaps, we're much better off without you, just leave us alone. Easy enough to answer for herself, but has she the right, *has she the right*, to answer for her kids? She hasn't told them he's written.

After the sausages (and Alan was proved right—while they were scorching fingers and blinking through smoke an imperious group assembled clutching fold-away chairs and a chilly bin, impatience glinting off their dark glasses) they move down closer to the water. To the soft sand, not yet hot enough to burn the soles of their feet. Maureen makes them wait before they go swimming. *Never swim on a full stomach*; the penance demanded of summer children every Christmas Day.

Mickey chews at the last piece of sausage, twice dropped in the sand and washed in the sea. Alan stands close enough to Carly so the soft sand he's sifting through his fingers will get in her hair and cling to her lips. When Maureen rebukes he justifies. 'She was giving me a sly look.'

'Go swimming then,' says Maureen. 'Get cramp. Drown. See if I care.'

'I'm going to wait.' Carly squirms with virtue.

Oh Jesus, God and Mother Mary, says Maureen in her seasonal heart.

She watches him in the water in case it's really true, what they say about cramp. He can swim well enough but on his own gets bored and comes out to lie dripping and sparkling, just far enough away from

318

them to make his point.

Carly is poking into the carton. 'Can we have some jelly beans now?'
She's putting on weight again.

'After lunch.'

'Then can we have lunch now?'

'You've just had sausages.'

'I'm still hungry.'

'Oh what the hell. Okay. We'll have lunch.' Alan will have to eat
a little humble pie before he gets to taste the ham.

After lunch he says, licking his fingers, 'I wonder if Keith'd be home?'
The innocent way he says it, Maureen knows it's been in his mind
all along but he didn't want to miss out on the food. 'Shall I go and see?'

She sighs. 'Okay, if you want. But you better be back before four
o'clock or you'll have to walk home.' The taxi is ordered again for
four. When they get home the kids will possibly crash from exhaustion
and she will watch the Christmas programmes on TV.

Alan glances ostentatiously at his watchface as he leaves. 'Hey,' she
calls after him. 'We've got some food left, if he's on his own and—'

She'd be prepared to try again if Keith was. If the worst happened
and they stopped her benefit and he didn't earn enough for them all
he could go on the dole as a family man. She's had time to think it
through.

Carly and Mickey make a castle down in the wet sand. Mickey doing
what he's told. Maureen takes out *Images of Women in Antiquity* but
can't get into it, certainly not here where a child could drown while
a page was being turned.

Daphne, last seen, had said she would be in the city for a day or
a few, ignoring Christmas. Yet here she is walking up the beach,
wearing black football shorts and a white business shirt with the sleeves
rolled up and the tails flapping. She sees the kids and looks about for
Maureen, who waves.

Daphne flops herself down beside the carton.

'I thought you were in the city?'

'I just got back.' She hammers at the sand. 'Like a fool I went to
visit my folks. Endured a whole Christmas Eve and half a morning
almost. I feel like a saint. Pissed-off. Saints feel utterly pissed off about
being saintly. Or would, if they were.'

Maureen nudges the carton forward. 'If you're hungry there's still
a bit left.'

'You ate early.'

'On demand.'

Daphne pokes among the debris and extracts a piece of bread from which she removes a couple of jelly beans. 'They're lovely people, my family. They torture themselves over how I'm all their fault. What a shame, they say, about Daphne.' She talks with a mouth full of bread. 'How's your day been?'

'Good,' says Maureen. 'Almost entirely good.' It reminds her. 'Is Alan at your place?'

'I didn't go up. I left my gear behind the shop. Thought I'd take a walk first, blow Auckland out of my head.' She watches the jet boat circle in, deafening and boastful. 'Hoons. Wish it was me out there.'

Maureen watches the boat sweep away, riding high on the water's surface. Down on the wet sand, beside their castle, a bullet-headed man in a green sarong has crouched to talk to Mickey and Carly. Maureen stiffens and watches. The man has binoculars slung around his neck and now he's taking them off, holding them in front of Mickey's eyes, fiddling to adjust their width or focus. Mickey looks out to sea then slowly turns inland. The telescopic eyes waver now in Maureen's direction. She waves when she thinks she might be in focus. The man sees her wave and nods in her direction. It seems to make him less of a risk.

Carly is demanding a turn, thrusting herself in Mickey's view. The owner of the binoculars transfers them to her. He may have kids of his own.

Maureen remembers Bruce's letter and searches among the towels for her wallet. 'I got a letter from their father the other day.' She hands it to Daphne.

The man slides Carly's spectacles off her nose and holds them while she tries again. Mickey wants the binoculars back for another turn.

Daphne hands back the letter.

'It doesn't sound one bit like Bruce,' says Maureen. 'Not at all.' She looks at Daphne hopefully, 'What d'you think?'

'What do your kids think?'

'I haven't talked to them about it. If he visits the kids—I'd have to see him too and I don't want to. We're all right the way things are.'

'They'd say he has a right, by law.'

'Oh, I'm sure they would.'

'If he had one of them, you think he'd be prepared to let the rest of you alone?'

'Alan, you mean?'

'Obviously.'

'I couldn't do that.'

'It would make things better.'

'Not for Alan.'

'For you. You're entitled to think of yourself. You're obliged to. You know the kid gives you a bad time.'

Hennie's been saying things. Maureen withdraws into a silence. She should've known better than to ask Daphne, who couldn't begin to understand.

A shout. A sudden gull-like clamouring of excitement at the water's edge, making Maureen turn sharply in search of her kids. And the second or two before she sights them is distended time that will show up forever in the fabric of her past like a dropped stitch or a purl where there should've been plain. But they are there still, and the man still with them. Carly with the binoculars held in place, and all three of them turned to look where people are pointing. At the flames that rage and dance on the water in front of the little beach across the bay, and are reflected in the water so that the sea itself seems to be on fire.

Then the fireball seems to contort, to be patterned for a second with darkness. And a part of it rolls off into the flaming water.

Carly begins to scream. The man in the sarong tries to take his binoculars from her clenched fingers but Carly twists away from him and dodges her way to Maureen.

'Alan,' Carly says. 'I saw Alan. It's him.'

'No,' says Maureen. 'No love, you just thought . . .' She hands the binoculars back to the man. 'You can't see through those things if you wear glasses.' She looks up at the stranger, 'Can you?'

He says he doesn't know. But people are shouting now and waving their arms. And a woman runs up to the man in the sarong and says, 'Hey, can you look through those things? We think there's someone in the water.'

'Room here for mother,' the man in the white coat says and Maureen is pushed forward and can hear Daphne saying, not to worry about things at this end.

'Mother?' The man takes her arm, 'If we just sit you here. That's right. All set?'

Maureen nods up at him dumbly, sitting in a plastic bubble, sealed off from the world now he's fastening the door behind her. Her feet

321

are tucked away from the stretcher and he's nearly all covered by blanket except his face and half of that hidden by the mask. But she can't keep her eyes off the bit that shows, that doesn't look like skin at all but like plastic left too close to the stove.

'We're on our way,' says the man. Then the noise is deafening and though his lips move she can't hear him. She sees the pity in his face, though he must see tragedies every day. She feels so sad for this man who is constantly eroded by disasters not even his own.

The thing rises unsteadily. As they turn Maureen sees that the little bay is smoking, small tongues of flame licking at the infinite shades of green forest. Alan would love this. You went in a helicopter. Honest to god. It came over just for you. First a jet boat, then a helicopter, both in the same day. The same hour. Perhaps he'll remember the boat. He was still conscious when they dragged him from the water.

Still breathing. In out in out. If it stops this man will have a remedy. Some ace up the sleeve of his white coat. If it stopped a minute from now, if it stopped forever, she would want to go back and stay in this second of time when there's still hope. As she wants already to go back to this morning and make it rain so they all stay home.

They'd laid him on the sand with someone's wrap-around skirt spread beneath and over him, tucked around his poor ear and his singed scalp. Leave it, they said, don't look, so she didn't. The water, they said, was the best thing that could've happened. But Maureen could feel the sting of the salt as they talked. Lucky, they said. Lucky the water was there. Lucky the boat was there. Lucky. She'd wanted to scream at them, but they were being so kind. Trying to keep her spirits up, as if that's what counts. Where was Keith, who ought to have been at home? Then none of this would've happened.

In that breathing apparatus with his scorched away hair and the melted bit he looks like one of the alien puppets in that stupid programme he likes so much. She'll remember that to tell him too. They'll fix his face so you'd never know. They can do that now, graft skin from thighs and bums where it won't be missed. It doesn't look too bad, they said when they didn't want her to see for herself. One hand, and an arm, and the face just by the neck. And maybe on his skull. But it doesn't look too bad. He's lucky.

Waiting. Everywhere she waits. On the beach and in the helicopter and in the ambulance to the hospital. And now at the hospital itself. They've taken Alan away somewhere and left Maureen with her worst fears and three anxious strangers. A man and a young woman sit together. She may be his daughter. They hold their faces away from each other and bite their lips. It's as though they're afraid that if their eyes met their fears would collide and become a certainty.

And there's a young man who paces. Sits. Stands. Walks. Sits and shuffles through a magazine. Stands. Walks. Sits down.

The staff seemed kind but their concern slid off Maureen as if she was proofed against it now and nothing could get through. A nurse, a receptionist . . . someone, had asked if there wasn't somebody she might want to come and be with her. Maureen told her, no. But now the need to talk to someone sends her in search of a phone.

'Nothing,' she tells Daphne. 'Not yet. I'm just waiting. How are the other two?'

'No problems.'

'You sure?'

'I'm sure.' Perhaps it's just sympathy that makes her sound so touchy.

'You don't know anything? About what happened?'

The slightest of pauses, then Daphne says, with certainty, 'No. Nothing.'

'And Keith hasn't turned up?'

'I haven't seen him.'

'And you're all right. With the kids? For tonight anyway? When I know some more I'll . . .'

'Don't worry. They're okay. I'm okay. You want me to say that they're just what I've always wanted? Would you like to talk to them?'

'No, no. Not now. I better go, in case they're looking for me here.'

Waiting again. The longer it goes on the harder it is to keep your mind in check. To imagine the worst increases the odds against being disappointed. But then the imagining could in itself become a prophecy inviting fulfilment. Thanks to Daphne's presence of mind Maureen has her wallet and also her sweater. She checks her money. Sixteen dollars and a few coins. Take away her boat fare and how much left to spend? If she doesn't go home tomorrow Carly and Mickey will munch their way through half of Daphne's benefit. Single people never believe the amount a child eats. Will they be hungry? Will they be homesick? Do they understand that she had no option but to leave them in Daphne's abrasive care?

She folds away her money and takes out Bruce's letter. She rereads the Westmere address and folds the letter up again.

Right now her strength needs to be concentrated, a force to sustain

Alan. She tries to picture in her mind the power of love—a greyish, goldenish body of air surrounding a stark white hospital bed. It seems wispy and unconvincing. The one time he makes no demands but needs, *really* needs her energy she's limp and depleted; spread too far and too thinly.

A male voice answers the phone. She wonders if she'd recognise his voice, but thinks her gut would remember if her head didn't. She asks for Bruce Harrison.

'I think he's just gone out. Hang on.' The receiver drops and swings twice against the wall. 'Yeah, afraid you've just missed him. You wanta leave a message?'

'Could you tell him his . . . Maureen rang. His son Alan's had an accident. He's at Westmore Hospital. I thought he would want to know.'

'I'll tell him.'

'Luckily,' says the doctor, 'most of it's fairly superficial. The most severe burning is on the scalp, also a section down on his back. But the right hand and arm, as you'll have seen, have suffered and this area up here.' She pats the side of her own face. She doesn't look any older than Maureen. 'I think we'll manage to save that ear. He's in no danger, but I should explain that burning is—have you ever experienced it yourself? Well is a very very painful experience. And perhaps I should warn you, so it doesn't come as a shock, that we put the patients in a sterile room in the initial stage. It may look . . . well you'll see for yourself.'

He's encased behind heavy glass like a museum exhibit. *Child with burns.* Naked except for the bandages. The mask is gone and his face— the part that shows—looks shorn and somehow unformed like a newborn baby. Maureen remembers seeing him this way when he was new, showing him to Bruce for the first time.

'Am I allowed to go in?'

The young man who showed her the way, after the doctor had left, seems to hesitate. 'We can mask you up. If you want. Hopefully he'll sleep for several hours so there's not much . . . But if you want to.'

She doesn't want to put him to that bother. Not just to go in and stand there. She supposes the young man is a nurse. Female doctor, male nurse. Daphne would love this place.

'How long will he be here? I mean the hospital, how long?'

'A while. I couldn't really tell you. It's not too severe—you should

324

see some we get. But burns are painful. They don't heal overnight.'

She doesn't go in. The young man fetches her a cup of coffee and says why doesn't she go home for a while? She looks as if she could do with some sleep. So she gives him Alice's phone number so they can ring her when Alan wakes and asks where the buses leave from.

He says she might have quite a wait, today's a Sunday timetable. On the way out she sees the decorations and remembers why.

She does have a long wait for the bus. She wonders if she should find a phone and ring Bruce again and say, he's asleep, you may as well wait till tomorrow. Now the danger's gone she wishes she hadn't rung Bruce at all. But it's done.

A couple of blocks to walk from the bus stop to Alice's. In her bare feet and sand still in the pockets of her jeans. If she wasn't a martyr, as Hennie'd often said, she'd have rung and had them come out to the hospital to get her. An accident gives you credit on kindness, people don't mind being asked to help. Disasters excuse presumption; she hasn't rung Alice to see if she could stay.

Alice is at home alone and scarcely Alice at all but some big dishevelled doll with funny eyes. She was watching an excerpt from the Queen's Christmas message, she didn't know why because she'd watched it right through earlier on.

Maureen explains why she's here at Alice's. And Alice says, 'How dreadful. I know what you need.'

Alice gets another glass from the pre-cut colonial cabinet and pours them both a sherry from the bottle she has on the little table right beside her chair. Maureen notices the present she sent Alice – a little wooden box, made in Taiwan but with such delicacy, such tiny perfection, and Alice is hard to choose for – lies under the cabinet still half-wrapped. It seems wisest not to thank her, not right now, for the biscuits, and Maureen stops herself just in time.

Apart from some vague and awkward words of sympathy Alice seems to have little to say. Maureen asks the whereabouts of Matthew and Simon. Alice taps her crystal glass (not simulated, nor tinted) against her bottom lip and says dreamily that Simon's out visiting a friend. Then, after a silence so long that Maureen has sipped her way through half the sickly sweet stuff in her glass, Alice says, suddenly, 'Matthew's out with his paramour.'

Maureen has never heard the word spoken. She wonders if it's some kind of small sea craft that Matthew has bought. Her bewilderment must show because Alice says now, with feeling, 'His floozie.'

Maureen, trying to digest this with a mind already overfull of fresh and painful images, blurts out, 'Since when?'

Alice's laugh is intended to sound gay, 'Oh, it's nothing to be concerned about. He'll come to his senses. I almost feel sorry for him, she's scarcely older than his pupils. Infatuation of course. She threw herself at him and what man ever refuses? I'm not worried.' She gives Maureen a wonderfully calm smile to prove it.

Maureen can think of nothing to say. Seeing Alice turning into the mother they share; each wrapped in her freshly laundered illusions. And safe, perhaps, in a crazy kind of way. Protected by their refusal to see the dangers. The two of them sit for a long silent time in front of the TV set. They sit through *Joanie Loves Chachi Christmas Show* and *Those Magnificent Men and their Flying Machines*. Halfway through *A Christmas Fantasy* Maureen goes into the passage and rings the hospital. They tell her Alan is sleeping soundly. She checks that they have the right number to call when he wakes.

Half an hour into the *Life of Nicholas Nickleby* Alice claps her hands and announces, 'I have to be up early. We're having a little Boxing Day party, nothing too exhausting. Just a little luncheon sort of thing. We'll fix you up with a room, shall we, before I toddle off?'

Maureen asks to sleep on the sofa, she's afraid the phone might ring unheard. Alice protests that would make her feel most inhospitable. She seems to have forgotten why her sister's expecting a call. Maureen has to insist. Alice calls out once she's in bed, wondering if Maureen expects to be here for the party lunch.

Maureen lies awake waiting for the phone. Simon finds her there when he comes in. 'Shall I get you one of her valiums,' he asks helpfully when she explains her presence.

'Aah,' says Maureen in her head. It's the first time Simon's struck her as being something more than Alice's son. He seems very grown-up on his own like this. 'Is she taking those a lot?'

He nods emphatically. 'It's creepy, the way she does. I just go out somewhere.' He sags and looks around the living room. 'You'd think, all the same, Christmas Day he could've . . .'

'How long's it been going on?'

'Months and months and months.'

'Poor Simon.' She puts her arm around him. He shrugs but doesn't quite pull away.

'Poor Alan,' he says. And he lets her cry against his shirt as if they knew each other well.

January

'I STILL HAVE fears, of course I do.'

'What kind of fears?'

'The same ones I've always had. That you'll leave me. That I'll leave you. That we'll never make a living out of this place. That we'll stay together because we're afraid not to even when there's no love left. All or any of those.'

'Why are women so negative?'

'Don't bundle me up in some stupid generalisation.'

'It's true though, they are.'

'Then maybe we've learnt to be; experience having taught us the pitfalls of optimism.'

'Ah, that's just shit talk.'

She refuses to humour him with a reply. Her picking hand automatically pops a strawberry into her mouth instead of the box. She lets the fruit rest for a few seconds on her tongue before her teeth pulp it to a teaspoonful of sweet/tart water. She's begun to think now it's there for the taking that the fruit is overrated, even though she insists their crop has much more flavour than those big bland ones that fetch the high prices. Appearance and convenience, that's what people go for now. The bigger each fruit the fewer little green stars they have to pluck for a meal. Convenience just a euphemism for laziness. Which may mean Geoff is that much more modern than she is.

It's an unfair thought right now because he's working at twice her pace. She kneels whereas he bends over the plants in a hovering crouch and his hands seem to take up a rhythm that the plants play along with, offering their babies up to him. Hiding those same babies away when her deliberate hands approach.

He's on the row behind her now, returning. She can tell by the way he drags it along beside him how much heavier his box is than hers. He'll be smirking like an idiot.

'You sulking?'

'You can't deny,' she says, 'that the common experience of women has been far more disillusioning than the common experience of men.'

He leers. 'I love it when you talk in abstracts.'

She pushes her box ahead of her and edges sideways, walking on her knees. They laid the rows well apart when they planted. 'So there'll be room for you down there—kneeling, the way a woman should be,' Geoff said at the time.

'Tell me,' he has to raise his voice to reach her, 'do you feel superior to all men or just me?'

They must've had this conversation before, it feels too familiar. They must've had every conversation that two people can have before they start making do with national issues and local gossip. Is that the reason people set such store by travel—something fresh to talk about? And does it matter, covering the same old ground? Is it something you just come to accept, like mowing lawns or doing dishes?

'All the ones I know, yes.'

His hands are still. He's taking it seriously now, as if he's about to unearth something she's been hiding. She feels so inhabited by him, so overexplored and familiar, then suddenly he'll amaze her with some question or comment that seems to suggest that he still regards her as a bit of a mystery. He says now, 'You're never moved to awe or respect for some individual male—never have been?'

She has to ponder this. 'Respect, certainly—but not the kind that implies complete confidence. And awe? I've been occasionally awed by men I guess, but men who are hardly more than strangers. On more intimate knowledge I'm sure I would've felt disillusioned.'

'And women?' persists Geoff. 'You have confidence in women?'

'Certainly more than I have in men.'

He squats on his heels to give this thought. 'Yes. You're right. So do I.' He turns back to the plants and she has no way of seeing whether he meant that or was just entertaining himself. Either way she feels suddenly full of smiles, blessed in her existence. If he meant it she loves his honesty; if he didn't mean it she loves his way of slipping tiny stones of aggravation into the old shoe of their life together.

This is their last morning. From the afternoon Sarah will be with them, the balance changed. Josie finds herself longing, now it's so close, for her daughter's peppery presence. Even Geoff seems eager, talking of parts of the island, people, that Sarah might enjoy. Coupling the child up already with young Harley though Josie objects that Sarah's too smart for him and wouldn't look twice.

Their year of grace has gone too fast and yet she has no complaints. Somehow she's settled her account with Geoff, the debt erased, this year beginning clean and straight on a fresh page.

Well, perhaps some residual guilt still oozing out of 1984's closed leaves. Geoff can't recognise it. Accuses her of inventing this guilt, an invisible cloying substance to clutch or chew or suck on along with all those other props she nibbles, clasps, inhales in order to maintain an image of bovine calm. Addicted. Guilt in beguiling little foil packets at every check-out counter, irresistible to women despite the small print; *Health Dept warning: guilt may endanger your happiness.*

On the subject of Keith, Geoff says stop thinking about it, you only make yourself depressed. In Geoff's opinion unhappiness is also an invention, self-induced by the self-indulgent. He's right in a way. The most grovelling of regrets won't help Keith now.

They attended the memorial service in the little hall at Toki Bay. The Presbyterian minister who seemed to have arranged it said a few rolling words about death and resurrection and they all mumbled their way through the Lord's Prayer and that was that. Maybe no one was sure if he'd ever been a Presbyterian or even any kind of Christian, so more may have seemed presumptuous. Josie had felt that with those few anonymous words Keith was being summarily and prematurely disposed of. They were being given permission to erase him from their minds.

Only a handful of people had gone though the service had been posted on the Parenga noticeboard and grapevined through the pub. Harley, Leon the fisherman, Peter, Leif and Helen, an old weathered guy called Jimmy Hastings whom Geoff knew, a couple of people she recognised vaguely from the pub and a little old hunchbacked thing in a floral, polished cotton dress which seemed to hold itself at a disdainful distance from the crumpled body within.

Outside the door a small crowd had gathered, peering in like a tour party, hushing each other between small explosions of laughter which in an awful way had been contagious. Josie had to fight back, once, a subversive bubble of a laugh. Which perhaps Keith had brought on himself, self-immolation being somehow *passé*–too gauche and flamboyant for a serious suicide.

They'd found a can, which seemed to rule out accident. Unless you chose to believe he'd gone down there with the intention of setting the island alight. And you couldn't be that crazy–even in this place– without someone having noticed. There only a few charred remains, whatever that means. Geoff brings home the news and speculation from the pub where disaster is appreciated and this one has enough drama and loose ends to ensure it a place in Parenga public bar mythology. Time will encrust it with tough jokes, hollow or full of slyly insinuating matter like oyster shells. How dreadful to die for nothing more than a few black jokes. How dreadful to leave no one behind except acquaintances.

Josie needs to know if she was, for Keith, a contributing factor. The thought that she can never be sure she wasn't seems unendurable. Shame makes her go over and over that night when a bit of black lace and nylon may have covered up more truth than flesh, obscuring the fact of her rigidly embarrassed self. Yet, to be absolutely honest, there had been a moment or perhaps longer when her sense of absurdity was smothered by the mood of need and possibility that she and Geoff had built up like a card house with such careful breathless delicacy. So one second she was the earth, she was Papa, she was Messalina. Then the mood collapsed about her and she was fat Josie McBride.

Geoff assures her it's different for men. They're not limited by selectivity, or subject to that inexplicable repulsion that women feel about the bodies of others. Men, according to Geoff, are as physically obliging as a sprig of impatiens — willing to sprout in any old jar or vase that comes their way and never wilting with resentment over being used for no higher purpose than other people's pleasure.

Even though Josie has long suspected that, despite all the satisfying generalisations, the *sameness* of male and female when you strip away all the crap of conditioning and expectation will prove, in the end, the one flaw in feminist logic . . . Even though she believes that, she's hoping that in this one area Geoff is right.

The vision of Josie bulging out of black lace may have been one of the minor compensations of Keith's last depressed days. After all Robert hadn't complained at all; she has that reassurance to cling to. But, as she's explained to Geoff; I liked that little guy Keith, he felt like a friend.

So even if he didn't mind a bit, we have abused him. Before and since, in our heads. Playing greedy games and never noticing that he was destitute. Guilty whichever way you look at it. Though not the only ones.

The women he'd shared a house with — the butch one who'd been on television and had rung Geoff that night — hadn't even turned up at the service. Geoff said the story going round the pub was that she'd told the young minister she had better things to do. But they'd want to put words like that into her mouth, the pub crowd. Like kids turning shadows into bogeymen for that thrill of fear.

The other woman, Maureen, would've still been over in the city, because of the boy, so you couldn't have expected her to go to the service. She'd told Josie the night she stayed, she and her kids, that she used to see quite a bit of Keith. Before he started drinking, she'd said. She didn't say if it was his drinking that caused them to break up.

Josie can see that losing a woman might be reason enough to kill yourself. Men who are without a woman seem to lack a sense of direction, flying blindly like untethered kites. When she thinks about Daryl swishing about in orange robes and flapping sandals groping for God or Buddha or whatever intermediary is currently in fashion she reassures herself that in time some nice sensible girl will come along and sort him out. She hates herself for thinking that way, conniving to burden some unwary and kind-hearted girl.

Anyway, such creatures may no longer exist; all the young women today being smart-mouthed and unashamedly selfish like Sarah. Girls evolving to meet the social changes engineered by their mothers and grandmothers while young men huddle unprepared, whinging and mooching on the edge of obsolescence. Who will take care of them, these casualties of progress? Not all of them young come to think of it. Keith must have been thirty at the very least, and Paul is middle-aged and one of many. It must be harder, even, for the older ones. Bewildering to suddenly discover mid-game that the rules have changed and the other team is playing to win.

Paul at least has found himself a replacement for Juliet. A letter from Collingwood where he dragged himself for Christmas was full of young love and old lusty appreciation. She's a goat breeder who's had a couple of short stories published. Figures, Josie said to Geoff when she was reading the letter out loud, hippydom is the last bastion of male chauvinism. Geoff gave her a long marvelling look and said, Jesus you're an inconsistent bitch—it must be exhausting scrambling back and forth over the fence the way you do.

Juliet? Juliet survived a Christmas alone. *Chose it*, she assured Josie, her phone voice youthful and limber as her body. She could've gone to her brother's but it felt necessary to prove she didn't need to. I went for a long walk, she said. It's hard to explain but I felt this enormous sense of inner strength; it just came flooding in. I knew I'd achieved something, she said. But Josie, who has always found protestation of abstract spiritual surgings a bit suspect, was convinced that all these hair-shirt confidences were just an oblique kind of reproach. About which she was sorry but not at all regretful.

In a way she can't quite isolate or explain Josie knows this year has

331

changed her permanently. It's as though after all these years the wind has dropped and Josie — Edie's big old butterfly — has dared to close her wings. Finally she feels safe. The twig she's chosen to settle on may look precarious but she has faith in it. To Geoff she may still seem to be fence-hopping (let him go on thinking that, the insecurity is good for him) but Josie knows that if it comes to a show of hands the side she's chosen is whichever side he's on. For richer or poorer, better or worse, flying in the face of all reason, against stupendous odds.

'Hello,' he says.

'Hi.'

'Fancy meeting you here.' He looks into her carton. 'Is that all you've got? This, I'll have you know, is my second box I'm onto.'

'I said we should've done it yesterday.'

'Fresh. Picked this morning. That's what they like.'

'Harry said no more than six kilos.'

'This'd be half that.'

'We still have to get changed. What's the time?'

'What the hell, knock off time. The more we pick the more we have to cart over. We'll get rid of the rest down at the village, they're just being over-cautious. They'll see.'

Josie heaves herself off her knees and wipes them free of soil. She has nice knees, nice calves, nice ankles, nice feet. They go with her face which she also likes.

From the shower he calls out suddenly, 'I wonder if Hogg'll remember her?'

'Of course he will, it's barely a year.' She pulls on the blue and grey dress, it's the first time she's worn it since . . . Since Christmas she tells herself briskly.

Geoff pads into the bedroom glistening and dripping and smelling of soap. When his hair's wet and hanging almost straight he looks much older and somehow comical like Ena Sharples in that wretched hair net. Drying his legs where the black hairs make mockery of the grey stuff on his head Geoff stops to examine a blemish on his thigh.

Lately he's always doing that — peering and probing at himself for signs of infection. Josie has tried to console him with overview; you're more likely to get cancer or get hit by a drunken driver. Then she says, I don't see how, and anyway it's a bit late now.

Maybe he just enjoys the suspense. In perfect health he talks suddenly about death as if his own is imminent. She thinks such thoughts may have more to do with Keith than it has to do with their

332

own indiscretions.

Josie feels philosophical about dying. She's had a fair whack at the world and her children are old enough to manage without her. She'd have no grounds for feeling cheated. All the same she'd prefer to think death would pick her at random. Not have been passed out and willingly, expectantly, swallowed like altar wine.

Josie's surprised to find she's coping with the aftermath of Christmas Day much better than Geoff. It left her with an almost cosy glow of an adventure shared and survived. Like Hansel and Gretel they'd let themselves be lured into the lollipop house. Where they ate and yet still managed to escape hand in hand into the sunset. Josie's imagination can transform what was Robert into some anonymous and purely sexual being. A great improvement. Josie's mind can inflate and deflate Brenda as the mood dictates.

Gretel has the witch under control. They're safe. But Hansel still has bad dreams.

On the boat they lean side by side against the railing and watch the island slide away from them. 'You haven't felt trapped,' he says. It's somewhere between a question and a statement and she's not sure what he means.

'The island,' he says. 'Remember, you weren't keen. In case you needed to escape.' Just recalling it he sounds offended.

'Well,' she says, 'I'm still here aren't I.' She rubs her head against his cheek.

He'd interrupted her thoughts of Sarah. She tries to take them up again but they've got tangled and she can't find a loose end. There's a nervous excitement crackling in her veins. Strange because she hadn't felt she'd missed the kids, not that much. But then airports have always made her jumpy and light-headed even in anticipation. Reporting times droned out, final as doom, and so much emotion spilling loose in the air.

If Sarah's plane's more than twenty minutes late they'll miss their flight home. They've booked seats on the little island plane and ordered a taxi from the airstrip. That had meant taking a taxi to the wharf too or the Rover would've been left there stranded. So much extravagance. But Dick has pots of money and the girl will have got used to luxuries, best to let her down gently. Besides there's the need to have her love the island – make a good first impression. This one has chosen to come back to them.

If the boy would write a bit more often and coherently it might ease away that small constant ache. There was a card that arrived just before New Year – probably in lieu of presents – wishing them spiritual health and happiness. A shiny blue heaven with stuck-on sparkling stars and inside several cramped sentences and a PS to say thanks for the gift, as if he couldn't remember what it was they'd sent. Sometime before that she'd written and asked, in what she hoped were tones of amiable interest, exactly what religion it was that he'd joined. Was it the same as Dick's? And what was that one anyway because she seemed to have forgotten?

In the card he'd remembered to answer. He belonged, he wrote, to the ONLY TRUE CHURCH of the ONE AND ONLY TRUE CREATOR. Well, said Geoff in mock comfort, now we know.

'We'll get the low-down on Daryl,' she nudges Geoff. 'I keep hoping it's one of those Eastern numbers. At least they seem kind of loose, an adventure of a sort. I don't think I could bear it if he'd gone all grim and fundamentalist and pure. I'd hate to think I'd raised and nurtured a member of the Moral Majority.'

'Whatever it is he was probably pushed into it.' He makes it sound as if that's her fault, for letting them go.

'I don't think Dick's fundamentalist material. He was always kind of loose. Scatty but loose.' It occurs to her she doesn't really know what she means by that word *loose*. The young ones use it all the time now and she likes the floppy comical sound it has. 'Besides he mightn't have needed pushing, he might've just inherited Dick's religious bent.'

Geoff gazes down at the sudsy water with nothing to say to that. Mention of genetics always makes Josie feel over-privileged; an urge to creep into his head and distribute comfort and hot soup. She can't believe he's as indifferent as he pretends about his parentage. Surely it can't feel right just to have popped up like a cork out of nowhere.

In the city they off-load the strawberries on Harry who was Josie's friendly greengrocer in the days of her second phase of solo mother-hood. Harry's always happy to see her, and prepared to pay a fair price. He'll take more of whatever they may have, any time they're coming to the city. Josie's glad she thought of Harry. The old shopping centre makes her nostalgic even though it's changing fast. Even Harry's is under renovation. A bustle of fashionability about the area now, though the street where Josie lived in the house her mother left to her . . . that street had always considered itself a cut above the rest.

In the bus from the city terminal she says, 'Maybe I ought to sell the house.'

He raises his eyes up as if to say these-foolish-whims. It startles her to think he's grown so cynical about her moot points. She longs to surprise him.

In the airport bar twenty minutes early, brandy and ginger ale tingling summery and festive on her tongue, she tells him, 'I want to marry you.' Then, when he smiles faintly but says nothing she gets badly afraid and her voice becomes sharp. 'You don't want to anymore.' It was *them* she thinks. She wants to scream at him, you set it up, not me.

But now he's smiling properly, easing the jaws of his gin trap off her poor heart. 'Okay,' he says. 'And soon. Before you change your mind.'

'I'll definitely sell the house. I'd like a proper greenhouse and we could extend a bit so I have a real study. And a garage, and a decent shed.' Once you've broken through recklessness comes easy.

There's not enough air in the bar for Josie's impatient lungs. When they've finished their drinks she urges Geoff out to the viewing platform. She holds his left hand in her left hand as if they're about to skate off the edge and onto the runway; it gives her a good view of his watch face. The plane glints in the sky with seven minutes to go to arrival time.

'Could be another one.'

'It'll be hers,' he promises.

Dead on time. Then the teasing business of pushing the steps into place, the hostesses lining up at the doorway like royalty, the baggage cart rattling empty across the tarmac. And finally the first passenger blinking his crumpled way into view.

'That's her,' says Geoff while Josie's still trying to make up her mind. Hair cropped and dyed piebald, thinner than Josie remembers, red hoop ear-rings, tight black trousers and loose white shirt. She looks straight up at where they're standing, her face split wide in a grin. She gives them a little open-fisted salute then jerks her thumb back over her shoulder, mouthing something urgent and humorous into the wind.

Daryl. Just starting down the steps. 'My god,' says Josie. The boy wears a grey suit, his hair's been cut short around the ears with just a bit of a fringe in the front. He looks pink-faced and uncomfortable and solemn like a child dragged along to a funeral. He's looking around vaguely but hasn't seen them.

'We've only booked for three,' she remembers.

'I can take the boat back.' Geoff already being squeezed aside, the odd one out.

'He can take the boat,' she says. 'If one of us has to. It was him who changed his plans.' She feels deflated and suddenly burdened. She imagines this grey and formal stranger sucking away their happiness.

'He might just as soon walk.' Geoff grins then waves his arms suddenly, a big signalling wave that catches Daryl's eye. He looks up at them and smiles a bit tentatively. Josie waves. Now he waves back, the stuffy grey suit coming to life and inside it's only Daryl after all, give or take a few fancy new ideas. Daryl's puzzled eyes, the old touch of bravado still about the mouth. An unfinished face, she thinks; but that's not her worry, not any more.

As Daryl walks out of sight beneath them Geoff's arm settles around her shoulders. Josie belatedly registers the joke in what he'd said before. She gurgles, the laughter coming up without the faintest sense of shame or treachery. She's aware of that—her new undivided self. She feels substantial, calm as marble, easy. Possibly loose.

*   *   *

These aerosol cleaners, she's always avoided them in the past because of the ozone layer but mostly because of the cost; twice what you'd pay for the powdered stuff. It felt like a wild indulgence when she bought the can but Maggie, who used to work as a commercial cleaner, said it was worth the extra. At the risk of sounding like a commercial, Maggie had said, I really do recommend the stuff.

All those times Maureen had passed it by on the shelves, sticking with what she knew. Condemning herself to rubbing at dirt as if it was some kind of necessary penance. Ashamed to splurge a dollar eighty, anyway, just to make her life a bit easier. Now she's tried the stuff a dollar eighty doesn't seem all that much. A dollar seems nothing now, except to Mickey. She can't think why anyone bothers with the powdered stuff, making it hard for themselves. And what's the good of worrying about the ozone layer if nobody else does.

She's done the living room and the bathroom and one wall of the kitchen. More than likely it's all for nothing because, as the agent said when he looked over the place and hammered his sign on the gate, it's really only good for firewood. Mind you, he said, looking from the living room, they'd get a great view of the city, especially if they topped those trees. If it was me, he said, I'd build right up the back and subdivide. The agent was on the doorstep just three days after Maureen wrote giving her notice. Maybe her landlord had been hoping she'd leave.

But even if the new owner does just bulldoze the place down Maureen feels compelled to leave it clean. Scoured surfaces have a dignity that goes some way towards cancelling out the disgrace of being poor. When these boards crash down they'll be grimeless. Cleaning them is a way of closing the door on the year of this cottage.

They're not moving until Saturday – three days to go. On Friday Wiki will come over on the vehicle ferry with her car and her furniture and she'll collect Maureen and the kids and they'll all go together to the Parenga house and help unload Wiki's stuff. Then Saturday Wiki and Janice, and maybe Daphne if she's around, will come and help Maureen and the kids to shift.

Last week Wiki and Janice came over with Maureen and Mickey and Carly after they'd been out to the hospital. They all went to look at the house (the people staying there, city people from Hamilton, were very nice about them all trooping through) which is handy to the wharf and the shops and only a few minutes walk to the beach. Since then the move has felt like some fabulous present peeked at but yet to be properly opened.

Maureen's half share of the rent will cost her as much as the cottage. But they'll save in other ways, buying bulk, halving the power bill. The house has a hot water cylinder, a proper bath and a shower as well, even a fridge and a washing machine provided. Wiki had laughed at Maureen's gleaming delight when they looked through the place. Over in the city Wiki's had at least a share of all mod cons.

They apportioned out the bedrooms on the spot. Janice and Carly sharing the one off the kitchen, Wiki and Maureen in the big one with the french windows, Mickey and a spare bed for visitors in the room at the end of the little passage. Are you sure, Maureen had asked; I don't mind sharing with Mickey. Wiki sniffed; you prefer his conversation to mine?

I just thought, Maureen said and left it at that. She doesn't know if she just imagines, sometimes, the way Wiki looks at her. But she doesn't mind anyway. It's reassuring. There's a motherliness about Wiki that feels like security. It's not just that she's older, or that she has a child. Wiki seems to be kind to everyone, to be loved is the very least she deserves.

Wiki was there that night at the Arawa Street house when Maureen had felt sufficiently shaken after a day at the hospital and sufficiently unwrapped by the talk around the table to confess. 'I feel,' she'd said drawn into the conversation, 'I'm a kind of a fraud.' She could feel her cheeks burning then because half a dozen pairs of eyes were watching and up until then she'd really only talked when she was spoken to; Daphne's friend Maureen, the timid visitor with the nuisance kids.

Now she told them, the truth a relief, that they seemed to accept her but she didn't know—she didn't even know how you could tell for sure about yourself—whether she was gay or straight.

Of course, they said. Of course. A chorus of understanding. You're coming up, they told her, smack against all that conditioning; what you're feeling is explosive so you try and reject it. What you're feeling in yourself right now is a perfectly normal reaction, you just have to work your way through it. Wiki, as far as Maureen can remember, had just sat and listened.

She'd stayed at Arawa Street until New Year's Day. It was on the bus route to the hospital. Jess and Linda gave up their room so Maureen and the kids could sleep in the double bed. Jess insisted, but after that Linda would come into the room and grab her clothes in a clamped-down fury. Maureen would've sooner slept on the sofa, but she could see they all wanted the kids out from underfoot, certainly at night. The Arawa Street household was used to being child-free; Carly and Mickey were briefly indulged then grittily endured. Maureen would take them with her to the hospital where they weren't much wanted either.

It was of course Daphne who organised them into Arawa Street. She'd arrived on Boxing Day, insisting she'd planned to come to town anyway, but Maureen thought Daphne had, already, that frayed look that children inflict on the uninitiated. Daphne had had the foresight to call in at Cashin Street on their way to the wharf and pack a few clothes for the kids and for Maureen. And Carly had left food for Jackson who couldn't be found in the time they had to spare.

The possible plight of Jackson had begun to seem like the very last straw. More than enough to have Alan with his silence and pain, Bruce like some cold fear not yet properly confronted, the bunched feeling in her gut whenever she thought about Alice, the tensions in the household where they were staying . . . What do you think I can do about it, she'd screamed unforgivably at Carly when the kid went on about the cat. Then she'd remembered that disasters entitle you, and had got Carly to ring her friend Tanya and ask her to tend to Jackson for a few days.

Her hours at the hospital left Maureen ragged. Jess offered to have the little ones one day, and did, and never offered again. In a way Maureen was quite glad to have them with her. At least they were company. Alan had so little to say. He lay there in his private world replying to her questions in such a remote considered way that she felt like an interrogator. There were things she needed to know but hadn't dared to ask. His eyes confused her, they seemed to have switched channels. The doubt, the suspicion she'd got so used to seeing there had gone. In its place there seemed to be a distant calm that demanded of her no response. She would remember her dream and think, this is it, I'm seeing him now from that echoing and precarious place high above. He's landed. He feels safe because he knows there is no further to fall. She would search his eyes to see if, in the midst of their new calm, there was also a gleam of satisfaction at having had his unspecified fears so thoroughly vindicated.

But it was Bruce who seemed to feel himself vindicated, to have that satisfaction. They'd met, unarranged, on Boxing Day in the hospital corridor. Daphne hadn't yet arrived with the young ones so Maureen was on her own. Bruce had stood in front of her in a cold and righteous rage, legs braced, chest stuck out, words spilling from his mouth.

'Call that looking after him, do you? My son, that's my kid in there. What kind of care do you call that? Scarred for life, he's gonna be. My son. A wonderful job, oh you have, you have done a wonderful job of taking care of him I must say.'

Bruce's friend, the one she'd never seen before who'd been walking beside him—a balding gingery greyhound of a man—had shuffled back a few paces and turned away.

Blame hadn't occurred to her. In thirteen months she'd forgotten the way his mind worked and was taken by surprise. But his voice had drawn attention—a man in a white coat was openly staring at them, a woman had turned to look, even the greyhound was peeking unhappily. And Maureen didn't have to put up with it, not any more and never again. She simply walked past him. 'Got nothing to say for yourself,' he hurled at her ram-rod back. She just kept walking. His power was gone long ago.

The next time they met she had Mickey and Carly with her and Bruce was quite polite in a strained and cautious way. He suggested he should do his visiting at night so they could avoid each other and she agreed most gratefully. By then Alan had been moved into a ward with other children. It didn't seem to be making him any more outgoing, but when Maureen looked at his room-mates she began to understand what the people on the beach had all meant when they said Alan was lucky.

Bruce didn't go to the hospital every night but she'd know when he'd been. First there was the lime green rabbit with its drunkenly swivelling eyes, the thing was bigger than Carly. Then the pocket calculator and a box of chocolates so big they couldn't fit in the locker. Maureen brought the boy books of puzzles, a jigsaw, little plastic roulette games, fruit and marbles. She had to square up with an ice-block each for Mickey and Carly on the way home. His Christmas watch was in his locker, it escaped the flames—his left wrist—but apparently wasn't waterproof.

It was hard to know how impressed Alan was by his father. Maureen would admire the gifts and Alan would watch her with his faraway eyes. You happy to be seeing him again, she'd ventured on encountering the rabbit. 'S all right, he murmured with a faint painful shrug.

Mickey, on meeting Bruce, had obliged with the instant affection he'd turn on for anyone. Carly was polite and faintly patronising. She kept glancing over at Maureen with her twitchy little smile.

Even the story of his helicopter ride didn't meet with much interest from Alan. Of course they were giving him painkillers. And his face would probably hurt when he showed emotion. The ward sister told Maureen he cried in his sleep and sometimes called out, not words but a frightened child noise. If he would talk about his accident, she said, it might help.

Lucky he's not a girl, that same sister had said. Looking at his arm, but mainly the burn that will show on his face just below the hairline. (Though they'll make it, eventually, almost like new. The skin must heal first. She'd never imagined it could be so complicated and protracted.) Then the father of the boy with both legs in plaster had said the same; *lucky they're not girls*. Maureen had bitched about it to Jess that night; as if for a boy it's nothing to be scarred. And Jess had said, well actually I'd agree with them—my reasons may be different but the sentiment's the same.

His injuries, and the rate and manner of their healing, was the one thing that did seem to hold some interest for Alan. He would describe in an academic sort of way degrees and location of pain. And this learned stoicism made him seem even more like a stranger.

'Give him time,' advised Wiki, whom Daphne had brought round to Arawa Street. 'The kid must've had a helluva shaking up. Give him time and he'll settle back the way he was.'

'Christ,' said Daphne, 'that's the last thing she wants.' And Maureen had spread a smile over her sense of things being worse than they seemed.

While she was staying at Arawa Street her life was so crowded and chaotic that Maureen would sometimes think back with a kind of disbelief to the winter at Kaimoana, so predictable and so lonely. Even before Wiki had suggested they might share the house at Parenga she knew she wouldn't ever go back to the way her life had been. In an awful way it was possible to argue that she had benefited from Alan's accident.

It was obvious from the start that she wouldn't be able to stay on in the city and go to the hospital every day. She couldn't afford it and it wasn't fair on Carly and Mickey who had rapidly grown bored with the confines of Alan's ward and outworn their welcome at Arawa Street. Nor could she land the three of them on Alice's crumbling territory. Besides, there was Jackson.

She explained this to Alan. He asked, 'What will you do over there?'

She wasn't sure what he meant. 'You know. Just the things we usually do.'

'But without me,' he said.

'Just for the meantime,' she reassured. 'I'll come over as much as I can. And your father'll still be here. I'm sure he'll be visiting you.'

She rang Bruce to make sure this was so. 'If I come over,' she told him, 'it'll probably mean bringing the other two with me and that costs heaps, so it won't be that often.'

He said, 'We still haven't talked about my rights concerning the kids. You realise they're going me for maintenance on your behalf? It's a bit of a laugh you moaning about costs. I bet you get a bloody site more than I do.'

She reminded him she'd rung to talk about Alan. 'Of course I'll visit the poor little sod,' he said.

Linda and Maggie had been beside the phone listening to Maureen's side of the conversation, giving support by way of raised eyebrows and rolled eyes. They told her she'd been much too polite and diffident. The bastard's got an obligation, they said. You should've laid it right on the line.

All the wimmin at Arawa Street took a real interest in Maureen's predicament. Sometimes she got the feeling that they were vaguely envious because having a husband she was in contact with put Maureen right out front in the firing line.

They also, once Maureen felt at ease and had become more talkative, took an interest in Alice, and wanted to help her. Kay, they reminded each other, had been in something of the same situation and look at the shit she's had to go through to get her head sorted out since then. (They knew about Hennie and Maureen, nothing is secret in Arawa Street. Their voices went spongy with consideration when they talked, in her presence, about Hennie and Kay who are making a fresh start in Dunedin.) Jess and even Wiki offered to go with Maureen to talk to Alice – the honest-to-god sister. Maureen had a warning vision of Alice's face and said it might be better, at least for now, if she went on her own.

She went the day before they returned to the island. Matthew was away, spending a few days on somebody's yacht. Alice didn't say if the floozie was with him. Simon was at the beach with friends. Alice was shocked to learn that Alan was still in hospital; she would've visited him. When Maureen hadn't come back Alice had just assumed . . . Maureen should've let her know. Alice's little luncheon party had been rather fun, Maureen should've stayed for it. The only *gruesome* bit had been Alice's forgetting she'd put some little canapé things in the oven.

If she hadn't known they'd ask her about it when she got back to Arawa Street Maureen would probably have let things be. Instead, dutifully, like an axeman confronting a glasshouse she demanded, what about this woman and Matthew? What are you going to *do*? Alice had sat up very straight as if she could hear the glass splintering around her. Matthew and I are fine, she said; it's just that occasionally I'm silly enough to let my imagination run away with me.

So Maureen, doing the best she could under the circumstances, had talked about herself. She'd discovered, she told Alice, that she didn't need a man around to be content with her life. Women friends, she explained, were infinitely more understanding and supportive. My only regret, she told Alice, is that I put up with living with Bruce for as long as I did. She looked her sister firmly in the eye and said, I've even started to feel as if I've got a future.

Alice leaned forward across the patio table and Maureen noticed for the first time how much weight her sister had lost. When her pink shirt fell away at the neck her collarbone jutted like a gravestone. '*Of course* you have a future,' promised Alice. 'You're still perfectly attractive when you make the effort.'

On the last day they went to see Alan in the morning and caught the midday ferry home. Wiki and Janice drove them down to the wharf; Wiki was describing the house, saying go and take a look. Wiki's aunt used to live on the island, Wiki had spent two summer holidays there and always dreamt of going back. Now she'd found this house through the friend of a friend. Excitement at the thought of it caught all of them up with its flicker and dazzle like the sunlit sea and the troublesome vision of Alan was obscured.

As the boat, packed with visitors, nudged its way around the bare yellow hills towards Parenga Maureen felt almost weepy as if she'd been away for years, an unnatural severance. Carly and Mickey were pointing and shouting, claiming ownership; their own, their very own island. We've put down roots, she thought, surprised.

On the wharf she saw Josie and Geoff spruced up for the city and protectively clutching cartons. She didn't want them to see her, perhaps call her over and start a conversation. She bent over the kids, hurrying them up, threatening that the bus might leave without them. Until it seemed safe to glance back and see that the crowd had closed in and the pair of them were hidden from view.

Sitting on the bus she'd tried to fathom why she'd needed so badly to avoid them. Not wanting to deal with kindly enquiries about Alan? Or because they reminded her of Keith when she'd prefer not to be? Another reason was there in her mind but she couldn't quite reach it. Seeing Josie, Maureen had felt a sharp and puzzling pang of loss; as if she'd just missed a plane she was booked on, or offered to do the dishes because she was too scared to get up and dance.

She went over twice to the hospital, each time with several days in between. On the first visit the doctor told her Alan could soon be discharged as long as Maureen was able to bring him in regularly for a change of dressing and then bring him back in three weeks for the last of the grafts.

At home things were very peaceful. She hated herself for noticing how much easier their life was without him. Carly and Mickey made her feel like a very good mother. *It wasn't me*, she would sing in her light head; it wasn't me, it was him. A difficult kid. Hennie had seen it with clear objective eyes. Maybe even a bad kid. Mothers all just stuck with what comes out. No guarantees, no right of return. Web-fingered or Mongol, no one in their right minds would blame the mother. *Difficult* being just the same, an accident of birth.

She talked it over with Daphne when the kids were out of earshot. 'For all I know,' she shrugged, 'he may prefer to live with Bruce; perhaps that's what he needs. And maybe we could come to a sort of bargain, me and Bruce. He has Alan and leaves the three of us alone, no rights or interference.'

'What a good idea!' said Daphne. 'But what if the kid refuses to go and live with his father?' Then, not giving Maureen time to find an answer, she said, 'I'd wondered how long Wiki'd be prepared to put up with your son. Mind you, Janice'd soon've dealt to him, she's a kid that doesn't take any shit.'

It being such a good cause Maureen dared to ask Daphne to have the kids when she next went over. She arranged to meet Bruce at his place before she went out to the hospital. That meant a taxi, but next week she'd be selling her washing machine and a few bits of furniture they wouldn't be needing and that should make up for what she overspent.

Bruce's place was a bedsitter with a shared bathroom at the end of the passage and a shared phone outside the bathroom door. Maureen wished she hadn't gone there; the rooms felt so desolate and transitory. A child living in such a place would be grown up by the time he was twelve.

So what happened to the six thousand? But she didn't really want to ask. She knew the way Bruce saw it his circumstances were all her fault. She refused the hard little kitchen chair he pushed towards her. Once she was alone with him and the door shut she was suddenly afraid. Waiting for his arms to spring at her in wild arcs, a year's grievances coiled up in that chest.

He suspected a trap, she could tell that. He hadn't bargained for the possibility of permanent fatherhood and yet the idea seemed to appeal to him. He was lonely perhaps. She made it sound like a sacrifice so Bruce would feel he'd be getting the bonus of her pain. 'What if he'd rather stay with you?' Bruce asked.

She said hastily, 'We can't force him.'

Bruce said what he'd meant was if Alan didn't want to live with him would Maureen then not try to prevent him from visiting all three kids.

Let's cross one bridge at a time, she said.

As she was leaving he told her, you realise they'll cut back your money? If you've just got two kids? When she didn't answer he wanted to know how much they gave her for being a solo parent. She told him, a bit less than you need.

They'd moved Alan to another, bigger, ward with a corner set aside with chairs and a TV. He was hunched there in front of the screen watching a plump toothy little man slice celery. Coming all this way to visit made Maureen feel a bit deferential as if this was his place and these were his patients. They watched Maureen on all sides, bored rigid. She and the bouncy little chef were the only things happening.

Because he was up she suggested they might go for a walk somewhere, there were things she wanted to talk about. But when he stood she saw that movement was painful, that walking stretched and moved the skin even right up on the back. He moved gingerly like an old man. So she followed him to the bed. He used a chair to help himself onto it, brushing away the hand she offered. She sat herself at an angle that was intended to shut out all the stray faces from her line of vision.

Alan looked into the bags she'd brought and chose the peaches in favour of a marbled lolly. He offered Maureen one and asked after Mickey and Jackson. He said he felt okay but it was getting boring. She said, 'I think you'll be getting out soon; that's what we need to talk about.'

'I don't care,' was all he'd say when she put it to him. 'I don't care. Whatever you want. Whatever he wants.'

'We want what you want,' she said. 'You must have some idea, love. You know you never seemed happy about living with us. It doesn't have to be forever, you can give it a try and change your mind. In lots of ways, at least until they've got you all patched up good as new, it would be much better if you were living with your father. If you want to live with us you might have to stay on here much longer because I don't see how else we could manage things. Whereas if you were with him . . .'

'You want me to,' he said. It was a statement, without blame, without surprise.

'Of course I don't want you to. All I want is whatever's going to make you happiest. What matters isn't what I want but what you want.' The words came away so easily like soft bark peeled from a tree. She wondered if the young woman in the bed behind her was listening. In Maureen's ears her own voice had sounded glib, slippery as vaseline.

Yet she'd done nothing she need feel ashamed of; he might still choose her.

'You can think about it,' she said as gently as possible. Knowing as she said it that Bruce would be visiting the boy any time he wished and had a way of getting what he wanted. Alan was perhaps having the same thought. Two tears were assembling on his lower lids.

Maureen sifted through the spilt lollies and loose change in the bottom of her bag and brought out a handkerchief. He took it from her before she could reach towards his face. 'It's all right,' she said. 'It's all right.' She was afraid his tears would trigger her own and their deluge would make nonsense of the rationality of her beckoning future.

'I want,' whispered Alan sniffing and streaming with the hanky clutched in his unharmed hand. 'I want Keith. I want to live with him.' His sobs broke and were sucked back in a hiccuping tide. Maureen was aware of her mothering being on display. She tried to calm him, to draw him against her, cautious of hurting tender skin. This was the first time, in her presence, that he'd mentioned Keith. She'd become afraid to probe at a memory that might be better erased. But now he says again, 'I want Keith.'

'You can't,' she whispers. 'You know that, don't you?'

He looks at her for a few seconds then nods, so she risks asking, 'Do you remember?'

He nods again and the tears stop coming. 'What did he do it for?'

Maureen shakes her head, a mystery. 'I suppose he was just very, very unhappy.'

'No,' said Alan, 'not down there. He can't have been unhappy.'

'You should've kept away.' She looks down at his burnt hand.

'I thought I could . . .' he looks away from her. 'He saw me, though. He knew it was me. He pushed me away. He knew it was me.'

'Of course he did,' she says.

'What's happened to his truck?'

Maureen didn't know. Daphne was still using her trusty pushbike.

'They should'a burnt that too,' he said it harshly, as if it had some secret significance. His face suddenly glittered with that shifty nervous look of pleasure it used to get when he'd pulled Carly's hair.

'I don't ever want to go back to the island,' he said, watching his mother's face.

'Fine,' she said. 'You don't have to.'

When she got home she asked Daphne what happened to Keith's truck.

346

Daphne said the local cop had come and towed it away. Last time she'd looked it had still been parked beside the Police Station, why? Maureen said she'd just wondered.

Maureen and Daphne hadn't really talked about Keith. Too many other things happening and besides Maureen couldn't help feeling frightened at how easily it could've been Alan dead too, and Keith in a way to blame. Such a crazy pointless thing to do that she's tried to think of instances when his behaviour might have suggested he was unhinged or even just desperate. And could there be some quality in herself that attracts the unstable ... Bruce, Hennie, Keith?

She asked Daphne, who was already worn out from a day of answering silly questions, why she hadn't gone to the service they held for Keith.

Daphne said she wasn't such a hypocrite. Besides the man had done what he presumably wanted to do, surely that was the end of it.

'But why?' persisted Maureen. 'Why did he? You must've wondered about it?'

'Well,' said Daphne slapping Jackson off the table so hard he almost hit the wall. 'Some men devise schemes for incinerating continents; Keith devised a scheme to incinerate himself. Same thing on a smaller scale.'

'That's not a reason,' objected Maureen. When Daphne talks that way—as if the whole world is a ledger of *us* and *them* with not even the odd exception scrawled in the margin—Maureen never knows whether to take her seriously.

'Maybe he ran out of people to blame,' offers Daphne.

Maureen reminded herself she'd asked Daphne's opinion. She says, 'He was very kind to me, to all of us.'

'He was after you, that's why,' said Daphne. 'And for godsake don't start believing that makes you in some way responsible. If you want a reason it could be that his mother was dying. There was a letter came, readdressed just after New Year so I opened it. It said his mother had "peacefully passed away".'

'He didn't even like his mother,' said Maureen. 'She'd been senile for years. She shitted in biscuit tins.'

'Poor mothers,' said Daphne, 'the universal scapegoats.' But Maureen was thinking about mad Mrs Muir passing on the seeds of her craziness to lie dormant for so many years until. Thinking that the womb itself was riddled with guilt for events that couldn't even be forseen; that fault was established the moment that a wriggling human beansprout

347

invaded the egg. The responsibilities being too vast and onerous for any one person to shoulder.

When she'd walked out of the ward in the afternoon it'd felt easy enough. Alan back in his old form, his words jabbing at her with that whining note they got when he felt compelled to be hateful. He'd followed her to the door and she'd had to walk slowly in pace with his cautious steps because they were being watched, but she'd wanted to stride away through those clattering corridors so fast she would feel the air brushing her face.

At the door he'd said, what about my bike and things?

'We'll send them over,' she promised bending to press her face against his unyielding cheek—the good side. 'Be happy,' she whispered and a cruel vision came into her head of Alan no older than Mickey watching as his father tauntingly devoured a Moro bar and licked his fingers clean.

Alan had said nothing in return. His lips were drawn in at the corners in that tense little smile he often wore. She should have avoided his eyes; that unguarded pleading that reached out and clutched at her.

Even when she'd reached the street she felt that his eyes were watching. Following her, grabbing, pleading, impeding her stride.

'The mirror,' says Wiki. 'You got to use that mirror.' And Maureen glances obediently in the oval mirror at the dust rising and the road curling up in the heat. 'Great,' says Wiki, and puts on her gangster voice, 'You're doin' good, pal.' Maureen doesn't reply because the Toki Bay bus is approaching and on these narrow roads the business of two vehicles edging past each other is a wonder demanding absolute concentration. She can hear Wiki holding her breath.

'I did it,' she crows in the haze of dust. 'I'm beginning to even enjoy this.' She can envisage herself casually taking keys from her bag, offering lifts. Entry to a club she's always been excluded from. A certificate of competency declaring her to be a real grownup. 'Home?' she asks.

'Why not,' says Wiki.

The freedom. Maureen still hasn't grown used to the wonder of being able to decide so casually, shall we go home. It's hard to believe that each day is open to so many options: to do things with the kids, or just Maureen and Wiki, or all of them together, or Maureen entirely, almost spookily, alone.

Janice is thirteen and capable. Maureen sometimes wonders if they don't expect a bit too much of the girl but as Wiki says Janice has her head screwed on and her boots laced up; no one stomps on Janice.

'That's right,' drawls Wiki, 'speed kills.'

Maureen is inching up the driveway, trying to remember is it the brake first and then the clutch? Wiki takes a droll pleasure in her mistakes but Maureen can't forgive herself so easily. Janice has been driving competently since she was eleven.

The house is empty. Wiki puts on the jug but Maureen says she needs a walk, the driving leaves her jittery. And it probably is mainly the driving but there's also been, these last few days a little drip, drip, drip of worry about Mickey. Perhaps she leaves him too often in the girls' care. Certainly he's become a bit moody and querulous. Boredom, Wiki says, he's ready to start school. And she's probably right. Soon the girls will be back at school anyway and Mickey will get more attention. Maureen's freedom will be trimmed.

Across the road, her view of the sea blocked here by tussocky sand dunes, and she hears Mickey bawling above the summer voices and the sea. A great boo-hoo bawling. The sand slides warm around her ankles, over the top she can see them now. Mickey with his fist dribbling sand and more sand stuck to his tearstreaked snotspread face. Janice and Carly standing on higher ground, twisting towards him. 'You little shit,' shrieks Carly who used to be his friend. 'You stinky little shiteater.'

'Yeah,' yells Janice. 'You better watch it, see, little shitface or you'll be kicked out too.' She yanks at Carly's shirt and the two of them run towards the beach.

Maureen slides a few soft steps until she knows Mickey has seen her. She drops down onto the sand and holds her arms out to him. The boy stands squinting across at her for several seconds then he wipes a bare arm across his wet and sandy face and turns away.

SUE McCAULEY

OTHER HALVES

Winner of the New Zealand James Wattie Award 1982 and the New Zealand Book Award 1983

Tug is an unemployed Maori boy of sixteen – orphaned, badly educated, already in trouble with the police and about to be sucked into the world of hard drugs and violent crime.

Liz is a married, middle-class housewife of thirty-four, suffering from suburban neurosis.

Their love affair transcends the barriers of age, class and culture. It is a raw, hard-biting story of astonishing power and vitality.

'Winner of New Zealand's counterpart to the Booker Prize, a just reward for this fine novel'
The Times Literary Supplement

'A beautiful love story and a bitter tale. McCauley marks herself out as a writer to be reckoned with'
London Standard

'Sue McCauley has succeeded in making an incredible story believable. She writes with authority about how the other half lives'
Herald Tribune

THOMAS KENEALLY

THE PLAYMAKER

Based on historical fact, THE PLAYMAKER is set in Sydney Cove, the remotest penal colony of the Empire where, in 1789, a group of convicts stage a play after travelling 'eight moons distant from their homes on the other side of the sun'.

As felons, perjurers, whores and thieves, captives and captors unite to reenact a story, their playmaker becomes strangely seduced. For the power of the play is mirrored in the rich and varied life of this primitive land, and, not least, in the convict and actress, Mary Brenham.

'Formidably good . . . strong, subtle, echoing and profound'
Bernard Levin in The Sunday Times

'A magnificent and moving documentary, a tribute to his roots'
David Hughes in The Mail on Sunday

'Keneally's mature fiction goes from strength to strength, finding ever new subjects to press within the vise of its historical imagination. He has now provided a brilliant fictional corollary to Robert Hughes' impressive THE FATAL SHORE . . . The Nobel committee ought to start looking at Keneally now'
Kirkus Reviews

Current and forthcoming titles from Sceptre

SUE McCAULEY

OTHER HALVES

THOMAS KENEALLY

**VICTIM OF THE AURORA
CONFEDERATES
GOSSIP FROM THE FOREST
SCHINDLER'S ARK
A FAMILY MADNESS
THE PLAYMAKER**

MAURICE SHADBOLT

SEASON OF THE JEW

KERI HULME

THE WINDEATER
BOOKS OF DISTINCTION